Also by Lynn Hightower

Flashpoint
Eyeshot
No Good Deed

About the author

Lynn Hightower lives in Los Angeles, works full time writing fiction, loves canoeing and horseback riding, and is witty after two glasses of wine. She is the author of three highly acclaimed Sonora Blair novels, all available in paperback from New English Library.

The Debt Collector

Lynn Hightower

NEW ENGLISH LIBRARY
Hodder & Stoughton

Copyright © 1999 by Lynn Hightower

The right of Lynn Hightower to be identified as the Author of
the Work has been asserted by her in accordance with the
Copyright, Designs and Patents Act 1988.

First published in Great Britain in 1999
by Hodder and Stoughton
First published in paperback in 2000
by Hodder and Stoughton
A division of Hodder Headline

A New English Library Paperback

10 9 8 7 6 5 4 3 2

A CIP catalogue record for this title is available
from the British Library.

ISBN 0 340 69590 0

Printed and bound in Great Britain by
Clays Ltd, St Ives plc

Hodder and Stoughton
A division of Hodder Headline
338 Euston Road
London NW1 3BH

For the world's best son
Alan Hightower, USMC
Semper Fi

ACKNOWLEDGMENTS

My sincere thanks to Detective Maria Neal, of the Lexington Police Department, and to Detective Jim Murray of the Cincinnati Police Department, for answering my endless questions. To attorneys John O. Morgan and James D. Lyon for information on credit collection and check cashing services, and attorney C. William Swinford for his stories. To retired FBI agent Charles Lewis for insights and answered questions, and to air traffic controller Duff Ortman for his information and stories. To Lynn Hanna, Physician Assistant, and Philip Wagner, Emergency Room Director, Georgetown Community Hospital, for all things medical.

To Amy Matthews, who let me borrow her candy business, KENTUCKY SEASONS. To Matt and Phil and Stewart, for support above and beyond the call of duty. And, as always, to my kids, Alan and Laurel and Rachel. My team.

Our records indicate that we have not yet received payment for your last bill. If you have already remitted payment, please disregard this notice. We appreciate your cooperation and attention to this matter. In the future, please mail all current charges upon receipt of each bill. Following this arrangement will avoid further collection activity, including possible referral to a credit bureau.

Chapter One

When it was all over, or as over as such a thing can be, Sonora could look back and pinpoint the precise moment when everything went wrong. There were times that she wanted to blame the case, times she thought that if she and Sam had not been on call that summer-soft night in March, things would be different, things would not have gotten so out of hand.

And other times she thought, no, she had handled other cases, some as bad, if not worse. The problem, maybe, was her. Maybe she was vulnerable then. Or maybe it wasn't her, who the hell knew, because life, when you come right down to it, life is a journey. You put one foot in front of the other and you choose a path, and stuff happens, good, bad, there aren't any guarantees. It's just a journey. A trip you've got to take.

Starting, as it often does in police work, with the ring of the phone.

She had dreamed the night before, a premonition, maybe, of something evil and old as original sin. But when the phone rang, Sonora, deep in a book, had forgotten the dream. She was tucked up on the couch reading *The Corinthian*, by Georgette Heyer, the smell of pork roast baking in a mustard-barbecue sauce warming the kitchen. She had cooked. A miraculous event. Clampett, the three-legged dog, lay in front of the stove, guarding the roast, all one hundred and six blond pounds of him.

The roast was safe.

Heather, fifth grade, and Tim, newly seventeen, were watching television, reruns of *Home Improvement*. *The Simpsons* up next.

No doubt they had homework. Sonora had looked up from her book twenty minutes ago at Tim, propped on couch pillows that trailed clumps of Styrofoam like popcorn, and Heather, legs dangling over a beanbag chair they'd bought at a garage sale for her birthday, and chose peace and quiet over proper parenting.

It was a good decision. A moment that came and went like such moments do, you could no more keep it than you could hold water in your hand.

She put the book down, not wanting to let go of the story, thinking it was past time to put together a salad. She got up to turn the rice down, and saw that Tim was handing her the portable.

'For you,' he said.

She was not sure who was more surprised. She leaned up against the countertop, nudged Clampett with a toe. He gave her a doggie smile. Drool had puddled on the floor. A tribute to her cooking.

'Blair,' she said.

'Sonora?'

'Sam. Darlin'. Haven't seen you for a whole two hours.'

'You want me to pick you up in the company car, or you going to meet me there?'

Something in his voice. 'Where is there, Sam?'

'You'll never find it. Let me come get you.'

'What we got?'

His tone went flat. 'Home invasion.'

Sonora put the phone down. Looked at the kids, who watched her. Seasoned cop kids. They knew something was up.

'Going to work?' Tim asked. She had only a sliver of his attention. Knew he would be on the phone the minute she walked out the door.

'Yeah,' she said. 'Eat without me, and be sure to leave the kitchen clean. You hear me, Tim?'

He nodded.

'Can I paint my toenails?' Heather asked.

'In the bathroom, not in here.' Not that it mattered, except on principle. Sonora glanced at the couch. Dusty rose, cushions stained with ink, coated in dog hair.

She got her purse. Turned off the TV. The children gave her looks drenched with annoyance.

'Go ahead and have your supper. Make a little plate of roast for Clampett. Heather, you take care of that.' She knew Tim would forget. 'And keep the doors locked. Did you hear me?'

Tim nodded. 'Eat and lock up. You load your gun, Mom?'

'Sam's picking me up, I'll do it in the car.'

'Turn the TV back on,' he said.

'Turn it on yourself.'

She grabbed her all-purpose black blazer and the tie she had draped over the back of one of the kitchen chairs, retied her left Reebok, and she was out the door, standing in the darkness, waiting for Sam.

Chapter Two

Home invasion. It was the kind of call Sonora dreaded, the kind of call no homicide cop, no matter how experienced or jaded, could approach without a flutter of dread; unhappy butterflies low in the belly.

She stood to one side of the porch, just at the edge of her garage. One of her neighbors pulled into the driveway across the street, raised a cautious hand. In a community of young families, all couples with small children, a widowed homicide cop with teenagers was an object of dread and fascination. She could not blame them. Teenage boys with loud bases throbbing from car speakers used to make her nervous, before she got one of her very own.

Sam hadn't given her the address of the call, but it would be a house just like that one across the street, just like the one next door.

Some cops made fun of John Q. Public for their naïveté, parents who did not see a pedophile on every corner (fewer and fewer every day), people who could not fully comprehend the concept of two-legged evil. Sonora knew this copper's disdain was nothing less than envy.

She never told anyone, not even Sam, how routinely she hit that book of mug shots, known child molesters who stalked the streets of Cincinnati. There were times of great private embarrassment when she saw a familiar face, say in Dairy Mart, or taking the kids to Graeters. And she'd be unable to remember if the familiarity of that face came from a chance meet at a PTA Open Parent Night, or a mug shot of a guy in and out of jail for raping eight-year-olds.

She glanced over her shoulder at her own house, curtains still open in the living-room window, Heather curled up on the couch, Tim pacing the hallway, talking on the phone. It seemed so bright inside, cozy, as sunlight drained away and motes of darkness grew thick in the air.

She felt off, somehow. Maybe it was just the sense she had, looking into that living-room window, that her babies were growing up and away; that dawning knowledge you gain as you get older that life cannot be static, everything changes just as you manage to take hold, and you have to let go, whether you want to or not.

She had a peculiar feeling, like homesickness, only she didn't know where home was. She pressed into the warm scratchy brick front of her house, looked down the road. The gold Taurus crept around the street corner and turned into her driveway, car lights milky in the dusk. She could barely make Sam out, there behind the wheel of the car.

She did not move. She had a bad feeling, like if she didn't turn around and go back inside the house, make some kind of excuse – she was sick, something, anything – that if she didn't she would go and come back and things would be different. Nothing would ever be the same.

She sensed, rather than saw, Sam looking at her. Listened to the engine idling. Knew Sam was wondering why she did not leave the hard comfort of faded red brick against her back. Sonora slung her purse over her left shoulder, the weight of the Baretta soft on her hip, and went to work.

Chapter Three

'It's in Olden,' Sam told her, something like regret in his voice. His clothes looked tired – khakis wrinkled at the waist and knee, tie knot slipping, blue cotton shirt pillowing from the waistband, collar unbuttoned and loose. He had run a comb through his hair, straight, brown, and baby fine, parted to one side, slipping over one eye. He was past the need for a shave.

Sonora frowned, mind suddenly flooded with dream images from the night before. Peculiar things, dreams, wild animals of the mind. Try to force them and they would hide and disappear. But relax, let them come forward on their own, and your conscious thoughts would be inundated with images, feelings and memories, as if dreams had to be coaxed out when you were not looking, as if they had to choose the time and place.

She had dreamed of her brother, Stuart, dead now these last four years – had it been so long? He had died at the hand of a small blonde sociopath who had been playing games of death with Sonora. Hazard of the profession, but it was not supposed to spill over on the family, inept evil that would not stay in the lines, and it had taken her brother.

The grief thing. Business as usual.

'Sonora? You okay over there?'

It was not normal for the two of them to be so quiet. Sonora gave him a sideways look, wondered if he was fighting with his wife again, or just tired.

'Sam, do you dream much?'

7

He looked at her. 'Do I dream?'

'Yeah. Dream.'

That he was not surprised or perturbed by her question was a sure sign that they had been working together too long.

'Only when I have hot peppers on my pizza. Or if I eat chili.'

'Chili makes you dream?'

'Among other things.' He turned the Taurus into the entrance of a new subdivision, passing a small pond. 'This is it. This is Olden.'

So many things Sonora saw here, senses raw, hair stirring on the back of her neck, that cop instinct and edginess keeping her hyper-alert. 'Pretty here,' was all she said.

Sam nodded. 'I got a cousin lives two streets over.'

'Really?' Sonora said.

'No, I made it up.'

'Like you're going to make up a cousin?'

'Lives two streets over, on Canasta.' Sam eased his foot over the brakes, bringing the Taurus almost to a stop, to let five ducks cross the road to the water. Sonora had never noticed before how they scrambled over curbs, pulling themselves up with their neck muscles.

Sam checked his rear-view mirror. Turned on his left indicator. 'You know this area?'

'Nope.'

'You will.'

Street lights, halogens, cast a muted aura over fledgling trees, concrete curbs that were white and crisp, houses trim with new paint and shiny siding – all the chirp and promise of raw wood and new construction.

Today was the third in a trio of soft summery days, winter hopefully no more than memory. The novelty of sunshine brought people out of their houses. A man in loose green scrubs walked a chesty golden retriever beside a woman pushing a dark blue stroller. The lawn of the house on the corner of Trevillain and Olong had been mown for the first time of the season, and a spray of freshly clipped grass fanned up and down the edges of the sidewalk. The front porch light was on, though it was sandy dusk out, and light enough to see. Three children in corduroys and sweatshirts rolled over the newly trimmed grass down the small hill. The air was just going crisp and chill. Tomorrow the children would wake up with raw throats.

Sam turned right, and the neighborhood changed, houses smaller, trees larger, providing actual shade, everything well kept, lawns edged, landscaping minimal but precise. The cars in these driveways ranged in age from three to twelve, not so many four-wheel drives and imports, just solid Fort Probes and Crown Victorias, with the occasional Firebird or Trans Am that bespoke a teenage population.

Someone had called the fire department. People were heading down the sidewalk, a few clutching the hand of a child, a look of easy curiosity that made Sonora sure they were drawn by the crowd, and ignorant of realities.

Two paramedic units flanked the fire truck, lights flashing, crews standing close together, talking, smoking.

'No survivors,' Sonora said.

Chapter Four

The house was at the end of a cul-de-sac, 436 Edrington Court. The dormant grass had stirred and grown and was ready for its first trim. It was not yet out of hand. It could wait a week, unless they got a lot of rain.

Sonora paused at the front walk, barely aware of the crowds on the circle of asphalt, the fire truck, men in blue shirtsleeves. She made note of the cars in the driveway, an older model Saturn, much dented, wedged next to a maroon Chrysler LeBaron.

She looked over her shoulder, counted three patrol cars, parked out of the way of the ambulances. Uniformed officers kept everyone a few feet from the curb, their voices on the edge of polite.

She moved ahead slowly, concentration wrapping her like cotton. The noise dimmed, in her ears, anyway, and she moved with a methodical unhurried precision like a diver at the bottom of the sea – it was the working mode, a rare stance for her, usually type A and manic about the small things of life.

She paused at the bottom of the driveway, looking at the mailbox. The flag was up. *The Stinnets* was painted in white letters on matte black, and there was a decal of a red-bird with a yellow beak.

Sonora slipped a pair of latex gloves out of her purse, turned her back discreetly to put them on, and opened the mailbox. Nothing inside. She heard the thrum of an engine and heavy tires. The Crime Scene Unit van crept into the cul-de-sac, driver wary of the ambulance and the children running amok.

She glanced back at the upright red flag on the mailbox, looked inside one more time. Something – a rock or a small gray pebble. Sonora slipped it into an evidence bag and left it. Crooked her finger at a crewcut boy in uniform. He glanced at the ID on her tie, the gloves on her hands, and moved out smartly.

'Yes, ma'am?'

She checked his name tag. 'Officer Byrd? Stay by the mailbox, will you, and ask one of the techs to give it a good dusting.'

He nodded, did precisely as told. Recruitment training was a wonderful thing. Sonora wondered if she could send her son through just for the experience.

My children, she told herself, are safe at home.

Her hair was in her eyes. She pushed it away with the back of her wrist, and headed up the driveway.

The LeBaron had the startled look of a car stopped suddenly, tires at an odd angle, driver's door hanging open. It gave off an aura of wrongness. As Sonora got closer she could see a set of car keys on the driveway, just under the open door. She bent closer. The keys, ten of them, hung from a brass ring with a leather tab that said *JEEP*.

JEEP? Couldn't they find a key-ring that said LeBaron?

The LeBaron's interior was black. A red and white Super America coffee cup was stuffed with empty Reese's Cup papers in a holder next to the console. There was mud on the nubby floor mats, which were brick red and did not match the gray carpet. Papers littered the back seat, pink invoices, a ball cap that said *Glidden*, and an overstuffed black vinyl case that had a swatch of yellow legal paper sticking out from the center like a tongue. In the back left corner of the seat was a baby carrier turned backwards.

The dome lights were dull but shining, and a red glow from the dash warned that the battery was low.

Sonora stepped away from the car, glanced over her shoulder

at the front of the house. Saw, next to the porch, a purple and lime-green tricycle – well-used plastic wheels battered and specked with old mud and black tar. A patrolman stood white-faced at the edge of the concrete porch, averting his eyes from the ambulance and the tricycle. He could have been made of stone. The front door, hunter green with a brass kick plate on the bottom, stood halfway open to the night.

Sonora glanced into the Saturn, parked neatly on the right-hand side of the drive. A pot of cotton-candy-pink lip gloss was stuck to the front dash on the passenger's side, and a Beenie Baby turtle hung from the rear-view mirror. A sweatshirt, buttercup yellow, was crumpled inside out on the passenger's seat, a bright red pair of *Keds* stacked on top.

Sonora made the first entry in her mental catalog. Female between the ages of sixteen and eighteen. Toddler, three to six. She opened her notebook. Wrote quickly. Her handwriting had never been good, but years of police work trained her to write legibly, if nothing else.

Someone had planted bulbs alongside the sidewalk that led in a direct line to the porch. Daffodils, purple and yellow and white.

Sonora stepped up on the porch, right behind Sam, who had stopped to talk to the uniform at the door – another youngster, with black hair, and sweat sliding from his temple.

'You okay?' she heard Sam say, in a low private tone.

The boy nodded.

Sam waited. Sighed. 'What are we looking at?'

'We canvassed the neighbors. Family of five is supposed to live here.'

'Supposed?' Sonora said.

Sam gave her his annoyed look.

'Supposed?' she said again.

'Yes, ma'am.' The Patrol Boy nodded. He cleared his throat, eyes lowered, attention riveted on his notepad. 'Adult male, mid thirties, the father, Carl Stinnet, accounted for, his body is in the living room. Female, adolescent, sixteen, Tina Stinnet, in a bedroom. Willis Stinnet, nicknamed Wee-One, two years old, in the living room with the father. Female adult, the mother, Joy Stinnet, missing. Female infant, two months, Chloe, nickname Baby-Bee, missing.'

'Anybody see anything? Hear anything?' Sam asked.

The officer nodded. 'A car, parked out front during the afternoon. An old Chevy Impala, four-door, paint primer on right fender and under the door, '87 '88.'

'Pretty specific,' Sonora said.

'We caught a break.' Patrol Boy inclined his head. 'Teenage boy down the street. Noticed it this afternoon when he came home from school.'

'He see anybody?' Sonora asked.

'Not that he recalled. But one of the family cars, a white Jeep Cherokee, '97. It's missing.'

'Put out an APB?' Sam asked.

Patrol Boy nodded. 'Done, sir.'

Sam slapped the boy on the shoulder and disappeared inside. Sonora looked back at the daffodils, then followed. Sam had stopped in the doorway, and she ran into him, nose bumping the center of his back.

'Oh, Jesus God,' he said.

She would remember that. The way he said it. Oh, Jesus God.

Chapter Five

They had killed the family dog. It had died bravely, leaving a fan of blood spray waist-high along the wall, a snarl on its face, a bullet in its gut, another wound in the left shoulder blade. The father had died about eight feet from the dog, and had been left still tied to a maple wood chair that had gone sideways under his weight, caught part way down by the edge of the couch. It had been one hell of a fight.

The chair, a stained, red-checked cushion tied to the seat, looked out of place, as if it had been dragged in from the kitchen. One of the legs had splintered, a bullet, Sonora guessed. Bits of tasseled cord, drenched with dark dried blood and knotted around the man's wrists, hung from the back slats of the chair.

Sonora glanced at the dog, thinking the shoulder wound had come first. The animal had run around a while from the looks of the blood patterns. She was well versed in splatter, and she wondered if all the blood on the walls was from the dog. She thought not.

She flashed for a moment on Clampett, protective of herself and the children, face white-flecked with age and doggie wisdom. Then she shut down inside, felt the shivery iciness wash over her – familiar this, something between shock and resignation.

She looked away. And everywhere at once.

It was a nice house, cleaner than most, under normal circumstances anyway, which these were not.

The bookshelves in the corner were built-in, white enamel, liberally speckled with blood and another thin dark substance. Coffee? There were glass fragments, and the base of what looked like a shattered coffee pot. Brown liquid had soaked into volume G of a set of *World Book Encyclopedias* and some scattered issues of *Scientific American*. A Pottery Barn catalog had been ripped in half and tossed on the floor.

The VCR was on, the television screen static, on mute. An empty case, open on top of the television, said *Wallace & Grommit and the Wrong Trousers*. Cartoon puppets. The dog on the cover, grinning.

Wallace, Sonora wondered, or Grommit?

The carpet was fairly new, a color called Irish Linen. She knew it from the swatches she had looked at when the desire for new carpet had been overwhelming enough to make her at least pick some out.

It would need to be replaced.

Sonora noticed drapes hanging loose over the picture window. The gold tasseled cord had come from there.

Opportunistic, then. Whoever it was had not brought their own rope.

She moved back to the father, squatted next to Sam, who was lifting the hands, still bound, as high as the cords would allow. A strip of white flesh on the left wrist looked stark against the deep brown of the forearm. Which told Sonora that this man spent time outdoors and that his watch had been stolen.

It was hard to tell from the battered face, but she would guess him to have been handsome. He wore loose tan chinos, bibbed with blood, and a polo shirt, open at the throat, which was open itself where a bullet had entered dead center the Adam's apple.

She wondered what he had looked like yesterday. She would have to check the family pictures.

His left eye was swollen shut and dried blood streaked from his nose, also swollen. There was vomit on the shirt, dry now, a yellow-brown crust.

Sam turned the hands from side to side, gave a low whistle. If force of will could have freed Carl Stinnet, he'd have been up and off that chair, but the thick polyester cords, a good three-quarter inch across, had proven impossible.

The man's right eye was open and unmarked, cool gray and bloodshot. Sonora looked at his right leg. A bullet had shattered the shinbone and exited through the back of the calf, the same bullet that had smashed the leg of the chair.

'Watch is missing.' Sam checked the man's trouser pockets. 'No wallet.'

Sonora bent closer in to the body. 'Sam, you got some tweezers or something?'

He raised an eyebrow, which annoyed her.

'Don't do that, Sam.'

'Do what?' He handed her a pair of red-handled needle-nose pliers.

'Raise your eyebrows at me like that.'

'Why not?'

'I don't like it, that's why not. Here, look at this.'

'What is it?'

'I don't know, that's why I'm asking you. It looks like a little pebble or something, but I found one just like it in the mailbox, and this one was stuck in this guy's hair.'

Sam took the pliers. Gave the pebble the sniff test, shrugged, pulled an evidence bag out of his pocket. The bag stuck, bringing out a train of three little bags. Sonora separated them and opened one up.

'What is it?' she said.

'A thingie, hell, I don't know. We'll send it to the lab. Probably just a rock.'

'But there was one in the mailbox, Sam, were you paying attention?'

'A rock?'

'Yeah, just like this one. I think that's weird.'

Sam squatted on his haunches. Gave her a heavy look. 'Don't get stuck on this, Sonora. There's lots of other stuff here to be looking at.'

'You think?'

Sonora heard voices, heavy footsteps on the porch, men in boots. Waiting. Crime scene techs.

Sam stood up, and she glanced back across the room to the dog. Something there, behind the couch, a bit of blue denim against the Irish Linen carpet. She didn't bother to stand up, but went toward the swatch of blue on all fours.

She saw it as she rounded the corner of the couch, a tiny little fist, chubby, nestled in a blue cotton sleeve. A small boy, two or three, lay curled next to the tail of the dog. The child's eyes were half lidded, like a coma patient, cheeks showing tear tracks that had long since dried. Sonora checked the soft, china-pale skin at the base of the neck, which, she could see, was broken.

A quick death. She glanced up the wall at the fan of blood spray left by the dog. Saw a dent in the drywall that looked like the mark of an errant baseball. Thrown up against the wall, she decided, which likely made the dog go nuts.

'Baby's behind the couch,' Sonora said. She put a feather-light finger on the top of the child's head, noted the thickness of a diaper beneath the Osh Gosh overalls, the little blue cotton turtleneck with Winnie the Pooh on the left shoulder. Young for the tricycle. Perhaps a hand-me-down, taken out of a corner in the garage as the weather turned nice?

'Quick, though, neck broken.' Is that my voice? Sonora thought. That cool professional woman is me? She stood up, knees rubbery.

'Got a blood trail,' Sam said, and she followed him to the hallway.

'Is it from the father?'

'What?' Sam asked.

'The blood trail. From the dad?'

'No, Sonora, see? It comes from the hall, stops there by the television, heads out to the kitchen.'

'*Wallace and Grommit,*' Sonora said, following the red and brown smear down the narrow hallway. Something gave beneath her feet and squeaked. She froze, stomach jumping. Sam clicked on his flashlight. Looked down.

A plastic hamburger.

'Dog toy,' Sonora said.

Sam nodded. 'Wallace and what?'

'Never mind.'

A strip of light blazed across the carpet. The bathroom door was open. The blood trail led from the carpeted hallway onto the yellow-gold tile. Sam took a step inside.

'Move over,' Sonora said.

The shower curtain had been torn from the blue plastic rings and left in a blood-smeared bunch in the corner. Sonora looked carefully. Nothing there but shower curtain, no hidden surprises.

Blood smeared the outside of the toilet bowl. One platform tennis shoe, hot pink and stained, laces still knotted in a double bow, sat atop a hunter-green towel, bloody and wet, wadded on the back of the tank. Sam crouched on his hands and knees.

'We've got a tooth here, looks like somebody got a fist in the face. And a strand of long brown hair.'

'Note it, will you?' Sonora headed down the hall. Stopped by a room on the right, door open. Canopy bed, pink bedspread. Clothes in neat little piles as if someone had been sorting the laundry. Sonora walked in, stood in the center of the room. Saw in a glance a white and rose picture frame that showed the pretty and still childish face of the girl who lay on the ruffled pink bedspread, hands folded on her chest, a gash zigzagging across her throat like black, bloody lightning. She wore one pink platform tennis shoe, a match to the one in the bathroom, a sagging white cotton sock on the other foot. Her shell-pink sweater was ripped at the shoulder, exposing a beige bra strap, but her jeans, baggy and low on the narrow, boyish hips, were still neatly bound by a thin leather belt.

Sonora put a gloved finger to the child's chin, touching the delicate, lifeless face, noting the bruising and swelling coming up under the jaw line. Not right for post-mortem pooling, the girl had been hit. Her hands were not tied. She looked as if she had been placed on the bed, and arranged by loving hands. A remorseful killer? No one had felt remorse over the baby and the father in the living room. Had the killer run out of time?

And yet. Bullets and cold carelessness for the living-room victims, knives and remorse for the girl in the bedroom.

Two predators?

Sonora crouched close to the bed. The spread, beneath the child's neck, was drenched red with blood, enough to soak through to the mattress. So she had been killed on the bed, and left there.

Sonora wondered who had bled so badly in the bathroom.

She took a penlight from her blazer pocket, shined it in the girl's mouth. Braces, white ones, not the clanky metal ones she remembered from her own childhood, but no missing tooth. And yet she would bet the long brown hair would match the strand Sam found in the bathroom.

Sonora looked back at the picture. What had the uniform said her name was? Tina?

She'd had prominent, heavy-lidded eyes, thin, sandy-brown hair and a wide happy smile. She stood with her arms over the shoulders of two girlfriends, all in red suits that said Brill High Swim Team. The three girls looked giddy, wet, and a little cold.

Sonora stood up, glanced around the room, which was immaculate around the pizza crust on the paper plate in the windowsill. The desk, a maze of papers and books, was dust free. Blue and yellow ribbons were tied to the bedpost. Sonora fingered them softly with the gloved hand that was free of blood. Swim meets.

She went back into the hallway, saw Sam in the next room, which was awkwardly over-furnished with a brand-new Juvie twin bed on one side and a crib on the other. Two babies in one room – a full house. The room was blue, a domain for little boys and Tonka trucks. Blocks were everywhere. A tiny soccer ball had rolled to the foot of the bed. A pile of Leggos sat next to an empty bin. They would have made a hell of a racket when they were dumped, Sonora thought.

She stepped over Leggos and Lincoln Logs. Saw the white wicker bassinet hidden by the crib's headboard. It was lined with ruffled yellow gingham, made up with a fresh cotton sheet that sported tiny little bears. A rainbow-striped blanket lay neatly folded at the end, another yellow pacifier on the sheet.

There was a changing table next to the bassinet, lined with Johnson & Johnson's baby powder, A&D Ointment, Baby Fresh Wet Wipes, and a bottle of dark brown liquid with an orange stopper. Vitamins.

Sonora had given her children exactly those vitamins, and she remembered that they smelled harshly of iron and stained everything rusty brown. She looked into the diaper stacker. Disposables, small ones. Took a last look around the room, inhaling the soft scent of powder that brought back a million and one images of her own children – late nights, early mornings, snugging up a diaper while their little legs cycled, kissing the bottoms of those tiny pink feet. Sonora wrote quickly and meticulously in her notebook.

She looked across the room at Sam. 'Anything?'

'No blood trails from this room, thank God. You?'

She pointed. 'The daughter's on her bed, throat cut.' She stepped backward, letting him go ahead. Was it her imagination, could she smell blood? 'You been in the master yet?'

'Not yet.'

'From the looks of this place, I don't much rate the chances of that mom and baby.'

Sam gave her a sideways look. 'They may have grabbed the mother to access the ATM. Took the baby along to keep the mother under control.'

'You ask the uniform who called this in?'

'Next-door neighbor. Saw the car door open on the LeBaron when she came home from work. Didn't think a whole lot about it. Came out after supper to take her baby for a walk. Saw it was still open. Tried to call. No answer. The front door was shut, and locked.

'So. The husband comes home, she tells him about it. He looks in the living-room window. Curtains closed. Gets a creepy feeling. Starts wondering why the dog isn't barking with him looking in the window. Decides to call the cops.

'Uniforms go around back to the kitchen, see a broken windowpane, blood trail, they go in.'

'And no sign of the mom or baby?'

'Nope. But a major blood trail in the master.'

'After you.'

Sonora paused at the doorway, noted the rumpled bed-spread, covered in towels, some folded, some wadded. The bed was at an odd angle, and there were indentions in the carpet, so someone had shoved it sideways. The lamp from the bedside table had crashed to the floor, shattering the lightbulb, and bending the frilled paisley lampshade that nicely matched the bedspread and curtains.

A battered but antique walnut dresser took up the entire far wall. A small rosewood crucifix hung over a bevel-edged mirror that had splintered and cracked from the impact of a bullet which left a hole on the right side, near the top. A bloody thumbprint streaked the glass next to a line-up of pictures that were tucked into the edges of the wood frame.

Sonora frowned. Looked at Sam. 'What?'

'What-what?'

'I thought I heard you say something. Did you say some-thing?'

'No.' He headed for the walk-in closet. 'Man, oh man.'

'What now?'

'Closet looks like World War Three. Or the closet in your bedroom, if you minus the blood.'

'There's blood?'

'*Oh* yeah.'

Sonora heard footsteps, saw a shadow in the hallway from the corner of her eye. 'Blair?'

She recognized the voice instantly. Deep, edgy and harsh. 'Crick's here.'

'About time.' Sam looked at her over his shoulder. 'How many guys you thinking?'

'Two makes the most sense to me. We've got the girl in the bedroom like she was placed, clothes intact, and her throat slit. Like the killer felt remorse.'

'He cover her up?'

'No, but her hands were folded over her chest.'

'Didn't look like remorse in that living room.'

'Different guy. Maybe there were two of them, egging each other on.'

'A couple-a team players in a psychotic pissing contest?'

'Something like that.'

'Blair? Delarosa?'

'In here,' Sam said, the same time as Sonora.

Crick's bulk made the hallway shrink. 'You guys been working together too long, you're worse than married. What you got in here?'

'A mess.' Sonora felt the level of tension rising in her stomach, neck and shoulders. Crick always had that effect. But she was glad he was here. Crick was nothing if not solid.

Sam stepped out of the closet. 'Blood trail here, one in the bathroom. Specks in the hallway.'

'Any problems I let some techs in?'

Sam shook his head. Sonora said no, but she felt rushed. She was still making notes.

Crick rubbed his chin. 'Uniform gave me a body count of one adult male, mid thirties, one adolescent female, one male toddler. We got an adult female, mid thirties, and an infant, female, unaccounted for.'

'That plus your assorted blood trails about sums it up,' Sam said. 'Somebody lost a tooth in the bathroom.'

'It wasn't the girl.' Sonora moved so Crick could go past her and into the bedroom. She glanced back at the bullet hole in the mirror, noted the bloody thumbprint, wondered, victim or perpetrator? It looked like a couple of the pictures that had been tucked into the seams along the edge were missing. There were gaps.

She took a closer look. A mix of black and white photos from the sixties, some new ones in brilliant Kodak color. A baby in a highchair dribbling cereal down its chin, a chubby long-haired girl holding a cocker spaniel that looked to be older than God. A woman in a wheelchair, hair gray and curly, wearing a Grateful Dead T-shirt and a big grin, one of a little boy with a Roy Rogers lunch box – this one in black and white. The man of the house, Sonora thought, during his cowboy phase?

Happy Trails.

Crick scooted past her, heavy on his feet, going the other way, this time. 'Neighbors say the LeBaron in the driveway belongs to the mom, Joy Stinnet. Dad's a paint contractor, owns a Jeep Cherokee, which seems to be missing along with the mother and the child. I've got uniforms looking around the backyard, but the initial check didn't turn up anything much. Kids' toys. I put the word out on the mother and the infant, and on the Jeep. Find me a checkbook or a bank statement so we can grab that end of it. They may be using the mom to access the money.'

'What we thought,' Sam said.

Crick was walking away from them, voice over-loud in the hallway. 'Got to be *something*, 'cause we got a headcount problem here.'

Chapter Six

Sonora, writing in her notebook, stopped to shake her pen, which was almost but not quite out of ink. Sam was in the closet. Maybe he had a pen. She took a step forward, then stopped, tilted her head to one side, listening. There it was again, the whisper. Had someone left a radio on? She looked over her shoulder, thinking it wasn't likely to be one of her co-workers; nobody in the cop business whispered, and the house had ignited with noise as soon as Crick gave the order for the invasion of techs.

There were too many people. Fear could saturate a room, and this crime scene was talking to her.

The techs were everywhere, voices a matter-of-fact, low-key rumble that was a comfort somehow. It gave her a solid feeling, familiar white noise safety, an antidote to black lonely feelings.

She glanced at the closet. Saw Crick, elbow braced against the door jamb, talking to Sam, neither of them whispering either, though with all of them, crime scene guys included, there was an almost hushed quality to their work, be it shock or respect or a mix thereof. You did not come across this kind of carnage every day in Cincinnati.

Sonora went back to the dresser. Wild English Garden lotion from Victoria's Secret, mascara, toner, eye gel and shadow from Merle Norman. Something from Estée Lauder, in a pretty yellow case that glittered with a spray of broken glass from the bullet-shattered mirror.

She saw a boom box on the floor in the far left corner, near the edge of the dresser. Maybe that was where the noise was coming from. The woman had probably been listening to the radio. Sonora crouched close to the floor, right hand, safely gloved, hanging on to the edge of the dresser. She could feel a gouge in the wood with the ball of her thumb, like someone had landed a hammer there.

A pinpoint of red light glowed by the switch. So the boom box was on. Sonora bent close, heard nothing. The switch was set on CD and the program light blinked. Had the music been playing when the killer or killers arrived? Sonora pictured the mom in the bedroom, music masking the noise of intruders.

She'd check it out later, when the techs were done.

She looked over her shoulder at the bed. A jumbled pile of clean towels on the right, a neat pile of folded towels on the left. If the mom – give the woman a name – if Joy Stinnet was right-handed that would have put her with her back to the bedroom door.

Sonora went to the bed, sniffed one of the towels. The scent of clean, dryer-fresh cotton was unmistakable. Laundry in progress.

Why was the woman's back to the door when there was a toddler in the house? Sonora would have expected her to be facing the hallway.

The bedspread was creased and bunched, towels closer together than she would have thought. The crime scene guys would look for semen and blood trace on the bedspread, but there was nothing visible.

She lifted a pillow at the top of the bed. Found a tiny yellow pacifier and an empty bottle, a Playtex Nurser, the plastic bag streaked with the heavy white residue of baby formula, tucked into the crease under the pillows.

So. Joy Stinnet was folding laundry, watching the baby take a bottle, music loud on the boom box.

Sonora headed for the closet, watched Sam and Crick, who were on their hands and knees studying splatter like engineers designing a bridge.

A huge amount of blood had pooled on the closet floor, leaking onto scuffed blue bunny slippers, flip-flops, gray polyester snow boots. Someone had gone down in a pile of jeans – maybe thirty pair in various stages of wear, jeans for whatever weight you were; it was a girl thing, your ego dependent upon what size you could fasten without passing out.

Whose blood? she wondered.

Not the father. He'd been shot sitting in the chair. And it wasn't the daughter's blood, her throat had been slit at the primary, right on the bed.

Which left the mother and child.

A stack of washrags had tumbled to the floor, as if they had been folded and dropped. Was Joy Stinnet holding them when she was attacked? Had the woman gone into that walk-in closet, been attacked there, and crawled to the bed? Lots of blood in the closet, and the pooling meant she had lain there a while. Left for dead? Which made no sense, if she'd been kidnapped.

In her mind, Sonora followed the trail of blood back to the bed. Why the bed? Was that where the baby was – still on the bed?

She shoved past Sam and Crick. The dust ruffle on the bed hung low, skirting the floor, as if someone had dragged it or yanked it down. Blood trail led right to it.

Sonora, down on her hands and knees, lifted the dust ruffle, exposing darkness and the smell of dust and the iron-flake odor of blood. She sensed it before she saw it, heard the whispering for sure this time.

The woman's head was close enough that Sonora's foot might have brushed the flushed and tear-stained cheek. Joy Stinnet's eyes were open and her mouth moved.

'. . . hail, Mary, full of grace, the Lord is with thee, blessed art thou among women, and blessed is the fruit of thy womb, Jesus. Holy Mary, Mother of God, pray for us sinners now and at the hour of our death. Hail, Mary, full of grace . . .'

Sonora took it all in in a heartbeat – the woman's pain-glazed eyes, her stomach ripped wide, left hand covering the long brutal gash, belly to rib, exposing a ripple of gray and pinkish-

27

white blue-veined intestine, globs of yellow fat. And in her right arm, a bundle, quiet but breathing, a china-doll baby, eyes shut tight, chest rising with every small breath.

The whispers. This was what she'd been hearing.

Chapter Seven

It was the closest Sonora had come to losing it in her entire time as a detective, and the steady sound of her own voice calling for Sam, shouting for someone to round up the EMTs, was at odds with the pulse in her throat and the tremors of her heart.

Sam was quick. He lifted one end of the bed while Sonora ran to the other side, and they slid it up and over, bedclothes dragging. The woman under the bed began to scream.

It did not add up in Sonora's head, how one human being could lose that much blood, and still have the strength to scream like that. The hair on the backs of her arms rose, and she went to the woman and crouched by her side.

'I'm a police officer, ma'am, you're safe now. We have an ambulance standing by, you're going to be okay.'

The woman turned her head and her eyes caught Sonora, and the intensity of that look made her flinch.

The woman stopped screaming, and Sonora could hear the baby crying. 'Thank God,' she heard Sam say, saw him reach for the child, who was slick with blood, the mother's or the child's, Sonora could not tell. Joy Stinnet reached for Sonora with her left hand, letting the stomach wound gape. Sonora peeled off the latex glove, took the woman's hand, which was cold and slick and sticky. Sonora winced and held tight.

'Men . . .' Her breath was coming quickly, in short gasps, like she'd been running, running, running.

'One man? More than one?'

'The angel came. He gave me the baby and told me don't come out.' The woman gulped and squeezed Sonora's hand. Something bit into Sonora's palm like wire, and she felt the leak of blood from slashed palms lacing their entwined fingers. She noted the slices of open skin on Joy Stinnet's forearms, felt a weird tingle in the small of her back. Defense wounds always got to her.

'I heard my husband coming home, I heard him . . .'

'Can you tell me what the men looked like? Did you hear a name? Did—'

'My little Rusty was barking.' Tears flowed down Joy Stinnet's cheeks. 'And they shot him, I heard him yelp.'

The EMTs came through the door like a crack of lightning, the marines of 911, heavy black boxes snapping open. A portly man with close-cropped red hair crouched next to Sonora, gave her a nod, smiled at the woman.

'My name is Chris, ma'am, you're going to be all right, you hear? Can you tell me your name?'

'It's Joy,' Sonora said. She moved back, waiting to be pushed aside, but Chris shook his head.

'Okay, Joy, you hang on, now. I just took a look at that pretty little baby girl of yours and she hasn't got a scratch on her. Detective Blair is going to hold your hand and talk to you, okay, Joy, so me and my partners here can get you a look.'

Sonora wondered how he knew her name, felt a tiny pang of disappointment that she knew, to her shame, was cowardice. She wasn't off the hook yet. She could not back away and let someone else take over.

'Joy? Joy, do you know who did this, did you recognize anyone? Can you tell me how many . . .?'

The woman's eyelids fluttered, her breathing shallow and fast. She had black hair, Sonora noticed, shoulder-length, matted behind her head. Her mascara-streaked face was dead white, with a haunted look of darkness around her eyes that Sonora had seen before, in other victims edging close to death.

The hand spasmed on Sonora's.

'Two men,' Sonora prompted.

'Two. And the angel.'

Another EMT, nametag of Hodges, stood next to Chris and pulled a radio out of his belt. 'Closest hospital, with that south exit closed, is—'

'Gillane's on duty at Jewish.' This from the young one, black hair gelled in place, working a blood-pressure cuff.

Sonora felt odd hearing the name, odd but comforted. Gillane.

'We'll go to Jewish,' the EMT named Chris said, and Sonora thought, good choice. 'Get a large-bore IV so we can get some fluid pumped into her.'

Sonora wondered what the hell Joy Stinnet meant by 'the angel'. People said all kinds of things when they took that final walk.

'Tell me, my babies, are they dead?' Joy Stinnet said, just as the young paramedic slid an oxygen mask over her face. 'Is Tina . . . did those men—'

Sonora heard a burst of static as the red-headed medic grabbed the radio from his belt, heard the note of fierceness in his voice. 'I've got a female, mid thirties, laceration from the umbilicus to the right costal margin. We got liver, we got bowel, we got major blood loss; 02 mask at ten liters a minute, BP eighty palp, heart rate one twenty.'

Sonora clasped the woman's blood-drenched hands between both of hers, saw what looked like IV fluid leaking from the wound. Whatever they were pumping into her was coming right back out.

She looked Joy Stinnet in the eye, wondered, just for a moment, how long she had lain under the bed clutching the baby. 'Joy, your husband got home in time.'

The woman watched her. Sobbed deep in her chest.

'Hell of a guy, your husband. Him and that dog of yours.' Sonora smiled, a stiff smile. 'I won't say they're not hurt, but it looks like they're going to be okay. Your little boy and your daughter, Tina, I think she told me her name was. Is it Tina?'

The woman was watching her, watching her face.

'Tina has your little boy, she just now carried him outside, and he's fine – scared though, but they're all fine, ma'am. Rusty will have to spend a night or two at the vet, but he and your husband really saved the day.'

Joy Stinnet turned her head sideways and tears leaked from the edges of the oxygen mask. The hands, clutched between Sonora's, were going icy. Joy Stinnet's sobs softened and faded and her eyes lost focus. Chris jerked his head, and Sonora, at last, stood up and out of the way.

Chapter Eight

There was a certain beauty in watching someone do something well, something they cared about. If you looked at it right, you could see the restrained intensity in Gillane's fingers, conducting the symphony of life over the woman on the narrow metal pallet.

Joy Stinnet's heart had stopped in her bedroom. The EMTs had not been able to start it back up, not with electric shock, fluids, or prayers. Gillane was having no better luck. The woman was gone, Sonora had no doubt, she was just waiting for everyone else to catch up.

She had always loathed doctors, hospitals, and their implements of destruction and resurrection wielded in an unfeeling, uncaring arrogance that was a ravage to the flesh and a blasphemy to the soul. But in Gillane's gloved fingers, white, worm-like, strong, in the focus drawn by the line of his jaw and the squint of his eyes, in the way he applied himself to a task he had done many times and knew very well, he had all the assurance of routine, and none of the boredom. He was there, mind clicking, powerful intellect focused, with an odd but constant air of being on the verge of discovery.

For just one second Sonora felt something like jealousy for the woman on the pallet. So vulnerable, so out of the loop, surrendered to the care and focus of a doctor so talented that he was like a painter confronted with a canvas on which some heinous event had drawn a picture of death, armed with sterile instruments like brushes he would use to change those lines of death to life, resurrection, and his best attempt at wholeness.

Sonora wondered if she had done right to lie to this woman, to give her an easy way out. Would she still be alive if she'd had children to avenge? Would anger and pain have kept her going long enough for Gillane to work his emergency-room magic?

She watched him, tall and fit, saw his catlike eyes in profile, the well-shaved cheek, a handsome man. The frantic movements slowed, plowing on relentlessly, but she saw the subtle heaviness that seemed to infect his neck, shoulders and jaw, and she knew that he had come to the same conclusion.

'Let her go,' he said.

Chapter Nine

Sonora stood with her back to the cold tile wall, arms folded, one foot propped behind her. She checked her watch, wondering how long it would be before Sam arrived to pick her up on his way back to the bull-pen.

An intern held Joy Stinnet's baby high in the air, under the eye of two nurses and one respiratory technician. One of the nurses fluttered her hands, as if she were on the verge of snatching the baby away.

He brought the little girl close and tucked a kiss into the folds of her neck. She had been bathed and snugged into a pink cotton nightie that was so long her tiny feet were a memory. The sleeves had been carefully folded back over the round pink balls of baby hands. She gave him a wide-mouthed grin, drool lapping over the rosy gums.

Sonora remembered how it had been, holding Tim and Heather up like that when they were babies, skin soft and new, growing their first serious head of hair, eyes wide. Holding them high and smiling at them, watching them extend their legs, and smile wide gummy baby smiles. They had been so cuddly, snapped into little terry-cloth suits.

Baby smiles and soft promise. No doubt Joy and Carl Stinnet had done the same with their three children, everyday ordinary parenting, everyday ordinary family. Dad coming home from work, teenage daughter in the kitchen getting a snack for the two-year-old, while mom did laundry in the bedroom and watched over the baby. It happened every day, everywhere. It was the arrogance of murder that stunned Sonora, the older she got.

Plastic curtains billowed sideways from the cubicle and Gillane was the first of a handful of medics, spilling out like ants from an anthill. A woman in pink headed in. Clean-up time, toe tags and the morgue.

Not the hospital morgue. Sonora would have to make arrangements. Medical Examiner and four autopsies.

Gillane was looking around. Looking for her? He did an abrupt change of direction when he saw her, and their eyes met. He was heading her way.

It was a thing sometimes, between a man and a woman. Unspoken and understood, like the silent p in pneumonia. Sonora used to think that one party or the other had to actually say something to sort of make it official, or the attraction could just all be in her mind.

She knew now to trust her instincts. When it was there, it was there. It didn't even mean you had to do anything about it. Better not to, sometimes.

'That crap all over your hands, is it hers? Not yours?' He was herding her, not waiting for an answer, moving her toward his private room where he could hang out or see patients, do paperwork or play the harmonica. The room, she knew from past experience, would hold a guitar, a laptop computer, a Kohner harmonica and most likely a box of Twinkies.

'I'm mango crazy right now,' he said. 'Want some fruit?'

'What, when I've got you?'

The smile flickered.

'I'm waiting for Sam,' Sonora said, but somehow she was walking beside him down that green tile corridor.

'I ain't exactly on break.' He punched the code in on his door, opened it, flicked a look at her over his shoulder. 'Your shirt's ruined.'

'Tell me something I don't know.'

Gillane took her elbow and shoulder and pushed her to the sink, started the water running. Squirted pink spearmint-smelling soap from a wall dispenser into his palms, and lathered her up.

'I've never understood why a woman in your profession always wears white.'

'I look cute in white.'

'You're the only cute homicide cop I know. Well. There was this one down in Houston. But he was short.' Gillane looked up at her. 'I *am* kidding.' He took folded paper towels and patted her hands dry. She stood still for it, she did not quite know why. She needed to go. Get to work. A million things to do.

'What are you holding in your hand, Sonora?' He peeled a long gold strand from her palm, held it up. A small golden cross dangled from a gold chain no thicker than a fine strand of wire.

'It belonged to her. Joy Stinnet.' She took a baggie from her jacket pocket, slipped it inside.

Gillane nudged her toward the slender bunk. 'Sit down, sweetie.'

It was a tiny room, smelling strongly of microwave popcorn and old coffee, spare and functional with a bunk, a desk, a sink. A shelf with a microwave oven parked next to a Gibson acoustic guitar. Absolutely nothing on the walls except a calendar from 1997. A horse calendar. Arabians.

'I've got to get out of here.'

'One cup of coffee, you owe me that. I want to know details.'

He pushed, she sat, still not sure why she wasn't up and on her way. Sam would be looking for her. Still, a girl had the right to get the blood washed off her hands, put on a new coat of lipstick.

'What are you looking for?' His back was to her; he was pouring coffee in a gray mug that said Kentucky State Police, filling it with cream and some kind of powdered chocolate.

'My lipstick.'

'Hang on, I'll get you mine.'

She was never quite sure when he was teasing.

He handed her the coffee, picked up a white thermal blanket

that was folded neatly at the foot of the bed, and tucked it around her shoulders. She realized that he was treating her for shock.

She wasn't sure she minded. The blanket was very soft, the coffee warm in her hands. She took a sip. Not too sweet and definitely chocolaty. 'God, this is so good.'

'If I had a dollar for every time a woman told me that.'

'Gillane?'

He sat beside her. Began rubbing her shoulders. Tiny firm motions with strong fingers. He was a tall man, long-legged, and up this close she could smell some kind of soap or aftershave, spicy and slightly sweet.

'She didn't have a chance in hell, did she?'

'You think I could have saved her and didn't bother?' It was a measure of his confidence, or his distance therefrom, that he did not seem offended.

'No. But we didn't find her for a while. She was under that bed, scared and whispering, and we were all over the place.'

'Drink your coffee. No, sweetie, she had an eight-centimeter gash in her liver and even if I'd had her in here the second after she got that gut wound, those small liver lacerations are hard to contain, you can't stop the bleeding. It wasn't a nice death, but if she hadn't gone then, she'd be hanging on for another twenty-four hours, going slowly from peritonitis, and that's nobody's idea of fun. Survive that, and she'd have worn her colon in a bag on her hip.'

'I see.'

'They used to tell us in medical school – and you never really know if they make this stuff up, do you? But supposedly. In medieval times. They get a victim with a wound like this, they feed them onion soup.'

'Onion soup?'

'Then you sniff the wound. If you can smell the onion, you know your patient's a goner.'

Sonora remembered the leak of IV fluid from the wound.

'What happened out there?' Gillane asked.

Sonora took a breath, knew she was starting up the rumor

mill. 'It was some kind of home invasion. Two men and an angel broke a pane in the kitchen window. She – the mom – was in a back bedroom, doing laundry and watching the baby.'

'I saw the baby.'

'She's okay. Everybody else, dead. Nobody went nice. Slit the daughter's throat. The little boy, God, Gillane, a two-year-old, maybe three. We found him in the living room with his neck broken. Quick though. Some time in the middle of all this the father came home. They took a chair out of the kitchen and tied him up with the drapery cords. Looks like he witnessed a lot of it, his hands were torn to shreds. And they had a dog. They killed that too.'

'Did you say an angel?'

Sonora shrugged. Took another sip of coffee.

'Are you still seeing that Jerk?'

'What?'

'Not my word. Sam's. He ratted you out. I heard you were pretty hot and heavy.'

'Nope, that one's history.'

'Good. I'll call you.'

'I'm not going to have one second to spare for you or anybody else, and by the way, your timing is absolutely crappy.' She put the coffee cup down on his desk, balled up the blanket.

'Offer you a Twinkie before you go?'

It gave her pause. The Jerk would never have offered her a Twinkie. He seemed to derive his greatest pleasure from doing without. Food eaten cheaply, no frills, simple nutrients, gave him more happiness than a really good meal. He would have made an excellent religious fanatic, a fabulous monk. In the boyfriend category, of course, that sort of thing didn't rate.

'Actually yes, I would like a Twinkie.'

Gillane bent down and pulled an open box from under the bed. Tossed her a cellophane wrapper that had two Twinkies, nestled side by side. 'I'll call you.'

'I won't be home.' She opened the door to the hallway.

'Sonora?'

'What now?'

'You said she was under the bed whispering? What was she whispering?'

'Hail, Mary, full of grace.'

'Ah. Her catechism.'

'Yes. Her catechism.'

Chapter Ten

When Sonora walked out of the automatic doors of the ER she saw Sam, heading in the other way, Taurus parked at an angle by the curb.

'How is she?' Sam asked.

'In a far far better place than you and me.'

'You and I. We got Joy Stinnet's next of kin, local anyway. A great-uncle – lives out in Indian Hills. Next-door neighbor says they're pretty close. Crick wants us out there tonight.'

Sonora nodded. Scooted past Sam and slid behind the wheel of the Taurus.

'What?' Sam said. 'I always drive.'

Sonora adjusted the seat all the way up. Raised it so she could see over the wheel. She glanced at herself in the rear-view mirror, thinking that she looked very steady.

Sam slid into the seat beside her. 'You keep fiddling with that, I'll never get it back where I want it. By the way, change lanes, you're headed for the wrong exit.' His radio crackled. He still didn't have his seat belt on. 'Delarosa, yes, sir.'

Sonora could hear the voice on the other end, wrapping information around static.

'Sonora?' Sam said. 'You get anything out of Joy Stinnet?'

'Never regained consciousness.'

Sam muttered into the radio, looked up. 'Where the hell are you going?'

'What did Crick say?'

'They're looking for the Jeep, they have an APB out. White Grand Cherokee, Marine Corps sticker on the back window.'

'Guy was an ex-marine?'

'Maybe he just thought the sticker looked pretty. Are you . . . what the hell? You're heading home?'

'You want me to go notify next of kin with the woman's blood all over my damn shirt?' It was a good excuse for something she'd thought up on the spur of the moment. She had the need to check the kids, see them in person, make sure they were both okay.

'I told Crick we were on the way.'

'We are.'

'Why don't you just button your jacket over the blood?'

'Number one it'll ruin my blazer, and number two, there's too much blood to be covered up anyway.'

Sam folded his arms. Stared out the window. Still no seat belt.

She felt weird turning down her street. Everything familiar, but different. She pulled into the driveway, put the car in park, left the engine running.

'Stay put, I won't be just a minute.'

'That's what worries me.'

'What?'

'Never mind, just go.' He got out of the Taurus, headed for the driver's seat. 'It'll take me that long to get the seat back.'

'*I don't give a shit.*'

Sam looked startled. Sonora felt the same way. She shook her head, and ran for the garage, feeling for the opener in her purse, catching the button with her thumb. Saw, too late, the next-door neighbors sitting on the front porch, their faces hard to make out in the dark, though she could tell that their heads were angled her way.

'Good evening, how are you?' Her voice was polite, friendly. She did not wait for a response, but wound through the garage, past two bags of garbage, an ancient green tent that started life as navy blue, a box of precious family pictures that should have been moved inside a year ago, a red canoe, sideways, under a white metal bunk bed, and a bag of old maternity clothes she was terrified to throw away.

Something rustled on the left.

Clampett met her in the kitchen, tail wagging, happy to see her. Mothers and dogs. Unconditional love.

She went to one knee and hugged him. He did not smell very good. His worn red bandanna was gone. He had probably taken it off and eaten it. It was his way.

She was immediately inundated with the look, smell, and overwhelmingly depressing feel of a dirty sticky kitchen. Pork roast on the cutting board, rice still stuck to the bottom of a pot on the stove, a mound of lettuce leaves, tomato ends, mushroom bits, onion skins in the sink, beneath the bits of pork, rice and bread the children had dumped from their plates.

The kitchen window was wide open, blinds hanging down to the sill, rippling with the breeze.

The men who had brutalized Joy Stinnet and her family had come in through the kitchen.

Sonora shut the window, locked it. Saw the milk spilled on the counter, the napkins on the floor, shredded by Clampett. She looked at the dishes, the open bottle of catsup. The numbness cleared, like headlights in a fog, and she felt a surge of happiness. Her world was still intact.

Outside a horn honked. What the hell was Sam thinking, at this time of night?

Sonora washed her hands, lemon-smelling Palmolive dish-washing liquid in the palms of her hands, making soft white bubbles that spattered overtop the food leavings clogging the sink, adding a clean smell to the scent of vegetable and cooked meat.

She ripped three paper towels from the dispenser, much too hard, and the roll kept coming, paper towels rippling over the countertop and settling in a pile on the floor. A pink and blue picture of a cottage with a heart that said *Bless Our Happy Home*. Heather had picked it out. She was into paper towels and she favored the expensive brands.

Sonora scooped up the pile of paper towels, opened the cabinet under the sink, and tossed them into the trash can.

Something leaped out at her and Sonora screamed, fell backward, lost her balance and hit the floor. The mouse, a big one by mouse standards, took off across the kitchen floor, with Clampett in pursuit.

Sonora stayed on the floor, letting her heartbeat slow. Remembered the rustling noise in the garage.

With any luck it was just the one mouse, and Clampett would take care of it.

She stood up, shoved the garbage can back under the sink, did not stop to look into the dark caverns behind, but headed down the hallway to check the kids.

The house was quiet, except for Clampett, who had run head-first into the couch and was now crouched, waiting.

Sonora checked Tim's door. Locked. Heather's too, the brats. She took a bobby pin from the bathroom, picked the lock, opened both doors in seconds.

Tim was sprawled across a bare mattress in a room as aromatic as a school gym. His hubcap collection was growing. He always told her he found them by the side of the road, but she was beginning to worry. She closed the door, moved on to Heather's room, found her daughter asleep in a tangle of blankets, a Hanson CD, evidently set on repeat, playing softly.

Happy music.

She stood in the hallway, saw that a dark stain had rubbed off the bottom of her Reeboks and streaked the carpet. Blood.

Sonora peeled the shirt off and balled it up to throw away. Scrubbed her stomach with a washrag. The bra was bloodstained too. She took it off, and threw it over the shirt. Dammit. She found another bra hanging from the closet door, put on another white cotton shirt. She threw the washrag into the pile of bloody clothes, felt a tingle of something like anticipation or, God forgive her, excitement at the base of her spine. She was the good guys. It was good to be the good guys.

Sonora closed her bedroom door, to inhibit wandering mice, wondered when she would get back home again, took what cash she had and put it in the emergency money box. She double-checked the kitchen window and filled Clampett's water bowl. He accepted a pat on the head, but stayed by the couch, hunting mouse.

Sonora took one last look around the house. Locked the doors, headed down the driveway to Sam, on his cell phone, probably talking to his wife.

He stuck his head out the window. 'Took you long enough. You stop to make a meatloaf or something?'

Sonora shook her head. 'There are fifty-seven frozen Lean Cuisines in the freezer – this time I'm prepared.'

'I heard you yelling.'

'I have a mouse.' Sonora got in the car. Closed the door softly.

Sam fiddled with the seat adjustment, going ostentatiously forward and backward, a pained look on his face. He looked at her across the driver's seat. 'I got news for you, Sonora. It's not an "it".'

'I don't care if it's a boy mouse or a girl mouse.'

'That's not the point. They don't travel alone, Sonora. You don't have a mouse. You have mice.'

'It was only one, Sam.'

He did not contradict her but he laughed, which was worse.

Chapter Eleven

It spoke to Sonora that the closest living relative Joy Stinnet had was a great-uncle who lived way out in Indian Hills. As a child she had taken the spread of grandparents, aunts, uncles and cousins for granted. The fourth of July and Memorial Day picnics were semi-duty, semi-fun.

Her family was scattered now, her mother and brother dead, grandparents hardly a memory. She worried about Tim and Heather growing up with only her.

And Clampett of course. The world's best dog.

'Do you see your family much?' Sonora asked Sam. She knew that he did, she just wanted to get him talking about it.

He squinted through the windshield, and she knew that look, the look of a man who would rather die than admit that he was lost.

'My *family* much? Don't I go home every night?'

'No, like aunts and grandparents and cousins and stuff.'

'Every major holiday of my life.'

'Hard to imagine, all those pickup trucks in one place.'

Sam squinted his eyes at her. 'You have been in a bad mood for seven months.'

'My record is a year and a half.'

'Yeah, Sonora, but don't you get the significance? Didn't you meet that guy seven months ago?'

'The Jerk? So? I'm done with him. Sam, you missed the turn.'

47

'That wasn't our turn. I think we were supposed to turn back at that T-section. Did it say Cricket Lane?'

'How the hell should I know? It's dark outside.'

'You ever hear from him?'

'No.'

'You call him?'

'No. You think I should?'

Sam stopped, backed the car sideways, started out the other way. 'No, don't do that, you'll break Gruber's heart.'

'Gruber? If he has a thing for anybody it's Sanders.'

'I didn't say he had a thing for you, Sonora. He won the pool, that's all.'

Sam rolled his window down, looked sideways. Seemed to come to a decision. 'Right or left?' he asked her.

'Left.'

He went right.

'What pool, Sam?'

'He picked August for when you'd be done with that guy. I would have taken July, myself. And Sanders thought you would get married.'

'Sanders was in on this?'

'She wouldn't bet in the pool, no, she said it was tacky, and you would kill her if you found out, but her opinion was that you'd get married.'

'You guys had a pool on the Jerk, like the one you had guessing when Molliter's wife was going to have her baby?'

Sam was nodding.

'You were actually betting on when it would be over with my boyfriend?' They had been betting while she had been crying?

'Actually it was more complicated. Would you dump him, or be dumped, were you—'

'Were I *what*?'

'Nothing.'

'Dammit, Sam.'

'Don't get mad at me, I didn't have any money in the pot.'

'Thank you for that, at least.'

'They wouldn't *let* me in, figured since I was your partner I'd have inside information.'

'So Gruber won?'

'Hundred eighty dollars.'

'I *hate* you guys.'

'Not me.'

'You especially. Dammit. You went right by that turn again.'

'It's a gravel road.'

'So? That's against the law, living on a gravel road?'

'It's not usual.'

'If you were out in the country as much as I am, Sam, you would not be surprised by a little bit of gravel road.'

'You know, ever since you got that horse, you act like some kind of hot-shot farm girl.' Sam slowed the Taurus, scattered rock crackling under the tires, announcing their presence to anyone within five square miles.

'I may be learning late in life, Sam, but I am learning.'

'Do you ever get to ride him?'

'Not much. He scares me and I never have time.'

'Get rid of him.'

'No way. I happen to love that horse. And I like hanging out in feed stores, and I now even concede the value of a pickup.'

'Will wonders ever cease.'

Chapter Twelve

Joy Stinnet's great-uncle lived on one of those strange little properties that started life as a moderate home in the country. But as the city stretched ever onward and the urbans sprawled, the land around this small place became a haven for people who wanted to spend their money on property that was close to the city proper with the advantages of the countryside. The best or the worst of all worlds, depending upon your viewpoint.

Sam stopped the Taurus about a hundred feet from the house. The driveway was lined on the right by a sagging wire fence, on the left by trees.

The house was small. Yellow clapboard.

Sonora followed Sam across the weedy grass, stepping on squares of crumbling red brick that someone had laid down as stepping stones in happy years gone by. The porch light was on, a yellow sixty-watt bulb in a black metal socket over a heavy wood door that was a faded country green.

The concrete steps led to a small porch that had pulled six inches from the house, leaving a leaf-filled gap that was likely a haven for things Sonora did not want to think about.

'No lights on in the house,' Sonora said. She felt embarrassed. What if they had the wrong house? It had happened before.

'Probably gone to bed.' Sam gave her a sideways look. Knocked on the door.

A dog barked and howled, a sort of chokey, panicked sound,

as if the animal had been woken from a sound sleep, napping on the job.

Sam and Sonora waited. The front of the yard was screened in by trees, evergreens, oaks, a Japanese maple. Plenty of places for someone to hide, Sonora thought, but shady and cool in the summer.

The dog quieted. Sam knocked again.

'No one home?' Sonora asked him.

'You wish.'

A light went on, in a window on the left side of the house. A bedroom. They waited.

There were noises, suddenly, on the other side of the door. A deadbolt, unlatching. The door sticking, a noise of suction, then the front door, a heavy old thing of solid oak, swung forward.

The man who stood in the doorway was six feet six inches tall, by Sonora's guess, and anywhere from eighty to eight hundred. He wore yellow and brown flannel pajamas that someone had ironed, and a heavy brown velour bathrobe belted tightly around his waist. He had brown leather house slippers on size thirteen and a half feet. The bones of his shoulders were prominent, his face thin, and though his frame could easily handle another fifty or more pounds, he was not gaunt or wasted. He looked like a man who'd been fit and active most of his life.

He wore glasses, wire frames curling over his ears, which stuck out from the closely razored white and gray-flecked hair.

'Who is disturbing me at this time of night?'

The voice aged him.

A basset hound stood quietly by the man's leg. The dog's eyes were red-rimmed and droopy. She had clearly been woken from a sound sleep.

Sam offered his ID. 'Sir, I'm Detective Delarosa. This is my partner, Detective Blair. We're police officers, sir, Cincinnati Police Department, looking for a Mr Franklin Ward.'

'That would be me. I'm Franklin Ward.' The man licked his lips, focused on the identification Sam offered, took it between both of his hands and held it at a distance. Far-sighted. His fingers trembled. There were age spots on the backs of his hands.

The man took his time. Cleaned his glasses on the sash of his bathrobe, put them back on, and read Sam's ID word for word, lips moving in an inaudible mutter.

It was something of a wait. The man's hands, like cold engines, did not seem to cooperate.

'Is something the matter?' Ward asked them. 'I have a clean conscience myself.'

'Yes, sir, no question of that. I'm afraid we have bad news.' Sam left it at that, voice steady, reassuring.

'You best come on in, then. Don't mind the dog, she's not going to hurt you.'

The biggest danger from the basset hound, Sonora thought, was that she might fall asleep on your foot.

The man waved them to a couch that was covered in an old tasseled gold bedspread, clearly the dog's favorite spot from the thick layer of hair coating the gold spread. Franklin Ward sat down in an old brown recliner, the vinyl repaired with duct tape on the right armrest. He sat with his back straight, large hands resting on his knees.

He reminded Sonora of her grandfather. He had died when she was two, but she remembered a tall lean man with glasses and a flannel shirt, throwing her up into the air, making her stomach flutter, catching her. Calling her his little cupcake.

Franklin Ward's quiet, trembling cooperation caught her more than the tears and hysteria of similar visits to other people, victims of mayhem. The wait to be told would be agony for him. He anticipated the blow. Waited for it. For once she was going to let Sam do it.

'Mr Ward, is there someone you can call to be with you?'

He nodded. Went to the phone, an old clunky black one with a rotary dial. His fingers shook and he dialed heavily, slowly. Looked up at Sonora. 'My niece, you know, m'great-niece. She looks after me. Here all the time with her babies. I keep her horse for her . . . hello, Joy? Joy?' He listened. 'Oh, it's the machine.' He frowned. 'Let me dial it again, she should be home this time of night.'

Sonora looked at Sam. 'Do something.'

Sam glared at her, stood up, held a hand out for the phone.

Ward looked at him. 'Just let me try her again. Maybe you better dial it for me.'

'Mr Ward, this is about your niece.'

Ward looked at Sam as if he'd threatened him. 'I better sit down.'

Sam hung the phone up gently. 'Mr Ward, when was the last time you talked to your niece?'

The man licked his lips. 'Yesterday afternoon. And she called me this morning, asked me to put some corn oil into Abigail's feed. Abigail is her mare. Joy used to board her out, but she and Carl have been having some troubles and I said I'd take the horse for a while.'

'What kind of troubles?' Sonora asked.

Ward did not want to tell her. 'Money troubles. Carl's business – he's a paint contractor, and one of his major clients went bankrupt and Carl never got paid. They had some unexpected bills with the baby, and everything just kind of hit them at once. It happens to people. They're good people. Please tell me what all this is about.'

'Mr Ward, I'm sorry to have to tell you that your niece has met with a serious accident.' Sonora wondered why it was habit to say 'met with'. As if Joy Stinnet had been introduced to a sociopath and a knife.

'Is she dead?'

'Yes, sir, she is.'

'Well, well . . .' Ward took off his glasses and polished them with the flannel belt. 'You are police officers? Was it an automobile accident? Is Carl at home?'

'Sir. Your niece was murdered.'

'Murdered?'

'Yes, sir.'

'How could that be?'

'Someone broke into their home.'

'Are you sure you got the right people? She had a nice new house in that new subdivision . . . oh, darn, I can't think of the name but the street was . . .' He reached in a drawer, took out a

Bible, the King James version, and took a stack of papers that were wedged in the middle. His fingers moved like thick sausages through the papers. 'Here it is, it was on Edrington Court, there in Cincinnati proper.'

Sonora sat forward. 'Mr Ward, we have the right house.'

'What about the babies? What about Carl?'

'Mr Ward . . .' Sonora looked at Sam. Why was she doing this again? 'Mr Ward, none of them made it.'

'None of them made it? You mean . . . all of them were killed?'

'All of them except the baby. A daughter. About three months old.'

'But I just can't . . . I just can't believe this.' Tears leaked from the man's eyes. 'What on earth happened?'

'We're piecing that together right now, Mr Ward. Someone broke into the house and killed everyone except the baby. Your niece managed to hide her under the bed and save her. Sir, is there anyone else we can call, to be with you right now?'

'Joy. She's the only family that I have.'

'We can get a social worker.'

'Mrs Cavanaugh lives down the road. She looks in on me and gets my supper three times a week. I can call her if I need someone.'

'We'll stay until she gets here. If you could tell me her number . . .'

'I don't remember. It's posted on the wall in the kitchen.'

'I'll make the call,' Sam said. Escaping.

'Mr Ward, may I get you a glass of water? Or make you some coffee? Or . . . anything.'

He did not answer.

A curious blankness settled over him, as if he were unable or unwilling to connect. The news had been too much for him. It was the kind of news that would be too much for anyone.

Sonora's first inclination was to think that his age would make him fragile, but she wondered now if the opposite were true, if life experience made him more able. He transformed right then and there. He was another person, a distanced person, his eyes like empty windows, his body a tense, tough shell. Endurance mode. Pain mode. No screams and wails, no denial, but a tortured acceptance. He had been there before. The only soft thing about him were the tears that gushed over the new-forming beard stubble on his chin and cheeks.

He was the last remaining one in the clan. Except for the baby. Down to two.

So many questions. She would have to come back. She gritted her teeth against impatience and the familiar feeling that time was slipping away.

Chapter Thirteen

The fifth floor of the Board of Elections building was lit like a torch, the parking lot behind the loading dock was full. Cincinnati's finest out in force.

Sonora noticed a smear of blood on the toe of her Reeboks as she walked past the glass booth, through the swing doors into the bull-pen. She frowned, replaying the scene in Ward's living room. She did not think he had noticed. But Molliter, her least favorite co-worker, was giving her a second look. He seemed preoccupied. His hair, orange-red, had been clipped in a burr that would bring tears of joy to a marine recruiter, and his skin, parchment thin, was webbed at the eyes and mouth with a stamp of finely etched wrinkles that overlaid as many freckles as there were grains of sand. He held a file close to his chest like he was pledging the flag. Sonora could see a fur of fine, red-gold hair on the backs of his hands. She had always wished he would use Nair or something.

He stopped abruptly. Looked her up and down. 'I'm praying for them,' he said softly.

Sonora looked over his shoulder, saw Crick, back to her, deep in conversation with Sanders, and headed his way. Felt Sam's bulk at her back as she headed down the hall.

Crick turned and looked at her and she felt a knot in her stomach as she waited for him to ask why they had been gone so long.

'Anything?' he asked.

Anything? she wondered.

'The woman is dead,' Sam said. 'Joy Stinnet died on the table in the ER.'

Sonora nodded. 'I was right there, she never regained consciousness.'

Crick rubbed the back of his neck. 'Damn. Okay. Sit down, right now, Sonora. Write down exactly what she said to you, word for word.'

Sonora sat at her desk. Looked at the typewriter. Drew a total blank. Crick glanced her way, and she started typing Js. JJJJJJJ . . . She glanced up. She wanted to know what the hell was happening.

Crick was talking in a low tone to Sam. 'Nothing yet on the Jeep. CSU is still out there, but Mickey's in the lab; he got in about fifteen minutes ago. He'll be over soon as he can, but he says those pebbles of yours are olive pits.'

Sonora looked up. 'Olive pits?'

'Type,' Crick told her. Glanced back at Sam. 'What about that baby?'

'Not a scratch,' Sam said.

'We got Sanders working on next of kin, Molliter's checking for prison breaks and ex-cons, and Gruber's coordinating the initial reports from the neighbor canvas. We've got three uniforms out there right now, working the crowd and going door to door.' Crick glanced up, saw that Sonora was not typing. 'Got it?'

'Almost.'

'Okay, get this entered into NCIC and see if we get any hits. How many men were there? Did the mother make any sense on that?'

'Two men and an angel.' Sonora noticed that Molliter had stopped and was listening.

Crick looked at her.

'It's what she said.'

'Two makes more sense,' Crick said. 'Got to be two.'

Sonora nodded. Two men, egging each other on. She'd seen that synergy before, a sort of heinous performance art, two predators playing *Can you top this?* A third didn't work. A third meant a gang, premeditation, a crime where money changed hands. Business. The curtain cords used to bind Carl Stinnet said crime of opportunity.

Sonora checked her watch. Wondered how much longer CSU would be out there, and if she could get back tonight. She typed more Js. She closed her eyes, put herself back in the hallway, remembered the woman's screams when the bed ruffle had been pulled away.

What the hell was it she had said?

Someone behind her called her name, right about the time her phone started ringing. She picked it up.

'Cincinnati Police Department, Homicide. Specialist Blair speaking.'

'Detective Blair or Delarosa, please.'

A man's voice. Businesslike, not unfriendly, a certain self-confidence in the tone. Not the slippery whine or cant of the typical informer.

'This is Blair.'

'I understand you caught yourself a bad one.'

Sonora sat up, tried to keep the wary tone out of her voice. 'Who's speaking, please?'

'Sorry. My name is Jack Van Owen, retired, homicide. I—'

Sonora leaned forward. 'Excuse me, did you say Jack *Van Owen*?'

'I . . . yes.'

'*The* Jack Van Owen? Crick's famous ex-partner, the guy who—'

'Guilty.'

The voice was younger than she'd have imagined. An attractive baritone.

'I . . . well, what can I . . . did you want to speak to Sergeant Crick?'

'Actually, no, I wanted to speak to you. You're Detective Blair, aren't you?'

'I are. I am.' Fumble, fumble. But who wouldn't? As baby detectives, they'd been weaned on stories of Jack Van Owen, cut down in his prime by a bullet to the head, pensioned off and sorely missed, for his detective work, his practical jokes, and his ability to charm a witness and nail a good ole boy confession.

Crick, impressed by no one, spoke of the man with an affectionate reverence that stunned them.

'I wouldn't be bothering you right now . . .'

Bothering? Sonora thought.

'But . . . you've got a home invasion. Did you, by any chance, find olive pits at the scene?'

Sonora felt the knot of tension in her jaw. 'Olive pits?'

'Police radio,' the voice said, just a trace of amusement. 'Old habits, you know? It's always on. When I heard about it I called Mickey in CSU. He let it out.'

'He told you there were olive pits?'

'Yeah. If he hasn't been across the hall to tell you, he's probably waiting to confirm.'

There was something wistful in his voice. He missed it. Before tonight, she would have missed it too.

'Anyway, Detective Blair, I had some information I thought I'd better pass along.'

Unbelievable. She picked up the pen she had dropped when he'd said his name.

'There's this guy I arrested about eleven years ago. He used to eat olives obsessively, had a jar of them all the time, worse than a smoker. He'd spit the pits on his victims. Last I heard he was in LaGrange, but he was due out last May. I was wondering what the odds are, that there'd be two guys out there like that.'

'Olive-eating sociopaths.'

'Yeah. Not too likely, you think?'

'I think not, no. You wouldn't remember this boy's name?'

'Never forget it. Aruba, Lancaster, AKA Lanky Aruba. Stone-cold sociopath, not very bright, or if he is he can't use it. Very disassociated. Dangerous as hell when you trigger the rage. Think Slingblade meets *A Clockwork Orange*. You remember—'

'Yeah, I remember the movie.'

'You don't sound that old.'

'My kid rented it.'

'Got you.' He paused a beat, and there was something in his voice, just a hint that he found her sharp, and he found her interesting. Or maybe she was hallucinating. 'Okay. Now our boy, Lanky, didn't specialize in home invasions way back when. He's kind of a nervous type, not organized enough to be a planner, and he lives in a whole other universe, let me tell you. Back then he was an opportunistic rapist, a petty thief. I think he had a few charges for dealing. He kind of drifts, you know, sort of an odd-job guy. By the time I got a hold of him, his crimes were escalating to murder, no matter what anybody hired him for. He's tough to keep in line, too out there.'

'Lanky Aruba,' Sonora said, going to the computer.

'Lanky's got a sister, lives in Kentucky, on the Woodford–Fayette County line, close to a small town called . . . let me think here. Versailles. Her address should be in his file somewhere.'

'If she's still there.'

'God knows people are transient these days.'

She paused. Had she sounded ungrateful? 'Listen, Mr Van Owen, I appreciate the call.'

'Call me Jack. Give my best to Crick, will you?'

'Sure.'

'Thanks for letting me keep my hand in. Good hunting, Detective.' The phone line clicked.

Letting him keep his hand in? He'd handed her the tip that might crack the case, and thanked her for it. Shown a gentle courtesy by coming straight to her and not going through Crick. The legend lived on.

Sonora worked the computer, entered Lanky's name again, tapped her fingers on the desk. The sister's address came up. Old Frankfort Pike, Versailles, Kentucky.

'Hey, Sam?' she said, craning her neck. 'You ever hear of a place in Kentucky called Versailles? Wasn't that where you and Louis the Thirteenth were born?'

Sam gave her a look, rubbed the back of his neck. 'Louis the Thirteenth was not born in Versailles.'

'No?'

'No.'

'So where was he born?'

'Somewhere up in Michigan, I think. And you're pronouncing it wrong. It's Ver-sayles, by local custom; anything else'll make you sound like a hick from out of town.'

'I am from out of town.'

'And no, you've got me placed at the wrong end of the state. This is down near Lexington. Remember that Daniels guy lived there.'

Sonora frowned. 'Of course I remember. About an hour from here, isn't it?'

'Maybe with you behind the wheel. Most people take an hour and a half.'

'How come they say Ver-sayles and not Ver-seye?'

'Sonora, when you go to Arby's do you order a chicken cordon bleu or a chicken cordon blue?'

'I order the chicken and bacon thing at Wendy's.'

'Then let me put it to you this way. People in Kentucky don't need some smartass from Ohio telling them how to say Versailles. Why are we on this subject, anyway?' He got up and looked over her shoulder. 'Why are you typing Js?'

Sonora pointed to the computer screen. 'One, Lancaster AKA Lanky Aruba has a sister who lives near Versailles.'

'Who in the hell is Lancaster Aruba?'

'You will not believe the luck. I just got off the phone with, wait for it, Jack Van Owen—'

'*Jack Van Owen?*'

'What he said.'

'Guy that used to partner Sergeant Crick?'

'Yeah, that's what—'

'Hell-fire, Sonora, that guy is a . . . he's a damn legend.'

'And me without my autograph book.' Sonora saw that Crick, on her left at the coffee pot, was looking their way.

He stopped his coffee cup in mid air. 'Somebody say Van Owen?'

'Yeah.' Sonora ripped the sheet of Js out of her typewriter and shoved them in her middle desk drawer. Easier said than done – the drawer was crammed tight and would not shut.

'*Jack* Van Owen?'

'What he said.' Sonora pushed harder, but the drawer was stuck.

Crick headed to her desk. 'Let me talk to him.'

'He hung up already.' Sonora shoved harder and the desk made a high-pitched squeak but came within an inch of shutting.

'Let me help you with that,' Sam said.

'*No*. Thank you.'

'See? Cranky for the last seven months.'

Crick left his coffee cup behind, signaling serious intent, and headed for her desk. 'Let me talk to him.'

'I told you, sir, he hung up already.'

'When Jack Van Owen calls you let me talk to him. What did he want?'

'He had information about some guy he arrested eleven years ago, guy named Lanky Aruba.'

Crick went back for the cup, swallowed coffee. Chewed it around in his mouth. 'Something about that name, Aruba, gives me that old bad feeling.'

'Van Owen, I mean Jack, he told me to call him Jack, did I mention that?'

Sam blew her a kiss.

'Jack says this Aruba is a sociopath, not all there, you know, like, disassociated, like that, but what is there is brutal, eats olives obsessively like some people smoke, and spits olive pits on his victims.'

Sam's mouth dropped open. 'You're shitting me.'

'Good old Jack,' Crick said softly. 'He may have just handed you jerks the case. Check it out.'

Sonora felt a tap on her elbow. It was Sanders, thirty pounds heavier than a year ago when she'd given up at long last on a toxic romance, but still wearing the soft straight sandy pageboy, the Peter Pan collars, and pleated skirts. The extra weight made her look older.

Her look was apologetic. 'I've got a couple of addresses for you, Sonora. Carl Stinnet's next of kin.'

Chapter Fourteen

It was a life of late-night work, Sonora thought. A cone of light, cast by a lamp against the press of shadow and dark, illuminated the papers on her desk. She put the typed two-page description of Joy Stinnet's last words in a file, inhaled the smell of fatigue and concentration, a human alone, at work, lonely. Strange for a Tuesday, giving her an out-of-sync feeling. The world was out at Applebee's and neighborhood bars, tucked up with Jay Leno and their significant other, and she was here, alone with the guys on the last shift, sweating beneath the halogen light, working on things to make the heart cringe.

She left the coffee cup half full on her desk, and headed home.

It was long, the drive out to Blue Ash. The death of the family Stinnet had infected her, settled into her mind like silt in the bottom of a dirty brown river. She could not stop things. She only saw the aftermath, in the hushed, shocky quiet after the noise and the shouting, the blood and the tears.

She would die too, one day. Step off that ledge. Sonora tried to shake the thought. Couldn't. The recognition of mortality was as familiar to her as desire.

She was way too tired, way too down. Police work was dangerous to the soul.

Clampett was glad to see her.

It dawned on Sonora, as she passed the kitchen table, that she had not looked into the fruit basket for a while. It was always her intention to keep it full of crisp apples, firm kiwis, and whatever else was in season. But it was not the kind of thing you could leave on its own for weeks at a time.

She passed it by with a twinge of guilt, carrying her plate of pork roast and rice, hot from the microwave, a thick white napkin not quite protecting her fingers from the heat. She sat down, Clampett at her side, looked at the newspaper, took a sip of ice water, ate one bite of pork roast.

Her appetite deserted her with a suddenness that made her spit the bite she was eating into the napkin. She put her fork down and set the plate on the floor for Clampett, who did not need the snack but was ever so grateful.

She took her gun out of her purse, made sure the safety was on. Headed down the hallway toward her bedroom, turning off lights as she went. She had touched the dark things before, walked through the wreckage, shoes sticky from those rivers of blood.

Speaking of which. Blood traces on her new Reeboks. Elf Reeboks, Tim called them, because her feet were small.

Sonora washed her face and brushed her teeth and put on a big white Oxford shirt that almost reached her knees. Her favorite shirt to sleep in. She deserved it tonight.

She thought she might be pathetic, having a favorite shirt to sleep in. There had to be more to life than that. Like maybe a favorite person to sleep with.

She opened the window, and Clampett came in and rested his wet black nose on the sill. He would not want to share the bed if the window was open. She could have it all to herself.

She curled up on her right side, lights off, one leg under the covers, one leg out. The room was growing chill and damp, dark and mysterious with the wind.

And on the night air came the resonant saxophone howl of a train, horn blowing, and the background presence of the engine and those massive box cars, streaking down the rusting iron tracks.

The noise took her back, back to a night like this one, with the smell of rain in the air, a paddock full of horses, the bay of a bloodhound on the scent, and the hunt for a missing child.

She pushed the memory away. The horn wailed again. Train music – it always made her want something, she just did not know what.

Sonora closed her eyes, willing sleep. Instead, she heard whispers. The voice of Joy Stinnet. *Hail, Mary, full of grace.*

Some noise, like a window opening, startled her out of a doze. Sonora shoved the covers back, jumped out of bed, headed down the hallway, snatching her loaded Baretta off the lingerie dresser as she went.

That Clampett stayed relaxed in front of the window should have tipped her off. She checked every door, every window.

Stood outside the children's rooms in the middle of the hallway, knees like jelly. She did not venture into the bedrooms, did not breach the closed doors. She stood with her back to the wall, thinking what a wonderful thing it was that the children were alive, asleep, unaware.

Her legs, suddenly, did not hold her. She slid down the wall and landed on her knees, slowly, softly, like a woman unwinding.

After all this time. After all she had seen and done. All the times she had touched those stiff lifeless wrists, walked through blood and broken glass, tearstains and spent cartridges. Was she losing her way? Why now?

Clampett padded out into the hallway and settled beside her with a groan, panting lightly, the tip of his tongue pink and wet. Kind brown eyes. The world was a weird place. On the one hand, dogs. On the other, the death of everyday America in the blood-soaked home of Joy and Carl Stinnet.

Chapter Fifteen

Sonora woke thinking of the old man, Franklin Ward. She was curled tightly in the fetal position, the room like ice beneath that open window. What, she wondered, stretching, was the attraction of the fetal position?

She looked at the bedside clock. Five forty-seven. The alarm hadn't even gone off. She was supposed to meet Sam back at the Stinnets' house at eight. She could take a quick shower, and she'd still have time, if she drank her coffee on the way, to talk to Ward again before she went back to the home of Joy and Carl Stinnet.

In the light of day, the place was easy to find. It had a sort of homey charm, and Sonora felt guilty for being the bearer of bad news to a house built in the 1940s and painted buttercup yellow.

The night before, when Sam and Sonora had broken their terrible news, Mrs Cavanaugh had been nothing more than a phone number on the wall, and a quick glimpse of a worried woman at the kitchen door. This morning she greeted Sonora at Franklin Ward's front door, and invited her into a living room that smelled of coffee and bacon.

Mrs Cavanaugh, 'call me Bonnie', announced that she had hot biscuits on the stove with the air of one whose biscuits were never refused. Sonora felt vaguely comforted by this evidence that there were still people in the world who baked before breakfast. She had the feeling that she had stepped into another world.

She followed Bonnie Cavanaugh past the couch, glancing at the picture Ward had shown her before she left the night before, a snapshot, faded and creased and framed in tarnished silver, of Ward and his brother in uniform before they had gone off to fight in World War II.

To fight in that war he would have to be . . . but there Sonora's education, or her early attention to her education, failed her. She did not remember the years of World War II. At a guess she'd say 1942 or 1943.

She paused in front of the picture, resisting the urge to pick up the frame. They were beautiful creatures form the past, Franklin Ward and his little brother, Emerson, tall and young in brand-new uniforms, immortalized by the local paper, teenage boys off to war. They had been no more than two years older than her own son was now.

It was only when you had children that you realized wars were fought by babies.

Bonnie Cavanaugh looked at Sonora over her shoulder, waiting politely. Her appearance did not add up to the sum of the whole. Taken in segments, she was almost comically unattractive. Crooked front tooth that protruded over her lower lip. Long, basset-hound face, sagging under years of excess poundage. Weird hair. Brown and frizzy, worn too long, pulled severely back from a face that had never been pretty.

She had a peaceful charm, that gave her a comforting glow. No doubt she had worries: the lines over the brows were too deeply etched to be merely age and sunshine, and the dual effects of stress and gravity had worn creases at either side of Bonnie Cavanaugh's mouth.

But there was something about her. Perhaps it was nothing more than the woman's quiet assurance, her air of life experience that had not marred the impression of a basic goodness.

Sonora had met people, men and women, who made the hair stand up on the back of her neck, men and women she would tear to pieces if they came to her front door and tried to cross the threshold into the air space of her children.

Certainly this woman led an ordinary life. But to Sonora, she seemed extraordinary. She wanted to pull up a chair at that kitchen table and tell Bonnie Cavanaugh her troubles, tell her the dream about her brother, and the whispers she had heard in her sleep, Joy's voice, saying her catechism.

She had not planned to talk to the woman and she did not want a biscuit. But that was before she met Mrs Cavanaugh, that was before she realized that this was the kind of woman you talked to.

Bonnie Cavanaugh led Sonora into the kitchen, and motioned her to a chair. Sonora settled in front of a worn, maple corner cabinet that displayed the multicolored pastels of Fiesta Ware, originals, with chips and cracks and faded colors. Mrs Cavanaugh put a pastel-blue plate and a plaid cloth napkin in front of Sonora, served her two biscuits, and poured her a cup of coffee in a bone-china cup that was white with deep rose flowers, a glued and glazed crack in the saucer beneath.

Nothing at the table matched, but somehow it all went together, like couples who've been married forty years.

'Cream?'

Sonora nodded.

Mrs Cavanaugh brought a small carton of half and half out of the refrigerator, set the carton next to Sonora's cup, gave her a tiny teaspoon that had the heft and balance of genuine silver.

Sonora cut a biscuit in half and reversed her original impression, which was that Mrs Cavanaugh was the kind of female who fell into the category of 'overlooked'. It was a popular opinion that women of a certain age became invisible. Sonora realized that this, like other popular and accepted myths, was total crap. This woman had an air of self-confidence and comfort in her skin that said she was rarely overlooked, and if she were, would not particularly care.

Sonora poured cream in her coffee, stirred, added more till she got the light-brown color she favored. 'Did you know Joy and Carl very well, Mrs Cavanaugh? Were they close to Mr Ward?'

'Oh, honey, Joy was here all the time.' Bonnie Cavanaugh set apple butter, Crock Pot margarine, and blackberry jelly within Sonora's reach. 'Two or three times a week, until the last baby. Then she couldn't get away so much.' She settled into the chair across from Sonora. 'She and Franklin just got on like nobody's business, have since Joy was a little girl. He never had no kids of his own, and believe you me, she *was* the apple of his eye. He's out there now, brushing Abigail, Joy's old horse. Bought that mare for her when Joy turned thirteen. She kept it here when she was a girl.'

Bonnie Cavanaugh leaned sideways on her left elbow, smiling and shedding tears. She grabbed a wad of yellow Kleenex from her pocket. 'You know, I can't help but cry, I hope you don't mind. I know'd Joy since she was . . . oh, eleven or twelve. She was a real sweet girl, and no bad mouth on her, not ever, not that I ever saw with me or Franklin. She was a good girl all her life, funny and lively most of the time, unless she was worrying, then she'd get real quiet.' The Kleenexes were called into use, sopping tears, wiping Bonnie Cavanaugh's reddened nose.

'How were things between Joy and her husband?'

'Carl was a dream.' Mrs Cavanaugh laid both palms on the table, yellow tissues showing beneath her right palm. 'I mean that now, I'm not just saying it. Not many people know this, 'cause she never liked to talk about it, but Joy was married once before, years ago, when she was eighteen. Lasted about six months, the boy just up and left her two weeks before Tina got born. Franklin stood behind her every minute, which was more than her own mama and daddy done, may they rest but not in peace.'

'They're both dead?'

'Eight years ago, in a motorcycle accident. They used to ride around on a Harley on the weekends, though they were normal enough the rest of the week. He worked for Procter and Gamble, shift supervisor, making peanut butter. Guy in a big green caddie never even saw them, ran them right into a guardrail on I–71, when they was probably doing sixty. She lived the night, poor thing, but he was dead on arrival. Killed instantly.'

Instant coffee, Sonora thought. Instant mashed potatoes. Instant death. She said, 'The ex-husband. Is he around at all?'

Mrs Cavanaugh gave her a blank look, then shook her head. 'Lord, no. She heard from him once, years ago, a few months after Tina got born, wanting bus money to come and see the baby. Which she sent and he never did show up. Joy just cried and cried. He called onst more, but Franklin took care of it, and we never did hear from *him* again. That's, Lord, sixteen years ago. Tina—'

But here her voice broke. She blew her nose. 'Excuse me. What I was going to say was Tina doesn't, Tina didn't take after him one tiny bit. We just liked to pretend it was a immaculate conception, you know, 'cause Joy never did like it when we brought him up.'

'What was his name?'

'Bobby Purcell. Last time we heard, he was out in Nevada somewhere.' Mrs Cavanaugh put her head in her hands. 'I'm sorry. I just cannot believe this has happened. It just seems to keep catching me by surprise.'

Sonora looked at her biscuit.

'Honey, I'm sorry, but this kind of thing, happening so sudden. What did whoever it was, what did he do to them?'

'Ma'am, he . . . he just killed them all. It was quick,' Sonora said.

'Social services called this morning about the baby. Franklin can't take her, and I offered, but they're trying to track down Carl's sister. Just as sweet as she can be. Franklin wanted to make sure they talked to Amber, not his half-brother, Eddie. Franklin gave them the number this morning.'

'A problem there, with the brother?'

'Not on a police level. He and his wife, Judice . . . you'd have to see them to believe them, is what Joy used to say.'

Sonora nodded, spreading a thin coat of apple butter on the biscuit. She took a small bite off the corner and nodded. 'Wonderful.' Bonnie Cavanaugh smiled. Sonora set the biscuit back on the plate. 'Mrs Cavanaugh, did Joy seem worried about anything, did she talk about strange phone calls, or . . .?'

The woman looked away. She seemed embarrassed.

An affair, Sonora thought.

Bonnie Cavanaugh placed her fingertips on the table. The skin on her hands was white and waxy-looking. 'They was hitting a pretty rough stretch with their finances. Lord knows we all go through it some time or other in our lives. I know Franklin was giving them as much as he could spare.

'See, what started it all was when Carl got hurt. He's a paint contractor, and he fell over a paint bucket, just a dumb thing, but he landed funny and broke his ankle and two ribs. And then he got the flu real bad, almost went into pneumonia. And with him being self-employed they just couldn't keep up with the health insurance, and her just having baby Chloe, they had quite a lot of bills, especially with Carl missing work. I know they were trying to get out of their car lease, but there wasn't nothing they could do without hurting their credit. And they'd just bought a house, which had taken most of their savings. It just seemed like everything come down on them at once. They still would of been okay, but one of Carl's major contractors went into bankruptcy, and he owed Carl for an awful lot of work. And another check he got went and bounced and Carl could not ever find the guy. And there's his workers needing to be paid, and taxes to the IRS. It just got really bad for them. Joy used to come here and just not say a word, she was so depressed, so worried, you know how it is, like she was so distracted and worried she couldn't even look at you, and bags under her eyes and I know'd she wasn't sleeping.

'So Franklin finally got it out of her. He took Abigail into his barn so Joy didn't have to pay board fees, and cashed out all his CDs so they could pay their workers and buy groceries. Carl was working all the time, even with his foot and all, and I think they were coming out of it. He was finally getting some of the money he was owed, and I think things were just starting to look up. Joy seemed more cheerful, and she was taking in typing jobs at home, which wore her out, with the baby to take care of, but it kept them in food. And Tina was working at Sonic and kicking her check in.

'I know their water got cut off a couple of times, and Franklin went down to pay that himself, 'cause Joy was so embarrassed she just couldn't face it. They had a couple long talks about strategy, like pay utilities first, that kind of thing, you know.'

'I know.' Sonora tore the biscuit in half so it would look like she was eating. 'You say Carl and Joy got along pretty well? Even with all the pressures of finances?'

'Oh, yeah, they stuck together. I mean, he'd been kind of down, but who could blame him?'

Sonora ran a finger on the edge of the table. Looked Mrs Cavanaugh in the eye. 'There was a certain amount of . . . anger, involved in this killing. Did either of them have any enemies? I know that sounds kind of dramatic for the suburbs. But was there any bad feeling with someone, anybody giving them trouble of any kind?'

Mrs Cavanaugh looked blank. 'No, ma'am. None to speak of.'

'Nothing at all?'

Mrs Cavanaugh narrowed her eyes. 'Well I shouldn't say no one. They were getting hounded to *death* over their bills. People calling early in the morning, late at night, and all day long. I know Joy was pretty tore up about it, and Franklin kept telling her that there were rules about that kind of thing. Now I have always paid my bills and I don't believe in charge cards, though that's the modern way, I know. But Joy and Carl was good people going through a tough time, and the way they got treated was shameful. Joy would sit here and cry, and she told me in private that she felt threatened, though Franklin and I both told her just to hold on and not answer the phone.'

Sonora nodded. Thought a minute, careful of her wording. 'I know how upsetting and annoying that can be, believe me, but that's not the kind of threat I'm talking about.' She tapped a finger on the edge of the tablecloth, wondering how to lead the woman down the nasty path of her own thought processes. 'You know, Mrs Cavanaugh, sometimes when people are under a lot of pressure, they might . . . they could do something they might otherwise not do. It doesn't mean they're bad people.'

Sonora watched the woman. Nothing but a blank look.

'For instance, one of them might have an affair. Which could lead to complications, like jealous lovers.'

Mrs Cavanaugh's mouth turned down, a look on her face that was cartoon comical, except Sonora did not feel like laughing.

'No, ma'am, there was none of that going on, as far as I know.'

'Would you know?' Sonora asked.

'Well, I was wondering, with Joy so upset all the time. And I know the signs, though you might not think it. I won't even tell you what my daughter's husband has put that girl through, and will continue to do unless she grows a backbone and throws him out. But I don't believe so. Not with Carl and Joy.'

'Okay then.' Sonora took her purse, put the napkin in a wad on the table. 'Can you get hold of an address on that ex-husband?'

'Oh, Lord, I doubt it. Well, maybe Franklin kept track of him. He might do that and just keep it to himself. He is an old-fashioned sort of gentleman, and he felt that was the kind of thing an uncle could take care of kind of behind the scenes, to shield Joy from getting upset.'

'If he's up to it, I'd like to ask him some questions.'

'He told me you'd be back. And he said he wanted to talk to you. Finish up your biscuits and I'll take you on out.'

Chapter Sixteen

Sonora walked toward the small, sagging barn under the benevolent but guarded eye of Bonnie Cavanaugh, the half biscuit she'd eaten sitting hard in her stomach. She paused at the lip of the barn aisle. Heard a man's voice, thin and tired, though there was no sign of the man.

'. . . lonely old thing. Hard to be queen of the barn when it's just you, isn't it, girl? Here you go, Abigail, have another one. I'm gonna have to be the one that spoils you now.'

Sonora recognized the nickering purr of a horse who anticipates the gastronomic ecstasy brought on by carrots, apples and sweet feed.

'Poor old Abigail, poor old thing. You miss her already, don't you, girl?' The voice broke.

Sonora took a step backward, counted to fifteen, then pushed against the already open barn door. She expected a creak of rusty hinges and was not disappointed.

'Hello?' she said. Stepping in.

The barn was small and cave-like, a dirt floor, tiny. Two stalls on one side and an open area on the right filled with hay bales, old feed sacks, a rusty wheelbarrow, bags of pine shavings, and a rusty manure spreader next to an aluminum ladder. Three dirt-encrusted window fans lay on an ancient moldy mattress.

'Who's that?' Ward stepped out of the stall, a red-bristled brush in his left hand. He wore faded tan corduroy pants and a brown flannel shirt. He looked creased, clean, and carefully groomed, right on down to the shine on his brown barn boots.

'Detective Blair, Mr Ward, Sonora Blair. I was here last night?'

'You catch him, Officer?'

There was real hope in the voice. Sonora never failed to be amazed by the optimism of the general public. Even the jaded ones, deep down inside, expected instant vindication.

'Soon,' she said.

He didn't answer.

Sonora kept moving, inhaling the scent of horse and hay, feeling the knots of tension in her shoulders ease as the familiar smells of horse and leather calmed the frayed feeling that was becoming as familiar as her own face. She paused outside the stall. It was twelve by twelve, a simple manger with an uneven dirt floor, liberally spread with yellow pinewood shavings. It was a simple barn, tar black, wood planks. A window had been rough-cut through the wood planks on the outside wall, and latched open like a crude shutter. A blue water bucket hung next to a black rubber feed tub. Hay was piled in the left corner, and the horse, mid bite, turned her head, gave Sonora a quick look, and went back to the hay.

'Alfalfa?' Sonora asked.

'You know your hay,' Ward said. He went back to the horse's right side, stroking her firmly with the brush, and Sonora started missing her own horse, Hell-Z-Poppin, an aptly named Arabian.

'She's too picky to eat timothy hay,' Ward said. 'Turns her nose up at orchard grass. She's as picky as a horse can be. Joy just spoiled her rotten.'

Her own horse, Poppin, was living on last year's timothy, and not too happy about it himself.

'Where'd you get that alfalfa?' Sonora asked.

'Friend of mine.'

'He got any more, I'll take it.'

'Have a horse, do you?' Ward said.

'Arab gelding. Hell-Z-Poppin.'

'He live up to his name?'

'And then some.'

Franklin Ward chuckled. 'Arabs do.'

The mare, Abigail, was large enough that Sonora wondered if she was in foal to twins, but she just smiled and said, 'Pretty horse.'

Ward kept brushing. 'Old piglet here is always a member of the clean plate club. We'll have to put her in a diet paddock in a few weeks when the grass gets sweet.'

Then why are you feeding her alfalfa? Sonora wondered, but she kept her mouth shut. There were as many horse opinions as there were horse people, and it paid not to say what you thought, unless you liked fireworks, open warfare, and hand-to-hand combat.

If she had learned one thing in the months she'd owned Poppin, it was when to shut up. Which, when it came to horses, was pretty much always.

'Mr Ward, I know this is a bad time for you, and if you want me to give you some time, so be it. But what I really want to do is ask you some questions.'

He nodded. 'Go on ahead. If you don't mind, I'll just keep on grooming. Abigail likes it and I find it settles my nerves. You have a horse. You know what I mean.'

She did know. She studied him, just for a minute. He had the curious mix of fragility and strength found only in elderly people who had led a certain kind of life. A wealth of life experience and a well-honed and finally trusted instinct that gave them a certain magic, trapped in a body that began to fail them when they had, at long last, figured so many things out.

Was she pushing too hard? She wondered if he had a heart condition. Could a man his age *not* have a heart condition?

Sonora opened her notebook. Leaned against the rough wood wall. 'I understand your niece and her husband were having money troubles.'

Ward nodded. 'They'd run into a rough patch all right, but they were climbing out.' He looked at Sonora. 'It's the kind of thing can happen to anybody. Even Donald Trump runs into problems with cash flow. Anybody says they never have that kind of trouble is lying.'

'Yes, sir, I understand. How was their marriage?'

'It was good,' he said.

Somehow, she was unable to pursue that one any further. 'You and Joy were pretty close, were you?'

'Fair on.'

Whatever that meant.

'Did she talk to you? Confide in you?'

'She'd talk about the kids. About Abigail. How Carl's business was going, that kind of thing. She wasn't one to bring me her worries.'

'Had she been threatened in any way? Had they been robbed? Did she talk about strange phone calls?'

'No. No, nothing like that I know of.'

'Did she or Carl have any . . . enemies?'

He stopped brushing. 'Officer, we're talking about a simple, middle-class, Cincinnati, Ohio, everyday average American family. They rented movie videos and ordered pizza on Friday night, and Joy stayed home with the kids. People like that don't *have* enemies. They don't sell drugs or government secrets, they just go grocery shopping on Saturday and church most Sundays.'

'What about Joy's ex-husband?'

'That pipsqueak? Who told you about him?'

'He's Tina's father.'

'No, he's not, not in my definition. Besides, he's long gone. I ran that boy off sixteen years ago, and we ain't heard from him since. And we won't hear from him either.'

'He have an address?' Sonora asked.

'Last time I heard of Bobby Purcell, he was in Kansas City, working at a Taco Bell. And overemployed, if you ask me.' He gave her a look over the back of the horse. 'You much good at picking hooves, Detective?'

Sonora looked up from her notebook. 'Picking hooves? Tolerable.'

'Kills my back to do it. That's the one thing Joy—'

She knew where this was going. 'Got a hoofpick?'

He pointed at a red plastic carryall. Sonora rummaged through the cotton rags, brushes, ferrazone ointment, until she found a black-handled pick. She stuck her notebook in her jacket pocket.

'The mare's gentle, right?' she asked.

'Hell, you own an Arab. This is just a little quarter horse.'

Sonora bent over, took the left hind foot between her hands. The mare had dainty feet, a healthy, springy frog, well-trimmed hooves. She dug packed-in manure, dirt and gravel from the horse's foot. She supposed Sam would call this bonding.

Chapter Seventeen

Sonora made Oldham in the thick of the early morning drive-the-kids-to-school-get-to-work traffic that clogged the primary roads and almost made a pretense of traffic in the Cincinnati subdivision.

She passed the pond, no ducks this morning, headed toward Edrington Court, took a sip of McDonald's coffee that made her wince no matter how much cream she added. Cincinnati might have pro sports teams, but she wasn't going to be content till there was a StarBucks on every corner.

Children milled on the curb, waiting for a school bus. Sonora passed a house where a little boy headed down the sidewalk from an open front door.

He wore huge white and black tennis shoes, and a Chicago Bulls cap – looked to be about seven or eight – and struggled down the walk with an aquarium too large and heavy for his arm span. Sonora could not contain the internal mommy cringe. A woman, large and pear-shaped in navy-blue sweat pants, closed and locked the front door, and followed the boy down the sidewalk, passing him by and opening the back gate of the red Honda Civic in the concrete driveway.

The boy reminded her of Tim, years ago. God, he'd grown up fast. She felt like crying, all of a sudden; why, she did not know.

Short on sleep, or going crazy.

She, who was usually lost on her own street, found her way to the Stinnets' house like a bee to the hive.

The gray stone ranch had taken on that hollow impersonal air – once a home, now a crime scene. Sonora was relieved to see Sam sitting in the Taurus, parked in front of the house. She double-parked beside him in the cul-de-sac. The Saturn was still in the driveway. The LeBaron, by virtue of that open door, was a possible crime scene, and had been towed away by CSU for scrutiny.

'You're late,' Sam said, handing her a cup of coffee. It was a mocha chocolate mix, no whipped cream, a hint of nutmeg. Precisely her favorite. He leaned against the car door, sipping from his own cup, which would, Sonora knew, contain a straight black Italian roast, provided he'd been able to get it. He looked tired, but crisp, showered. He gave her a lazy smile. 'Sleep in, did you?'

Sonora took a tentative sip from the white plastic top that rested on the thick cardboard cup. 'You've been here all of five minutes.' She headed up the sidewalk. He hadn't gone in without her. She didn't blame him. She wouldn't have gone in without him.

He walked behind her, closer than usual. 'Five minutes? Says who?'

'Says me. Coffee's still hot.'

He whistled. 'What a detective. Ever—'

'Think of going into police work?' It had come to this. Finishing each other's sentences. 'Maybe when I give up the exotic dancing.' Sonora broke the tape across the front door, unlocked the Cincinnati PD padlock. She glanced back over her shoulder. Three of the daffodils had been flattened. Probably when the EMTs had wheeled the bodies out.

She went inside, paused in the living room, waiting for Sam.

It was warm in the house, too warm. The air seemed oddly thick and expectant, and there was a heaviness to the room, as if the walls had been saturated with emotion. Sonora went to the phone, checked the caller ID. When they'd left last night it had been suspiciously clear – no calls showing on a caller ID box that had the capacity to store sixty-five names and numbers. Between last night and this morning there had been six calls, one from

Franklin Ward, made from his living room while she and Sam were there to break the news, and five unavailables.

The answering-machine light flashed red. Two messages. Sonora hit play.

Please call American Express at 1-800 . . .

Please call Star Bank Visa at 1-800 . . .

Sonora looked at Sam. 'I stopped at her great-uncle's place on the way in.'

'Ward's place? How did they take a cop on the doorstep at that time of the morning?'

'They fed me biscuits.'

'Some people have all the luck. Get anything useful?'

Sonora shrugged. 'Not much. The family was in a serious money crunch.'

'You think?' Sam pointed at the answering machine.

'And there was an ex-husband, but so far back in the picture the odds are pretty remote. Not much else, just that the Stinnets were exactly what they looked like. Average, middle-class family.'

'Average middle-class families don't get butchered, Sonora.'

'This one did.'

'What have you got on the ex?'

'Teenage marriage, shotgun wedding. The girl, Tina, was hers from that relationship, but the guy had cut out by the time she was born.'

'Tell me one I haven't heard.'

'Last seen at a Taco Bell in Kansas City.'

'Serves him right. Anybody bothering them? Lawsuits, affairs, feuds with the mailman?'

'Just Visa.'

'If that could kill you, we'd all be dead. Start in here, then?'

'It's where we are.'

Sonora sat at a kitchen desk, looking through bills and paperwork, all piled up in no particular order, just like her own house. She wished people would get their lives organized.

A glance through the refrigerator and the pantry had revealed careful shopping – peanut butter, generic cereal, bologna and macaroni and cheese. Frozen burritos. A six-pack of Miller Lite with one twelve-ounce can missing, an unopened bottle of Blue Nun. No other alcohol in the house. She and Sam had searched the usual places for joints, searched the medicine cabinets for sleeping pills and happy-face self-medications. Nothing but Excedrin Migraine, Benedryl, ChlorTrimeton, and a wealth of children's medicines; Tryminic, Orajel for teething infants, little orange tablets of Johnson & Johnson's baby aspirin. Liquid Advil for children. Fifty-milligram tablets of Diclofenac for Carl Stinnet, three times a day or as needed for pain. Probably for that broken ankle. St John's Wort.

'Ah ha!' Sam said.

Sonora looked up from her papers. They were spending a lot of time in the kitchen, going into the bedrooms only as needed.

'Overdue movie. *Whatever Happened To Baby Jane?*'

'How late?'

'Three weeks.'

'That solves it. They were taken out by those blueshirts at BlockBuster Video. Any clue about library fines?'

'Go ahead, have your fun. When we break the chain of video terrorists you'll have me to thank for the collar, the promotion, the interviews on Montel.'

'Maybe I'll get a book deal.' Sonora stacked papers, yawned.

'Anything?' Sam asked.

'Just bills.'

'Feel right at home, do you?'

'Shut up.'

Chapter Eighteen

Sam was humming. 'You're darn tootin, I like Fig Newton.'

Sonora paused in front of the elevator in the Board of Elections building. 'It's Newtons,' she said.

'What?'

'It's Fig Newtons, with an s. "You're darn tootin, I like Fig Newtons."'

'No, it isn't, that doesn't rhyme.' Sam grabbed the doors before they closed, went through the familiar struggle. 'Get in the elevator, will you?'

She shook her head. 'Go on up. I forgot something.'

'What?'

'Just go.' She dashed off, went around the corner. Leaned against the wall. What the hell was the matter with her? Why couldn't she get on the stupid elevator that she'd ridden almost every day of her working life, which was close to almost every day of her life?

Maybe it was a psychic thing. Maybe it was going to get stuck. She'd be able to rescue Sam. She wandered down the hallway, wondering whether the staircase was behind door number one, door number two or door number three.

She ran, ten sets of twelve steps, and was winded and sweating when she burst through the doors of the bull-pen. Sam was at the coffee maker with Crick and Gruber and a man she didn't recognize. The man was punching Crick's shoulder, the two of them grinning at each other like a couple of dogs who've been offered a ride in the car.

'That was fast,' Sam told her. 'Did you get it?'

Both Crick and the other man turned and looked at her.

'Get what?' she asked.

'Whatever it was you forgot.'

'Oh, sure.' Sonora smoothed her hair back. The stranger was looking at her with a smile that seemed so knowing Sonora could swear he read her mind. He raised a red can of Coca-Cola in salute and took a sip. Everything about him, other than the cup of coffee that should have been grafted on to the end of his hand, said cop. Were they getting a new guy? Nobody ever told her anything.

He put the can down. 'Detective Blair? We talked on the phone. Jack Van Owen. I'm not haunting you. Crick called and asked me to sit in.'

They shook hands, his warm and dry in her palm, nice grip. He was a definite surprise. She had expected him to be a whole lot older, and in bad health. She had not expected late forties, trim, bottomless brown eyes and, for God's sake, dimples in his cheeks.

She knew that he had retired on disability, injured in the line of duty, a bullet to the left cortex of the brain. She looked for a scar. Saw none. Well, no, there it was, just at the hairline.

There was something about the man.

There were people who had theories about karma, people who believed you dealt with the same souls over and over. Sonora was cynical and pragmatic and she thought karma would make a great name for herbal tea. A new line from Celestial Seasonings.

'Nice to meet you. I appreciate the help.'

He winked. 'Thanks for being kind to one of the old guys.'

Crick glanced over at Sonora, shook his head at Van Owen. 'Blair doesn't think there ever was a time before my time.'

Van Owen grinned at Sonora. 'He was a cop then, Detective, about as raw and green as they come.' He turned to Crick. 'Weren't you?'

'Something like that.'

What like that, Sonora wanted to know, but knew better than to ask. Crick had always seemed like the kind of man who had seen it all and never been surprised. Jaded at birth.

'Something amuse you, Detective?'

'No, sir.' It was the idea of Crick as a baby detective. She couldn't wrap her mind around it.

She snuck another look at Jack. So this was the famous Detective Van Owen.

If Sam was the cowboy in the tan pants and blue chambray shirt, a sweat-stained Stetson and a ready smile, Jack Van Owen was the man in the silk flowered vest. She pictured him smoking a fat cigar, thinking shrewd thoughts, immaculate in tailored black pants, smelling of expensive cologne, the best bourbon on his breath.

'Okay, people.' Crick included them all in the boom of his voice. 'Jack's graciously agreed to sit in with us today, as he's provided the best lead we've got, and Mickey's waiting for us in Interview Three. Sonora?'

'Sir?'

'You coming?'

'Yes, sir.'

Van Owen motioned her ahead, frowned like he'd forgotten something, then gave her a half smile that showed the dimple. 'I'm sorry, I know this is out of line, but what perfume is that you're wearing?'

'Escada,' Sonora said, aware that Crick and Sam and Gruber were looking slightly stunned by the turn of conversation. She felt a sense of dread. The guys would never let her get away with this one.

Van Owen was nodding. 'I'm sorry, that was personal. It's just that my wife loved that scent, God bless her.'

She knew that the wife was dead, that there was some sort of tragedy there, but she didn't know the story. There was the kind of pause in the conversation where the living were brought up short by memories of the dead.

Crick inclined his head. 'Detective Blair? You planning to grace us with your presence?'

'Coming, sir.'

Crick waved a hand at Jack. 'After you.'

Van Owen picked up his can of Coke. 'Let's see if I still remember the way.'

Chapter Nineteen

Sonora sat beside Sam who leaned close and whispered in her ear, 'What kind of perfume is that you're wearing, anyway? Eau de Horse?'

'Leave me alone.'

He pushed her chair sideways with his size twelve and a half foot.

Gruber pushed her chair back in place and sat on her other side. 'What's that perfume you're wearing, Sonora?'

'It's deodorant, Gruber, you should try it.'

'She shoots, she scores.'

Mickey was looking at her. 'We haven't identified the prints yet, but we've got some good ones. Including a few of yours, Sonora.'

'Me? Where?' Her face was going red.

'The bed.'

'Well, excuse me for trying to save a life.' Damn them. She heard that woman's voice in her head every time the world went quiet and she closed her eyes. She looked up, saw that Van Owen was watching her.

'Bad,' he said. Not a question.

She nodded.

Mickey looked at Sonora. 'Gillane ran an AIDS test on her. He was worried about your exposure. Clear, by the way.'

Silence in the room.

Sonora had held the woman's hand while she died, she

should not have taken the risk. She had been rattled. Way too rattled. Trying to be human instead of a pro.

Never again.

Mickey rambled on. 'Prints everywhere, like I said, except on the caller ID box, which was wiped clean.' Mickey, a short man, barrel-chested with dark hair showing on his arms beneath the short-sleeved striped shirt, rested his backside on the edge of the table. 'The little gray pebbles, as you called them, Blair, are olive pits, as per my early suspicions.'

Van Owen was nodding.

'We found them in the mailbox, on the body of the father, and one in the hair of Joy Stinnet.'

'Anything on the missing Jeep?' Crick asked Gruber.

'Nothing yet.'

'What did you get from the next of kin?' Crick looked from Sam to Sonora.

'We've only talked to Joy's people.'

Sam loosened his tie. 'Nothing but average ordinary folk.'

'Any drug paraphernalia in the house?'

Sam was shaking his head. 'And we were looking for it, believe me.'

'What'd you get from the neighborhood canvas?' Crick was back to Gruber again.

'Seemed fairly well liked. Nobody noticed anything unusual about the people who went in and out. Sometimes painter guys that Stinnet used in his business as a contractor, some of them were a little rough-looking. Here's something. One of the neighbor boys did see some guy in a uniform.'

'A uniform? Cop?' Sam said.

'He wasn't sure. Military, he thought. Other than that, the worst complaint I got was some of Tina's friends played their car stereos too loud. But she was well liked, baby-sat for some of the neighbors when she wasn't training or competing with the swim team. No strange people coming in at night. Next-door neighbor said the lights were usually out by eleven, but you could see that the TV was going in the master bedroom. Her theory is they went to bed with Letterman every night, 'cause she and Joy used to go over the best of the top tens.'

Crick leaned back in his chair, rubbed the bridge of his nose. 'This isn't adding up.'

'They were in a severe money crunch,' Sonora said.

Crick frowned. 'You get the impression they were borrowing from the mob or something?'

'No, sir. Visa and American Express.' Sonora looked at Sam, knew he was thinking about the Blockbuster Video joke. He narrowed his eyes and shook his head, ever so gently.

As if she would.

'Okay.' Crick pushed his chair away from the table. 'Jack, how about you give us what you know on this olive-pit whacko.'

Van Owen turned so he could see them, that half smile spreading across his face. Sonora found that it was not in her to resist that smile.

He was an average-looking man, speaking objectively, a hard thing to do if you spent more than five seconds with him. Sonora tried to figure it out. Decided a lot of it was the smile. It made him attractive, to men and women. There was something knowing in his eyes, something that saw you, and gave the impression that he knew all about you and liked you anyway.

'This guy I'm thinking about—'

'He eats olives.' Gruber. Interrupting.

Showing off, Sonora thought, embarrassed for him and annoyed.

Van Owen nodded. 'Yeah. Green olives, with the pits. Not a pimento man. You a pimento man, Detective?'

'I am at that,' Gruber said.

'This guy's not. His name is Lancaster AKA Lanky Aruba, probably got a picture here, in the file.' This to Crick, who nodded and opened a manila envelope. 'There you go. Take a good look, and go carefully with this guy. He's really out there, paranoid and dangerous. On all the secret service and FBI lists, just can't quite get his shit together well enough to assassinate anybody, thank God.'

Gruber handed the picture over to Sonora. She frowned, thinking that there was something peculiar about the mug shot. She chewed the inside of her cheek, decided it was the total absence of self-consciousness. People in mug shots showed emotion – they were sheepish, angry, bewildered, intensely annoyed. Either that, or they went to the other extreme, ranging from blankly stoic to the prison-yard stare.

But this guy – as well snap a Polaroid, he seemed indifferent to the camera. The shot caught him looking up, to the left, squinting his right eye, as if something on the ceiling puzzled him. His hair was curly, cut close to his head, and he needed a shave. Cleaned up, with normality in the eyes instead of that puzzled coldness, he might have been attractive, but he had an alien out-there quality that would never get him on *Suddenly Single*.

'Six two or thereabouts.' Van Owen looked at the file. 'Six one. Blond hair, blue eyes, scar down the right side of his chin since that mug shot was taken.'

'You remember that?' Sonora asked.

Van Owen gave her a crooked half smile. 'I gave it to him. He went after the girl in reception when we were walking him out. She wasn't behind glass back then.' Van Owen showed her an open palm. 'Totally unexpected, came from nowhere. Guy was cuffed, had two uniforms to baby-sit him. I was following them out, talking to him, just trash talk. I have no clue what set him off. What was it he said?' Van Owen looked up at the ceiling. 'Something about Hopi Indians voting the straight Democratic ticket, as I recall. No rhyme or reason. Weird guy.'

'What's he drive?' Sonora asked.

'No license. He can't pass the written test,' Van Owen said. 'He told me it was graded by Democrats. And on that note' – he looked at his watch – 'got to go.'

Crick was on his feet quickly for a man who bulked out like an ex-fighter. He shook Van Owen's hand. 'Thanks for coming in, Jack.'

'Anything to help.' Van Owen nodded to all of them. Headed out the door.

Gruber wheeled around in his chair. 'Hey, one more question, a quick one.'

Van Owen looked backward, the expression on his face reminiscent of a parent asked for one too many drinks of water at bedtime. 'And what would that be, Detective?'

'How'd you get this guy to talk to you? He did talk to you, didn't he?'

'Confession that held. It convicted him.'

'It's that old Van Owen magic,' Crick said.

Van Owen smiled. 'I just took the guy a jar of olives.'

'So if I get this guy a jar of olives, no pimentos, he'll tell me everything I want to know?'

Leave it alone, Sonora thought.

Van Owen shifted his weight. 'Let me tell you a quick little bedtime story. Aruba disembowels his landlady on the second-floor landing right outside his apartment. Goes straight to his kitchen, gets a bunch of stuff to clean up the mess. Gets caught mopping up by one of the neighbors, whom he also kills. Now, the way old Lanky remembered it, the way he tells it to me, is one minute he and this lady are arguing about whether or not to replace the linoleum, the next thing he knows he's mopping up the blood. Doesn't remember a thing about grabbing her from behind and cutting her open.'

'He actually told you that?' Gruber asked.

Van Owen nodded. 'And if you catch this guy, Detective, and if he's your man I sure hope you do, make sure that whatever you do, his wrists are cuffed, his legs are shackled, and the bastard's chained to the floor.' He waved a hand and headed out the door. 'Stay safe, fellas.' He winked at Sonora. 'Ma'am.'

Chapter Twenty

Sanders stood with her back to the sink in the women's bathroom, watching Sonora put on lipstick.

'It's too red,' Sonora said.

'I like it. Better than the purple. Here, let me see that.' Sanders held out a hand.

'What's wrong with the purple stuff?'

'MAC? Is this new?'

'Yes, it's new. What's wrong with the—'

'I just didn't like it, you asked me to be honest.'

'No, I didn't.' Sonora looked at her watch. Eleven thirty.

'Hey, what did you think of that Van Owen guy?'

'The legend? Let's go to lunch and dissect him.'

'I thought he was cute. Can't do lunch. I'm on that Jenny Craig. I have to eat this little can of chili and a salad. But I get half a pear this afternoon.'

'*Half* a pear? Not the whole pear?'

'You know what? I'm losing weight on this plan, so shut up.'

'Give me back my lipstick.'

Sanders took a comb off the back of the sink, let it glide through her fine, silky hair. 'I've had some thoughts on your third man theory. Hey, did you cut your hair?'

'My hair? Yeah. Three weeks ago, you just now noticed?'

'Looks good. Kind of kicky. Kind of Marilyn.'

'Manson?'

'Monroe.'

'What third man theory?'

'I read the notepad on your desk.'

'Dammit.'

'There's no privacy around here, you know that.'

'Just don't bring it up yet. I'm not ready to throw it out for ridicule.'

'Anyway, I do think you have a point. I mean, to me, it looks like somebody came in and put a stop to things. That poor kid wasn't raped, she was laid out on the bed like that. Somebody got hit, they lost a tooth.'

'The kid could have done that. Or the father.'

'I read your notes. No sign of bruising on either of their hands.'

'It's hard to come up with a theory that makes sense of all of it.'

'Maybe it was an angel.'

'Picture me going to Crick with *divine intervention*.'

'Speaking of divine.'

Sonora put the lipstick back in her purse. Straightened her tie. 'It's the tone of voice. You need advice.'

'At least this one isn't married.'

'So she does have a brain.'

'It's Gruber.'

'*Gruber?* Are you just the definition of dumb?'

'I'd appreciate it if you wouldn't say his name like it was something on the bottom of your shoe.' Sanders ran a finger along the edge of the sink. 'You don't think he's attractive?'

Sonora took a breath. 'No, I do. So do most women in greater Cincinnati, or the whole east coast, if you get my drift.'

'It's just dinner.'

'Tell me another one. Hell, Sanders, he's your partner, why do you want to have *dinner*? You eat with him all the time.' Sonora looked into the mirror, catching Sanders's reflection. 'You slept with him?'

'*No.*'

Sonora read yes. 'Listen, Sanders, this guy is your partner.

98

You see him every day, you're working with him, where can this go but wrong?'

'I really like him, Sonora.'

'Yes, hon, and he really likes you.'

'You think so?'

'Don't even *start*. It's a wreck in progress, and you know it. On the plus side, you'll have a lot of fun till the crash. Keep me informed.' Not that she would need to be told. She knew exactly how it would go, it would just be a matter of damage control on down the road.

'*Wait* just one minute. Are you telling me you never slept with Sam?'

'Certainly not,' Sonora lied. 'Sorry to run out on you, but I really need to go.' She scooted out of the bathroom and ran right into Sam. He grabbed her elbow.

'Keep moving, girl, I got a home and work address for one Barton Kinkle, known associate and distant relative of Lanky Aruba.'

'Why not an address for Aruba?'

'No luck.'

'Are they really related?'

'So I'm told. Weird names must run in the family. We'll get lunch on the way. I called . . . that's kind of red, isn't it?'

'What? The lipstick?' She followed him down the hallway. 'You don't like it?'

He stopped. Backed away. Cocked his head to one side. 'Give me some time to get used to it. I like it better than the purple stuff.'

'Did I *ask* you—'

'As I was saying, I called the locals down in Kentucky, Lexington, talked to some woman, Detective Mai Yagamochi—'

'Sounds like your typical steel magnolia.'

'She's going to do a driveby past the sister's place, whose last name is Kinkle too, imagine that, and look for the Jeep, or anything else, kind of just scope it out. She checked for me, the address is definitely Fayette County, so it's their jurisdiction.'

'How does she sound?'

'Pretty good. Kind of excited. Must be on the quiet side down there, right about now.'

'Yeah, what a shock.'

He headed through the swing doors and she had to run to keep up.

'I figure we'll do Kinkle's apartment, grab some lunch, then hit his place of employment.'

Sonora slung her purse over her shoulder. 'Where's he work?'

'Night auditor at the Hampstead Inn over on Montgomery.'

'Over on Montgomery? Over where on Montgomery? That road's about a hundred miles long, give or take a kilometer.'

'Exit seven.' Sam pushed the down button on the elevator.

'Oh, yeah, where the exit goes six, eight, seven?'

'I bet that's hell on out-of-towners.'

'No rule that says numbers have to be numerical.'

'Not in Cincinnati.'

The elevator door opened. Sam stepped in, looked at her. Sonora took a breath, stepped in. Stupid elevator.

'Sam, let's do lunch first, I'm hungry.'

'Oh, come on, the apartment won't take that long.'

'Unless he's *there*. Then we could have a gun battle or something. Who the hell knows what could happen.'

'It's better to get shot on an empty stomach, Sonora.'

Chapter Twenty-One

'You want to hear my prediction?' Sonora said.

Sam pulled into the parking lot of the Kilmar Arms. He squinted at the four-story, weathered red-brick building. 'First stop on our tour, the Heartbreak Hotel.'

'What's that mean?'

'This is the first place every divorced guy in Cincinnati goes, right about when he first separates from his wife. It's cheap, close to downtown, in walking distance of three small dark bars, a McDonald's, Arby's, and Arlene's House of Laundry, which has a drink machine, pinball games, and a coin changer.'

Sonora slammed the car door. 'And you know it well because why?'

Sam slid into his tan raincoat, yesterday's sunshine a memory. 'A lot of my buddies wind up here, during the transition. We go down the road to grab a beer and watch football.'

'It's good that you've got so many happy memories associated with this place, Sam. I'm glad to know that your friends' depressions and life-shattering events don't, you know, spoil it for you.'

Sam locked the Taurus. 'Hey.' He opened his arms. 'Might as well enjoy a divorce when you can. I keep the guys cheered up. Move them in, move them out. Part of the cycle of life, Sonora.'

She followed him up six brick steps bordered on each side by an ornate, black, wrought-iron railing, and through a wide, heavy door with a fanned glass window over the top, like a transom. Sonora paused in the foyer, craning her neck to study a dirt-encrusted chandelier that would have been at home in the ballroom of an old-style Chicago hotel, brightening wedding receptions and New Year's Eve parties.

'What the hell,' she said.

'Quite a place, isn't it?' Sam grinned at her, like a boy with his first car. 'Built in the twenties.' He pointed up. 'High ceilings, a man can breathe in here. It could be cleaner, sure, and there's no air-conditioning. Look, see, it's got those neat grill heater things along the wall, don't see those around much any more. Hell of a place.'

'It's the fried-fish smell that makes it.'

Sam went ahead on the staircase. 'I've never been able to figure that smell out. These suites—'

'Suites?'

'Don't have kitchens, there's no cooking allowed, but most of these guys don't take the kitchen stuff when they go anyway.'

'They do allow power tools?'

'Funny.'

'No elevator?' The stairs were wooden and creaky. The banisters would have been a work of art had they been cleaned, buffed and polished. Sonora felt a rough spot under her thumb. Someone had carved their initials. S-D-M.

'Nope.' Sam puffed a little. 'This guy's on the fourth floor. D eight.'

'Sam, how can they not allow cooking?'

'They let you have a popcorn popper.'

'What more does a man need?'

'What was your prediction?' Sam said.

'My God, you were listening?'

'I always listen to you.'

'Man, it really is quiet in here. Nine-to-five guys.'

Sam shrugged. 'Or night-shift day sleepers.'

'Okay, my prediction is, Kinkle is home, asleep, like a good night auditor.'

'Maybe not.'

Sam sounded pathetically hopeful, Sonora thought. She paused on the third-floor landing to catch her breath. Her left side ached faintly, like a memory. That ribcage had been kicked in fifteen months ago by another mild-mannered, low self-esteem type who engendered pity. Sonora took her gun out of her purse. She was starting to prefer the hard cases.

'It ain't ever this easy, Sam.'

'What about that antiques dealer who dropped his business card?'

'Okay, but other than him?'

'There's the River Front Strangler.'

'Yeah, but, dammit, Sam, that guy confessed.'

'You don't call *that* easy? I like it when they walk into the office.'

'Okay, you want easy? Let's hope this Kinkle is in the National Guard or something.'

'The guy in the uniform? Gruber's on top of that.'

'That's not all he's on top of.'

'What?'

'Nothing.'

Sam held up his left arm, gun in his right hand. They stood to either side of a battered mahogany door with a brass number six hanging over a peephole. Sam knocked and moved away.

'Hey, Sam?'

'*What?*'

'Didn't you say eight?'

'Huh?'

'Didn't you say this guy was in D eight?'

'Oh. Yeah. I did.'

The door to six opened. A man in sweat pants and a clean white V-neck undershirt said, 'Cloris?' in a hopeful tone of voice. His dark thinning hair was wet and slicked back like he'd just come out of the shower. 'Oh.' He gave them a hangdog look of depression. 'Yes?'

The smell of popcorn and cigarette smoke wafted from his 'suite' into the hallway. Sonora saw a temporary bed, steel frame, a striped mattress, twisted blue sheets, an open suitcase, and a huge brand-new television.

'Wrong apartment,' Sonora said.

'Okay.'

'Sorry.' This from Sam as the door shut.

Sonora shook her head. 'Guy didn't say word one about the guns.'

'Other things on his mind.' Sam led her around the open staircase and across the landing to number eight.

This time Sonora knocked. It was her turn.

No one came to the door. They waited. Listened. No response.

'Okay.' Sam sounded cheerful. 'The Hampstead Inn it is.'

'I want lunch.'

'There's a McDonald's right down the road. Walking distance.'

'Dammit, I'm sick to death of McDonald's.'

'They have Beenie Babies.'

'Oh, okay.'

Chapter Twenty-Two

The parking lot of the Hampstead Inn was newly paved, newly painted, and almost empty. Sonora, turned sideways in the front seat of the Taurus, took one of the meat patties off her Big Mac, and threw it back into the brown, grease-stained bag.

'Hey,' Sam said. 'My fries are in there.'

'They won't mind.' Sonora took a bite of her hamburger, ate one French fry, and took a long drink of Coke. Nothing in the world like fizzy cold Coke.

Sam reached across the seat and wiped dressing off her mouth with his thumb. 'Why do you do that?'

'Do what?'

'Take the meat off.'

'I keep one. I just don't want two.'

'Then order a quarter-pounder.'

'That's not at all like a Big Mac. Here, take your fries. Sam, do you think Gruber is sleeping with Sanders?'

Sam stopped in the act of cramming a fistful of French fries in his mouth. 'What brings this on?'

'Come on, what do you think? You're going to choke, eating fries like that.'

'They taste better this way. It's like eating popcorn, you got to shove in a whole bunch at once.'

'Pretty too, when food falls out of your mouth.'

'Oh, yeah, I lay awake at night wondering if I eat pretty.'

He tapped the straw of her coke which showed a red ring from the new lipstick. 'I decided I do like the red. It's kind of sexy.'

'You know the biggest problem with Aruba?'

'You don't like his haircut?'

'That too. It's just I don't get the connection. How does a guy like Lanky Aruba wind up at the Stinnets' house?'

'I been thinking about that.'

'And?'

'I don't know.'

'What about Sanders and Gruber?'

Sam chewed. Wiped his mouth with a napkin. 'Let's say they did sleep together once or twice. We did it.'

'Sam.'

'Well, we did.'

'That was ages ago and you're not supposed to bring it up.'

'Yeah, but we did.'

'Okay.'

'It's not like I'm going to forget.'

'*Okay.*'

He gave her a sideways smile which Sonora decided was supposed to be sexy. She offered him the rest of her French fries, and he took the red cardboard box delicately between his thumb and forefinger.

'What's your take on Van Owen?' Sam said.

'Cool to meet the legend.'

'He likes you.'

'Does not.'

'Does too.' Sam grabbed her hand. Brought her wrist to his lips. 'What kind of perfume did you say this was?'

'The kind that appeals to you, Sam. Eau de fried potato, a musky hint of grease, the floral bouquet of iodized salt.'

'Stop it, you're making me hot.'

'Are you *still* eating?'

'No, I'm done.'

'Are you?'
'Yeah.'
'Then can we go?'
'Sure. Just freshen up that lipstick, baby.'

Chapter Twenty-Three

The Hampstead Inn was a minimalist suite hotel, catering to business travelers on a budget. The lobby, which smelled of Pine Sol and overbaked coffee, was carpeted in a color that was now a slightly worn butterscotch, though, for all Sonora knew, it had come that way. It was conceivable that someone had actually selected it.

A peculiar linoleum-floored anteroom off the lobby had a dairy case filled with ice-cream bars and frozen burritos. A Coke machine hummed and glowed. An orange light warned that the machine was out of change. A small assortment of magazines was displayed next to a paltry selection of paperback novels, and small individual packets of pharmaceuticals and drugstore sundries were displayed next to a small microwave oven.

Atmosphere sacrificed on the altar of convenience and practicality.

Beyond the front desk, the lobby spread out into an area filled with small round tables, half of them sporting circular foil ashtrays, the other half with white plastic placards displaying a burning cigarette with a red circle and a slash. A big-screen TV was tuned to the inevitable CNN, and a long empty banquet along the wall, coffee machine mercifully up and running, hinted at bagels and croissants from seven to eleven, every single day of the week. A newspaper rack that said *USA Today* came up empty next to the half-full bins for the *Post* and the *Enquirer*.

A man in a yellow shirt and brown tie stood behind the front desk, hovering over a trim woman, permed brunette hair cascading over her shoulders, long nails attacking a computer keyboard at an awkward angle.

Sam laid his ID on the countertop. 'Would you ask the manager to come out, when you have a minute?'

Sonora would not have added that *have a minute* patter, but Sam was from the South, and therefore polite – to a fault, by Sonora's way of thinking.

The man sidestepped the girl, who looked up in panic at the desertion, and pressed his stomach against the edge of the countertop. He was bald on the top, hair tufty and overlong at the sides, and his ears were neat and small. He had the general physique of the Pillsbury Dough Boy, without the endearing smile.

'I'm the manager.' His nametag said Kreski, Jim, MGR.

The words were just out of his mouth when a man in chinos, white shirt, and hound's-tooth sport jacket laid both his palms on the countertop and crowded Sonora closer in to Sam. 'Excuse me, is there anywhere I can get a caffe latte?'

'Vincent's,' Sonora said. 'Right down the road. Best coffee in town.'

The girl behind the desk gave her a puzzled look.

'How far?' The man was persistent.

'You can walk it,' Sonora told him.

'Thanks!' He slapped the desk once and headed out the front doors.

Sonora looked at Kreski, Jim, MGR. 'Is there somewhere we can talk?'

Kreski did his peculiar sideways slide, a crab on ice, and came from behind the front desk, leading them to one of the larger rectangular tables at the far end of the lobby. He waved them into chairs. 'Coffee? Either of you?'

Sonora shook her head, sitting with her back to the TV.

'No, thanks,' Sam said. 'Mr Kreski, we're here about an employee of yours, one of your night auditors. Barton Kinkle.'

'Barty?' Kreski's eyes were on the big screen, behind them.

Sonora leaned forward. 'Mr Kreski, would you switch chairs with me?'

'Oh. Sure.'

Sonora glanced at Sam as she moved across the table, saw he was trying not to smile. Sonora settled back comfortably in Kreski's chair, and rested her elbows on the table. 'That's better.'

'Is there something wrong?' Kreski asked.

'You tell us,' Sam said.

'Look, you're the police.'

'We know.' Sonora leaned back and crossed her legs. 'Mr Kreski, when did you last see Barty?'

'He worked Sunday. Monday was his day off. He was supposed to work last night, but he never showed.'

Sam's look was mild, almost uninterested. 'He call in sick or something?'

Kreski shook his head. 'Never called, never came in.'

Sam snapped the photo of Aruba down on the table, two degrees south of a sticky ring of coffee. 'You ever see Barty with this guy?'

Kreski frowned down at the picture, face close to the table.

'You can pick it up,' Sonora said.

Kreski picked it up. Sonora saw it, that genuine flicker of recognition.

'Yeah, I've seen him, a couple of times. I'll tell you the truth, he gives me the creeps.'

'Why is that?' From Sam.

Kreski's face went tight. 'Hard to explain. Something . . . he has this sort of off-ness. And he's always saying weird stuff that doesn't relate, like paranoid conspiracy stuff, but sort of incoherent. Like, one day he looks at me, but not direct, sort of off to the side, and says the Arapaho Indians own all of the Holiday Inns, and they're just a front for . . . hell, I don't remember. Charter Ridge, I think.'

Sam looked at Sonora. Definitely their guy.

Sonora scooped up the picture. 'He wasn't eating olives, was he?'

Kreski looked at her. 'Yeah, as a matter of fact, he was.

How'd you know? Anyhow, I told Barty not to let him come around any more. 'Cause he'd sit in the lobby, drink the coffee, try to talk to people. He bothered the guests. He was a nut. Barty says he's like some kind of mentally defective uncle. I hate to be unsympathetic, but I can't have somebody like that bugging people.' Kreski slammed a hand on the table. It would have been impressive if his palm hadn't landed smack in the old coffee. 'You know, this is pretty much it, as far as I'm concerned. I was ready to let him go anyway.'

'He pull the no show thing quite a lot?' Sonora asked.

'No, this is the first time he hasn't called first. But he does get sick a lot, he has asthma and allergies.' Kreski assumed the air of a man who thinks allergies are a myth perpetuated by lazy employees. 'Up till now, he's always called and given plenty of notice. He's usually very good about that. Give Kinkle a rule and Kinkle follows it. That's another problem in itself.'

'How so?' This from Sam.

'He offends the guests. He's not very smooth. He makes things harder than they should be. For instance.' Kreski leaned toward Sam. 'Say you want a hair dryer and call down and ask for one to be sent up. That's not a problem, we're happy to do it, though technically the guest is supposed to sign for it at the front desk. Kinkle won't take it up or have it taken up. He's going to insist the guest come right then and there in their bathrobe or whatever and sign at the desk. Dumb stuff. Makes people mad. But that's Kinkle. Give him a rule, you know? Don't know when to bend, don't know when to break.'

'Does he kind of get off on that? Giving people a hard time?'

'No, ma'am, he doesn't mean to. He just can't handle people. He gets intimidated so he just sort of shuts down and sticks to the straight and narrow because he is so afraid of screwing up. Which makes him screw up even more. I mean, if somebody even looks at him sideways, his hands go shaky. He puts people's backs up. Plus, and I know this sounds picky, but he gives terrible directions – same thing, I think, just gets nervous and doesn't think about what he's doing. Hands out our preprinted maps and highlights routes with no real idea what he's talking about. In his behalf, I will say I don't think he does it on purpose.'

'That makes it all better,' Sonora said.

'And twice this month I've caught him sleeping on the job.'

Sam waved a hand. 'I thought that was tradition for night auditors.'

'Not here, it isn't. I know he's got a day job, and I'm sorry for him, but he gets paid to be awake. Consciousness. It's one of our major qualifications.'

'You know what the day job is?' Sam said.

Kreski opened his arms. 'Some kind of collections, can you believe it? Guy couldn't intimidate a flea. But you know.' Kreski scratched his chin. 'He'd actually be pretty good door to door. He's kind of weird when he goes all shaky. I'd pay, just to get him off my porch.'

'Collections these days is pretty strictly phone work,' Sonora said.

Kreski nodded. 'I hear they'll hire just about anybody. But I bet you got to be conscious.'

Sam stood up. 'Thank you, Mr Kreski. If he calls in, or comes back to work his next shift . . .'

'Which would be tomorrow,' Kreski said.

Sonora handed him a card. 'Just give us a call.' She followed Sam to the front doors, overheard the girl behind the desk recommending Vincent's to a woman in a slim brown skirt and oversized sunglasses.

Kreski ran up behind them. 'If I should see Barty, do I mention you came by?'

Sam said. 'We'd prefer not.'

'What about the other guy?'

'Aruba? Call me or call 911. Be careful. He's a dangerous man – don't handle him yourself and don't piss him off.'

Kreski went paler. Nodded and told them thanks.

Sonora shook his hand, thanked him again, and followed Sam into the parking lot. He slowed to let her catch up. 'What say we stop at this Vincent's place? Get a cup of coffee, and let me tell you if it really is the best in town.'

'We can't.'

Sam opened the car door. 'And why is that?'

'Because I made it up.'

'You made it up? Why'd you do that?'

'That guy was a jerk, he interrupted me and shoved me.'

'So you made up a coffee shop?'

'Imagine him, Sam. Walking up and down Montgomery, looking—'

'Remind me never to piss you off.'

Chapter Twenty-Four

'Sam, something's bugging me.'

'Something's bugging me too, Sonora, which is what did you do with that cherry pie thing?'

'I'm saving it.'

'For what?'

'Sam, you know my brother loved those things.'

'I know Stuart is dead and he can't eat it. I know you owe it to me.'

'How you figure that?'

'Made up that big coffee house. Got me all excited. Best coffee in Cincinnati, she says.'

'I can't figure out who hit who in that bathroom. Who lost the tooth? I talked to Mickey and he says there was actually some kind of olive residue—'

'Olive *residue*?'

'A piece of the skin or something. I can't believe this traffic, we've sat through this light twice.'

'So what about the olive residue?'

'It was on that tooth we found in the bathroom.'

'What's so hard about that?' Sam looked over his shoulder, started to pull the Taurus into the left lane, then stopped when a Pontiac LeMans scooted in to take up the inch of space. 'Dammit. Look, Sonora, two things. Number one, give me that cherry pie. Number two, if there's olive residue on the tooth then the tooth belongs to Lanky Aruba. Talk about a forensic gold-mine.'

'Gold-mine. But see, my point is, you don't think there was a third man, Crick doesn't think there was a third man.'

'If you look at the psychology—'

'Yeah, okay, if you look at the psychology, I don't think there was a third man. But Joy Stinnet said there was an angel, Sam.'

'Are you sure you heard right, Sonora? Maybe she meant that guy in the uniform.'

'You thinking an *angel* uniform, Sam?'

'No. Just maybe she said . . . soldier. Or how about airman?'

'Or navy seal. That sounds a lot like angel.'

'Give me the damn pie.'

'I told you I'm saving it. I'm stopping by the cemetery on the way home. I haven't been in a while. But what I can't figure out is who punched Aruba in the mouth hard enough for him to lose a tooth. I mean, can you see Barton Kinkle doing that? 'Cause I can't see him doing that.'

'But he must have. Unless it was Carl Stinnet.'

'No, I looked at his hands. A hit like that is going to leave a mark on whoever it was knocked out the tooth. Somebody dragged Joy Stinnet under that bed, somebody saved that baby, and somebody decked Aruba – who looks like a damn scary guy, if you ask me.'

'Okay, then it's an angel.'

'Sam, I'm serious.'

'Yeah, Sonora, so am I. Hell, if you take pie to your dead brother, why can't you go for an angel? Listen, I'll make you a deal.'

'What?'

'Split it. Half for me, half for Stuart. It's not like he'll care, since he's dead. It's the thought that counts, right? Like flowers, except you take weird stuff. Is it that you can't afford the flowers?'

'No, Sam, it's that I want to take him stuff that he liked.'

'Very Buddhist of you.'

'Okay, we split the pie, but we have to stop by the cemetery now, on our way back to the office.'

'It's a deal only if you promise to be quick, Sonora. Zip in, zip out – no big tears and shit.'

'Sam, you are a sensitive, caring individual.'

'Well, I am. Look at the traffic.'

The black iron gates were wide open in welcome. Sam turned right and followed the narrow asphalt drive that looped and wound around headstones and crypts and dying flower arrangements, driving a little faster than might be considered respectful. In one hand he held a little more than half of a fried cherry pie. Syrupy red filling oozed over his fingers.

'I still don't know why you couldn't give me the little cardboard holder.'

'I'm not going to just leave the pie out there naked on the stupid headstone.'

'Excuse me, I didn't know there were rules.' He parked in their usual place along the right-hand side of the drive, under an ancient elm tree that looked unlikely to survive the next storm. 'Want me to go with you?'

'No, be just a minute. There's napkins in the back seat.'

She slammed the car door, crossed the drive, and wove her way through the familiar maze. Hawkins; Baldwin, Mr and Mrs; Theodore. A soldier's grave with a tiny American flag, and a reference to the Tet Offensive. The headstone for a teenager who had died in a car accident in 1987. There were always new balloons and flowers on this one, arriving on the last day of the month.

It came to her again, the dream she'd had, two nights before she'd been called away to the home invasion of Carl and Joy Stinnet.

It had started with sunlight, so intense she had not been able to open her eyes without squinting. There were people and the scent of flowers, sweet and cool, and the murmur of a crowd at a happy occasion. Her children had been there.

And she had been getting married. There were flowers in her hair, flowers everywhere, she was outdoors, with tables and a white tent over a wood platform floor. There was music.

Somehow the children were behind her, and she was wearing a wedding gown, very ornate, with pearls and lace and covered buttons. And she had looked down and seen blood, bright red, so much blood, soaking the front of her dress. She held the skirt high, feeling the happiness drain away because something bad had arrived, something dark and terrible and she had been afraid.

And then there was Stuart, standing in front of her, and she looked up at him, to say the ridiculous and the obvious – *What are you doing here? Why aren't you dead?*

And he had smiled at her and lifted his right hand, palm out, to ward off the terrible thing.

And everyone in the garden, the whole crowd, froze. Only she and Stuart could move and talk, him smiling, her with tears running down her face, tears of happiness, tears of relief.

And he had smiled at her. *I'm alive if you need me to be alive.*

Sonora checked the row of McDonald's cinnamon rolls, three cardboard boxes side by side. The rolls were gone. They always were. Squirrels? The homeless? She set the portion of pie next to the boxes, adding the leftover French fries that had been in the bottom of the bag.

Chapter Twenty-Five

Sonora had gone straight to the bathroom to wash cherry-pie filling off her hands, thinking that she was being smart, that Sam would have to report in to Crick and take the brunt of the man's temper, only to find Gruber had set her up for the interview from hell. She sat behind her desk, facing Judice Stinnet, wife of Eddie Stinnet, estranged half-brother of Carl Stinnet. She heard Gruber's voice, low and muted, as he talked on the phone at the desk directly behind her own. Sam had disappeared into Crick's office to report in, just the way she'd planned. The man was just lucky, that was all. She'd take Crick over Eddie and Judice Stinnet six times to Sunday.

'That's J-U-D-I-C-E.' Although Eddie was the blood relative, Judice was doing the talking.

'Yes, ma'am, I got that.'

'Most people spell it wrong.'

Sonora was tired and she frankly did not give a shit. 'When was the last time you talked to Carl?' She directed the question to Eddie, in the dim hope that he might be the one who answered.

He did not, she thought, favor his brother, from what she remembered of Carl's pictures tucked into that bedroom mirror. Eddie was short and lean, quite a bit older, with matchstick arms and legs and a tiny bowling-ball stomach. He had a camera slung around his neck like a dedicated tourist. Sonora didn't like him.

'Carl called us three months ago, demanding money, was

what it was.' Judice, into the breach. The word 'demanding' interested Sonora. It did not fit her picture of Carl Stinnet.

Eddie turned red. Brick red. High blood pressure, Sonora thought.

'That's not the way it was.' His voice had a hard edge, and Judice went suddenly tight-lipped. Eddie could clearly rein her in, which came as a surprise to Sonora. 'He just hinted that a loan would come in handy, and he said he'd pay me back.'

The tension between the two of them was surprisingly thick, and Sonora had a flash of pity for Judice, though it was difficult not to find the woman annoying. The large, Cheshire cat earrings, the tedious, long-winded conversation, did not help. Judice was a big-boned woman, and she wore an olive-green caftan in that annoying color that cannot decide if it is green or brown and flatters no one who does not look good in mud. A silkily fringed shawl was knotted around her shoulders and she had quite a lot of coarse brown hair, curly to frizz, lifted on both sides with matching turquoise combs that allowed the hair to cascade across the broad, meaty shoulders.

Sonora had shaken the woman's be-ringed hand twenty minutes ago with a flutter of sympathy in her stomach and pity in her eyes. Both had evaporated at the first question, this from Judice, inquiring about the possibility of life insurance.

'Were you able to help Carl out?' Sonora asked. Mainly to annoy them. But their reactions would be interesting, and she was a typical cop. She had to poke that stick into the ant-hill.

'I am an artisan.' Judice bowed her head, as if accepting homage.

Which pertains to what? Sonora wondered, fresh out of homage herself. She leaned back in her chair and crossed her legs. 'You paint? Like Carl?'

'Art-i-*san*. I throw pots. You've seen them in catalogs, I'm sure. Pots By Judice. It's not a name you'd be likely to forget.'

'I don't buy a lot of pots. Sorry.'

The woman's face went dullish pink, but it took some time, so Sonora figured that, of the two, Judice's blood pressure would land in the healthier range.

'It doesn't *upset* me when people don't know the name, it just *surprises* me. There is no need whatsoever to apologize.'

Eddie crossed one leg over the other. Sonora got the impression he'd heard all this before and was feeling restless. 'So what happened exactly?'

'We're not releasing details,' Sonora said. 'But your brother—'

'Half-brother,' Judice said.

Sonora thought perhaps the woman simply could not help herself. 'Your brother was murdered, Mr Stinnet, the whole family was killed, except for the baby.'

'We can't take her in,' Judice said. 'I have my work. On no account can I raise a child. Or, if I did, there would have to be some kind of financial arrangement where I could hire a nanny.'

'A nanny might work,' Eddie said.

Sonora doubted either of them had ever even met a nanny. She knew she hadn't. 'The baby is with your sister.' She looked at Judice. 'Half-sister?'

The woman turned her head slowly and looked at Eddie. 'You didn't tell me that *Amber* had the baby.' Her head swiveled back to Sonora. 'Has she set herself up in that brand-new house out in Yuppieville? I can just hear her, saying it would be *best for the baby*. The same *environment*.'

'Nobody's in the house, we have it taped off.'

'And how long will *that* last?'

As long as I want it to, Sonora thought. She chose her words. 'It's not exactly livable, just now.'

That shut her up. Eddie stood up, went to the window and looked out. He raised the camera to his lips like he was going to kiss it or take a drink, and started shooting pictures.

Nervous habit? Sonora wondered, craning her neck so she could see him. A way of distancing himself? It was getting to be a toss-up which of these two was the bigger pain. This interview was going on forever, and she hadn't gotten anything useful out of either one of them.

'Mr Stinnet, sit back down, please. I won't keep you too much longer.'

Eddie circled back to the chairs in front of Sonora's desk. She was aware of Gruber, ever watchful. 'Mr Stinnet, did Carl talk to you about any problems he was having? Did he seem troubled to you?'

Judice lifted her head. 'We sent him a check for fifty dollars three months ago when he asked for help. My art is only just getting to the point where the money is catching up with my fame.'

'Did he cash the check?' Sonora asked.

'Yes. Sent us a real nice note,' Eddie said. 'Promised to pay it back as soon as he could.'

Poor desperate bastard, Sonora thought.

Judice opened both arms. 'I cannot take this child unless there is compensation. It is the best I can offer – a nanny to care for the child, maybe do some light housekeeping, so that I can do my work.'

'They've made other arrangements.' Sonora spoke slowly, hoping it would sink in.

'Then I lay down my karmic burden.'

That tore it. It was past time for her to go home anyway. Sonora stood up and shook their hands. If they had information, she'd get it somewhere else. 'Mr and Mrs Stinnet, I'm afraid there are reporters camped outside. I'll get a uniform to show you the back way out and get you safe to your car.'

Judice looked at Eddie. Sonora saw it pass between them, the psychic communication inherent in people who know each other very well. Eddie Stinnet stood up, fingering the black plastic camera strap.

'We'll be okay.'

Chapter Twenty-Six

Sonora, who had been sorting through the freezer looking for something to cook, glanced up at the television screen, catching sight of Eddie Stinnet. 'Damn. Like I didn't see this one coming.'

'Mom?' Heather was growing up beautiful, wearing pigtails today, hip-hugger jeans and a monkey T-shirt.

'Heads up, Heather, it's soundbite time.'

'You could cook that for dinner.'

'Soundbites?'

Eddie had more camera presence than Sonora would have guessed, Judice oddly small and shy at his back. But any wife might shrink behind the red-faced anger Stinnet modeled for the camera.

'Is that a threat, sir?' A pretty brunette with lush red lips had the grace to look appalled. Probably new in the business.

Eddie edged sideways. They had caught him in the street next to the Board of Elections building. 'He was my *brother*.'

'Half-brother,' Sonora muttered.

'I don't know what folk around here do, but Carl was family, and back where I come from, we look after family.'

Sonora went back to the freezer. 'A man from the clan, who'd of thunk it? Bet you five bucks Judice holds up one of her pots.'

'Judice who? Mom, are you even *listening* to me?'

'Of course I am.' She wasn't.

'I mean, Susan is such a *feminist*, and she's in the Virgin Club at school, she actually thinks you should never have sex till your wedding night – like is that for real in this day and age?'

'*Feminist* is *not* a dirty word. If you . . . ho, ho, wait a minute, what's this about having sex?'

'Mom, you've said yourself you should never marry anyone you hadn't ever slept with.'

'I never said any such a thing.'

'Yes you did, to me and Tim, one day in McDonald's.'

'Was I drinking?'

'Mom, you did, I remember. Tim thinks it makes good sense—'

'I just bet he does.'

'Mom, it's my life, you're just going to have to accept that.'

Sonora shut the freezer with her foot. 'Speaking of Tim, he's not going to be here tonight, it's just you and me. What say we grill a couple of steaks, that sound good?'

'But I'm sleeping over at Megan's!'

'Not on a school night.'

'We're finishing our Egyptian project and the costumes are over there because we have to dress up and you already said I could last week. Her mom's going to drive us to school in the morning. I mean, it's not like *you* ever have time to drive me anywhere.'

Sonora put the steaks down on the countertop. Had they had this conversation? The children knew all too well how absent-minded she was and they milked it.

'Are you in the Virgin Club?'

'Me? No way, Mom. If you join the Virgin Club, you get click-kicked and have to hang with the Christian right. They pray in the lunch room. Lots of kids do it.'

'Pray in the lunch room?'

'Have sex.'

'Oh, for God's sake, Heather, most of them are lying. There aren't that many eleven-year-olds out there having sex.'

'You wish. Don't worry, I don't even want to right now, I'm waiting till high school.'

'*High school?* Heather, you're not going to have sex in high school.'

'But why not?'

Sonora knew when she was being baited, which did not give her any particular guidance. 'How about venereal disease?'

'I'll use a condom.'

'Don't forget pregnancy.'

'Condom.'

'Be sure and belch the alphabet first.'

'Mom, you are like *so* trying to sabotage me.'

'Heather, girls in high school who have sex almost always regret it. They get taken advantage of. They're not ready to handle the—' Sonora realized that Heather was making a hand puppet with her fingers and mocking every word.

'Sorry, Mom, but you've like told me this a thousand times.'

Sonora rested her elbows on the countertop, and beckoned her daughter closer. 'Okay, Heather. Here's the real truth. You can't have sex till college because no boy in high school is good enough at it to be any fun, and I guarantee he will go right back to school the next day and tell all of his friends and hurt your feelings and embarrass you in front of the whole school.'

Heather frowned. Sonora, a veteran of interrogation technique, knew when she'd scored. 'Get your stuff together, hon, and I'll take you to Megan's. Load the dishwasher first.'

'I don't have *time.*'

'Make time.'

Chapter Twenty-Seven

It was going to be an all-alone night but Sonora was not panicked. She was looking forward to it with at least three-quarters of her heart, the other fourth still crumpled up over The Jerk. The worst thing about that relationship was the void.

But tonight she had Clampett and the mice and the house to herself.

She put her hair up on her head, allowed herself a brand-new pair of thick white cotton socks, and shrugged herself into a gray T-shirt that she'd bought at the Gap when it was still the Gap. The white stenciling on the front was a distant memory, the sleeves and neckline frayed and as soft as a baby chick. It had turned cold out again but she wore the cut-off jeans from Abercrombie and Fitch that were loose and comfortable. She stopped for a quick look in the mirror and decided that she looked pretty cute. She felt damn good when she could keep her mind off that Jerk.

Sonora stole the boom box out of Heather's room and turned it on to whatever CD was in the slot. Tub-thumper — Chumbawamba. She cranked up the volume and opened a bottle of wine that she had been saving, and began chopping garlic.

Halfway into her first glass of wine and she was moving a little, not exactly dancing, not really, garlic flying from the wide blade of the knife, Chicago Cutlery, an indulgence, and sticking to the bottom of the cutting board. Clampett started barking.

Sonora ignored him. The kids were safely tucked away at friends' houses and there was no one she wanted to see. Unless . . .

She headed for the door. It would not be the Jerk, but she had to check.

A car in the driveway, something familiar about it. And the man on the porch. Keaton Daniels. Her past coming back to haunt her.

'Oh,' Sonora said. Her stomach immediately filled with butterflies and her hands started shaking. *Dammit*, she thought.

'Hello, Sonora.'

Something about the deep throaty way he said her name made the butterflies die on the wing. The drama of it, the lurking sympathy.

'Come in?' she asked.

He gave her that old half smile she used to love. 'Depends on what you plan to do with the knife.'

She looked down. 'You would only have to worry if you were a clove of garlic.' She waved her hand, and he smiled and followed her in.

'Letting your hair down tonight?'

Sonora put her hands behind her back, pinking the palm of her left hand with the damn knife. She felt blood trickle across her palm, wet and oily, and she made a fist. She looked down at herself, the loose old cut-off jeans, trailing threads, the ancient ratty T-shirt with the hole under the arm. She felt dumpy all of a sudden. Sloppy. Definitely not cute.

She was closing the door with her hip, hands fisted behind her back, when a huge white Cadillac convertible, 1958 maybe, with the top down, pulled into the street in front of her house.

Keaton walked back to the door and looked out. He was a handsome man, tall, big-shouldered, dark curly hair and brown eyes. He had lost an estranged wife and a beloved brother to the same psycho who killed Sonora's brother, Stuart. It had been a year of portents and the winds of change, and the small blonde serial killer who had brought them both such unhappiness still wrote to Sonora from her cell at regular intervals. Nothing was ever over in police work.

'That guy in the car.' Keaton inclined his head to the caddy. 'What's he doing? I saw him at the stoplight, he cut me off. I'd be surprised if they couldn't hear his stereo system all the way to Cleveland. What the hell is he doing?'

Sonora looked out the window. Damn, if she didn't like that car. She'd always wanted a convertible, and that one could pull a horse trailer. Imagine riding in that with the top down, a saddle piled in the back.

'Do you know this guy?'

Did she imagine the note of disapproval in his voice? Had he been this . . . pompous before?

He looked wonderful. Freshly showered, crisply ironed khakis and a blue striped shirt, and gray sweater. He headed through the small foyer and up the stairs to her living room and she caught a tiny whiff of familiar cologne.

The bastard.

She ran up the stairs behind him, slipping in the socks, catching herself on the handrail. She executed a round-end maneuver behind him in the kitchen and ran to turn down her own music, which also might be heard all the way to Cleveland.

'There's your friend,' Keaton said, and Sonora looked up and jumped sideways. Opened the sliding glass door.

'Gillane, dammit, what are you doing on my sun deck?'

He pulled back. 'Did you or did you not leave a pathetic little message on my machine saying you couldn't sleep and did I have anything that would help . . .?'

Sonora felt the heat creep from her neck to her face, though why it was an embarrassment to be too stressed to sleep, she did not know. But nightmares were private, as far as she was concerned.

'Come in,' she said.

Keaton was standing almost at attention, as if he had caught her with her neighborhood connection and was embarrassed to witness the deal.

Gillane looked at him over his shoulder. 'It's just Benedryl, prescription strength. And only one a night, Sonora, as small as you are. You won't need much, and you don't want to start taking any of the serious stuff.' Gillane wandered into the kitchen, literally sniffing around. 'What you cooking? Hey, how's the horse?'

Keaton was staring.

'I bought a horse,' Sonora said. 'Hell–Z–Poppin.'

'You what?'

'A horse.'

'You bought a horse?'

Gillane opened the cabinets till he found wineglasses. 'Clos de Bois Pinot Noir 1996. Keaton, can I get you a glass? Good stuff.'

'Sure.'

Gillane served. 'No need to introduce me, Sonora.' He turned and held out a hand. 'Gillane.'

Sonora liked it that he didn't push the doctor bit.

'I'm a physician at Jewish, work in the ER.'

Sonora rolled her eyes.

'You speak English like a native,' Gillane told Keaton. 'I can't hear your accent at all and I've got a pretty good ear.'

'Those of us over in Mount Adams have learned to blend in.'

Gillane frowned.

'It's not him,' Sonora said. 'He's not the Jerk.'

Gillane gave her a look. 'You mean this is *another* one?'

It was at that precise moment that Clampett streaked by, moving like a young dog, hot on the trail of three very desperate mice.

Chapter Twenty-Eight

Gillane was clearly enjoying himself. Sonora was not. Keaton, who was holding one end of the couch very high off the ground to expose the mice who had taken refuge beneath, clearly was not. Clampett, hot on their trail, had them cornered, and he went belly flat on the carpet, tail wagging, poking the mice with a paw.

'Can you please get your dog out from under there before I drop this thing?'

Sonora knew the couch was heavy. '*Clampett. Heel.*'

Clampett exercised his ability to perform selective doggy hearing. Either that, or he was ignoring her.

'Clampett!' Sonora grabbed the dog's hind legs and dragged him into the bathroom and shut the door. Clampett yelped and scrabbled at the door.

'He's going to mar the paint!' Keaton yelled.

'*Shut* up.' Sonora kept it under her breath.

'What was that?' Gillane's voice, angelic.

'Nothing. How are the—' Sonora walked back in the living room, saw Gillane on his stomach after the mice, and both men turning to look at her feet as the three tiny brown rodents ran to her for sanctuary. 'Dammit, no! Why are they coming to me!'

'I'll get them,' Gillane said.

'*No.*' Sonora, still holding the dishtowel, draped it over the top of the mice and scooped them up in the cloth. 'Open the front door, quick, they're hopping around!'

Gillane opened the door and Sonora ran out like a freight train. She went straight for her neighbor's yard and laid the dishtowel gently in the grass. The mice wiggled out but showed no inclination to run for the woods.

Sonora squatted down and looked at them. 'Don't come back. Find another home. If you come back, I'll let the dog get you.' She reached for the dishtowel, changed her mind, and headed back to the house empty-handed.

Gillane was sitting on the couch, wineglass in hand, and Keaton stood over the fireplace, arm resting on the mantel like he was posing for *Town & Country* magazine.

Gillane stopped mid sentence, something about his car speakers, and grinned at Sonora. 'What did you do with them?'

'I let them go.'

'They'll just run around back and come in again,' Keaton told her.

'She's probably hoping they'll go into the neighbor's house.'

'Well, what am I supposed to do?' Sonora said. 'They ran to me for help, am I supposed to just kill them?'

Gillane looked at Keaton. 'This woman carries a gun. She probably kills people.'

'Not people who run to me for help.' Sonora took a sip of wine, mentally counting steaks. Should be enough.

'Don't forget to let the dog out,' Gillane said. As if she could forget, with the ruckus Clampett was making.

'Please don't,' Keaton said.

Sonora, who had no intention of letting the dog loose, felt a prick of annoyance. 'Gillane, why don't you start the grill and I'll cook.'

'I can't stay.' He stood up, set the half-full glass of wine over the fireplace. 'Sonora, your Benedryl is in that cabinet of junk over the stove. I make no comment except to warn you that cold medication becomes inert three years after the expiration date. Bye, sweetie. Don't get up, I'll let myself out. Call me if this doesn't do the trick.'

Sonora walked him to the door anyway, marring his exit line, mainly because she wanted another look at that car. He drove sedately away, waving, and she locked the door behind him and returned to the living room, where Keaton had taken Gillane's place on the couch.

She sat in the rocking chair. Her feet were cold, even in the new socks. 'So,' she said, taking a sideways look at Keaton's face. He had lingered in her subconscious all this time, and she had not even been aware he was there, he was so much a part of the landscape of her mind.

She wanted to run upstairs and put on that red lipstick Sam liked. She laughed a little, nerves, the wine, and the man – and the realization that she had lost sleep and shed tears over that stupid Jerk, who was insignificant, and hey, one door closes and another door opens, isn't that what they say? She was glad to have this door open.

He smiled at her very gently. 'Something funny?'

'Just glad to see you.' She had always known he would come back.

'Sonora, I can't stay for dinner, but thanks anyway.'

'No?' Had she asked him?

He put the wineglass down, rubbed his hands together. 'Did I tell you I'm getting married?'

'Are you?' Her lips felt stiff, like she'd been standing on a corner in cold weather. 'Congratulations. Who is she?'

'Another teacher . . .'

He kept talking but she did not listen. She got up and let Clampett out. The dog raced for Keaton, shed some hair and drooled on the khaki knees, before returning loyally to Sonora, who was back in the rocking chair.

She rubbed Clampett's ears and he gave her a look of pure love that made her feel a little better, but not a lot.

'So why are you here?' Sonora asked, then realized from his startled look that he must have been mid sentence. Pull yourself together, she thought.

'Trudy—'

'And Trudy would be?'

'My fiancée.'

'Ah.'

'She teaches high-school biology. She has this student, kind of a marginal kid, an alternative kid, not a regular attender but he's doing better. Doesn't get along with his dad, so he's been spending a lot of time with his grandmother. He absolutely worships the woman, Trudy says. Anyway, he's been worried sick, and she got him to tell her – Trudy is so good with her kids, they really trust her.'

'She sounds wonderful, Keaton.'

He smiled. 'Anyway, this boy says his grandmother has been threatened.'

'By who?'

'Some kind of bill collectors. I'm afraid the details are hazy.'

'Those people are shits, Keaton, but they can't hurt you.'

Sonora got the distinct impression from Keaton's look that Trudy would not have said 'shits'. It hurt her feelings, that look. After all this time, she had not given up on him. She thought she had, but there they were, all those old feelings, astonishingly close to the surface, ready to slash, burn and destroy her peace of mind. Not that she had any peace of mind. Maybe the timing was good here. She was already feeling miserable. He couldn't destroy her happiness if she wasn't happy.

'Sonora? What do you think?'

She had missed something. 'You say she's being threatened by bill collectors. Keaton, there are laws about that sort of thing. All kinds of consumer protections. Tell her not to answer the phone for a while.'

'She says they told her that something was going to happen at a house on Edrington Court, and she'd read about it in the papers.'

Sonora leaned forward. 'The hell. When?'

'Two days before it happened.'

'You're talking about—'

'Yeah, that home invasion. I knew it was your case. She's scared, Sonora.'

'I just bet.'

'Will you see her?'
'Give me the address.'
'Home, or work?'
'Where is she *now*, Keaton? Don't fuck around.'

Chapter Twenty-Nine

Sonora fed Clampett and locked up the house, checked her watch. Fifteen minutes to get to Sam's place, another thirty-five to find this grandmother, whose grandson had confided in Keaton's Trudy. The woman's name was Martha, and she made candy, and rented a deli out at night to fill her orders according to the specifics of the health department. Her grandson spent his nights with her at work, helping make the candy, doing homework. Right now he was standing guard.

Sonora had absolutely forbidden Keaton to pick up Trudy and come with her, and he'd left in a tight-lipped aura of annoyance. As if, by bringing her information, he was now allowed to be a part of the case. He had thanked her with a gratitude he did not feel, but to which, to her way of thinking, she was definitely entitled. She did not bother to explain that people did not talk freely before an audience, particularly when it came to their finances, and that extra civilians wandering through an investigation were as welcome as head lice, and about as much trouble.

Not that she wasn't curious to get a look at the amazing Trudy, but that was personal and she was working here.

Sonora felt a prick of nerves as she drove away from her house. Everyone else was home, eating dinner, settling in. She lived in an alternate universe.

She felt edgy, aware of the possibility that she could walk into that deli and find the kind of carnage she had seen at the

Stinnets. Could a massacre so brutal possibly be connected to collections gone incredibly bad? It didn't seem possible. And yet. The killers had left wallets, purses, and cash, but had gone through the mailbox, wiped the caller ID – phone and mail, the two avenues of collections. Sonora drove faster than usual, and hoped Sam would be ready for her. She had that been-there-done-that feeling. Keaton had taken too long and talked too much.

Sam headed out the front door as she drove up, so he'd been looking for her. She'd always liked his house, an older home, a Cape Cod, with windows and arched doorways and a sort of Beatrix Potter charm. Sand-colored shingles, front door and shutters freshly painted in that shade of blue Sonora thought of as early American. Lots of older trees in the yard, many of them the flowering kind, and everything was trimmed, neat, and perfectly maintained.

Sonora just lately had such envy for the world of Beaver Cleaver, such longing to live in Mayberry RFD, such a need to come home to Aunt Bea, the smell of cornbread, a clean house.

She envied the men. She knew better. Knew that they came home to the same messy life she did, but in her mind she could not help picturing them walking into a clean house with dinner in the oven, and children who were polite, respectful, and loving.

She knew that Mayberry RFD was a magical but mythical place. She knew that the men arrived on the doorstep ahead or behind a wife who had put in a long day already, that they'd all head out to Fazolis, just like she did, and that she was having a thing, a mood, a phase, a bout of hopelessness that was infecting her life like the flu, and that, like the flu, it would pass. In her head she knew she would feel better in time, but in her heart she did not believe it.

Chart your glories, she told herself. She had made a good dent in the Visa bill, she had scrimped all summer, no vacation, grilling hot-dogs, she had paid cash, hard money, for all the back-to-school expenses and also for that form of hell for moms otherwise known as Christmas.

What was the matter with her? She liked Christmas. Now she was kicking Christmas?

She looked at herself in the rear-view mirror. 'Get your ass up off the floor.'

Perspective arrived in the form of Sam's little girl, Annie, who ran out the front door to hug him goodbye. Sonora could not stop the automatic scrutiny of the child, two years younger than Heather. Did she look tired? Did she look thin? Sam lived with the threat of leukemia in retreat every day of his life.

Annie gave her a wave. Sonora smiled and waved back and Sam settled in the seat beside her. It was her car, so she would drive.

'That's a pretty weird-looking smile you got on your face.'

'Hey, Sam, I'm trying to be cheerful.' She handed him the directions she'd scrawled on a paper towel. 'Annie looks good.'

'Yep, that she does. What are you upset about, Sonora? Is it that Dawson guy, out in Blue Ridge?'

'I have no earthly idea what you're talking about.'

'You haven't heard.'

'Heard what, Sam?'

'Sheriff's Department, Barry Dawson. Found him sitting up against a tree in his backyard.'

Sonora knew what he was going to say before he said it.

'Ate his revolver,' Sam said.

'The unspoken cop disease. I always think there should be a special clause in a cop's insurance policy, a sort of double indemnity. If a cop eats his gun, it pays double. Society owes us that.'

'Like suicide is something you catch on the job?'

'Isn't it?'

'The statistics bear you out.'

'They ought to take care of your family when something like that happens.'

'You ever think about it?'

The air went electric suddenly, and Sonora made sure not to look at Sam. He knew her too well. 'Of course not. I just understand when a guy wants to step off the merry-go-round, don't you?'

'It's no shame, Sonora. To think about things like that.'

Sonora gave him a huge smile. 'What you think the fat content is on a chunk of lead?'

'Only a girl cop would ask a question like that.'

'Next thing you know I'll be wanting pink bullets.'

'I thought you put a voucher in for those last week. Hey, watch it, didn't you see the truck?'

'He shouldn't have been there.'

'It's not worth a head-on collision just to make a point. Do you know where you're going?'

'You've got the paper towel, you navigate.'

'This is a bunch of storage sheds.'

'Offices and small businesses is what Keaton told me.'

'Keaton Daniels? This is the same Keaton, this is your Keaton?'

'Not mine. He's engaged.'

'Ah.' They were silent. 'That explains it.'

'Explains *what*, Sam?'

'Why you've been talking through clenched teeth.'

'It's not that big of a deal, Sam, it's been four years.'

'Bad timing, after you just broke up with that Jerk. Take a left there, you're going to want the third exit.'

'What's the actual exit number?'

'I don't know, but it's the third one.'

'I need specifics, Sam.'

'If I *had* specifics, I'd give you specifics. You think I'm holding out on specifics?'

The windshield fogged and misted with the beginnings of a drizzle. They passed the backside of a Wal-Mart. Everything was gray and dreary and Sonora wanted spring.

'You know if the sun would come out I might not be so depressed.'

'The sun doesn't come out at this time of night except in Iceland.'

'You know what I mean.'

'Honey, Keaton isn't worth being depressed over, it was years ago, and he always kind of got on my nerves.'

'It's not him. It's just . . . Sam, do you ever stop and say to yourself, hey, I can't do this any more?'

'No. When I talk to myself I usually say stuff like, hey, don't eat that, you pig, save some for somebody else. Listen, Sonora, you don't want this Daniels guy. I mean, as I understood it, you guys had totally great sex and true love, that right?'

It was the order in which men looked at things.

'And then, he gets all upset, because his wife who he's in the middle of divorcing anyhow, for Christ's sake, gets murdered by the same chick who stalked him and killed his brother, also your brother, so it's not like he's the only one who suffered. So then he's all mixed up and he doesn't know what he wants or how he feels and he's got all this weird guilt. I mean, please.'

'These are the kinds of things that upset people, Sam.'

'The guy's a whiner. A whiner and a waffler. Aren't you the one who said you'd had enough wafflers and that one too many waffles might just put you off the whole idea of breakfast?'

'When did I say that?'

'A couple months ago when you dumped the Jerk. You were running on adrenaline then.' He grinned at her. 'Being married ain't perfect either.'

They eyed each other, single to married, looking at each other over the fence to see who got the better deal.

'Hey, Sonora, that's the exit.'

'It's not the third one.'

'It's the *right* one, so please the hell take it.'

Chapter Thirty

Sonora turned left from the main road on to a limited access highway that looped down and around prefab sheet-metal buildings that were new and hopeful, a self-made low-end industrial park. At the top of a hill she saw a sign that said 'Judy's Deli'. Not a bad idea. Entrepreneurs had to eat.

'There it is,' Sam said, squinting through the windshield. Street lights reflected off the soaking asphalt. 'They look closed.'

'I told you, Sam. It's a lunch place. Martha Brooks rents the kitchen at night and makes candy.'

'What kind of candy?'

'I don't know.'

'Maybe she'll give us a piece.'

Sonora turned left, aimed the Pathfinder up a steep concrete hill. 'We're supposed to head around to the back.'

Metal storage units stood in rows behind the deli. Sonora frowned, some half-remembered bad association with storage units. She parked along the back next to a green metal dumpster. Saw a truck unloading at a building at the end of the drive. The area had the shiny shoestring aura that was a by-product of fledgling businesses. Here and there lights shone from a building window, but for the most part the place was shut-down silent. Sonora could see why the grandson felt the need to ride shotgun. He went up in her estimation on that alone.

Sam rapped his knuckles on the aluminum frame of the

screen door that Sonora hoped led to the back kitchen of the deli. They waited.

'Maybe we've got the wrong door.'

'Somebody's in there. I can see a light and I can hear music.'

They waited, listening to cars on the highway, the pat of rain on asphalt.

'Knock again, Sam.'

He knocked, harder this time. Looked at Sonora over his left shoulder. 'Music's stopped.'

They waited. The door opened finally, no more than three inches. Sonora heard whispers, an adolescent male and a woman. 'It's okay, we're cops. Keaton Daniels sent us. He's engaged to Trudy . . .' Trudy who? Sonora wondered. 'He's engaged to Trudy the teacher.'

Sonora did not look at Sam. It felt strange, saying Keaton's name after all this time. *Trudy the teacher?* he muttered. But it worked like abracadabra.

The door opened wide and a woman bent forward, a tall, lank boy at her back.

'Could I please see some identification?' she said softly. She had to open the screen door to take Sam's ID, and Sonora could see that her long white fingers were trembling.

She was a plain woman, with a broad and interesting face. Thick black hair, marbled with gray, was combed straight back from the wide forehead and rolled loosely into a bun. Her eyes were black and kind. She was handsome, with heavy arched brows and a cleft in the round chin.

'I'm Martha Brooks.' Her smile held more than a hint of apology. She wore a milk and flour-smudged apron tied around a plaid jumper, navy tights, and sensible shoes, black rubbery-looking Easy Spirits, designed more for comfort than pizzazz. Her only jewelry was a wide gold wedding ring and a watch on a thick leather band. 'This is Davy, my grandson and my guardian angel.'

Sam offered a hand. Davy hesitated, as if he were unused to this social convention. But he shook hands with Sam, then stepped backward out of the doorway.

He wore a newish pair of Timberland boots on his large feet, jeans so baggy they evidently stayed up by magic, and an open flannel shirt layered over a short-sleeved T-shirt layered over a long-sleeved T-shirt. His hair, spiked heavily with gel, was pink on both sides, yellow and green in the middle, giving it an over-the-top, over-the-rainbow, sort of effect. His only piercing was in one ear, fairly sedate for a boy sporting tutti-frutti hair. He had an awkward physical presence, all legs and elbows and height that he seemed unsure what to do with. He slouched sideways and told Sonora hello in a deep but barely audible monatonic mumble.

Martha Brooks beamed at him, and could not have seemed prouder if she'd just announced his election to president of Harvard University. Nothing in the world more wonderful than a doting grandmother, Sonora thought.

Martha Brooks returned the ID. 'Thank you so much for coming. Please, come in.'

She led them through a narrow hallway, past a tiny bathroom cum storage area that held mops, buckets, paper-wrapped towels, pots, pans and industrial-sized boxes of detergent. Both the woman and her grandson gave them looks over their shoulders, a mix of relief and awe. Sonora could see they were both afraid.

'We're making bourbon balls,' Martha Brooks said.

Sam's head came up. 'Bourbon balls? What kind of bourbon do you use?'

She smiled at him over her shoulder. 'Now, if you were from Kentucky like I am you would know there is only one choice.'

Two minutes ago, Sonora thought, this woman was shaking like a lamb, and afraid to open the door. Now she was flirting. 'That old Delarosa magic,' she muttered to Sam. She knew he was after the candy.

'Maker's Mark,' said Sam, as if stating the obvious.

Brooks moved behind a huge rectangular island that dominated the large, square kitchen. She wiped her hands on the apron. 'You're not.'

'Oh, yes, ma'am, western Kentucky, down around Owensboro. Born and bred.'

'*I'm* from Owensboro.'

'No.' He shook her hand over the table. 'What the heck got you stranded in Ohio?'

'My *husband*.' She caught Sonora studying the cluttered cabinets. 'That's all deli stuff, please don't blame it on me.'

Sonora nodded, somewhat in shock. Huge frozen rolls of ground beef had been left to drip and defrost overnight on countertops that showed pink and wet beneath. There were pies on the counter, apple and cherry, and large chocolate-chip cookies, all from the Kroger deli. She had never realized pie ordered in a restaurant might have been bought from the grocery store down the road. She wondered what they charged for a slice.

'I think the chocolate's melted,' Davy said.

'Stir it for me, will you, hon?' Brooks said.

Davy went to a double boiler that sizzled on a huge gas stove, pushed a rubber spatula round and round, lifting it up so that Sonora could see the thick coating of dark chocolate. Like any child, he could play and work at the same time.

'Do you mind if I work while we talk? I've got to make six hundred bourbon balls by Sunday.'

'Go right on ahead,' Sam said.

'There's a couple chairs,' she said, the hostess taking over from the businesswoman. 'Davy, hon, go on and take that off the burner. We're not going to dip for a few minutes, and if it gets hard, we can just heat it back up. Use that glove, honey, don't get burned.'

Davy did as he was told, easing the double boiler off the burner with the air of one who has done this before. He took a small plate out of a cabinet, and arranged about six misshapen chocolates in a spiral.

Martha Brooks took a huge stainless-steel bowl out from under an industrial-sized mixer, tucked it into the crook of her left arm, and stirred with a large wooden spoon. 'I hardly know where to start.'

'Don't be embarrassed, Grandmom.' Davy offered the chocolates to Sonora, then Sam.

Martha Brooks, pink in the face, said, 'Hon, don't give them the rejects, give them the pretty ones.'

For a teenage boy, Sonora thought Davy was doing just fine in the host department. She would never have dreamed of complaining.

'These are perfect,' Sam said. 'They're wonderful.'

And they were. Huge candies, the size of small eggs, coated in dark chocolate, sweet white bourbon-zapped filling, and a pecan on top. Sonora's teeth ached with sweetness. She held the candy in her left hand, chocolate melting against her fingertips, flipped her notebook open and rested it on the far edge of the island.

Sam swiveled from side to side in a desk chair, upholstered in black.

'It was that home invasion that scared us.'

Davy stood next to his grandmother, nodding. 'We knew it was going to happen before it did.'

'Well, Davy, we didn't know exactly *what*. But we knew something, and we knew where.'

Davy began covering the island with sheets of waxed paper.

'How did you know?' Sonora asked.

Sam's look said listen first, ask questions later. She edged sideways so she didn't have to see him.

Martha Brooks stirred. 'It was that man that called. The one from the check-cashing service.'

Sam raised one eyebrow at Sonora. 'What check-cashing service?'

'That one over near Indian Hills, on Delaney Road.'

'You've seen their ads,' Davy said. 'They're on TV. You know, we'll cash your check and give you the money till your pay comes in. They've got a whole bunch of those places up near Patterson Wright Air Force Base.'

And near Fort Knox, and in every town where people had trouble making ends meet, which was every town Sonora had ever heard of. She wondered how a woman like this, a woman whose simple clothes came from expensive shops, a woman whose grandson's jeans, shoes, and Abercrombie and Fitch T-shirts added up to a good four hundred dollars, wound up in the hands of people like this.

'I am so embarrassed,' Martha Brooks said.

'Just tell 'em, Grandmom. I'll tell 'em.'

Martha put the bowl on the table. 'Please don't take me for the kind of person who does not pay her bills.'

'Cash flow is the biggest problem for any new business,' Davy said.

Martha patted his arm. 'I should have gone to my husband for help—'

'No, you shouldn't of.' This from Davy, with the unbecoming belligerence that skimmed beneath the surface of the adolescent male.

'I've wanted to start my own candy business all of my life. Three years ago, I decided I had waited long enough. I had raised my kids and kept my home and now it was time for me. But nobody would take me seriously! My own children, who I put through college, mind you, into careers of their own, they treated me like some kind of a joke. They'd say, Mama and her candies, like it was funny to them.'

'They're always first in line to eat the candy,' Davy said. 'Especially Aunt Vee.'

'Davy, hon.' His instant obedience to the woman's gentle tone fascinated Sonora. 'My husband was the worst – he gets so jealous of my time, though, Lord, we've been married over thirty-eight years. Anyhow, I just got tired of dealing with the whole kit and caboodle. I just did it by myself, and nobody knew, till one day I got in way over my head with an order of twelve hundred bourbon balls, and two orange cakes, and Davy here came to the rescue.'

'I skipped two days of school.'

'*Shush*, hon, now that's our secret.' She opened the bottle of Maker's Mark, and Sonora inhaled the sweet crisp scent of bourbon. 'I haven't let him skip any school days since. He'll be graduating with a B average.'

'Maybe.' Davy sounded dubious.

'You can do it, hon, you just need to apply yourself.' Martha stirred bourbon into the mix, then scooped filling into her fingers, rolling little white balls of candy insides and resting them on the wax paper. 'So anyhow. I ran into a problem where I had to buy supplies and couldn't pay till I got the order filled, so I cashed a check with those people. And my money came just like I knew it would, but they wouldn't let me pay it back.'

'Wouldn't *let* you?' Sam asked.

She shook her head. 'No, sir, they would not. Have you ever heard anything like it?'

Sonora was afraid that she had. 'They want you to roll the debt, not pay it off.'

'I told her they can't do that,' Davy said.

'And I told him that they did.'

Sonora frowned. 'What exactly did they say?'

'Well, let me think.' Martha rolled a bourbon ball. Two more. 'I went all the way out to Indian Hills because I didn't want to run into anybody I know. And the girl behind the counter, she was just so nice, that first day. Then some *man* starts calling me up, even before the money comes due, and says I've got to go in that day in person and make a payment on the interest. I tried to tell him that I wasn't supposed to pay yet, but he said he was going to get the sheriff in after me.' Her hands were shaking again as she rolled the candy.

Sonora felt the sick stir of anger in her stomach, and the candy she was nibbling felt heavy in her hand.

'Well, I was plenty upset, but Davy said he'd go pay it for me – he had some money from his band. Davy plays guitar for Dead Head Devils. Have you heard of them?'

Sonora was sorry to admit she had not. Sam ate another bourbon ball, crunching the pecan. How, Sonora wondered, could he eat such a huge bite of candy without getting sick?

'They play for parties at the high schools. And they came in third in the battle of the bands. They should have come in first.'

'*Grandmom*,' Davy said. Though it was clear he agreed.

'Anyhow, he goes and pays, and three days later they are calling me again. And this time neither of us has anything to spare. And this man on the phone, he gets nasty and says for me to watch the papers, and see what happens on Edrington Court, and maybe *then* I'll pay them. And he—' Her voice broke and she put a sticky hand to her forehead. 'He called me a deadbeat and he said I would be sorry if I didn't pay.'

Sam was up and off his chair, wetting a paper towel and handing it to Martha Brooks to wipe candy filling off her forehead. Sonora knew he felt the need to do something, she felt the same way. Davy watched them with a palpable sense of relief, and Sonora imagined that the two of them had been feeling very alone, backs to the wall. A feeling she knew pretty well herself.

Davy's jaw was tight. 'If those people try and come here, they'll have me to deal with.'

The slam of a car door made them all jump. The creak of the screen was barely audible.

'Stay put,' Sam said, drawing his gun. He inclined his head toward Sonora. 'Take the front.'

She fished the Baretta out of her purse and followed Sam into the narrow dark hallway. She took one backward glance into the kitchen. Martha Brooks had a hand to her mouth. Davy looked excited.

Chapter Thirty-One

Sonora parted ways with Sam, heading past a dishwasher, a sour-smelling mop, and a deep sink piled high with dishes. You wouldn't catch her eating in this place.

She went around a counter into a tiny, dark dining room that held five round tables, chairs perched on top. The floor looked like it had been swept, but not mopped.

She saw no headlights, no shadows, through the tight-lipped ivory miniblinds in the picture window. The front door was bolted, a nothing lock. She unhooked the dead bolt, opened the door a crack, and looked out.

A car went past on the street below, came to the dead end, circled and headed back out. She watched till it disappeared down the limited-access highway. The parking lot was empty.

Sonora stepped out, eased the door gently shut, making sure the spring lock on the doorknob clicked into place. She moved left along the side of the building, listening.

Voices, coming from around back. Two men, and a woman. The woman surprised her. Could the third man be a woman?

She saw the car by the side of the building, a Jeep, which made her heart jump just for a second, till she realized that this one was red, not white, like the one stolen from the Stinnets' garage.

The voices, still low, took on a little more distinction. She thought she heard Sam. The woman said something and laughed. Sonora could have sworn she sounded embarrassed.

'Sonora?' Definitely Sam, definitely annoyed. 'Ollie ollie in come free.'

She came in out of the shadows, and a woman, tallish, jumped sideways and squealed. She put a hand to her heart. 'Well, where did *you* come from?'

The man next to her, in khakis and a gray sweater, encircled the woman in his arms. 'Hello again.'

'Keaton? What are you doing? I thought I told you not to come.' Sonora tucked her gun into the back of her pants, where it rested snugly.

Keaton shrugged, but had the grace to look embarrassed. 'I wanted to check on things. If it wasn't for me, you wouldn't be here.'

'My mom used to say the same thing.'

Sam opened the screen door and motioned everyone in. 'Hang here a second, and I'll tell them it's okay.' He glanced at Sonora. 'I hope your gun's on safety.'

'Just remind me not to sit down.'

Chapter Thirty-Two

Sonora could not hide a covert fascination with Keaton Daniels's fiancée. Physically she was amazingly like the wife who had been murdered before she'd become the ex – a tallish, slender thing, long brunette hair. But the first wife had been a sharp dresser, high heels and business suits, worn with a daunting air of competence that would have taken her to the top of the glass ceiling.

Why, Sonora wondered, trying not to stare and failing miserably, would any female, over the age of, say, eight, wear a striped dress with a big red bow at the waist? With little red Pappagallo flats to match?

Impossible for her to understand the mindset. Which seemed to include a printed agenda with a cover picturing orange fuzzy kittens, which the woman had laid on the countertops, avoiding the watery beef. She had used a red felt-tip pen to check off her handwritten commitments. Sonora edged closer, checking out the puff sleeves banded on the thin little arms.

Steph's b-day gift!

Dog to the groomers!

Sonora admitted that this Trudy person looked good in red. But she thought the white hose a bit much. Sonora would have bet money that Trudy dotted her i's with little hearts. She was chewing gum, something with a cinnamon smell. Gum seemed out of character.

It made Sonora feel oddly better, seeing Trudy the Teacher

in the flesh. If this was what Keaton wanted in a woman, he was not going to get it from her.

She noticed Sam looking at her. Again. She wished he would stop. It was like old home week in the kitchen, with Trudy embracing Martha Brooks and giving Davy a quick awkward hug that seemed to take him by surprise.

'I cannot thank you enough for your help,' Martha said, and Trudy ducked her head in demure acceptance. 'Keaton, and Trudy, thank you so much for setting this up.'

Trudy tossed her head. 'I am *not* one of those people who can just *stand* by.'

'Maybe you could be one of those people who leave,' Sonora said, just under her breath. Sam looked up and grinned at her, though she knew there was no possible way he could have heard.

'Mrs Brooks, perhaps you'd like to come into the office tomorrow, and make a statement,' Sonora said.

There was a moment of stunned silence.

'Oh, but *no*,' Trudy said. 'You can't just leave them here, not without protection!'

If it sounded, to Sonora, like a plea for condoms, she chalked it up to sour grapes. 'Mrs Brooks, did you use your home address in any of your . . . transactions?'

'Oh.' Martha waved her hands. 'No. I didn't want . . .' She glanced at Keaton and Trudy.

'Perhaps you could step into the dining room here, with me.'

Martha nodded, waving Davy off to find more chairs. She and Sonora huddled next to the sink of dirty dishes, the crock pot soaking in tomato and soap-tinted water.

'Mrs Brooks.' Sonora smiled, giving the woman a moment to catch her breath and gather her thoughts. They kept their voices low. 'You were saying.'

'Because of the way that my husband . . . that things are, with this business?'

Sonora gave her a nod.

'I was really careful not to leave any kind of a paper trail that would lead to my home.'

'You said they called you? To pressure you?'

'I have a cell phone. I got it to carry in the car, but I've been using it for the business.'

'What address do you use? For the cell phone, and on your checks? Do you have a checking account for the business?'

'Yes, but I use a post office box.'

'Okay, good.' This lady had it covered. 'Did you ever call these people from your home? Even once?'

'No. No, ma'am, not ever. Douglas keeps track of all my calls, and I didn't want him to know.'

'Are you absolutely sure? They'll have caller ID. If you've ever called from your home, they'll have made a note of it.'

'No, never.'

'How about Davy? Did he call them? Do they know where he lives?'

'No, I never let him call them.'

'Okay. Have they ever called or contacted you at your home?'

'No.'

'Have they been in touch since . . . what happened at the Stinnets?'

Martha shook her head. She was biting her bottom lip.

'Ma'am, I don't think you have a lot to worry about. Just to be on the safe side, stay away from that post office box till I talk to you again and clear it. If you absolutely have to go, we'll send you with an escort. It's a small risk that they'd follow or bother you, but it's one I don't want you to take. And don't make any attempt to get in touch with them.'

'What do I do if they call me, or if they ask me to pay?'

'Any chance you'd be willing to lend me your cell phone? I'd like to be on the other end when they call.'

'I guess . . . sometimes I get calls for orders and—'

'I'll take messages for you. You can check in with me every day and pick them up. We could have your calls forwarded, Mrs Brooks, but that takes time to set up, and sometimes it doesn't work, I don't care what the technicians say. I know it's a hardship, but in a situation like this, I don't like to leave any room for error.'

'No. No, Detective, what they did to those people was so awful. But you think I'm okay?'

'Yes, ma'am, I think so. But if something, anything, happens to scare you, or even make you uneasy, call me. And if they somehow find your home number or you get even a hint they know where you are— Where do your cell bills go?'

'How would they get that?'

Sonora cocked her head sideways. 'We live in the age of information sharing, Mrs Brooks. Where do your cell bills go?'

'The post office box.'

'Smart lady.'

Martha ducked her head. Smiled. Sonora handed her a business card. 'My home phone number is scribbled there on the back. Can you read it?'

'Yes, no problem. You really have very pretty handwriting, Detective.'

'Thank you.' She didn't, but she appreciated the compliment. It was a girl thing. Martha Brooks was returning the favor of approval, a commodity every woman craved, no matter how independent. Sonora glanced at Martha Brooks for a moment, thinking of her mother, who had given her approval every day of the week. 'Call me any time, day or night, if you have even the tiniest reason to be worried or afraid.'

Martha held up the cell phone. 'I'll have a direct line. But I promise not to use it unless I have to.' She leaned forward, surprisingly, and gave Sonora a hug.

Chapter Thirty-Three

Sonora lay rigid in her bed, eyes wide and gritty after two of the Benedryl tablets Gillane had left her, and another glass of wine downed while she had cleaned up the kitchen after the dinner she'd never cooked. If the mice had returned they were sleeping quietly. Clampett paused at the foot of her bed, took one mighty leap and landed beside her, nose wet. He paused, waiting to be told to get down.

Sonora patted his neck, and he stretched out beside her.

I am afraid, Sonora thought, fear like an ache that became more acute every night. She did not know what she was afraid of, which made it hard to deal with. But she felt the weight of the fear, piled on top of the weight of her responsibilities. The children needed her, financially and emotionally, and would for years and years. And, like the Stinnets, like Martha Brooks, like everyone else in the world, she had bills to pay that looked like they would go on for ever and ever. And if she did get ahead, there was college to think of.

What if she slipped up? She was alone, there was no safety net. Her children would be as vulnerable as the Stinnets' little baby girl.

And in the meantime, she had to catch their killer. Who was she to catch a killer? It was getting to be a burden, this homicide gig.

Think on it, she told herself. A victim. A human being. Their life is over because someone steps out of bounds and kills them.

Who the hell? Who the hell would have the arrogance, the anger, the cold-hearted selfishness? And yet. Homicide. A daily occurrence.

And she was going to put this right? She was going to find the killer in a city full of people and possibilities? She would find the right one?

She cocked her head, considering cases solved. Every year. Statistically speaking, sometime in her career, what were the odds that she would put the wrong one in jail? Or let somebody dangerous slip away, because she just wasn't smart enough to get it right?

Had it already happened?

The phone rang. Not Martha Brooks's cell phone, which was tucked next to her pillow. Her own phone.

'Blair,' she said.

'Sonora, it's Keaton.'

Sonora looked at the clock beside the bed. Three forty-seven a.m. 'What's up?'

'Nothing.' The voice was wistful and exhausted. Like her own. Should she mention that it was almost four o'clock in the morning? 'Sonora, I'm sorry to call so late. I couldn't sleep.'

'Why can't you sleep, Keaton?' My God, she was as patient with him as she was with her children, on good days, anyway.

'I feel this sense of . . . obligation, I don't know. You were so good tonight, with those people. And I sort of sprung it on you, the engagement, it just seems kind of mean now, as I think about it. I'm afraid . . . you're upset. I just felt . . . like I should call you.'

It was the word 'obligation' that stung. That, and the dramatic pauses that were incredibly . . . irritating.

'Look, Keaton. I was doing my job tonight. And if you have information about a crime, particularly one like this, you are morally and legally obligated to bring it to me. Other than that, I'll tell you the truth. I would rather scrub toilet bowls in gas stations with my own personal toothbrush, than talk on the phone to a man who is calling me only because he thinks he should.'

'I . . .'

Dramatic pause.

'You?' she prompted.

'I want to be your friend, Sonora.'

'So? Be my friend.'

'That's okay by you?'

'Actually, no.'

'Don't you stay friends then? With your exes?'

'It's been known to happen, but very rarely.'

'That Gillane guy is gay by the way.'

'Oh, bullshit, Keaton.'

'Guys know, Sonora.'

'That's nice, Keaton. But just so you know, when it comes to staying friends with exes, no thanks. I usually hate their guts and never want to see them again.'

'That's not very mature.'

'Fuck mature.' Sonora hung up. If Sam were there she would tell him that she wasn't mature. And he would say tell me something I don't know.

The first wave of sleepiness kicked in at last. The pills were taking effect. Sonora turned off the light, clutched the cell phone, and cuddled up to Clampett. She missed the children, their quiet presence down the hall in the middle of the night.

She closed her eyes, and it came again, the whispers. The voice of Joy Stinnet. *Hail, Mary, full of grace.*

Chapter Thirty-Four

Sonora stopped at the coffee pot, nudging Molliter aside, and pausing at Gruber's desk. 'Was that you, calling my name?'

Gruber tapped a pencil against the desktop, impossible as always for him to sit still. Sonora would not have wanted to be his kindergarten teacher.

She put her hand over his. 'Be quiet.'

He pulled the hand away and kept tapping. 'Hey, you know that lady that was in here yesterday? Where'd she lay that karmic burden? I don't want to be tripping over it.'

'This is what you called me over here for?'

'Nope. I had a talk with our witness who saw the man in uniform go into the Stinnets' house.'

'Reliable?'

'Fifteen-year-old kid. We went over some pictures, you know, of guys in different uniforms. Definitely military, and he kept picking out marines.'

'A marine? When?'

'Day before the murders.'

'Any chance he got the day wrong? Maybe the day of instead of the day before?'

'He seemed definite, but anything's possible. I gave Mickey the heads up. If it's solid, military prints are on record.'

'Hey, Gruber, is there some kind of military unit called the Angels? Like the Flying Angels, like that?'

'Air force, I think. I'll check.' He frowned, fingers still at last. 'By the way, Sam's been looking for you.'

'Where'd he go?'

'Took off a little while ago – got off the phone like he had ants in his pants.'

'Sonora, there you are.' Sanders came through the swing doors from CSU.

'Like she's been hiding somewhere?' Gruber grinned at Sanders and Sonora saw the look that passed between them. Definitely sleeping together.

Sanders turned to Sonora. 'I've got Carl Stinnet's sister in One. Amber Wexford. She's been waiting a while. She got here at seven thirty this morning.'

'Seven thirty? Man.' Sonora grabbed her coffee mug, filled it, added cream, looked over her shoulder at Crick's office. The door was shut. And she didn't like to keep relatives waiting.

'Hey, Sonora, your purse is ringing.' Gruber again. Everything amused him these days. He was in too good a mood not to be sleeping with somebody.

Sonora rummaged. It was Martha Brooks's phone. She answered. Cautious. 'Hello?'

'Yes, I'd like to order some of those bourbon balls?'

'Ah. One minute.' She handed the phone to Gruber. 'Take an order, will you?'

Sonora headed down the hallway to Interview One. Checked the two-way out of habit before she went in.

Amber Wexford was crying. She sat stiffly at attention in a folding metal chair, legs crossed at the ankle, a roundish woman with long legs in neatly pressed jeans and a golden sweater. Tears ran freely beneath the large square glasses as if they were in endless supply, and she wiped them away from time to time with a crumpled blue tissue.

Sonora went back to the coffee maker, filled a cup half with coffee, half with sweet chocolate-cocoa mix, and stole the box of white, lotion-soft Puffs off of Molliter's desk. Amber Wexford was blowing her nose vigorously when Sonora pushed the door open with her hip.

'Here, can I help?' The woman was up and off her chair in a split second, taking the box of tissues out of Sonora's hands, leaving her to juggle the two coffee mugs.

'Help yourself,' Sonora said, inclining her head to the box of tissues. She handed Amber a mug. 'This is for you.'

The woman took the cup with a blank expression that did not betray whether or not she wanted coffee at the moment.

'Go ahead, sit down,' Sonora said. 'Are you cold? I can turn the heat up.'

'No, thank you though, but I'm fine.'

Fine she was not. Eyes bloodshot, nose red, a look of stunned bewilderment with which Sonora was much too familiar.

Amber Wexford was the type of girl you saw a lot of in high school, pleasant to everyone with no stir of what she really thought penetrating the mask of amiability. All knees and glasses, long hair freshly washed and blown dry with a hint of a flip at the bottom. Perhaps, to her intimates, she was quite dashing. But any pizzazz she had was buried under layers of conventionality that she used as armor to the casual brutalities of everyday life.

She was reasonably attractive, hiding like a hedgehog behind a large bulky sweater. She would never be seen in short, cut-off bluejeans, and for that matter, might have no aspirations to. In the summers, her uniform would be cotton shorts, longish, cuffed and pleated, bound in the middle with a canvas belt. Her watchwords would be comfortable and decent; pretty enough, and attracting only the right kind of attention, provided any attention was attracted at all. Might as well tattoo *I'm a very nice girl* on her forehead.

Sonora wondered what she was really like, thinking it possible that no one knew.

She put a hand on the woman's arm. 'Mrs Wexford, I'm Detective Blair. I just want you to know how sorry I am for your loss.'

Amber Wexford nodded, and Sonora thought she might not be trusting her voice just yet.

'How is the baby?'

'Oh.' Amber cleared her throat. 'Excuse me. The baby is

fine.' Her voice cracked and she cleared her throat again, took a grateful sip of the coffee. 'I'm sorry.'

An apologizer, Sonora thought. Not surprised. 'I'm just curious, Mrs Wexford. Do you know if you're the child's legal guardian?'

Amber nodded. 'Yes, unless Carl changed the will. Both he and Joy asked me to take the kids if anything happened to them. And I made them guardian of my two.'

'Chloe's lucky to have you,' Sonora said.

'Thank you. You must've met Eddie.'

They both laughed, but Amber was already backing away. 'I'm sorry, that wasn't kind.'

Sonora didn't pursue it. 'I really appreciate you coming in to help us out. It saves us time. But I can see how upset you are. Will it be okay to ask a few questions?' It was something of a dirty trick. She could appear sympathetic, secure in the knowledge that a woman like Amber Wexford would be accommodating. The world ran on the shoulders of women like Amber Wexford, dutiful, hardworking, and above all, pleasant.

'Yes, that's okay.'

Sonora leaned back in her chair. 'Tell me what was going on with your brother.'

Amber slid forward on her seat with the look of someone about to take a very difficult test. 'My brother was a good man, a good man, Detective, but he was having money trouble.'

'A lot of people have money trouble, Mrs Wexford. A lot of very good people.'

'Yes. Yes. But Carl – or Joy, I should say. The family was being threatened.'

Sonora waited. But Amber looked at her steadily, waiting.

'Tell me about the threats.'

'Some man would call and say that if they knew what was good for them, they better come down and pay.'

'In person?'

'In person.'

'Do you know who made the threats, Mrs Wexford?'

'No, Carl never did say. He didn't tell me about it. I don't think he knew. Joy told me. They always talked to her.'

'But she didn't tell her husband?'

'Oh, Detective, Carl was so upset about his business and the Jeep—'

'What about the Jeep?'

'They repossessed it. He was so ashamed.' This brought on a new flood of tears, and Sonora peeled off five tissues and folded them neatly, handing them over to Amber Wexford who blew her nose. 'I'm sorry. I just felt so bad for him. Joy didn't want to do anything to make him feel any worse.'

'And she didn't say who?'

Amber shook her head. 'I'm surprised she told me that much. She kept that kind of thing to herself. But I was over there, I took them a little something, and she broke down and told me.'

'What did you take them?'

'Just – something.'

Sonora waited.

'I have an IRA with my job, and I cashed it out. And Carl was already starting to pay me back before . . . this happened.' She sobbed and blew her nose. 'And he would have, Detective. He was going to pay me before the year was out so I could roll it into another account and not get the tax hit.'

'You are very generous,' Sonora said.

'He would have done the same for me. He *did* the same for me, he helped me through nursing school. He always had some extra money for me before I got married. It was good to get a chance to pay him back some. But he didn't tell me he was in trouble till after they took the Jeep.'

'Mrs Wexford, do you know if your brother or his wife went to one of those instant check-cashing places?'

Amber eased back in her chair, frowning. 'It's funny you say that.'

If ever a phrase got a copper's attention. 'Yes?' Sonora said.

'Joy said something to me once. She told me never to go to

one of those places. She said they were the newest breed of loan shark.'

'She was right,' Sonora said.

'I wonder if she went back again?'

'Again?'

'She called me, the day before . . . before it happened. She said she had money, two thousand dollars, and did I need any of what I had lent them paid back, or could she keep it for groceries.'

'Two thousand? Did she say where she got it?'

'She wouldn't tell me. She said she wasn't going to pay bills, she was going to keep it as a stash for groceries. Of course, I didn't take it. I don't really think that's why she called.'

'Then why?'

'She asked me to tell Carl I gave it to her.'

Sonora looked up. 'Where do you think she got that money?'

'I have no earthly idea.'

'What did you tell Carl?'

'Nothing. I never talked to either of them again.'

Chapter Thirty-Five

Sonora put her feet up on the desk, listening to Frank Sinatra singing 'I Did It My Way'. She hated being put on hold almost as much as being in voice jail when she banked by phone. The door from CSU swung open and Mickey slid in front of her desk like a man on skates.

'We got a match, my beautiful baby. You're the first to know, after me.'

Sonora pulled her feet off the desk and leaned forward. 'Aruba?'

'Beautiful forefinger on the front door jamb. And a smear on the doorbell. Dipshit.'

Sonora kissed her fingers at him.

'And we got another hit. I found you a marine.'

Sonora sat up. 'Seriously?'

'Seriously. Sergeant Robert J. Purcell.'

'Oh, my God. Bobby Purcell.'

'Who is?' Mickey said.

'Joy Stinnet's first husband. Tina's father. He ran out on her before Tina was born.'

'Looks to me like he ran back. Better tell Crick.' He went in without knocking, something only Mickey had the courage to do. Sonora, tied to the end of the phone, was aware of missing an opportunity. She got a quick glimpse of Sam standing up and Crick on the telephone before the door shut.

Dammit, she thought. She was going in there as soon as she got off the phone with this Quincy David. 'Dammit.'

'Quincy Da— I beg your pardon?'

'I said this is Detective Blair, trying to get in touch with Quincy David, Attorney at Law.'

'Jeez, it sounded more to me like you said dammit.' The voice was mild. Amused. A slow day in the office.

'Is this Quincy David?'

'You got me.'

'Mr David, I'm working an investigation and I understand from our District Attorney that you're the man to call about these check-cashing services that are going up all over the city.'

His voice went from amiable to grim. 'Like anything bad, Detective, they're everywhere. What can I tell you?'

'Tell me everything, Mr David.'

'Okay. Can I put you on hold a minute, while I grab a cup of coffee?'

'Go on ahead.' She considered her own mug. Decided against it. Waited. Jim Croce this time, singing 'Roller Derby Queen'. If she kept not sleeping at night, maybe she could make it up napping while being on hold.

'Okay, I'm back, thank you.' Sonora had the impression of a man leaning back in his chair, so she leaned back in hers.

She took out a pen and paper.

'Once upon a time, Detective. Blair is it?'

'Sonora Blair.'

'Sonora. It all started up in a little town called Cleveland Tennessee, then it spread into Kentucky, and now it's swept the country like venereal disease. In the beginning, it centered around the military bases, preying on the enlisted guys, giving them an advance on their next government check. They called them payday loans.'

'How does that work?'

'Joe Blow comes in and writes a check. They'll take anybody, so long as they have a job, a social security number, a bank account, a pay stub, or some other ID, like a utility bill. These guys let them cash a check and hold it for two weeks. Then, at the end of the two weeks, they let you roll the check over for payment. They might keep rolling it every two weeks for a year, which would wind up with the customer paying about nine hundred dollars in interest on a one hundred dollar check.'

'Is that legal?' Sonora said.

'Nope, I don't think so. We've got some murky rulings handed down. As far as the check-cashing guys are concerned, they take the position they're immune. There's a statute which gives the right to cash checks and collect a fee where said fee is not considered interest. This kind of thing doesn't fall into that category, no matter how many times these people say it does. This is a loan, because these people know there is no money in the account when the check is written, and it's a rollover scheme. They're violating the truth in lending laws, RICCO, a million and one consumer statutes.

'And they're in a sweet position. If people don't come in and pay the interest, then they cash the check they're holding, which they promised not to do, and run up all kinds of charges when it bounces. Sometimes they'll send the sheriff after people, to collect, maybe put them in jail if they can't pay – debtors prison is alive and well, Detective. It's not legal, but the deputy sheriff doesn't know better. Hell, even a lot of attorneys aren't up on this, and when these people call their lawyers, they get told there's nothing they can do. It's tied up in Federal court, right now, with Judge Hood. I mean, come on, Detective, we got the Gambinos in South Florida in on this, if that tells you anything.'

'Why this instead of their usual?'

He laughed. 'No longer profitable. The damn credit-card companies get twenty-four per cent, they've put the loan-sharking boys out of business. Do you know what the largest profit maker is for any bank?'

Sonora did the parrot thing. 'Credit cards?'

'Yep. There isn't any money in loan sharking any more.'

Crick's door opened, and Mickey came out, then turned on his heel and stood in the doorway, back to Sonora. She heard male voices, but she kept her mind on David.

'. . . and the credit-card companies are making so much

money they don't even go after bad accounts any more, they just write it all off. They don't even file a claim on their tax returns. It isn't worth their time. They spend all *their* money lobbying to make it harder for your average Joe to file bankruptcy and get the hell *out* of credit-card hell.'

She had pushed a hot button. She took notes, hand cramping, pen flying. 'You sound angry, Mr David.'

Mickey headed past her desk, waving. Sonora craned her neck, looking for Sam.

'I am angry, Detective Blair.'

'What kind of people get caught up in this kind of thing?'

'All kinds of people, Detective. Victims range across the board, from the extremely well off to your single mom living on welfare. They've got one thing in common – immediate financial crisis. They need food, they have to make the mortgage, they have to make the rent.'

'What kind of collection methods are we talking here?'

'Okay, they're not out breaking legs. But there's no profit in that anyway, and to tell you the truth, they don't have to. Most of these people are embarrassed. They feel guilty already, for having to go there in the first place, they're usually under a lot of stress. And the ones at the low end of the financial scale, they're poor, they don't have good experiences with the law, so they're not going to complain. Most of the methods are psychological. They call, day and night. Read people that collection Miranda that goes on everything, even bubble-gum wrappers these days. We have the right to collect, bla bla bla. That little notice scares the Bejesus out of people, God knows why. It looks official and threatening, and by God, people feel threatened.'

Sonora caught sight of Sam out of the corner of one eye, heading for her desk, skidding to a stop when he saw she was on the phone. He threw up his hands and she heard a curse. Headed back behind her to his own desk.

'You mentioned horror stories?' Sonora said, trying to keep her mind on David.

'I got a million of them.' He stopped, gulped. She pictured him drinking coffee, black probably, the perfect brew for a no-

nonsense tough guy. 'Most of them slide around within the bounds of the law. But I've had people in chapter thirteen bankruptcy with check cashers going after them, bouncing checks through their accounts and running up fees when these people can't pay their water bill or feed their kids. They've had people arrested, and they threaten it all the time. They've told people that unless they pay, they'll be taken into custody, and the jail will report them to Human Resources and take their kids away, or they tell them they'll be convicted felons and then they'll lose their kids. I had a woman, she's at home with three little kids, in the middle of a snowstorm. They call her and tell her to come down and pay the rollover or pay the check and the fee or they're going to deposit the check. There's nothing in her account over the checks she's already written to pay her bills, so she says she'll come down there with the grocery money; they give her till three o'clock. She goes with her kids four and half hours on the bus on roads that are covered with snow and ice, gets there at two thirty, and they already deposited the check. Bounced everything else in her account, ran up over a hundred in bloody bank fees, and she's got another four and a half hours home on that bus. You know what these people are, Detective?'

'Predators, Mr David.'

'Shits, Detective. They're shits.'

A legal term, Sonora thought.

'And by the way, that tough guy calling about your Master Charge at eight a.m. Saturday morning is probably a hard-core con in a maximum-security prison.'

Sonora winced. A new service, put together for your hard-core predator, Dial-A-Victim, courtesy of your credit-card company.

Sam waved a note under her nose, then handed it to her like a bouquet of roses. She nodded at him, fingering the folded paper, still listening to David.

'I had a lady, they wouldn't *let* her pay. She told them to send the check through. They said no, she had to pick it up. That way they can get her in the office and convince her to roll it over. I got people, they come into my office and cry. Nice people,

Detective, hardworking. Had a girl last week, they swore they were going to have her baby taken away if she didn't pay up.'

'Ever had anybody get physical?'

He paused. 'Not that I've heard of. It's not the norm. But I've heard . . . rumors.'

'What kind of rumors?'

'People coming to the house. Ringing the doorbell, standing on the porch. One lady said some guy spent all afternoon in her porch swing – by the time she got me on the phone, she was hysterical. I don't know if it's true, I haven't got anything concrete on that. People do get scared. Mostly what I see is psychological. And that works because people are embarrassed. It quits working when people have had all they can take, and they just get hard about it.'

'What is the usual collection rate?'

'Depends on the part of town. Anywhere from twenty-five to forty-five per cent. Thirty-three is the norm. But that's normal collections. Not these guys. I've known check cashers to make seven hundred per cent.'

Sonora set her pen down. Seven hundred per cent? That she would remember. 'Can you give me anything at all concrete on the rumors?'

'I don't really have much. Just people, scared people. I can tell you this. The scaredest people come from that place over in Indian Hills. On the other hand—'

'You were saying?'

'It's this Indian Hills place. Just this one. I've heard of it a time or two, and actually had it happen to a client.'

Sonora waited.

'Got to give the devil his due, I guess. Once in a while, some of these people – like the single moms with kids and stuff? – the debt just goes away.'

'Where does it go?'

'All the people say is it's been forgiven. By the angel.'

'The *angel*?'

'Yeah, I know. And always from that place in Indian Hills, as far as I can tell, but most of this is whispers, it's hard to pin it down.'

'Who owns it, do you know?'

'I been trying for three months to unravel that paper trail. I'm nowhere yet, but maybe your people are better than mine. All I can tell you is, whoever that guy is, he's either your best friend or your worst nightmare.'

Sonora opened the note. Focused on Sam's neat block handwriting.

DETECTIVE WHITMORE FROM LEXINGTON, KENTUCKY REPORTS THE PRIMER-STAINED CHEVY IMPALA AT THE SISTER'S ADDRESS ON OLD FRANKFORT ROAD. DMV CHECK SHOWS CAR BELONGING TO BARTON KINKLE. SUBJECTS MATCHING DESCRIPTION OF ARUBA AND KINKLE SEEN GOING IN AND OUT OF THE HOUSE. CRICK HAS THE PAPERWORK UNDERWAY.

'Thank you, Mr David, you've been a lot of help.'

'Uh, you okay, Detective, you sound kind of funny? Not having a heart attack are you?'

'No, I'm fine, Mr David, and very grateful for your help.'

'That so? Because if you're really grateful, Detective, spread the word there with your colleagues that it's not legal for you people to be out there picking my clients up.'

'I'll do that,' Sonora said. It seemed too rude to tell him it wasn't her department.

Chapter Thirty-Six

Sonora walked through the Dairy Mart, elbowing her way around every other person there on their way home from a long day at work, wondering if they'd have anything she could use for dinner. The kids were getting tired of Lean Cuisines and she could not face the lines and jazzed-up chaos of a major grocery store during the pre-dinner after-work panic.

She wanted to buy something quick, she wanted to buy something easy, so she could take a hot bath and get to bed early. Tomorrow she would be up at dawn for the drive to Kentucky. She ought to be excited.

She wasn't excited.

Frozen pizza? Burritos? Pimento loaf, pickle loaf, stale doughnuts? What the hell was she doing shopping here anyway when she should be at home doing something wholesome like making chicken and dumplings? Unfortunately, she did not have the first clue how one made chicken and dumplings, the kitchen was a mess, and the thought of clearing the rubble and cooking was enough to make her want to leave the country.

A man in corduroy pants that sang with the movement of his legs walked around her with an exaggerated air of polite tolerance that told her, one, he felt she was in his way but he was going to be civilized about it, and two, she didn't like his face. He did not look happy. She looked around, trying to find someone who did look happy.

No luck.

The door opened and closed, opened and closed, the line at both registers got longer. She decided on bacon. They would have BLTs, unfortunately without the tomatoes. Not the best dinner in the world, but not the worst. She would get the kids their favorite chips, totally unhealthy, but it would fill them up, and she was too tired to think of anything else. Unless . . . soup? Was there soup anywhere? Soup and sandwich, that was lunchy, but definitely wholesome, according to all those Campbell's commercials.

She found chunky soup, got into the end of the line. It wasn't moving. The woman at the front was buying cigarettes, and she wanted them in the box, Marlboros in the box.

The clerk found the right cigarettes. Now the woman wanted lottery tickets. Sonora gritted her teeth and made a fist. She hated waiting for people who wanted lottery tickets; people who wanted lottery tickets and cigarettes at dinner time.

Maybe it made them happy. This woman looked happy now, the first happy person Sonora had seen in the Dairy Mart of the thirty or so who passed through while she was trying to make up her mind.

She bit her thumbnail. Waiting in a line that was going so slow she genuinely thought she might prefer to die than wait her turn.

Here I am walking through Dairy Mart and I want to die. Everybody here who wants to die, raise your hand.

Sonora wondered what the percentage would be. Low, surely, but deep in her heart she was convinced that it could be pretty damn high. Which showed how far gone *she* was.

The BLTs were a hit with Heather. Whether or not Tim would have been pleased was a moot point, as he had not come home.

Sleep. Bubble bath. Catching her breath. All out of the question.

On the one night she actually felt sleepy, had actually fallen asleep on the couch, had to get up very early the next morning to catch two desperate and dangerous killers, for God's sake, this would be the night the boy did not come home, the boy did not call, this would be the night the boy, her son and firstborn, chose to disappear.

Sonora, a mother, a cop, a woman with a great deal of common sense but a lot of imagination, did a mental review of all the things that could happen to him – a list as long as the list of things she would do to him once she had him home and safe.

By midnight, the witching hour, Sonora left Heather asleep in her bed, and took Clampett out in the car to keep her company while she cruised the streets for her son.

She had made all the phone calls, hospitals, the city jail. No news is good news, this pearl of wisdom courtesy of the clerk on duty at the city jail.

She stopped at a red light. She turned the heat on. It was cold out for cut-off jeans, but her sweatshirt was warm, and she was comfortable. Clampett, banished to the back seat, made a move for the front, which is where she would put Tim if she ever found him. She cruised slowly past the after-hours clubs and other places Tim better not be. Where the hell was he?

Cincinnati was quiet, she should be home in bed, so should all two of her kids. She closed her eyes, waiting for the light to turn. She felt alone and back to the wall, thinking maybe she just couldn't do it any more. The light went to green. She found a blues station on the radio. Something from *Hot Flash* by Blue Sapphire.

They call me a tramp. They don't understand. I just want one good man.

She wondered what Gillane was doing, if he was working the night shift. She considered calling him to help her look. Changed her mind.

The dark thoughts were with her like never before. They touched her forehead with sweat, they sat in her stomach like an ulcer pain, made a knot in her chest that was becoming as familiar as her reflection in the mirror.

The thoughts scared her. They felt a long way from safe.

Another red light, she was catching them all. A black Trans Am, brand-new, pulled up in the right lane beside her. The windows were tinted, Sonora could not see the driver. She had the uncanny feeling he was looking at her, and when the light changed, she took off.

The tires of the Trans Am screeched and he was with her neck and neck. She accelerated, looked at the speedometer. Eighty-five, and increasing. Traffic ahead. The car fell back. Sonora kept the speed up an extra second to make it clear who'd won, then braked hard, a red light ahead. Clampett slid forward into the dash and she grabbed his fur, keeping him in the seat, one hand on the wheel with the car weaving right and left and all over the road, till she got the speed down and the Pathfinder's nose straight.

'Sorry, Clampett.'

He was a good boy, he didn't deserve being slung into the dashboard. Sonora eased up to the light slowly like any middle-aged heavy, a BMW purring in the lane beside her. They both pulled away with a quiet decorum befitting a week night.

Clampett licked her arm.

Her cell phone rang and she grabbed it. 'Tim?'

'Detective Blair?'

'Who's this?'

'I'm sorry, this is Jack Van Owen. I got your message about Barton Kinkle?'

'Oh.'

'I called your house. Woke your daughter up, sorry, but your message said urgent. Are you . . . out and about?'

'You could say so.'

'Want to meet me at Denny's for a cup of coffee?'

Anything beat going home alone to worry. 'Sure. Which one?'

'First tell me where you are.'

Sonora was watching for him, snug in a booth and drinking coffee and orange juice. She almost didn't recognize him in jeans and a worn blue sweatshirt. He looked damn good for a man on disability. He smiled and slid into the seat across from her.

Sonora wasn't sure if it was the dimples, or the air the man had, but the waitress was at his shoulder in seconds.

'Let me buy you breakfast,' he said.

'Coffee's fine.'

'I'm starving, eat with me.'

She found it impossible to tell this man no. That smile again. That air of knowing her very well.

He had the Grand Slam breakfast, and she ordered potato pancakes. Carbohydrates were tranquilizing. She could use some tranquilizing.

'You're upset.' He said it quietly. An invitation to talk, a flash of sympathy. But a little distance. She did not feel crowded. More like invited.

'My son didn't come home tonight.'

'Ah.' He winked at her. 'A teenage boy. How well I know it.'

'You have a son?'

He nodded. 'How old is your boy?'

'Tim's seventeen.'

'Ouch, is he driving?'

She nodded.

'I know how you feel, Sonora.' She thought he was going to touch her hand, then changed his mind. 'I know it feels like the end of the world, but it isn't. It happens every day.'

'That doesn't help me sleep.'

Her potato pancakes arrived, followed by his breakfast. He slathered them with butter and maple syrup. 'Listen, Sonora. You do what you can for your children, then you have to let them walk their path. Get some distance.'

'From my son?'

'It's not a sin, it's survival. You do what you can and you live.'

'Impossible.' Her potato pancakes were lumps on the plate.

'Not impossible. Just damn hard.'

She took a sip of coffee. It was going cold. She was not the magical Jack Van Owen. No one appeared to fill her cup. 'What about Kinkle?'

'Barton Kinkle?' Van Owen shook salt and pepper over two eggs, cooked over easy. 'Don't know him. But isn't Kinkle, isn't that Aruba's sister's last name?'

'He's some kind of nephew.'

'Crazy as Aruba?'

'Not what I hear.'

'Can I give you some advice?'

'About Kinkle?'

'Crick says you're going after Aruba tomorrow.'

'Yeah.'

'Go home and take a pill or something. Get some sleep. Your boy will be in twenty-four hours.'

'I can't just assume that.' But weirdly enough, she believed him. He had that effect.

'You want me to sort of ask around? I still know a lot of guys. I can find out if something . . . I can rule some things out.'

She was wary of favors. But for her kid. Anything. And this was the legendary Jack Van Owen. 'You've got time?'

'I'm retired. Remember?'

Chapter Thirty-Seven

Sonora was annoyed that Kentucky, reputed to be part of the South, if you believed the natives, was socked in with an overcast gray miasma that rivaled the worst you would endure in Cincinnati.

'Pretty here, isn't it?' Sam said.

Always the man with the cup half full. But it was pretty here, in spite of the weather, cruising down the two-lane road, pastures greening up on either side, a huge red brick Civil War mansion on the left, gravel drive leading to the front door, and a new barn going up on the right. New four-plank wood fencing on the right, wire fence on the left. Horses in the field, next to a pasture full of cows. Since the acquisition of her very own horse, Sonora had developed an appreciation of barns bordering on the obsessive. Where once she liked to look into people's windows as she drove by, imagining the home within, she now wanted to wander in and out of barns, checking out the stalls and tack rooms.

The road dead-ended into Old Frankfort Pike. A small black sign said *Pisgah Pike Historic District*. Sam pulled the car off the pavement and opened a map.

Sonora looked up and down the road. Sam had picked his spot carefully. No one around to ask for directions.

On the left, an old cemetery, crumbling white headstones sagging tiredly against one another beneath the branches of a giant barren oak. It would be beautiful and peaceful come spring. Across the road, an old Baptist church, red brick. A tiny rural congregation. Trim green lawn, well-kept Kentucky blue-grass.

Sam pointed at the map and Sonora looked over his shoulder, pretending to make sense of the lines and splotches of color. They both knew better.

'We take a right here,' Sam said.

'Do we?'

'There should be a restaurant about a mile on the left. Some kind of barbecue place.'

Sonora looked up and down the road. On the right was an old stone fence, built, according to the sign, by Irish laborers before the Civil War, and much appreciated by the clusters of cows eating the grass.

'Way the hell out here? Sam, who would go to it? The cows? This is screwed up. We're lost here, admit it.'

He frowned at the map, looked up, squinting. 'The land-marks are right. Church, cemetery.'

'There's not going to be a barbecue place out in the middle of nowhere.'

'This isn't no*where*, Sonora. It's Woodford County.'

'I thought this place was in *Fayette* County.'

'Yeah, well, maybe we cross the county line somewhere around here.'

'Sam, we're lost.'

'We're not lost.'

'We should have met this guy, this Detective Whitmore, in Lexington, like he offered.'

'Why go all the way to town and then come all the way back out here? Don't you want a look at the place on our own, before we deal with those SWAT guys?'

'Yes, you know I do.'

The cell phone rang. The Martha Brooks's phone.

'Yes?' Sonora said.

'Yes, is this the place that makes those Kalua candies?'

'I'm sorry, sir, my secretary called in sick today. Could you get back to me day after tomorrow?' She hung up.

'*Sonora*,' Sam said.

'Shame on me. Yes, I have guilt.'

'You should never have taken that phone.'

'Excuse me for trying to keep a witness alive.'

Sam refolded the map, restarted the car.

'How do you do that, anyway?' Sonora asked, stuffing the phone back in her purse.

'Do what?' Sam checked over his left shoulder, and turned out on to Old Frankfort Pike, going right for the mythical restaurant that Sonora knew they would never find.

'Fold that map up just like it was.'

'It's a guy skill. Beats the hell out of wadding it into a huge ball and throwing it into the back seat.'

'I only did that one time.'

Sam drove slowly. The houses were smaller here, closer to the road. They passed a sagging, boarded-up cement-block building that had never been pretty, though it had once provided groceries, beer and car parts. The faded sign said FLOYD'S BARGAIN HOUSE. She still didn't see any sign of a restaurant, but the road was leading them through an area that could pass for rural congestion if one were optimistic. But a restaurant. That was going to be stretching it.

'There we go.' Sam had that superior tone of voice. 'Good Ole Days Barbecue Restaurant.'

Sonora squinted out the window. It was new-looking, a log-cabin air about it, not a place she'd be afraid to walk into. A sign on the door said *CLOSED*. The place looked like it had been closed for months, though it had the spruced-up air of some-where that was reopening soon.

A beige Dodge Ram pickup was parked to the side. No driver. Sam pulled into the small square parking lot of a grocery store separated from the restaurant by a sagging wood fence. Two ancient gas pumps stood in front of the grocery store, one in use.

'Step two. The restaurant. The one you said doesn't exist. Only thing missing is Detective Whitmore.'

'That's his car?'

'Yeah, his personal ride. What, you think we should have a meeting of the Taurus and the Crown Victoria way the hell out here, stand around in suits, and talk into radios? Might as well send these guys a fax and let them know we're on the way.'

'So how come we didn't take your pickup?'

He paused. 'Didn't think of it, that's why.'

Sonora looked around the rectangular parking lot, counted three pickup trucks and a '78 Mercury Cougar.

'I bet they make great sandwishes in that place,' Sam said, looking over his shoulder at the grocery.

'Sandwich.'

'Not when you're this hungry.'

'It says they've got chicken salad on that sign in the window. Go on in, Sam.'

'What are you going to do?'

'Call home and see if I've got any messages.'

'Sonora. You've called every ten minutes since I picked you up this morning. Tim knows your cell number, doesn't he?'

'Yes, Tim knows my cell number.'

'Come on in with me, Sonora. The one who eats the last biscuit gets to kiss the cook.'

Only Sam said things like that. 'No, thanks.'

Sam shrugged, got out of the car. Hesitated. He walked around to her window and Sonora rolled it down, cell phone clutched in her left hand.

'What?'

'Honey, you called all the hospitals and the jail, right?'

'At least twice.'

'Okay, then. I was a teenage boy once. And I'm telling you, Tim is okay. He's holed up at a friend's house, in some kind of trouble that seems real big to him, like skipping school or something. Right now he's sleeping late instead of going to school, and when he wakes up he'll fool around trying to work up the courage to call you.'

'Sam, the kid has got to know I'm half out of my mind.'

'No, Sonora, he's hoping, stupidly, but kids live in La La

Land as you well know, he's hoping that you're so absorbed in this case you haven't had a chance to miss him.'

'Sam, I am not the kind of mother that gets so absorbed in her work she doesn't know when her kids don't come home! And I can't think of one good reason for him not to at least *call* me. Pick up the damn phone!' Her voice broke and she gritted her teeth.

'I know. He'll call, in his own good time. You just have to keep your sanity till then.' He leaned into the open window. 'Sonora, do you want to go home? You don't have to do this.'

'No, Sam.'

'Did you get any sleep last night?'

'Some,' she lied. She didn't tell him that she didn't sleep under the best of circumstances. Teenage sons not coming home were not the best of circumstances.

'Are you going to be able to keep your mind on the job? These guys aren't exactly a cake walk. You don't want to be worrying about Tim when we're bringing down a guy like Aruba.'

'Sam. Get your sandwich and let me make my call.' She hadn't meant to sound quite so brusque, but that's the way it came out.

'I hope it makes you feel better, taking everything out on me. I like to know when I suffer for a good cause.' But he smiled at her while he said it, and she would have felt better, if it had at all been possible.

Chapter Thirty-Eight

A ratty pickup truck, much dented and minus a working muffler, passed slowly on the road, coming to a crawl as it approached the grocery store parking lot. The front seat was stuffed with four men, short, dark-skinned, black-haired. In the back of the truck were hay bales and a rusted-out wheelbarrow. The truck slowed and the driver stared at Sonora, who stood with her back resting on the dirty bumper of the Taurus.

The front door of the grocery store opened, and the driver of the truck changed his mind about whatever it was he'd been going to say. Sonora looked over her shoulder.

She would have sworn, if she hadn't known better, that the two men coming out the front door had grown up together as friends, if not brothers, so easily did the conversation flow, both with that relaxed air of men who know each other well enough to tell dirty jokes, complain about their jobs, and, a huge sign of trust, take each other's recommendations on mechanics. They had the matched stride of tall, broad-shouldered men who support the same football team.

Detective Whitmore, Sonora had no doubt. A tall black man, skin the color of midnight, seeming oblivious to the casual dressing down that was the new trend in police work. He seemed as comfortable in his wrinkled suit as Sonora was in her oldest, most worn-out Reeboks.

He turned sideways, answering a question from Sam. The suit, creased along the backside, could not quite disguise the man's broad pear shape, and the suit coat swayed from large, rounded shoulders. But the lines down the side of his cheek and the sloping, tired shoulders, said salesman after one too many meetings, or an overworked cop.

Whitmore inserted the last bite of a hot-dog in his mouth, wadding a catsup-stained piece of white tissue into a tight ball. He looked over at the Taurus, raised a hand at Sonora. Sam saluted her with an Ale-8-One. She knew, from past experience, that he would have bought a packet of peanuts and funneled them into the bottle, a bizarre Southern custom Sonora did not understand. She always expected him to choke.

'Police Specialist Blair, meet Detective Ron Whitmore.'

'How cha do?' Whitmore had a coarse, gray-streaked mustache, and a weary but understanding face. He was taller even than Sam and his large, square hand dwarfed Sonora's.

'How's it going?' she said.

'Pretty well. I was telling your partner here we're in shape, almost anyway. Still a little paperwork but I've got Mai working on it downtown. Been watching your boys for the last twenty-four hours, got a man out there right now.' He glanced over his shoulder at the grocery store, flexed his right shoulder like a man who ached, and leaned sideways on the back of the Taurus.

'The older guy, the blond. Aruba?'

Sonora nodded.

Whitmore scratched his cheek. 'Far as we know, he's still in there.'

'Where's there?' Sonora said.

'Two miles down, on the right, just past the Woodford–Fayette County line. About five or six little white row houses.'

'Row houses? Out here?'

Whitmore shrugged. 'Whatever you call 'em. Built cheap out of concrete block and shingle, whitewashed, no more than one or two rooms inside. Tiny little places, built maybe thirty years ago. The car's out back, the Impala, paint primer on the right front fender. Registered to Barton Kinkle.'

'Sister there?' Sam said.

'She's there, and so are her three children. Baby, a toddler, and a five-year-old boy. We've been watching and hoping the sister will bring the kids on out of there, but except for taking the dog to the bathroom, they've all stayed inside.'

'They've got a dog?' Sonora said.

'Rottweiler, from the looks of it.'

Sam sighed. 'Why is it always a Rottweiler?'

Whitmore went to the trunk of his car, opened a briefcase. Handed a picture to Sam. 'This is Kinkle. Never been convicted of anything except possession of marijuana, twice, misdemeanor both times. Juries feel sorry for him. Hell, I feel sorry for him. He's a weak link. Falls into things. Easily manipulated, easily intimidated. Possibly the lowest self-esteem on the planet.'

Sam passed the picture to Sonora. Damn, if she didn't feel sorry for him. Maybe because he looked so scared. He had brownish black hair, in something resembling a bowl cut, a bald spot in the back like a monk's tonsure, showing from the side view. His eyes were black like little buttons, his brows sparse and arched. His skin looked unhealthy. He was the kind of guy whose palms were always moist and sweaty.

'There's a note there from his social worker.' Whitmore scratched his cheek. 'Kind of a sad case. Mom dumped him in a tub of hot water when he was a toddler, didn't check the temperature. Just about boiled him. He couldn't have been more than two or three at the time. According to her notes, it was an accident. Evidently the mother wasn't real bright, but not a bad sort. The thermostat wasn't working and it jacked the water temperature up to boiling. Left a patch on the top of his head where the hair won't grow, scar tissue on his hands, arms and legs. Barton Melville Kinkle, everybody calls him Barty. Five feet nine inches tall, light-brown hair, wiry build, about one fifty-five. Reasonable IQ.

'They sent old Barty out to do the marketing a couple hours ago. Went to the Meadowthorpe Bread Co-op, last I heard he was at Krogers.'

'Buying milk,' Sonora said, making a mental note that she needed some herself.

'Or beer.' This from Sam.

'He's got the car,' Whitmore told them. 'I got a guy on him. Soon as we get our paperwork through, we'll pick him up.'

'I'd like to grab him before he goes back home,' Sonora said.

Whitmore nodded. 'Mai will give me a call soon as Judge Hooper signs the order. Paperwork straight on your end?'

'Murder warrants in hand,' Sam said.

'It's a high-risk entry, clearly, so we've got our emergency response unit on board. Captain's calling them in as we speak, briefing at five o'clock.'

Sonora checked her watch. Noon.

'When is it set to go?' Sam asked.

'Captain hasn't said for sure, but I suspect it will be the usual.'

'Four a.m.,' Sonora said.

Sam grimaced. 'I wish we could get those kids out of there.'

'Can't wait forever,' Whitmore said.

Chapter Thirty-Nine

The Meadowthorpe Grill sat in a depressed-looking shoestring of a strip mall that hadn't seen pretty in a long long time. According to a sign on the front windows, the office next door had been a dialysis center. It was empty now.

Sonora cringed. She could not imagine walking through that door with anything remotely approaching confidence. Whitmore had explained that the center had relocated, because the doors were too narrow for hospital stretchers.

A blessing.

Sonora resisted a backward glance at Whitmore, who sat in his pickup truck, smoking a Marlboro Light. He had warned them that one, there was a back door from the store room beside the bathrooms at the back of the grill; two, subject Kinkle had been observed going inside twenty minutes earlier, presumably for lunch; and three, the food was excellent.

Sonora got her first look at the primer-stained Chevy, parked crookedly out front. She resisted the urge to look through the windows. Kinkle might be watching.

Sam went in first, holding the black mesh door open for Sonora. Suddenly they were a couple, out on a lunch date. It took the cop patina off them, in case Kinkle was watching.

The grill was cramped, tables in the front, booths and more tables crowding the narrow dining room on the right. The place was packed with a lunch crowd that ran the gamut – most of them men, some of them in uniform, UPS, NTW, BP

Oil. Men in three-piece suits. Tobacco smoke mixed with steam from the open, cafeteria-style kitchen, where people dragged trays on metal bars and ordered meat and three or burgers from the grill.

Sam headed for the food line, handing Sonora a plastic tray and silverware wrapped in a napkin. She was hungry. She scanned the lunch room. A dark-haired boy at a table on the left, well to the back, looked like he might be Kinkle. Too far away to be sure.

My God, did she need glasses? *Dining room too hazy with cooking steam and cigarette smoke to make positive ID.* That's how it would go into her report.

'What'll you have?' The woman behind the counter had a round, doughy face, pale gold hair in a net behind her ears, and a large smile. Her lipstick was very red, and she wore a floral apron over her jeans and tailored white shirt.

'I'll take the fried shrimp,' Sam said.

'Coleslaw?'

'And mashed potatoes. With gravy.'

'There's your bread counter next to the wall there, right by the drinks.'

They might not be regulars, Sonora thought, but they were welcome. Sonora snapped her order out. 'I'll have the Salisbury steak, mashed potatoes, and green beans. And tea.' That should sit well on her stomach.

'Got your mind all made up!' The woman's tone said congratulations and we appreciate you not holding up the line. Sonora felt complimented.

The food came on heavy Chinet plates, overwhelmed beneath generous portions and pools of gravy.

'Find us a table,' Sam said, reaching for his wallet. 'I'll get the drinks and the bread.'

'Okay, but I've changed my mind, I want Coke.'

'Gotcha.' He leaned over and gave her a kiss on the cheek. 'Just for authenticity,' he murmured so only she could hear.

She headed for the booths, blood-red leather, much mended with steel-gray duct tape. Sonora felt conspicuous as she navigated the thin spaces between the tables and tried not to look at Kinkle.

He was looking at her, though, but so were several others, and she was relieved to settle into the booth after walking the gauntlet. But it was a man–woman thing, not a cop–killer thing. It was annoying to feel this vulnerable.

She salted her green beans, hand hovering over then rejecting the pepper shaker. She unrolled her silverware as Sam slid into the seat across from her, trampling her new white Reeboks with his shiny black shoes.

'Ouch, Sam.'

'Sorry, move your feet.'

'Move yours.'

He handed her a large, yellow-gold yeast roll. 'It was this or the garlic toast.'

'How well you know me.'

'Not exactly. It's bad stake-out etiquette, eating garlic.'

'Really, Sam? Could we please stretch this rule to apply to chili?'

He waved a hand. 'No. So.' He leaned close. 'What's happening?'

'He's eating a sandwich and reading a . . . looks like a comic book. One of those Japanimation ones.'

'What kind of sandwich?'

'It looks like a BLT, why?'

'Just curious.'

'Okay. What now?'

'We could arrest him in here, but there's a lot of people around. I told Whitmore we'd let the guy have his lunch, make sure he doesn't duck out the back, and grab him in the parking lot when he goes for the car.'

'Fine. Pass the Worcestershire sauce.'

'Are you ever going to learn to pronounce that right?'

'Are you ever going to hand it over?'

'Remember our first stake-out? You were so nervous you couldn't eat. We must have sat there twelve hours.'

Sonora reached across his plate for the Lea & Perrins. 'We grow old and jaded.'

Sam took a huge bite of garlic bread, crumbs falling on to his tie. 'How's your food?'

She poked the green beans with her fork. 'Sam, I think the beans are bad.'

'What?' He reached his spoon across the table and took a bite. 'They're fine. They're good.'

'But they're . . . limp.'

'That's how you're supposed to cook green beans.'

'But they don't crunch.'

'No. But they taste good.'

'But they're not crisp.'

'No. They *taste* good. Don't they?'

She carefully ate one bean. 'Yes.'

'That's the point, here in the South. It's supposed to taste good.' Sam swiped crispy brown shrimp, red sides showing through the batter, through a plastic cup of cocktail sauce. 'This place is a helluva find. Don't you think?'

Sonora nodded, the yeasty roll sweet and fresh in her mouth. She took a bite of homemade mashed potatoes. 'Remind me, later, to thank Kinkle.'

'Stop staring at him.'

'I'm not staring.'

'Does he look like his picture?'

'I can't tell, with that stupid ball cap on his head. Want me to go peel it off him?'

'Maybe later. When we thank him for leading us to the Meadowthorpe Grill.'

Sam sat with his elbow on the table. 'Pass me the rest of that chuck steak, if you're just going to leave it.'

'It's not chuck steak, it's Salisbury steak.'

'It is not. I know chuck steak when I see it.'

'Look on the menu, Sam. S-A-L-I-S-B-U-R-Y.' She checked her watch. 'Come on, dammit, let's take him.'

'Let him finish his pie. He'll head out of here in a minute or two. You have no patience, Sonora. Anybody ever tell you that?'

'You, every day.' The restaurant was beginning to clear. She checked her watch.

'Will you quit with the watch? Is that all you're going to eat?'

She shoved her plate across the table. 'We better grab him, Sam. Get him squared away.'

'Girl, you are type A to the max.'

'And I need to call home and check on Heather.'

'Why not call her now, it'll look natural.'

'I can't concentrate on my kids and a perp at the same—'

'Good point. Maybe you should go outside with Whitmore.'

'Oh, and that won't look suspicious?'

'We could stage a fight.'

'We don't have to stage one, we're . . . whoa, whoa, here we go.'

Sam forked the final chunk of Salisbury steak into his mouth. He wiped his mouth with a napkin. Took her hand across the table and looked lovingly into her eyes. 'Don't be impatient. Give it a second. Make sure he's not headed for the men's room.'

'By the way, Sam, I am positive that Sanders is sleeping with Gruber.'

'I cannot believe he's not stopping to pee. That kid had three refills on his Coke, he must have cast-iron kidneys.'

'You're getting old, Sam.'

'You've been to the ladies' room twice.'

'You're not supposed to *count*, Sam. A gentleman isn't even supposed to notice. A gentleman – come on, dammit, he's getting away.'

Chapter Forty

'Getting away' was something of an exaggeration. Kinkle kept his elbows in tight to his body and he slid sideways between the tables, heading for the door. He kept his head low, a man accustomed to not being noticed.

He was thinnish, his Wrangler jeans did not fit well, too loose in the seat, too long at the bottom, hem flaring in an unattractive cut reminiscent of a style popular in the unattractive seventies, a style making an inexplicable resurgence. He wore a mud-brown, polyester-filled vest, stained on the back, a red ball cap and wire-rimmed glasses. Sonora got a quick glimpse of his face, one side mottled with whitish scar tissue. He seemed young, she would have guessed early twenties, not thirty-one. For some reason, she felt sorry for him.

Out of the corner of her eye, she saw Whitmore flick a cigarette on to the pavement, squashing it into the asphalt, smoke streaming out of his nose.

Kinkle, unaware, went straight for his car.

Sam moved in behind him, hand in the small of his back, shoving him hard into the side of the car. '*Police*. Hands on the roof. *Hands on the roof.*'

Kinkle froze, and Sam grabbed both arms at the elbow and raised them to the roof. Sonora heard the meaty smack of Kinkle's palms, knew it had to hurt.

'Are you Barton Kinkle?' Whitmore had his badge out, and a hard edge on his voice. The patrol cars were circling the wagons, hordes of them, lights flashing. Lexington took their backup very seriously.

Kinkle shrugged.

'I *asked* you a question. Sir, are you Barton Kinkle? Get his ID.' This to Sam.

'I'm Barton Kinkle, yes.' The voice was a strangled vanilla tenor.

'I can't hear you.' Sam kicked Kinkle's legs apart.

'Yes, sir, I'm Barty Kinkle. What'd I do?'

'Mr Kinkle, you have the right to remain silent . . .'

Sam patted the man down. 'Face me, Barty.'

'. . . you have the right to—'

'Sir?'

'Turn around, son, unless you want your hands cuffed *behind* your back.'

Kinkle turned slowly. His face had gone dead white, lips bluish with shock. 'But what did I do? Would you please just tell me what did I do?'

Kinkle's eyes welled with tears. Sonora shook her head as Whitmore crammed Kinkle into the back of his car. Could this nebbishy little guy be responsible for a crime as brutal as the Stinnet home invasion?

Sonora was aware of a familiar disappointment. It was often this way. Pathetic little men trying to make themselves large through a big crime. She kept staring at Kinkle. Could this really be their guy?

Sam looked at her over his shoulder, inclining his head toward the Taurus. 'Follow us in, okay, Sonora?'

One of them present at every point. She nodded. 'Don't lose me. It's not my town.'

Sam waved, slid in beside Kinkle. She hoped he would not fight extradition. She wanted him now, she wanted him in Interview One, she wanted him on her own turf. She could crack him open in an hour, tops.

Chapter Forty-One

All four lanes of Main Street in downtown Lexington were clogged with after-work traffic. The streets were lined with government buildings, empty storefronts, an old theater called the Kentucky. A beautiful but almost empty newly built Victorian office structure. It was the usual mix, a downtown sucked dry by suburban sprawl, kept alive by attorneys' offices, eclectic restaurants, antique stores, and the kind of hopeful entrepreneurs who opened aerobic juice bars. A sidestreet storefront advertised Pamela Dee Wigs.

Hard to tell if downtown Lexington was going under, or just resurfacing.

Whitmore made a left turn, then another, on to a narrow street of back entrances and a graffiti – and trash-strewn underpass on the right. He got out and opened a huge metal garage door, Sonora waiting, Taurus engine idling. She followed the patrol car into a cavernous underground loading dock, and parked catty-cornered from a huge white van with the windows covered in blackout curtains.

She rolled down her window. 'Okay if I park here?'

Sam stepped out of the patrol car. 'Didn't you see us waving at you when we passed the annex garage?'

'Nope.'

Sam looked at Whitmore. 'I told you. Oblivious.'

'You're okay.' Whitmore smiled at her gently, and took Kinkle's right elbow. 'Let's make tracks, my friend.'

Kinkle moved stiffly, gave Sonora a hint of a shy smile, which she returned with stiff lips and a wave of nausea. Sam took Kinkle's left arm. Kinkle looked back once at Sonora over his left shoulder. She exchanged looks with Sam.

Kinkle was intimidated by the men, the cuffs, the police car and the procedure, and he was desperate for a kind word, clearly expecting it from Sonora. So his rage, unlike so many others, was not triggered by women. She'd be the best bet in interrogation.

She had a stab of worry over Tim. What kind of trouble was he in? Was he in jail somewhere? Had they handcuffed her son? Had he been afraid and looking for a kind word? Had he had anything to eat?

Focus, she told herself, stepping on to the elevator, back against the wall. Kinkle had that stunned look but at least he was not crying. Sonora heard Joy Stinnet's voice in the back of her mind. Saw the woman holding her stomach together. This *boy* was thirty-one years old. This *boy* had a lot to answer for.

Chapter Forty-Two

The third floor of the Lexington Police Department was nicely turned out with new carpet, walls and floor in a maroon and gray color scheme, a maze of cubicles stylistically laid out, providing each detective with semi-private work space that included a comfortable padded chair, file cabinets, a computer terminal and telephone. Most of the detectives were dressed down, jeans, khakis, sweaters and flannel shirts. They could have been a group ad for the Gap or Old Navy. Whitmore was an aberration in the wrinkled suit, but Sonora did not think the difference had ever occurred to him. All, of course, were decked out with police jewelry – handcuffs, gunbelts. The usual.

The room had a muffled quality, brought on by new carpet and low voices on the phone.

Sam looked at Sonora, raised an eyebrow. 'Poofie.'

'Jealous.'

They sat side by side in a sort of annex to a cell/interrogation room on the far wall. It was a tiny room, the size of two bathrooms side by side. Kinkle was handcuffed to a bench that was bolted to the floor. On Sam and Sonora's side of the two-way window was a video camera and microphone.

Sam yawned. Checked his watch. 'Briefing in eight minutes. Let's go find Whitmore.'

'In a minute.' Sonora watched Kinkle. His head was bowed. He'd called an attorney. Gone to the bathroom twice – Coke refills kicking in. 'I want to talk to him.'

'You can't talk to him. He's called his lawyer. What's he doing, bent over like that? He doesn't have to go to the bathroom again, does he? He's been pissing like a weasel since he got here.'

'I think he's crying.' How did a weasel piss? Men had odd minds.

'You don't feel sorry for him, do you?'

'I wouldn't want to *be* him.'

Sam swiveled his chair back and forth. 'You know, it comes to me, Sonora, that we are doing this interrogation thing all wrong anyway.'

'Yeah?'

'Yeah. We should sit these guys down and make 'em watch *Titanic* and *Waterworld* back to back unless they talk.'

'You make me watch *Titanic* and *Waterworld* back to back and I'd talk.'

The door was pushed open and Whitmore stuck his head in. He'd loosened his tie and unbuttoned his top button. 'You guys ready?'

Chapter Forty-Three

Whitmore led them down the side of the bull-pen, through a heavy door, that led past a room of cubicles, into another room of cubicles, and into a meeting room, tile floor, new wood table, folding metal chairs, huge green chalkboard covering one wall.

The emergency response team, the SWAT team, filled the room. Twenty-odd, three women, the rest men. Everyone looked tense. Everyone looked like they used their gym memberships.

The chalk board was covered with Xs and Os, like football strategy. It looked like the meeting was in progress. Sonora gave Sam a sideways look. He leaned up against the wall and did not sit down. A sign that he was wary.

She was exhausted. She sat.

Whitmore held up a hand. 'Gentlemen. Ladies. Say hello to Detectives Blair and Delarosa, in from Cincinnati. They'll be riding shotgun tonight; this is their baby. You've all got the memos – confidential, I don't have to remind you. The subjects are suspected of perpetrating a home invasion, body count of four, a middle-class family in the suburbs. There was some torture involved. The guy we're going after, Aruba, is a pretty hard case.' He looked over his shoulder at a man who was pale, very blond, with unhealthy-looking skin. 'Taleese?'

'I'll take it from here.' Taleese stood. He looked serious, his manner sucked dry of any humor, good or funny. 'I'm Captain

Taleese. I run the emergency response unit.' He nodded at Sam and Sonora, glanced over at Whitmore, who was taking a seat. 'We got a dog out there?'

'Looks like a Rottweiler.'

There was a groan around the table.

'Boggs, Mirren, you're the dog team.' Taleese pointed his chalk to a team marked DT. 'Mirren, take the sleeve and the baton. Boggs, you take the gas.'

'What kind of gas?' Sonora asked.

Whitmore leaned close to her. 'It's liquid nitro. Scares the hell out of them, but doesn't hurt them.'

'Unless they get so scared they jump through a two-story window.'

Sonora looked around, wondering who made the remark. Saw a smirk or two. She studied the chalk board. The men were divided into teams of three. One with a ballistic shield, one with a submachine-gun, one hands free. There were variations. Men on command. Men armed with gas. First and second hammer men with a sixty-five-pound ram.

'That house have a storm door?' Taleese asked.

'No,' Whitmore said.

'Good. We'll take the hooligan anyway. Mai, as usual, videographer.'

A thin oriental woman along the middle of the second table gave a small nod. This, Sonora realized, was Whitmore's partner, Mai Yagamochi, doing double time as ERU videographer.

Taleese pointed to a mark on the board. 'This is Old Frankfort Pike. We'll hit at four a.m. and we will pull over right here, about a hundred yards before we get to the first house. We're hitting house number four. The houses are on the left. Subject is Lancaster as in Lanky Aruba, and he is armed and extremely dangerous. Some indication of mental illness, he is going to be a handful. Also inside are Belinda Kinkle, aunt of Barton Kinkle, currently in custody, and sister of Aruba. She has three children, so heads up. One baby, one toddler, one five-year-old boy.

'It's going to be complicated. Aruba is going to be nervous.

Kinkle got sent out this morning, and he didn't come back. This man's jacket says he is capable of anything, up to and including harming the sister and the kids. And don't forget the dog. We got just about everything working against us on this one.

'Fifteen seconds tops to get everyone inside secure from the time we bust that door. Any questions?'

There were none.

'According to our Cincinnati detectives, it's possible Kinkle and Aruba took small items from the primary, pictures, maybe even jewelry.'

It was a stretch, Sonora knew, but it enabled them to get very specific with their search warrants.

'This means our warrant allows us to look virtually anywhere you could hide a picture or a piece of jewelry, which means anywhere.

'I want everyone assembled and suited up at 0 two thirty. Any questions?'

Sonora checked her watch. Wondered where the hell her son was.

Chapter Forty-Four

Sonora woke suddenly, the van lurching sideways, throwing her up against Sam. Unbelievably, she had dozed off, in the middle of a before-dawn raid on a hard case like Lanky Aruba. What panache. Sam put an instinctive hand on her knee, steadying her.

The hand did not go unnoticed. Mai, Whitmore's partner and the ERU videographer, studied Sonora openly, unsmiling. She had the personality of a videographer, watchful, uninvolved, stoic − wise little face, a poker face, impossible to guess her thoughts. Her body was compact and petite, but taut and muscular for her size. She was definitely a presence.

A woman, Sonora thought, who had secrets. A woman who would reject much, who would pare the world down to white polished bone, allowing no sharp edges, meat or gristle. She would be judgmental. Thoughtful. Obscure.

The woman watched Sonora more than she liked, studying, probably habit. She'd make a bad enemy. A rare but elusive friend. Her friendship could be as scary as her enmity.

Sonora took a breath, feeling car sick. It was a tight fit inside the van. Cushioned benches ran along either side, leaving Sonora and Sam near the driver, beside and facing the twenty-man unit, all of them dressed in black and riding quietly. They looked impressive and impersonal, in black Kevlar helmets, weighted down with forty pounds of equipment. Radio frequencies were coordinated and set.

There was a surprising lack of conversation, to Sonora's

mind, the tension as thick as fog. They would be worrying about the children, she decided. Wary of the dog. And what they knew about Aruba would make some of them nervous, and some of them aggressive. He was every cop's nightmare, disassociated, disturbed and unpredictable. Men like Aruba reacted in unexpected ways. They fought like animals, they felt no pain. Logic did not apply to the Arubas of the world, who ran on instinct – warped, ego-saturated instinct – and an inexplicable agenda coupled with an otherworldly strength.

Anybody with brains would be worrying about Aruba.

The van was a world unto itself, housing a range of weaponry that included MKs, AZs, and the weapon of choice, MPS submachine-guns. There was a Remington II 87 semi-automatic shotgun, tools for the sniper on the team, silencers.

Sonora shuffled her feet, toes sticking on the metal floor. It was claustrophobic inside, too many people crowded too close together, Whitmore up near the front with Captain Taleese and the driver, who had the only roomy seat in the van. Blackout curtains muzzled the windows. A phone system – the command center – was installed behind the driver, just under the television and the microwave oven. The team could survive long stake-outs, and watch the action on television if the raid was complicated by the predatory press.

The guys across from Sam and Sonora had the worst seats, bench bolted in front of slots for the shields.

Outside, Sonora could hear the frizzy noise of tires on wet pavement. Still raining. Sam had accused her of bringing the rain back from Cincinnati, but as far as Sonora could tell, Kentucky had plenty of its own.

The weather was a mixed blessing. It would give more cover, less visibility, and muffle some of their noise. But it would also make the ground slippery, and spread wet misery over the team, who were technically not supposed to care. And Sonora had always been of the opinion that weapons did not function as well in heavy humidity, though Sam was prone to arguing the point.

The van slowed. Sonora hoped they were close. She was

getting very car sick, riding sideways, with no window to see out of. Captain Taleese was on his feet, they must be close. At his command, the team stood up and grabbed plastic straps that hung from the roof. They were like a parachute team, readying for a jump.

The van shifted sideways and stopped, resting at a tilt that said they had pulled off the road. The neighborhood dogs sounded the watch, background music to every raid Sonora had ever been through. No doubt the Rottweiler was a member of the chorus.

Sonora thought of the children in the tiny white house, uneasy in their sleep. She thought of Aruba, edgy now that Kinkle had not returned, alerted by the barking dog.

Someone once said that massacres were all the same.

The back of the van opened with the creak of a metallic hinge, and things happened quickly. Sonora felt oddly detached, with a panicky sense of being out of control. Each man jumped out, shouting *Off the truck*. She followed Sam, Whitmore and Taleese out of the front of the truck, around the side to the teams filing out the back doors, moving toward the house in a stylized shuffle step. When the last team was out of the truck and in the line-up, Taleese gave the signal and the teams broke into a slow jog, heading in a direct line toward house number four, ground giving wetly beneath their heavily booted feet, like a line of black army ants after a picnic.

Sonora looked up to the wet mist of rain, feeling it settle on her face, knowing that it would make her hair curl. She was damp all over. They'd smell like wet dogs by the end of the night.

She imagined looking out one's living-room window, spotting the white van and the line of darkly dressed men and women, intimidating in helmets, equipment and that confident and inexorable threat that emanated from well-trained men on a mission.

Call the police, would be the first thought. The second, sinking, helpless, this is the police.

There was a surreal quality here, the men and women

jogging in the rain, the first team, the ones with the sledge-hammer and ram, turning now, veering across the dormant grass to the tiny house, that showed not a light to the face of the world. She felt uneasy. A sense of dread. She felt as if she and she alone had set this in motion, as if she would be responsible for what would happen next.

She thought of the three children and the sister. Were they all that different from the Stinnets? Lower on the socio-economic scale, with the unsettling vulnerability of a family in the orbit of predators. In the back of her mind, she could hear Joy Stinnet, *Hail, Mary, full of grace*, as the ram thundered into the flimsy front door of the small row house and knocked it splintering backward off the hinge.

The house erupted in an explosion of noise, men in heavy boots, clustering for a critical and vulnerable three seconds as they all tried to fit through the gaping door.

The dog howled, a bay that set the hair rising on the back of Sonora's neck. A little girl screamed *Mommy*, and Sonora heard a shout go up – *He's got a gun!*

She stood outside the house, feeling the straitjacket of her disinvolvement, no choice but to stand and wait, while rain ran over her hair and down her face, mixing with tears as she listened to the dog yelp and squeal in macabre harmony with an infant's wail.

Was this what it had sounded like, the night Aruba and Kinkle invaded the home of the Stinnets?

Chapter Forty-Five

Sonora heard the fight all the way out in the front yard. She looked at Sam, who nodded, headed in through the busted front door. She followed without hesitation, and they made two unnecessary people in an overcrowded house.

A woman in a white nylon nightgown, heavy breasts loose and in motion, was wrestling the dog into a tiny bathroom. Sonora got a quick glimpse of curling linoleum, and the white flecks of liquid nitro on the dog's muzzle, where he had been sprayed with CO_2. The woman's hair, pale reddish gold, like Aruba's, swung in a plait down her back. Her eyes were large and dark, the right one swollen shut, purple and black with a brand-new bruise. The Rottweiler showed the face of a dog with a dilemma, but thankfully listened to the woman's whispers of reassurance and entreaty, as she ignored the man with the submachine-gun, and locked the dog away.

The front of the house was partitioned into two rooms, a living space on the left, dominated by a big-screen TV, kitchenette on the right, a tiny room in the back a closet-like bedroom. The couch was upended – one officer going through the cushions. Sonora counted all three children safe in the arms of men who were fathers in their off time.

The action was in that back, dark bedroom, and Sonora heard the shouts of the officers: *Down, now. You are under arrest – cooperate and we will not hurt you.* Words tossed like pebbles into the abyss of Aruba's rage. If he saw the officer training the submachine-gun on his midsection, he gave no sign, and it took a five-man pile-up to get the arms locked behind the body, working pressure points and using brute force to get the leg hobbles tight around the ankles, and still one man got caught by Aruba's powerful kick.

But at last, Aruba stopped moving, his breath coming like a tornado through a sieve. The couch had been searched, set upright, and the woman sat in handcuffs, head turning, as she tried to keep an eye on all three of her children.

A blessed sort of quiet began to descend, the baby soothed by the rocking of a muscular man, six feet if an inch, mustached. The scar that ran down his left cheek wrinkled the keloid tissues as he smiled down at the baby.

The toddler, a golden-haired girl with blue eyes and a white-lipped look of shock, reached for her mother, and the police officer sat her on the couch. She lay sideways, thumb in her mouth, head on her mother's lap. The woman stroked her head carefully, keeping the slender cuffed wrists a safe distance from the child's flushed, delicate skin. The five-year-old boy buried his head in one of the men's shoulders, legs wrapped around the officer's waist, and the man made no move to peel the boy away, but carried him wherever he went.

Captain Taleese called an ambulance and Whitmore read the search warrant word for word to a disinterested, shell-shocked audience, with background chants from Aruba, complaining, 'You fuckers broke my fucking arm.'

The man going through the coach cushions made a guttural noise deep in his chest, held up a white envelope to Sonora.

She looked over his shoulder. 'What?'

'Money. Looks like . . . seventeen hundred twenty-eight dollars.'

Sonora looked at the address on the envelope. Preprinted. Carl Stinnet. The remainder of Joy's two thousand.

'Jackpot, baby.'

Sonora looked up, wondering what a jackpot was if it wasn't the money. The uniform pulled a four by five snapshot and a .32 Smith & Wesson out of the cushion, like a magician pulling a rabbit out of a hat.

Chapter Forty-Six

Someone had given Lanky Aruba's sister a raincoat, which had almost gone double around her thin angular body. She held it tightly across her chest, arms folded. She had nodded once, when Mai Yagamochi asked her to confirm that her name was Belinda Kinkle. She had asked twice about her children, and when no answer was forthcoming, had set her lips, and found a place, inside herself, to go into full retreat.

Sonora handed her a chemical ice pack for the black eye. 'Who gave you that?'

Belinda Kinkle spoke through clenched teeth. 'Ran into the door.'

'What is Aruba to you?' Mai asked.

'He's my stockbroker,' Belinda said. Her thin face seemed ready made for pain, so quickly did it settle into lines of stress.

Mai, sitting upright in her chair, ran a pencil through her slim fingers, tapping the eraser on the edge of the desk. Sonora wanted more than anything to smack her hand. 'Let me explain what will happen to you, Miss *Belinda*, if you do not care to answer my questions.

'You will be charged as an accessory to murder. Your children will be put into protective custody. Your dog will be taken to the pound. If you cannot raise bail, your children will be put into foster care and eventually put up for adoption. If you are found *guilty*, your children will be put into foster care and put up for adoption. It may take some time to place your oldest boy, but the baby girls will find a home very quickly. Certainly the infant.'

Almost none of the above was true, and Sonora was not sure what surprised her more, that Belinda seemed to believe every word, or Mai's clumsy handling of a woman who might have been able to give them a great deal of insight, as well as solid information.

'Sit and think, Belinda. I'll give you some time.' Mai got up and headed for the door. She glanced backward at Sonora, who waved her on. It was clear from Mai's expression that she did not care to be waved on.

As soon as the door shut, Belinda began to sob. She seemed exhausted, eyes bloodshot and bleary, nose red and puffy. The black eye seemed even more swollen than it had before. Belinda put her head in her arms, crying into the oak-veneer table.

Sonora had a sudden memory of the conversation she'd had with Quincy David, the expert on check-cashing sharks. Thinking that they were using pretty much the same techniques.

She rubbed her face in her hands. Maybe she was just tired, but it was getting hard to tell the good guys from the bad.

Sonora scooted her chair closer, spoke in a low tone. 'Belinda? They can't put your kids up for adoption. Not unless they prove you're an unfit mother.'

'If I go to jail, I'm unfit, aren't I?' Belinda looked at her with a stunned woefulness that signified a loss of hope.

'No, it doesn't.' Sonora leaned forward. 'You're afraid of him, aren't you?'

'Who?'

'You know who. Your brother. Aruba forced his way in, threatened your children. Gave you that black eye. You didn't have a choice, did you, Belinda? Did you?' Sonora looked at her. *Say yes*, she willed the woman. Say yes, please say yes.

Belinda opened her mouth, swallowed painfully. 'Step-brother.'

'Step-brother. You were afraid. He threatened you and your children. You didn't have a choice. Yes, Belinda?'

She nodded slowly. 'That's right. I didn't have no choice.'

Sonora repeated it one more time. Belinda nodded and said yes again. Sonora let her breath go, relaxed. It was on videotape, exactly what Belinda Kinkle needed to say to keep clear.

She leaned across the table. 'Belinda, I want you to just listen for a minute. You don't have to say a word, okay, just listen, will you?'

It was hard to know if she was getting through, from the stunned look, the haunted eyes. But Belinda nodded and leaned toward her.

'Lanky isn't getting out of this one. I know you've heard it before, but this time he's really going down. This is a death-penalty issue, do you understand that, Belinda?' Sonora watched her, trying to read her thoughts.

'He could get out,' Belinda whispered.

'No, he couldn't. But if he did? Somehow? I promise I would call you and warn you.'

'No phone,' Belinda said. Still whispering.

'I would see that someone came and told you. I'd make sure. I would come myself if I had to.'

The woman looked at her as if she were insane.

'There's something I need to know,' Sonora said. 'I need to know if your brother and Barty worked with somebody, a third man. I think there was somebody else, and I need to know who he is. Did Lanky or Barty mention anybody else? Someone they worked with? Anyone at all?'

Belinda put a hand on Sonora's arm, and it seemed, for a moment, as if she would speak, but no words came.

Sonora patted the hand that gripped her arm. 'It's okay, Belinda. I know you're scared. Tell you what, I'm going to give you my card, okay? If you ever want to talk to me, just call, any time. You can call collect, I'll accept the charges. And Belinda? We boarded up that door we broke, and locked your house. And I left your dog some food and water.'

She grimaced, remembering the twine Sam had tied to the bathroom door, so they could let the dog out of the bathroom from outside the house. How many times the twine slid off and they had to start over. Mai's amused looks.

Sonora stood up and headed for the door. She could not remember being this tired, ever. 'Take care of yourself, Belinda. If anybody wants to talk to you, ask for Detective Whitmore. If you can't talk to Whitmore, don't say word one till you get a lawyer.'

Belinda looked like a woman whose last hope is walking out the door. 'He forced his way in,' she whispered. 'He hit me. He scared my babies.'

Sonora gave her the thumbs-up sign, and left, wondering if she was losing her way, or finding it.

Chapter Forty-Seven

Kinkle's attorney arrived at a relaxed nine fifteen the following morning, and by ten thirty word had gone out that Barty Kinkle was not going to fight extradition to Ohio.

Sonora sat in the small interrogation room with Sam, Whitmore and Drew Manson, Attorney at Law. Manson was a large man, with well-oiled black hair, thickly brushed back from a square, handsome forehead, and a broad, sad, puppy-dog face that said, *We've seen it all, haven't we, folks?*

According to Whitmore, Manson was a semi-competent local criminal defense attorney who was well known among local drug dealers and homegrown wiseguys.

Kinkle's story was simple. He had heard about the killings on the radio, worried he would be suspected because he'd been at the house that day, and had run with Aruba for his sister's to wait things out. Yes, they had gone there to collect a debt. Yes, they had gone inside. Yes, the woman had given them two thousand dollars cash. Sonora saw that Kinkle was looking at her. He seemed more relaxed today, more suited to the role of victim wanting only to please and be a very good boy. He gave the impression of someone who would do as he was asked for a cookie.

But he looked older up close, one side of his face a pale white webwork of scar tissue, the back of both hands a match of damaged skin, ancient history. Sonora squinted her eyes, thinking about Kinkle being dumped in an overheated bath, a three-year-old on the way to hell.

'Can I ask a couple of quick questions?' she said.

'No,' from the attorney.

Kinkle balled his hands into fists on the table. He wanted to speak. But he would not disobey Manson's command. Sonora could see the lawyer relax just a little. He seemed to be enjoying his morning. Cop a quick fee, cut this guy loose to his representation up in Cincinnati, who would get the glory and headaches inherent in this case.

'Look, you're not fighting extradition,' Sonora said. 'We appreciate being saved the paperwork. On the other hand, we've got Aruba now, and he's not fighting it either.'

Manson watched her, wary but not particularly expecting to catch her in a lie that he could so easily check.

Later.

But he didn't have the edge of a player who knows he'll have to try the case himself.

'What exactly are you saying, Detective?' Manson had a nice voice, which he clearly enjoyed the sound of. He would present well in court, Sonora thought, as long as he avoided a tendency to talk just for the pleasure of listening.

'You tell me,' Sonora said.

The invitation surprised him. But she knew from the narrowing of his eyes that he would not be able to resist taking her up on it. He put his fingertips together over the steel-gray vest, pursed the thick lips. Playing out the mannerisms, to give himself some time. It would be tedious, if he used this strategy in court.

'I think what you're trying to tell us, Detective Blair, is that Mr Aruba is trying to work some kind of deal.'

Sonora smiled gently. This guy was too smart for his own good.

Kinkle, staring at the center of the table, raised his head slowly, like a carrion bird interrupted in a meal in the center of the road.

'Am I right?' Manson said.

Sonora opened her arms. '*You* know how these things play out, don't you, Mr Manson?'

Kinkle watched his attorney like an acolyte before a priest. Which had its effect on Manson.

Manson tapped a finger on the table. 'I will tell you this. My client suspects that Mr Aruba went back to the Stinnets' house, after the initial visit. Since they've been holed up at the sister's, Aruba has done a certain amount of . . . bragging. We think that Mr Kinkle's story will be borne out by . . . certain forensic evidence, which you yourself have collected. Certain little gray pebbles which are, in fact, olive pits. Mr Kinkle would like to cooperate with you, and tell you what Mr Aruba said, for certain concessions.'

'Such as?'

'Immunity. Complete and total immunity.'

'Mr Manson, I would appreciate it if you would come down to earth.'

Kinkle looked at his attorney, who nodded. 'My client *wants* to tell you the truth. He wants to help. He's been traumatized by this guy Aruba. He's a victim like everyone else.'

Sonora looked at the faces of her fellow detectives. There was not much flow of sympathy in the room.

'We'll certainly take your thoughts to the district attorney,' Sam said, no hint in tone that the guy was dreaming. They'd get him to Cincinnati first. 'Of course, whatever happens, we'll want a polygraph. You going to cooperate on that one too?'

Manson pursed his lips. 'It is a future possibility. After we talk to the DA.'

Sonora had no trouble sounding annoyed. 'What you guys need to understand is somebody is going to make a deal. It can be Barty here, it can be Lanky Aruba.' She looked at Kinkle. 'The best thing you can do is give me a reason to choose between the two of you. We've got Aruba in custody, and we're going to go talk to him right after I finish with you.'

Aruba was in the ER, sedated, having his arm set, talking to nobody, but Sam and Whitmore stood up, heading for the door, playing right along, God bless them both. Sonora, last one out, stopped and looked at Kinkle, with as much understanding and sympathy as she could muster.

'I want everybody, do you understand me, Barton? The more of you there are, the more we can spread the blame around.'

Kinkle leaned close to Manson, who held up a meaty hand, as if this would shield their conversation.

'Detective, do you understand, we're going to hand you Aruba?'

'Counselor, do you understand, I've *got* Aruba?'

Manson frowned. 'Cards on the table, Detective. What do you want?'

'I want the third man.'

Kinkle's eyes widened and he swallowed. His body took on a tense stillness, like a mouse in the paws of a cat. He looked at Manson, shook his head vigorously.

'My client has no comment at this time,' Manson said. Ending the interview.

'Whatever you say.' Sonora turned away, heading for the door. Kinkle might not have told her in words, but he had told her. There was a third man. Scarier even than Aruba.

Could a marine, who made his living, after all, scaring recruits for life, scare Kinkle that bad?

Chapter Forty-Eight

When her cell phone rang, Sonora was sitting sideways in the driver's seat of the Taurus, waiting for Sam to complete the paperwork so they could finally go home. The driver's door was propped open, and her elbows were on her knees, chin in hand. Not exactly relaxed.

The phone was in her lap. She sat up, leaned against the seat cushion. 'Blair.'

'Sonora?'

She was aware of a sinking disappointment. Her son called her Detective Mom, from time to time, but never Sonora.

'It's Jack.'

They were Jack and Sonora now. 'Hello, Jack. You hear the news? We got 'em.'

'You got Aruba?'

'Aruba and Kinkle.'

'Are they—?'

'No, both intact. Aruba's in the hospital with a broken arm, but we're bringing both of them back.'

His voice was warm. 'Good job, Detective. I have news for you too. I found your son.'

Sonora got out of the car, catching a glimpse of her face in the side-view mirror. She had gone very white. She walked back and forth along the driver's side of the Taurus, feet making crunching noises in the gravel.

'Do tell.' She amazed herself – the calm worldly mom voice flowed like melted butter over the thud of her pulse.

'He's okay, Sonora. He got caught up in some minor trouble in Boone County.'

'*Boone* County? Good Lord.'

'I know.' Van Owen's voice was kind and soothing. 'I didn't get the impression it amounts to very much. But I don't think the bumper sticker on his car helped.'

'The one that says *I'M DRIVING THIS WAY TO PISS YOU OFF*?'

Van Owen laughed. 'No. The one that says *BRUNO'S PIZZA AND BLUES, CHICAGO, ILLINOIS.*'

'That was on there when we bought the car. He bought the car.' She never liked people to know she helped.

'Yeah, but you know.'

She did. Interstate seventy-five between Miami and Chicago was a major drug route and the boys from Burlington drew a pretty tight net.

'Guy that arrested him is pretty decent. I think you'll be able to get things worked out okay.'

'God, Jack, I am so relieved. I can't thank you enough.'

'No, no, I'm glad I could help. You sleep at all in the last forty-eight hours?'

'Some.'

He chuckled. 'Liar. Listen, I'm going to let you go. I have a feeling your son will call in the next, oh, three minutes?'

'Jack, I mean it. Thank you.'

'They're the children of our heart, aren't they? God bless, Sonora.'

Chapter Forty-Nine

'Caught by the Boone County Cowboys.' Sam chuckled, ate another bite of his Egg McMuffin. 'Jeeze, Sonora, didn't you ever warn him about those guys?'

'Many times.' She ate the last bite of her hash browns. Yawned. 'Dammit, Sam, when is he going to call?'

'It hasn't been—' The cell phone went. 'There you go. I'm taking a walk, I hate violence.'

In spite of being in jail, Tim sounded pretty much like his normal self, with the overlay of charm he reserved for times of trouble. Sonora was trying to figure out how she felt. Decided, on the whole, that *relieved* summed it up, with the possibility of annoyance in the very near future. Rage was not as strong a possibility as she might have thought. Her son was alive, semi-well, and returning home as soon as she posted bail.

'How much is it?' she asked.

'Nine dollars.'

'Nine dollars?' Her son, the criminal.

'Yeah.' He sounded good-natured. He usually did when he was in this much trouble. Tim was invariably at his best when he was in deep with Mom, his survival instinct kicking in. 'I mean, I had eleven dollars in my wallet, but they took that.'

'That's what they do. Tell me again why they arrested you?'

'The computer said my license was suspended.'

Sonora paused. 'Is it? I *will* double-check this.' She was a cop, dammit. She pitied the vulnerability of the average parent.

'No, honest, it's some stupid-ass computer glitch. I explained it to the guy.'

'But there had to be a reason they pulled you over in the first place, Tim. How fast were you going?'

'They said they clocked me at eighty-five.'

Carefully worded, Sonora thought. Why did teenagers think their parents were stupid? 'You got clocked going eighty-five miles per hour through *Boone County*? Are you completely insane? Haven't I told you—'

'Yes, ma'am.'

'How fast *were* you going?'

He hedged. 'About that.'

'I still don't see why they didn't just call me to come pick you up.'

'It was probably the machete thing.'

'The *what*?'

'Mom, you know that machete, the one I always take camping?'

She did, indeed, know the machete. 'What was it doing in the car?'

'It isn't now, it's evidence.'

'Evidence? How so?'

'The guy asked me if there was anything in the car he should know about, and I said, just the machete. I thought it was okay. I was trying to be honest. Anyway, they got me for speeding, driving on a suspended license, and carrying a concealed deadly weapon.'

Sonora shut her eyes. The boy was clearly overdue for a lecture on 'How to Handle the Uniformed Police Officer'. Subtitled 'The Policeman Is Not Your Friend'. 'That's a bullshit charge, hon, it'll never stick. A machete is not a concealed weapon, they were just slamming you. God, I hate cops.'

'Mom, you are a cop.'

'Whatever. Okay, kiddo. That still doesn't explain why you didn't call me for two nights straight.'

'Mom, I know you're cracking a big case, and I didn't want to disturb you.'

'Totally pathetic. Try again.'

'I called my friend Walter and he and Brock said they'd come get me out. Mom, seriously, I know how busy you are.'

'I am so unimpressed. So what happened to your buddies?'

'Their car broke down. I was wondering if . . . you're coming, aren't you? To get me?'

Interesting, that bit of uncertainty in his voice. 'Yes, I'm coming.'

'I was wondering if, on our way back, could we stop and pick them up?'

'Where are they?'

'BP Subway.'

'Dammit, Tim. Is there anything else I should know?'

The deadly pause. 'One thing.'

'Yes?' Her heart was pounding. *Please*, God, no drugs.

'They got me for driving barefooted.'

Chapter Fifty

It felt good to get some alone time, Sonora thought, bombing down I–75, heading for Boone County, which bordered Cincinnati and would almost take her back home. She had dropped Sam off and gone to an ATM – it was going to cost her more to feed Tim than to bail him out.

A fine mist of rain blew up as she headed north, turning the ground to muck, and making it hard to see in the dark. Headlights from oncoming traffic glared off the wet pavement.

Sonora gritted her teeth. Her biggest problem was going to be staying awake.

The road construction started around Florence, and Sonora reduced her speed. No point falling into the same trap as her son. She took the Burlington exit, turned left, braked until she was going thirty-five. The only good thing about this town was its size – even she could find the courthouse without any trouble.

Sonora stopped outside of the courthouse long enough for Tim to put on his shoes.

'Thanks, Mom. Where'd you get them?'

'Out of your car, which is still in the impound lot.'

'Can't we get it?'

'Not till we get this business straightened out about your license. You're lucky they didn't strip it and tear it up looking for drugs.'

He winced. 'You think they might do that before we come back and get it?'

'No. I stopped at the Dairy Mart and got a disposable camera. Took a few pictures, let them know I was doing it. I didn't make any friends. We need to get it out of impound ASAP.'

He nodded. Tied his shoe laces. Followed her through the dark parking lot. If she had expected a cowed, frightened little boy, she was once again tricked by the mysteries of male adolescence.

'Where's the Pathfinder?' he asked, searching the near empty lot.

'Home in the garage. I'm in the company car.'

'How come?'

'How come? Tim, I'm in the middle of a shit load of a case. I just came off a night raid.'

'You mean those guys that did the home invasion?'

'Can't say.'

'Mom.'

'Yeah, Tim, that's what I mean. And as soon as I get you fed and back home, I've got to go back to the office.'

'You look pretty tired.'

'I am pretty tired. I hope you feel guilty.'

He ducked his head. 'Yeah, I do.'

'Good. This can't happen again, kiddo. If I have to get you an attorney, and I don't know yet if I will, you get to pay for it.'

'I'll pay you every penny.'

'Yes, you will, even if it means you sell the car.'

He swallowed. Definitely a hit.

'Come on, get in, Tim. We still need to go get your buddies?'

The hug was swift, sudden, the first she'd had in months. 'You really are a great mom.' He retreated to his side of the car. 'You know, Mom, we could think of this as quality time.'

'May we always do our felonies together.'

*   *   *

Tim entertained Sonora and his buddies, all starving and happy to be treated to McDonald's Extra Value Meals, supersized of course, with the various plans he had thought of for making his escape from the Boone County Jail. Sonora, well aware that the jail was run so tightly it squeaked, listened without comment. The boys had been cold, broke and hungry, and the sight of a parent with a working car and enough cash and goodwill to buy them dinner had been a welcome sight. She supposed that to the average Joe they looked like tough little fellas, but to her they still seemed like babies.

They were amazingly polite, grateful, helpful. Sonora, who felt that teenage boys were best kept busy, put them all to work at the BP station. Walter pumped gas into the Taurus, Tim checked the tires for air, and Brock cleaned the windshield.

'You should have just escaped that place,' Brock said, as Sonora let him off in front of his house.

'Yeah, why didn't you?' Walter asked.

'Nine dollars seemed a whole lot easier,' Tim said.

It was the most sensible thing Sonora had heard all night.

She and Tim were greeted with ecstasy by Clampett and Heather, who were both glad to see Tim, and delighted by the sackful of cheeseburgers.

Sonora checked the kitchen windows, told the kids goodbye. They both looked at her with great big smiles.

'Is it going to be on the news?' Heather asked.

'We may make CNN again.'

'Congratulations, Mom,' Tim said.

'Thanks. Look, I won't be home till . . . hell, I don't know when. Get your butts off to school.'

'We've already missed half the day,' Tim said.

'Your point?'

'We'll get our butts off to school.'

'Let me write you both a note. Tim? I can count on you?'

'Oh, *hell*, yes.'

'Plus you owe me nine dollars.'

He opened his wallet. 'Money's still there,' he said, putting a five and three ones and three quarters into her palm.

'Thanks. Stay locked up.'

'Load your gun,' Tim said.

'Yeah, yeah. Now he tells me.' She did not want to leave them. She paused at the front door, turned and pointed a finger at Tim. 'Twenty-four hours. Can you stay out of trouble that long?'

'Sure, Mom. Piece of cake.'

It made her nervous, kids saying stuff like that.

Chapter Fifty-One

The bull-pen felt like Christmas morning, though technically it was the afternoon. But what it lacked in flashing lights and foil-wrapped packages it made up for in a palpable excitement. Crick, sitting next to Mickey at the conference table, had his Sunday-Go-To-Meeting suit on, and a brand-new tie. He'd be *Alive At Five* by the end of the day, and likely a presence in *Details At Eleven*.

Sonora leaned her elbows on the table, reading through the autopsy report. A bruise on the girl's sternum – her killer had rested a knee there while cutting her throat, in the opinion of the Medical Examiner. The toddler, the boy, had died instantly of a crushed skull and the resultant hemorrhaging, no other marks on the body. Carl Stinnet hadn't been so lucky, histamine levels indicating extreme suffering.

Sonora read the reports back through for the third time. There was no reference to marks on Carl or Joy, or, for that matter, Tina Stinnet's hands, no broken or grazed knuckles. Somebody had punched Lanky Aruba in that bathroom, so hard he lost a tooth; someone had crammed the blood-soaked towels on the back of the toilet.

Sam slid into the chair beside Sonora, opened a pink Dunkin Donuts box. 'Did Gruber tell you they got Clara Bonnet coming in? Grab a donut, Sonora, before the pack gets wind.'

'Clara's coming? Why now, after we've caught the guys?'

Sam shrugged. 'She's a forensic psychologist, she's interested.

Seems she's met this Kinkle before, which'll give us some insight. I thought you liked her.'

'I do. A lot.'

'Any problem if she's in on the interrogation?'

'No, she'll probably help us make our case.'

Sam rattled the donut box encouragingly. Sonora looked at the display – sprinkles, caramel, nuts, white-powdered and plain. A few glazed, some with chocolate.

'No, thanks, Sam. Looking at them makes my stomach hurt.'

'Sonora, have you eaten anything since lunch yesterday?'

'Yeah,' she said. She hadn't. 'Have you seen these autopsy reports, Sam?'

'Yeah, I read them.'

'And?'

Sam picked up a powdered white donut. Took a huge bite. 'I know what you're thinking.'

'Do you?'

'Sure.' He took another bite before he had chewed the first one. 'You're thinking who punched Aruba? You're working that third man theory.'

'Maybe I'm thinking you shouldn't talk with your mouth full.'

He crammed the rest of the donut in his mouth and licked his fingers. 'You think it was the marine, this Purcell. Like maybe he walked in on the whole thing. The big problem with that theory is why the hell didn't the guy go to the police? Walk in on something like that, then go home? Makes no sense. Kinkle hit him, Sonora, and Kinkle wore gloves. That's why there weren't any marks on his hands. I saw you looking.'

'So where *are* the gloves?'

'He ditched them.'

'He ditched the gloves, but kept the picture he stole, the money he grabbed, and the gun he used and hid them in his aunt's row house?'

'What's this about?' Crick had called the meeting to order, or everyone had gone quiet at the same time. At any rate, Sonora found herself the center of attention.

'We're talking about the tooth in the bathroom, if—'

'Sonora? We'll get to that. Mickey's going to do a recon-struction, theoretical. Mickey?'

'Fine,' Sonora said. 'I'll just sit here and wait for the rest of you guys to catch up. What's another hour when I've been awake for forty-eight straight already?'

Crick turned his head slowly, like a bird of prey. 'Did you say something?'

'No, sir, she didn't say nothing.' Gruber took a chocolate donut and put it on a napkin, slid it to Sanders, who slid it to Molliter, who slid it to Sam, who put it in front of Sonora.

Crick waved a hand at Mickey. 'No point waiting for Clara, she said she might be late, and it looks like certain people are impatient. Get on with it.'

Mickey turned away from Crick, gave Sonora a slow wink. He put an eight by ten color glossy up on the board with a clip. 'Looks like they came in from the kitchen.'

The picture showed the kitchen window, pane broken out, glass spray over the stainless-steel sink, a red and white dishtowel wadded on the cabinet. The paper towels said *Bless Our Happy Home*. Mickey kept clipping pictures up. More of the kitchen. The hallways, the bedrooms, the Stinnets in the throes of their long and unhappy last hours.

'Got some mud in the sink from the bottom of somebody's shoe.' He pointed to the teenage girl lying on the bed, throat bluntly cut across the middle, clotted with blood. 'Tina. She was in the kitchen spreading peanut butter on saltine crackers. Those are her prints on the knife.' He pointed to another picture, this one of a table knife, thick with peanut butter, on the floor next to a shattered jar of Peter Pan, Extra Chunky.

With little kids in the house, Sonora wondered why they hadn't bought plastic.

'We pegged Aruba as the guy who did the little boy. Got a print on the kid's left buckle of his little overalls. Looks like Aruba grabbed him and slammed him up against the wall. We're thinking the little boy was the first casualty. He was probably in the kitchen with his sister. Aruba grabs him and the dog goes for him. He slams the kid up against the wall, somebody shoots the dog. Probably Kinkle. He was the guy with the gun, from the angle of the shots, and the height of the shooter. Kinkle's like six inches shorter than Aruba. Everything points to Kinkle as the shooter. The weapon recovered in Lexington, in Belinda Kinkle's row house, is being worked by the Lexington PD, and it looks like a match.'

'But no gloves,' Sonora said.

Crick glared at her.

Mickey pointed. 'Hard to figure what happens when. Sometime about now the dad comes walking in the front door. We're thinking Tina's still alive. There's a struggle. She runs and they catch her in the bathroom. She maybe was running for her mom. We got strands of Tina's hair in the shower curtain and a piece of her shirt, just a fragment. Somebody, Aruba we think, tackles her in the bathroom, we've got subcutaneous bruising along the jaw line, takes her in the bedroom and cuts her throat in there.

'Now here's an oddity. There were blood-soaked towels on the back of the toilet and the blood belongs to Tina. Somebody pressed those towels to her throat, gave up, and wadded them up in the bathroom.'

'The father?' Molliter asked.

'Which father?' Sonora asked. 'Carl Stinnet or Bobby Purcell?'

Mickey shook his head. 'Neither. The only prints we got on Purcell were on the money, on a coffee cup in the dishwasher, and on the side of the couch. We don't have any of his blood anywhere. And we've got no blood in there for Carl Stinnet, he put up his fight in the living room. But it's an interesting point – Tina gets laid out on the bed with a certain consideration, if you take a look.' He pointed to the picture. Tina resting on the blood-soaked mattress, hands folded neatly across her chest.

The door opened slowly, as if someone were trying to be discreet. Sonora looked up and saw Clara Bonnet slipping in. She was a black woman, way past retirement age, with advanced osteoporosis that bent her back and was on its way to crippling her knees.

Gruber was up on his feet before anyone else, giving Clara his arm, guiding her to a seat. Clara Bonnet was extremely popular, full of insight and compassion, but blessed with a streak of realism that made her recognize a predator when she saw one. She was as far from warm and fuzzy as any psychologist Sonora had ever met. They had worked together before. Clara had a knack of being right more often than not.

Mickey waited till Clara was settled, gave her a nod. 'The mother, Joy Stinnet, was in the closet. The baby, the infant, was lying on the bed, kind of circled by stacks of towels, the mom folding laundry. She had music going. We checked the volume control; it was turned up medium loud, but if she was in the closet, at the back of the house, with the music going, there was a minute or two when she couldn't hear. They took her from behind, Aruba we think, slit her from the umbilicus to the right costal margin, lacerating the liver, to wit, evisceration. Her killer, and we're pegging Aruba, leaves her bleeding in the closet, ignores the baby. We think this is the point where the father walks in.

'We've got the dog and the little boy dead in the living room, Tina locked in the bathroom, the dad coming in. Aruba's got no clue who might be coming in that front door. There's enough confusion that he ignores the baby and goes to help Kinkle with the father.

'The dad comes in knowing something is wrong. He leaves the car door wide open, drops his keys in the driveway. We don't know if he heard something, saw the car, saw something through the window. We may never know. Anything we get will be from the killers. But it would explain Aruba hightailing it back to the living room to back up Kinkle, who's trying to handle the father all on his own, and from the looks of the fight he put up, the father took a lot of handling.' Mickey waved a hand.

'From here it's anyone's guess. Aruba slits the girl's throat, leaves one of his trademark olive pits in her hair. Kinkle shoots

Carl Stinnet. Nobody goes back and looks at the mother, who crawls from the closet, gets the baby, and goes under the bed.'

'Wait a minute,' Sonora said.

'Why don't you let me finish?'

'You said anybody's guess, but there wasn't any blood on that bedspread, not on the top, where the baby was. So Joy Stinnet couldn't have taken that baby off the bed after she got eviscerated. I saw the bed, not possible.'

Mickey nodded. 'We'll grant you that. Moving back to the bathroom, where we think Tina may have tried to keep Aruba out. There were cracks along the hinge, new ones, looks like somebody forced their way in. And we've got a tooth, left incisor, definitely belongs to Aruba. So somebody punched him a good one.'

'Are you telling me Tina did it?'

Mickey was fidgeting with his top collar button. 'Gee, Sonora, did I tell you Tina hit him?'

'No. I'm making a point.'

'Make your point later,' Crick said.

'No, I want to make it now. You're reconstructing with two guys, and I think it's clear to anybody with a brain that there were three. Somebody took that baby off the bed and tucked it in with the mom. Somebody hit Aruba. Somebody kept that girl from being raped. Look at Aruba's case file – he's hard core. Somebody tried to stop the bleeding, somebody laid Tina out on the bed.'

Molliter raised a hand. 'What happened to this third man? You think he got scared away?'

'By who?' Sonora said. 'They shot the dog. Had the father tied to a chair, the mother dying in the closet, the other child dead on the floor. Aruba and Kinkle had time to go to the mailbox, take the mail out, spit an olive pit there—'

'How do you know they took any mail?' Molliter said. 'Did you find any mail at that sister's house?'

'Okay, maybe they stole mail. They took pictures out of the bedroom and Joy's two thousand dollars she got from God knows where. We'll be sure and let the Postmaster General know if it turns out they stole mail.'

'It's a federal offense,' Molliter said.

Sonora gritted her teeth.

'Were they family pictures? That would be very much like Kinkle,' Clara Bonnet said. She had a voice like an electric blanket on high on a subzero night.

'They took a couple of snapshots, family pictures, like you say. Kinkle's fingerprints. They went through the papers. I think they were grabbing anything that implicated that check-cashing service.' Sonora turned to Clara Bonnet. 'You've looked at the file on this?'

'Oh, yes.'

'Clara, what's your take on this?' Crick said.

She leaned forward just a bit. 'I've met Kinkle, so that gives me a pretty good insight. I don't know Aruba personally, but I've read his file, looked at his test results. Of the two, he is without doubt the most dangerous. Without throwing you a lot of jargon, he is conscienceless, dissociated, disorganized, running on a kind of predatory instinct. He doesn't live in anything resembling the world you and I know; our reality comes and goes in his head like a not so strong signal from a distant television station. He is brutal, completely unable to hold a job of any kind, unable to maintain any kind of social inter-course. You might find him leading a very marginal kind of life; anything he has he probably took from somebody else.

'Barty Kinkle, on the other hand, Barty Kinkle never had a chance. Always a nerd, never parented well. Rewired as a child to expect a sort of benevolent neglect. Nobody beat him, but nobody gave a damn. His mother was in the high-end retarded range, she should never have been allowed to raise a child. With the right help at the right time, Kinkle might have made it. He's able to hold down a job, but he's very weak. And he has a lot of rage he turns inward that comes out as depression. The two of them together? A match to gasoline. Would he have the stuff to stand up to Aruba, Sonora, I think that's what you're asking, isn't it?'

Sonora nodded.

'Hard to say. I would have guessed not, but it is conceivable. And it looks like he did.'

'And the third man?' Sonora asked.

'What's your theory?' Crick said. 'Bobby Purcell?'

'Maybe he was there. Somebody was. Somebody . . . intervened.'

Crick glared at her. 'Let's say you're right. Where'd he go afterward?'

Sam nudged her and she ignored him.

'If he came in on something like this, and tried to save Tina and the baby, help out the family, where did he go? Why didn't he call the police? Why didn't Aruba kill him, or vice versa?'

'I admit the pieces aren't fitting, sir. But that doesn't make them go away. Somebody was there.'

'And you still clap for Tinkerbell,' Gruber said. '*Ow.* You kicked me?'

Crick rolled his eyes. 'What's your take, Clara?'

Dr Bonnet pursed her lips. 'I won't say not possible, but it would be an aberration. Purcell doesn't make sense. If not him, who? Three implies a gang, and this doesn't have that professional look about it. They used curtain cords to tie up the father, they didn't bring rope, they didn't cut the phone lines. Things happened haphazardly. I don't think any of it was planned. I don't know why they were there. I just know once they broke that kitchen window, that's when it would get out of hand. Aruba's inner predator kicking in, Kinkle swept along and weak and finding some anger of his own. It's not a three-man job, but anything is possible. It's also possible that Kinkle felt remorse in the middle of it all, and he's responsible for laying the girl out and tucking that baby in with the mom. Do you have any forensic indications there was anyone else there?'

Mickey took it from there. 'No prints. Some unidentified hairs, but that could be anything. Repairmen, friends, previous owners. Guy who laid the carpet. Nothing definitive.'

'She said she saw an angel,' Sonora said.

'Talk to him,' Clara said. 'Talk to Kinkle yourself, Sonora. You would have an excellent chance of him telling you. Men intimidate him, but he relates very well to women. His mother was a poor parent, but she did have some nurturing instinct, and she did love him. Where is he now?'

'In transit. He wants to deal. For total immunity, of course.'

Clara smiled. 'No point in giving Aruba a polygraph, except for the clinical interest. But give Kinkle a poly and sort it out. I'll sit in if you like.'

Crick nodded. 'I like.' He pointed his gaze at Gruber. 'What's going on with Purcell? Last you told me you had talked to his CO.'

'Military channels are a maze, sir. I was going down there—'

'Where is there?'

'Parris Island, South Carolina. He's a drill instructor. Chops up recruits. Last I heard they're coming here.'

'I want to talk to him when he gets here,' Sonora said.

Crick pushed back his chair. 'If he's not here in twenty-four hours, go get him.'

Chapter Fifty-Two

Sonora put the phone down, listening to the murmur of her co-workers. Molliter was talking to his wife – she was making a special dinner in celebration. Sanders and Gruber kept exchanging looks, leaving no doubt about how they'd be celebrating.

'You call your kids?' Sam asked.

'Yep.'

'Where you taking them for dinner?'

'Nowhere. One's got a sleepover, the other a rendezvous at the *Rocky Horror Picture Show*.'

'What did Clara have to say?'

'You were there.'

'I don't mean in the meeting. I mean when she took you aside in the hallway.'

'Nothing special. Just small talk.' Sonora bit her lip. Clara had told her she looked tired and asked her if she was okay. She had asked her in a tone of voice that said she did not think Sonora *was* okay. She had told her to call if she needed to talk.

What? Sonora thought. Am I giving off that glow of bad mental health?

Sam waved a hand in front of her face. 'Sonora? You still with me here? I was thinking you might want to come home with me tonight, I'm taking—'

Her phone rang and she picked it up.

'Is this the world-famous Detective Blair, the girl who always gets her man?'

'Depends on who's calling.'

'Why, the world-famous physician, who would love to take you out tonight to celebrate, so long as you will forgive me for being on call. Deal time. You can be on call for murder, and I'll be on call for mayhem. I make a hell of a designated driver.'

'But, yes, I'd love to.'

'I know it's kind of last minute, but we just saw it on the news in the ER and I thought you might . . . you just said yes, didn't you?'

'I did.'

'When can I pick you up?'

'I've got some paperwork to slog through. Any chance you can come here? Board of Elections building, on—'

'I know where you are. I'll be there at eight.'

'Is it Twinkies again tonight, or maybe margaritas?'

'Twinkies for me. Margaritas for you.'

She smiled and hung up. 'No thanks, Sam, I've got a date.' She looked around at the avid faces and realized that she had been overheard. Word was spreading like the flu, Sonora has a date, the period of the Jerk is officially over. Was this what celebrities felt like, Sonora wondered, with people watching their every move?

She was an idiot. She was being paranoid. No one was paying the least bit of attention.

She went through the paperwork like a zombie, mind everywhere else. Found herself typing Js again. The hell with it; she turned off the typewriter, slammed her desk drawer, and grabbed her purse.

Molliter waved at her from across the room, gave her the thumbs-up. 'Have a good time tonight, Sonora.'

It was not in her to snub him, not tonight, not after they'd all worked together to bring home the Stinnet Home Invaders, according to a headline that Sonora had heard not more than ten minutes ago on CNN. She gave Molliter the thumbs-up. Turned the lamp off over her desk. Headed for the bathroom to comb her hair and put on lipstick and refresh her entire scheme of makeup. She found a jean skirt in her locker, a pair of black tights and a sweater. She'd been looking for that sweater. She put the lipstick on, not the purple stuff, the Angel Red that had been getting such rave reviews.

She slid out of the bathroom door, hoping not to be noticed.

But they were waiting for her, all of them lined up and down the sides of the walls whistling and making catcalls and she decided that it had been much too long since she'd had a date.

'Thank you, thank you, to all the little people.' She tried and failed at dignity, walked past the gauntlet and through the swing doors, took the stairs because just now she did not like being trapped in elevators, and made it out the front door to the sidewalk below.

Darkness had come softly while she'd been doing paperwork. Gillane was waiting for her, parked illegally, standing by the beautiful white caddy. She saw him before he saw her. He wore a white shirt, simple but incredibly expensive-looking, medium starch, bright white cotton, sleeves rolled back twice, accentuating the strong tan wrists. It hit her quite suddenly how attractive he was. She felt nervous suddenly, and then he saw her and smiled. She glanced up at the fifth floor, wondering if that was really Sam peering out the window.

'I've got the top down.'

'I noticed.'

'Do you think you'll be too cold?'

'No, I'll be fine.'

He brought a black leather bomber jacket out of the back seat, and handed it to her. 'Just in case.'

He opened the car door and she settled back into the cushion and closed her eyes. Fabulous car. Fabulous night. Tonight the Cincinnati Police Department was made up of heroes, and she was one of them. Tonight she was not going to celebrate alone.

He started the engine. 'Don't let me forget to tell you that you look pretty.'

'Don't forget to tell me I look pretty.'

The engine caught. Sonora snuggled under the bomber jacket and the car jerked forward. He was speeding, right in downtown Cincinnati in front of a whole slew of cops going off shift.

Of course, knowing her co-workers, they'd leave Gillane in the dust given half a chance. Cops were closet speed freaks no matter what they said to your face.

'Margarita?' Gillane asked, loudly, over the noise of the wind.

'Yes, please.'

'Music?'

'Loud. Can we dance?'

'We'd be fools not to.'

Heat. Bright colors flashing on a dark, smoke-hazy dance floor. The pulse of music in her ears. Sonora was feeling the margaritas, and the lack of sleep, and she smiled at Gillane, feeling herself melting away, a heavenly sensation after the week she'd had.

It came to her like a memory, like something she had known by heart, in years gone by, something that was coming back in little bits and pieces. Happiness. Sufficient unto the day. The music was party stuff, familiar, rhythms she had grown up with, and what woman could resist dancing to 'YMCA' with a man as handsome as Gillane?

He almost carried her to the car. 'Do you always go under this fast?'

'How many drinks did I have?'

'One and a half, sweetie.'

'Tired, Gillane.'

'When is the last time you slept? Or ate, for that matter?'

She curled sideways in the car, trying to think and having no luck whatsoever. These questions were just too hard.

'You're cold. Let me put the top up.'

'No, don't, I'm not cold.'

She felt the leather jacket being tucked over her shoulders. Heard the squeak of Gillane's car door, the sound of the engine as it caught. Then he leaned across the seat, took her chin in his hands and kissed her.

He smelled good, and tasted of lime and club soda and breath mints, and her head was spinning with tequila, fatigue and

Gillane. She opened her eyes. He had such a way of looking down at her, with a sort of world-weary attentive kindness that stripped the cynical defensive veneer she showed to the world, making her feel young. And yet.

He could not be that much older than she was. He had a non-judgmental quality she found very attractive. She had seen it before, in cops who had been on the job a very long time. A quality they would acquire at the end of their tour, a quality that seemed to come with a stillness, too often tempered with a look in the eyes that let you know this state of mind had come at cost, this state of mind had inflicted damage.

And she began to wonder about Gillane, a man who could have such a look in his eyes, and be so young, and self-confident, and kiss so well.

'Did I forget to tell you that I find you unbearably attractive and that I am fascinated by the tornado you call everyday life?'

She traced the line of his jaw with an idle finger, so tired she could barely form the words. 'I love your chin . . . and I love your car.'

He laughed. Kissed her on the forehead, and buckled the seat belt around her waist. 'Come on, Cinderella. Let's get you home.'

And your voice, she thought. I really like that too.

Chapter Fifty-Three

Sonora inhaled the musky sweet scent of alfalfa hay, the dark fragrance of grain. She had bought a hay bale from Franklin Ward, and was making an overdue visit to Poppin. She felt a flash of guilt. She had not liked the way the horse looked the last time she'd been out.

She checked her watch. Seven-o-four. The sun was new and her body was still awash in the stunned discomfort of early morning fatigue, though she had actually slept the night before.

The coffee was waking her up, even the harsh brew of McDonald's that she could never drink without wincing no matter how many little buckets of half and half she poured in through the opening along the side. The plastic lid caught her lip. But still. It was coffee. And the warmth eased the tightness in her chest, and charged the synapses in her brain, and she started to feel better.

She turned off the rutted two-lane road on to a gravel one-lane grass-pitted stretch that raised a fine white cloud of dust. No sign of life from the farm owner's yellow-brick house, mud-stained at the base. The barn doors were closed.

It was an old tobacco barn, sagging sideways, with an uneven dirt floor, overflowing trash cans, rusty farm tools with blades and odd shapes in a pile by the door. Grass and weeds grew up through the rusty metal. Poppin always danced around the mound of farm implements, feeling one of those mysterious horse threats that come from unexpected places and seem to involve no logic whatsoever.

Sonora pulled the Pathfinder to a stop along the fence line. Poppin had his back to her. He gazed longingly over the fence at the two mares in the next paddock, then put his head down in search of grass with the undying optimism of a horse on very bad pasture.

He had been here two months. All the weight Sonora had managed to put on him was steadily dropping off. She was paying for full care and, from the looks of the horse, getting no care at all.

He looked up, saw her or the car or maybe smelled the hay, limped over. He was in no hurry – a good indication that he was not in the habit of being fed. Sonora waited till he made it to her side of the fence, let him rub his nose on her arm and lick her wrist before she stroked his neck, and moved to the back of the Pathfinder. Under Poppin's curious eye, she cut the orange string that held the hay flakes together, and scooped a third of the bale into her arms, tossing them over the fence. The hay fanned out into five flakes, and Poppin bent his head close to smell them.

Sonora, brushing alfalfa leaves off her shirt, watched Poppin cautiously lipping the hay. He might be two hundred pounds underweight, you might be able to see the shadow of his ribs and the bony thrust of his hips, but he was a hay connoisseur, and he would make up his own mind.

He snorted and began to eat, fresh sweet alfalfa and grass mix, with more enthusiasm than he had ever shown for mere timothy. He lifted his head and considered her while he chewed. She was going to have to move him. Again. And there would be no guarantee that the next place would be any better than the last.

Selling him was not an option. No one would buy this horse, no one with good intentions. She leaned over the fence to rub his neck, but he moved away and concentrated on the hay, ungrateful as always.

She headed for the water trough, to make sure it was clean and full. She was going to be late for work.

Chapter Fifty-Four

Sonora looked into Interview One. No sign of Sam. She went back to his desk. No Sam. Checked her watch. Looked out the window. The streets were quiet, too early for the lunch crowd, late enough that everybody was safely at work.

She glanced over at Gruber, who was hanging up the phone. 'Yo. Dude.'

'Me, dude?'

'You, dude. I need to drive across the street and grab Kinkle. Sam was supposed to go with me, but I can't find him. Want to go stretch your legs?'

'Did you know you have twigs in your hair?'

Sonora patted her hair, found a wadded stick of hay. 'Those aren't twigs, Gruber, that's alfalfa.'

'What's the difference?'

'About five dollars a bale.'

'I'm not even going to ask you why it's in your hair, Sonora, but I can't help you out. Sergeant Robert J. Purcell is in Interview Two with his wife and commanding officer. Wonder which one has rank?'

Sonora looked up. 'Purcell is here? Can I sit in?'

'No kicking?'

'No kicking.'

'Right this way.'

*   *   *

Sergeant Robert J. Purcell sat in Interview Two between his commanding officer and his wife, Bethany Purcell, and Sonora, looking in at them through the two-way, saw no trace of the teenage deadbeat dad.

The marines sat stiffly, in dress blues, hats on their left knees, and if you could sit at attention, that's what they were doing. The wife was a plump brunette with a curly perm, wearing a navy-blue dress with a hemline that hit mid calf, dark hose. Her hands were knotted demurely, if worriedly, in her lap, and, astonishingly, she wore a pair of short white cotton gloves.

They were there to impress.

Sonora walked in behind Gruber and the marines were instantly on their feet. Purcell's CO was tall, thin and black, with arms and shoulders that showed the result of daily PT. He introduced them all.

'Ma'am, I am Staff Sergeant Eckler, here with Sergeant Purcell and Mrs Purcell. We're here to assist your investigation into the deaths of Carl and Joy Stinnet, and their children, Tina and Willis.'

Bethany Purcell looked at Sonora. 'How is the baby, how's Chloe?'

'Carl's sister Amber has her. Last I heard she's fine.'

Bethany Purcell nodded, like a woman who had some familiarity with the children. Like a woman determined to show compassion, with no trace of resentment.

It could be genuine, Sonora thought.

She glanced at Purcell. The face of a marine was not meant to show emotion, but she saw something register in his eyes. Grief? Guilt? Rage?

Strong emotion, she just didn't know what flavor.

'I'm Detective Blair, this is Detective Gruber.' She shook hands with both the men. Bethany Purcell stayed in her chair, hands in her lap.

'There's coffee,' Gruber said.

'No, thank you.' This from Eckler. Sonora was not surprised. 'Detectives, if I may come to the point? Sergeant Purcell had contact with Joy Stinnett the day before she was murdered. As soon as he was aware of the killings, he came straight to me.'

'When was that?'

Purcell was motionless. No more than five eight, a good five inches shorter than his staff sergeant, hair sandy brown, cropped in the marine corps burr. He had brown eyes and a thin face, and old acne scars on his cheeks and neck. He was wiry and muscled and had an air of self-confidence that was as strong and as palpable as aftershave.

'The day after the killings,' Eckler said. 'That afternoon at o three hundred.'

'Three o'clock,' Gruber told her.

She let it go. Put a fresh tape in the recorder. 'Would it be possible for us to talk to Sergeant Purcell alone?'

Eckler nodded, waited for Mrs Purcell, who smiled warmly at her husband, squeezed his hand, and walked out.

No doubt she was ready with his alibi, Sonora thought, waiting for the click of the door. Gruber gave her a look and followed them out. He was going to talk to the wife and the CO and let her have Purcell herself. The sweetheart. She ought to kick him more often.

Purcell sat back down, hat on the left knee, giving her the impenetrable marine façade.

'Tell me about it,' Sonora said mildly.

'I met Joy Ward in high school. We flunked algebra together, and we both got a job at the Dairy Queen. She was my first real girlfriend. I was seventeen when I got her pregnant, eighteen when Tina was born. By then I was long gone.'

'But you married her?'

'Yes, ma'am, and we were together about six, seven months before I took off. I was a scared little punk and I cut out on her. I'm not proud of that time in my life.'

'Go on.'

'I tried to call a couple of times. Then her uncle kind of run me off. Don't blame him. About fourteen years ago I wrote Joy a letter. Tina would have been about two. I sent it to Joy's uncle, Franklin Ward.'

Sonora nodded. So far so good.

'I just . . . I apologized to Joy. I wanted to get squared away, face up to my mistakes. I was a new man, a new marine, but I was still responsible for my past. The letter came back, unopened, with a note from Mr Ward. He asked me not to get in touch again.'

I just bet, Sonora thought, wondering what Ward had said. Purcell's face gave nothing away. Damn marines.

'I tried again, two years later. By then I was married and had a baby of my own on the way. I sent a letter to Joy and told her I was sorry, and if she ever needed help, I had her back.'

Had her back, Sonora thought. Someone to watch over her.

'I'm not good at writing stuff, but I tried to tell her I didn't want to interfere, or disrupt her life. Basically, I wanted to let her know that I was there if she or Tina ever needed me.'

'Did she answer the letter?'

'No, ma'am, not then. I wrote her one more time. Told her I'd been through Desert Storm, sent her a picture of my kids – I have four, ma'am, besides . . . besides Tina. One boy and three girls.'

'And she wrote you then?'

'Yes, ma'am. I had told her that Tina would get a share of my life insurance, if and when I die. I guess . . . she seemed reassured by me having kids of my own. She said she was glad I had made it through Desert Storm okay, and she sent me a picture of Tina, said some nice things about my own kids, and said that we both had families of our own and it would be best not to disrupt either of them.'

'By that you mean tell your wife and her husband?'

'No, ma'am. I don't know what she told her husband. I sent the letters to the house with my return address. I wasn't trying to hide, I wasn't trying to push. My wife knew before we got married. I have always told her the truth.'

Sonora let that one go.

'Four weeks ago I got a letter out of the blue.'

'From Joy?'

'Yes, ma'am. She asked me for a loan. She said she was in trouble, it was temporary, and could I help out. I have never paid any . . . child support, though I offered a couple of times. She always told me I had enough on my plate.'

Sonora took a sip of coffee.

'I spoke to Bethany. We took money out of savings, two thousand dollars. She . . . Joy didn't want a check or any kind of paper trail. She asked me for cash, and that's what I brought her, two thousand dollars cash.'

And there it was. The mysterious two thousand.

'I want you to know that on the day she died I was on the road, on my way back to Parris Island.'

'Alone?'

'Yes, ma'am.'

'No witnesses?'

'There's a waitress at a Waffle House outside of Asheville who might remember me. She reminded me of my Aunt Geneva. I left her a big tip.'

Sonora scooted back in her chair, wondering if she believed him. Thinking that she did. 'Would you object to making some donations?'

He frowned. 'Such as?'

'Blood. Hair. Saliva.'

He stood up. 'Whatever it takes.'

'May I see your hands, please, palms down on the table?'

He obeyed instantly. The military man.

'Can you tell me where you got that bruise on your right knuckle?'

'A demonstration of hand to hand, for my latest batch of recruits.'

Sonora cocked her head to one side. 'How many in a batch?'

He almost smiled. 'Depends on what they send me. I started with fifty-eight. I've got fifty-two right about now.'

Sonora stood up. 'Let me introduce you to my buddy in the CSU.'

Chapter Fifty-Five

Sanders, standing beside Sonora in the lobby of the Hamilton County Jail, glanced out at the street, then back at Sonora. 'What happened with the Purcell guy?'

'Shush. Tell you later.'

The Hamilton County Jail, conveniently located just across the street, was Barton Kinkle's current though temporary home. He wore the uniform, orange jumpsuit, and his hands were cuffed in front. A guard, black, female, kept a firm but kindly hand on his elbow.

'You want him hobbled?' The guard looked at Sanders. Kinkle looked at Sonora, gave her a hesitant smile.

'No,' Sanders said.

'Yes.' From Sonora. 'Every precaution.'

Sanders nodded, unoffended. The guard wound chains around Kinkle's ankles.

Sonora gave him a grin. 'Think of it as a sign of respect.' Sam would have killed her for saying something like that. Her radio went. 'Yeah?'

'Sonora? Where are you?' Sam's voice.

'At the jail.'

'You couldn't wait five minutes?'

'You sure it would have been just five? Sanders was around, she didn't mind helping with the pickup.'

'Man, when I think of all the times I've waited on you. Gruber just called up from the back lot. There's a press truck out there – he thinks they're camping, looking for a perp walk.'

'Crick says no perp walk till he gives the okay. I think he owes some favors.'

'Yeah, well they're out there. You got him processed?'

'Signing him out as we speak.'

'Walk him over, why don'tcha?'

'What, there's nobody out front?'

'Nah, Kinkle's a badass, they figure we'll bring him over in the car. Listen, I'll come down, head out the front, make sure the coast is clear. Give me thirty seconds.'

'Thirty seconds? For *that* elevator?'

'I'll take the stairs.'

'Done.' She put the radio away. 'Ready, Barty?'

'Am I going to be on the news?' He looked apprehensive, excited.

'Not this morning, but you cooperate and we'll get you on maybe this afternoon.'

'Is my attorney coming?'

'He's coming. He'll be here after we do the poly. You don't want him sitting around, running up your tab, do you?'

'No,' he said.

Agreeable already. Good, Sonora thought, signing forms. It was an embarrassment of riches, both Kinkle and Aruba wanting to confess. But there were enough forensics that nobody was going to get anything sweet for the deal – unless they came up with the third man.

And there she would have to be careful. The department was ever old-fashioned. A bird in the hand, in this case two, forensics up one side and down the other, the DA's office rubbing their hands over a slam dunk. Sonora was getting hostile vibes – don't muck with it. You got a conspiracy theory, go bother Oliver Stone. Straight and forward suits us just fine.

But she wanted him. That third man. The angel. The man who forgave debts, saved babies, invaded a home in the suburbs.

'Okay, he's ready to go.' The guard stood up, back popping. Her nametag said Stubbens, Marika.

Sonora took Kinkle's arm. 'Sanders, look out, would you, see what we got? Sam says there's press in the back lot, but the front's clear, if you believe it.'

Sanders headed to the front door. 'Looks okay. What, we're running him across in hobbles?'

'He can hop. You can hop, can't you, Barty?'

'Sure, Detective. But don't let me fall, okay?'

'I'll keep a hand on you,' Sonora said. Her radio crackled. Sam.

'Looks good out here, darlin', come on down.'

Sonora looked at Sanders. 'I keep a hand on him, you ride shotgun.'

'Shotgun it is.'

Sonora paused at the door, looked north, west, up and down. Nothing unusual. There was Sam, heading out the front door of the Board of Elections building. No little news Pintos, or trucks with antennas. No skinny girls with microphones, stoic cameramen, ponytails hanging out the back of a ball cap.

'It's a go,' she told Sanders.

The guard held the door for them, and Sonora led Kinkle out. He picked up the rhythm pretty quickly, Sonora thinking he'd done this walk before. He slid his feet across the sidewalk. She took a good grip of his elbow going over the curb, but he gave a little hop and landed on the asphalt with a grace that surprised her.

'Nice work, Twinkletoes.'

Kinkle sniffed. 'I always wanted a nickname.'

'I wouldn't take *that* one to prison.'

Sonora glanced up, grinned at Sam. He smiled back at her, hair falling in his eyes, and it was then that Kinkle jerked, dragging her sideways, going down like a rag doll.

'What the hell?' Sanders, crouching, spinning sideways, gun drawn. A bullet hit the curb, pocking the concrete, and Sonora, pulled sideways, twisted and landed in front of Kinkle, shielding him, hoping she wouldn't be taking a bullet for a low life like this.

Nobody was getting it.

People on the sidewalk kept walking past, trying to avoid them, like they were homeless and hapless. Then she heard a scream, and the breath went out of her chest as Sam landed on her, smashing her into Kinkle.

No more shots. It surprised her, the sudden silence.

She was breathing hard. Sam wasn't moving. Why wasn't he moving?

'On the roof,' Sanders shouted, taking off, and Sonora swam out from under Sam.

'Watch the civilians,' she shouted, like somebody's mother. 'Sam?' There was blood on her shirt, and she wasn't feeling any pain. 'Sam?'

A groan.

'Shit,' she said. Stubbens, the guard, coming toward her. 'Stubbens, we've got an officer down.' Sonora rolled him. Eyes shut tight, face drawn and dead white, looking like he'd never wake up, and his left leg looked like he'd been attacked by wolves.

But breathing, please God, breathing.

Chapter Fifty-Six

Lights, camera, action. The press edging out from behind the barricade in waves, uniforms yelling, blowing whistles, somewhere a child was crying. Sonora stared down at Kinkle, strobe lights flashing across the orange jumpsuit. He looked vulnerable, crumpled over the curb, legs hobbled, wrists cuffed, entry wound in his chest like a star, an exit wound the size of a bowling ball torn from his back. Blood, still sticky, trailing from the side of his mouth. He'd have drowned in it, if he'd lived that long. Death semantics, but she did not think he had.

She felt guilt.

A flash snapped as the CSU guys took more pictures. She smelled exhaust from the ambulance, motor running, saw Sam, dead to the world, IV drip, blood soaking through the sheet from the waist down.

An EMT touched her shoulder. 'You sure you're not hurt?'

Sonora looked at the blood that spattered her sleeve and soaked the front of her shirt. 'No. Thanks. Get him moving.'

The man nodded. She thought he looked familiar. One of the guys that had responded to the call on the Stinnets?

Sonora went toward Crick, arms folded. She was shivering. Cold. Sanders was out of breath, face flushed, hair flying, a smudge of dirt on her forehead.

'Anything?' Sonora asked.

Crick turned slightly to include her in the huddle. 'We got nothing.'

'Lots of time between the shots. My guess would be a Remington II 87.' Sanders still sounded out of breath.

'What made you decide to walk it?' Crick said.

'Media in the back lot. Sam called, said you didn't want a perp walk.'

Crick ran a hand over his face. Somebody snapped it, photo op, Sonora saw the flash. Crick dropped the hand like it was burned. 'Yeah, okay. How's Delarosa?'

'Alive,' Sonora said. This wasn't the point where medics told you Jack shit. This wasn't the point where they knew.

Crick nodded. 'Okay. Angle of the shots says the guy was up on our damn roof. We got uniforms up there now, looking. Sanders, you get with the press, see who was back there, see if they saw anything, got anything on tape. This bastard . . . I want somebody on top of Eddie Stinnet. You saw him on the news?' He looked at Sonora.

'That little weasel? You're kidding, right?'

'You psychic now, or you know something I don't?'

'Where was Purcell?'

'Sitting with Mickey getting his hair snipped. It wasn't him. Eddie Stinnet made threats on national television. We check it out.'

'You check it out. I'm going to the hospital.'

Chapter Fifty-Seven

There were static noises in Sonora's head, like hissing, and she woke suddenly. She blinked in the harsh white fluorescent light that reflected off the squares of cream linoleum in the waiting room outside the fifth-floor intensive care unit of Jewish Hospital. The hushed quiet of the middle of the night reminded Sonora why they call it the graveyard shift.

She was acutely uncomfortable, cheek plastered against the drywall, sideways in a chair that had a low comfort level at best.

When she had fallen asleep, there had been several people in the waiting room. Some of them Sam's friends, others waiting the wait for other ICU inmates.

Sonora felt bereft. As if the world had ended, and everyone had escaped, not turning to see that she had been left behind.

She wanted a shower and her own bed, she wanted to curl up with Clampett, to see to the kids. But she did not feel like she could leave. She had the weirdest feeling that Sam might need her.

She stood up, walking down the hallway to the nearest ladies' room. Looked at the large round clock, second hand moving in little jerks. Just after three a.m. No one had called her cell phone. No one had touched her arm and sent her home.

She dashed water on her face, the light over the mirror casting an unflattering edge on the fatigue that aged her. She stared into the mirror, feeling disconnected from the reflection, as if the woman she saw was someone she felt sorry for.

'Don't be sad,' she said.

A strange whisper, a strange woman, talking out loud in the public rest room of Jewish Hospital at three in the morning. 'Sam will get well. He'll come back. He won't leave you.'

What if he didn't?

Sonora opened her purse and made the effort to find the latest and greatest tube of lipstick. Opened the metal case, rolled the lipstick out of the silver cylinder.

She wondered what lipstick was made of. She wondered why she was putting it on at three o'clock in the morning.

It used to amuse her. Something she always did; it started out as a way to get in the faces of her male co-workers – putting on lipstick during stake-outs, before raids and interrogations. It used to feel brave, it used to feel flashy, it used to be 'her'.

She rolled the lipstick back down into the tube, capped it and dropped it into the depths of the purse. Knowing she was well and truly lost.

Chapter Fifty-Eight

'Mrs Delarosa?'

Sonora turned, frowning, at the plump redhead in royal-blue polyester pants, a matching smock, thick white shoes soiled with the dirt and wear of hospital corridor miles.

'I'm sorry?' Sonora said. The man had to be talking to her. There was no one else in the room.

'Are you Mrs Delarosa?'

Sam. 'Is he okay?' She stood up, took a step toward the man, who patted her arm.

'He's okay, he's just having a restless night. He asked me to come look for you. He said a short woman with red lipstick and an attitude.'

Sonora smiled. She did not mention that the real Mrs Delarosa was a tall and willowy woman with hair the color of mouse. Or that she had gone home hours ago. Or that she wore no lipstick, God forbid red. It was full slips, harness bras, and large cotton underpants for the real Mrs Delarosa.

'Would you like to step in for a few minutes? Might do him some good, he's been asking for you.'

'Can I?'

The nurse smiled. 'He might rest a little better if you'd sit with him for a while.'

Sonora grabbed her purse and followed, thinking that night-shift nurses were often the kindest.

The ICU ward blinked with lights, mechanical gasps, hisses and beeps. The annoyance level was very high.

Sam was awake, in a small room of his own that had enough equipment to run a nuclear reactor. His face was gray and clammy, his leg in traction, swathed with enough bandages to give it a width of about a foot and a half. Sonora pulled a green metal chair to his bedside and held his hand.

'Mrs Delarosa, I presume.'

The voice was weak, but it was Sam all right, under all that pain and equipment.

'When did I get the demotion?'

It looked like a definite attempt at a smile on his face. Sonora squeezed his hand.

'You okay?' he asked.

'It's not me we're worried about.'

'You got any idea who?'

'Crick is working on locating Eddie Stinnet. Soon as they pin him down, Gruber and I are bringing him in.'

Sam turned his head.

'Was that a laugh, Sam?'

'The best I can do. Not that twerp Stinnet.'

'Not the marine either, he was with Mickey.'

'You got a theory?'

'Not a clue.'

'Your third man?'

'I didn't want you to laugh again. But yeah, why not?'

He seemed to sink into the pillow.

'Quit worrying, Sam, and leave this to me.'

He grabbed her hand. 'Make me a deal.'

'Sure, Sam.'

'If something ever happened to me. Like I died or something.'

'You're not—'

'I know. But look how fast that happened out there. If it ever did. You'd keep an eye on my girls. Annie and . . . the other Mrs Delarosa?'

'You know I will.'
'I'd do the same for you. Heather and Tim.'
'Promise?'
He squeezed her hand.

Chapter Fifty-Nine

Eddie and Judice Stinnet were staying at the Knight's Bridge Inn, one of those motels where there aren't any phones in the room, and you make a deposit if you want a blow dryer for your hair. Sonora wondered how long before they'd make the towels a coin-op deal.

Gruber yawned, not bothering to cover his mouth. He was starting to look unshaven. He shifted in his seat.

It was four o'clock, they'd been there since noon. It was now past time for Sonora's kids to be home. She and Gruber had gone into the Stinnets' hotel room four hours ago. Gruber's comments on Judice's wardrobe would have sent her howling at any other time.

Martha Brooks's phone, still in Sonora's purse, began to ring.

'Hello,' Sonora said. Ready to take an order.

'Detective Blair?'

'Mrs Brooks? Are you all right?'

'Well, yes, dear. I'm so sorry to bother you. But I saw you on the news, by that ambulance, your shirt all covered in blood. Are . . . are you and Detective Delarosa all right?'

'I'm fine. Sam caught a high-velocity bullet that broke the bone of his thigh.' Eleven pints of blood, Sonora thought. 'But his surgery went okay, he's just going to be laid up a while.'

'Thank goodness. Um . . . have I had any calls?'

'Heads up,' Gruber said, voice tight.

'The Heedly Ad Agency wants two gift baskets and Sloanes Market returned your call.'

'Sloanes? Do they need more bourbon balls?'

'They didn't say. Mrs Brooks, I have to go, but you can come in to get your phone any time.'

'I did wonder, since you caught those two awful men.'

'Just stop in at reception on the fifth floor of the Board of Elections building. I'll leave it with Ellen.' Sonora cut the connection, put the phone in her purse while she leaned forward, squinting through the windshield.

Gruber put a hand on the door handle. 'I still say we take them in the hallway. It's too cramped in the room. Hell, they could go out a window if they get in and lock the door.'

'I don't want them in the hallway, with John Q every which way, I want them rounded up.'

'What about at the car? Look at 'em, see, a thousand packages. Let's go get them with their arms full.'

Sonora looked across the parking lot. Not a civilian close. 'Okay, but quick, Gruber.'

'Aw, gee, and I wanted to do it slow. You think *she's* dangerous?'

'Only if you let her talk.'

Chapter Sixty

Sonora went straight for Eddie Stinnet, ID flashing, waving a warrant, leaving an annoyed Gruber with Judice.

'Eddie Stinnet, you are under arrest.' ID flash. A wave from the warrant. 'Turn and face the car, sir, hands on the hood. Hand on the hood of the—'

'What the—'

Sonora kicked the inside of his leg and flipped him to face the car. 'Hands on the *hood*, Eddie.'

'But what—'

'*Hands on the hood.*'

He was shaking. But he bent his head, slapping his hands on the warm dirty metal. The car was pinkish gray, like an unhealthy liver. An almost new Mercury Cougar.

'For heaven's sake, I lost an earring, let me pick it up!' Judice. Not getting it.

'Legs apart, Eddie.' He didn't move fast enough, and she kicked his feet apart.

He might not be the one, she reminded herself. Not that it mattered. She'd wanted to throw him up against a wall and cuff him since he'd told her what he put his brother through for a whole fifty dollars.

'Eddie Stinnet, you have the right to remain silent.' She snapped the handcuffs in place. 'If you—'

'That's too *tight.*'

'Pipe down, and listen, I'm reading you your rights.'
But she checked his wrists. They were fine. The
whiner.

Chapter Sixty-One

They'd put Molliter in Interview One with Judice at Sonora's malevolent suggestion. Later, she would allow herself the pleasure of watching. Now, she stood, arms folded, back to the wall, one foot propped on the baseboard.

Gruber sat behind the table, leaning back in his chair, tie loose, still needing that shave. He looked rough. So did Eddie Stinnet.

'So you were shopping at Wal-Mart,' Gruber said.

Stinnet folded his arms. 'That's what I told ya.'

'For six hours? You were shopping at Wal-Mart for six hours?'

'We got lunch.'

'Where'd you get lunch?' Sonora asked.

'At *Wal*-Mart. They got this McDonald's.'

'Yeah? What'd you have?'

'Quarter pounder with cheese, extra-value meal.'

'What number is that?' Sonora said. Kind of playing with him.

'What you mean what number?'

Gruber leaned forward. 'She *means* what number extra-value meal, you shit for brains, and you raise your voice again—'

'Okay, okay, I'm sorry. I don't know . . . number three, I think.'

'It's four,' Sonora said. She had no idea. 'This is a fucking joke.' She spoke to no one in particular.

'Okay, four.'

'Okay four? Okay two? How about ten?'

'They don't have a—'

'Yeah, they don't have a ten,' Gruber said. 'But that don't matter 'cause you weren't there, were you, Eddie?'

'What, 'cause I don't know what number happy meal?'

'Extra-value meal, Eddie.'

'Look, check out the bags in the car, we got a ton of stuff, we were shopping.'

'Not for six hours. What kind of *guy* shops for six hours?' Gruber made it sound perverted.

'Judice had a lot of stuff she wanted to get. I bet we spent five hundred dollars.'

'In Wal-Mart?' Sonora said. Five hundred? And he lent his brother fifty?

'Look at the receipts. They give the time, don't they?'

Gruber looked at Sonora. 'Listen to that. Receipts with *time*. Detective Police Specialist Blair, did you ever go shopping and check the receipt for the *time*?'

'Can't say as I have.'

Gruber looked at Stinnet. 'I can only think of one reason you would look for a time on a receipt, and that's if you were trying to set up an alibi. You trying to set up an alibi, Mr Stinnet? You own a gun?'

'Guns? A couple.'

'A couple? You own a rifle?'

'I used to. But I don't have it any more.'

'Registration says you do.'

Good bluff, Sonora thought. Computers made people assume they had all the information at their fingertips instantaneously.

'I *had* one, but I sold it.'

'He *had* one,' Gruber said to Sonora. 'But he *sold* it. So you don't mind, then, we test your hands for residue?'

'I don't know.'

Gruber looked at Sonora. 'He don't know. Okay, Eddie boy, maybe you want to change your mind about that lawyer. If you killed this guy, you better get an attorney, and you better call him now.'

'Well, but you said if I cooperated—'

'But you're not cooperating, and I'm getting tired of talking to you.'

'Look,' Sonora said. 'Suppose he did kill Kinkle. Kinkle killed his brother, he butchered the whole family. Let's keep that in mind, Detective Gruber. You think a jury is going to hurt him for that? Hell, he's going to make more than you and I make in a lifetime selling his story to *Twenty-Twenty*.' She looked at Eddie. 'Spell my name right, okay?'

Gruber pushed his chair away from the table. 'Yeah, go on, get a lawyer, Eddie. He'll get thirty per cent of your take—'

'Thirty per cent?' Eddie said. Outraged.

'For your story,' Gruber said. 'There'll still be plenty left, after the IRS gets its cut.'

'I didn't do it,' Stinnet said. 'But I wish I did.'

Sonora shoved a yellow legal pad across the table. 'Make me a list. Everything you bought at Wal-Mart.'

'How'm I supposed to do that?'

Sonora rolled a PaperMate Gel-Writer across the table. 'Try with this.'

Eddie Stinnet uncapped the pen. Licked his lips.

'Write your name at the top,' Sonora said. Getting him started.

The door to Interview Two opened abruptly, and Sonora looked up, trying to hide the flash of temper.

It was Sanders. 'Crick wants you.'

Chapter Sixty-Two

Sonora, heading for Crick's office, could see that Molliter was there, Mickey in the doorway, Gruber at her back.

Sonora pushed past Molliter. Crick looked up from his desk. 'Aruba's been hit.'

'What? Aruba?'

Crick nodded. 'We called Whitmore down in Lexington PD, soon as Kinkle got splattered, told them to beef up their security. They kept two guys on him. Aruba's dead. Shot through the mesh of the hospital window, bolt-action Remington, high-velocity bullets, just like Kinkle's shooter.'

'Same guy.'

'Eddie have a Remington?'

'Yeah, but he sold it.'

'Oh. He sold it.' Crick popped his knuckles. 'Whitmore's still working the crime scene, but they'll keep it fresh for you. Take a camera and get some pictures if you can do it without stepping on toes. Maybe even one of the shell casings, if they find any.'

'Third man,' Sonora said.

'Not if it was Stinnet. What's Eddie got to say for himself?'

'Eddie says he was at Wal-Mart.'

Chapter Sixty-Two

Chapter Sixty-Three

Sonora parked illegally in the restaurant lot of an all-night place called Tolly Ho. She was pissed off. She'd been sent to the University of Kentucky Hospital by some paper pusher, because that was where prisoners usually went, but for reasons no one had an explanation for, Aruba had been on the fifth floor of Good Samaritan.

Street lights made yellow pools on the pavement – Euclid, quiet this time of night. The rain had stopped, but the streets were wet. Did it always rain in Kentucky?

The hospital was surrounded, patrol cars, press vans, everything with the quiet air of after the fact, but at least this time she was in the right place.

A couple of uniforms in the lobby looked her over. She flashed her ID.

'Don't mean much in this town,' one of the uniforms said.

Sonora gave him a second look. 'I'm looking for Captain Whitmore, Officer . . .' She checked the name badge. 'Robie, is it?'

'Captain Whitmore is busy.'

The other officer, younger, trimmer, likely more intelligent, had the grace to look startled.

'Officer Robie, I'm tired. I've had a long day, and I don't like your haircut or your round and nasty face. Tell me, Robie, do you walk your beat in those nerdy little shorts during the summertime?'

She could tell from his face that he did.

'So?'

The other officer was fighting a grin. 'Ma'am, I'll be glad to take you to Captain Whitmore. He's upstairs on five.'

'Lead the way.'

'*Ohio* bitches.' They left on a trail of Robie's muttering.

'Tell me, Officer Darnell. Any particular reason for the fifth floor? Better security, or was that just where they had a room available?'

'Well. Number four is maternity.'

She laughed.

'Five is the psyche ward, ma'am.'

The elevator door opened to Whitmore and Detective Yagamochi, another one of Sonora's favorite people. Yagamochi seemed anxious to get on the elevator.

'Sonora. Hey.' Whitmore, suit more wrinkled than ever, took her by the arm. 'Glad you could make it.'

'Thanks for the heads up.' Officer Darnell started for the elevator. 'Hold,' Sonora said. 'Listen, Whitmore, this Darnell is great, but I had a problem with your other guy downstairs.'

Whitmore frowned. Mai stepped on the elevator, punched the button. The doors closed, stranding Darnell.

'By the way, hello,' Sonora said to the door as it shut. Typical Mai behavior.

'What kind of problem, Detective Blair?'

Detective Blair now.

'It was Robie, sir,' Darnell told him.

'Robie? What, again?'

'Yes, sir.'

'Want some overtime, Darnell?'

'Yes, sir.' Darnell, from the look on his face, did not want some overtime.

'You tell Officer Robie that Captain Whitmore said to go home, and that I'll be in touch with his lieutenant.' Whitmore looked at Sonora. 'I'll take care of it. Guy's a cowboy.'

'Guy's an idiot.'

'That too.'

'Tell him if he ever needs a job, don't come looking in Cincinnati.'

'He'll be a security guard somewhere, before the year is out. Come on, we got other things to think about. Let me show you what I got.'

Sonora followed him down a wide, clean corridor, wrinkling her nose at the medicinal gym-sock scent found only on a hospital ward, thank God. The psyche floor was different from the usual. Potted plants. People in street clothes, not scrubs. Orderlies carrying leather restraints.

Rubber rooms, buffed attendants, fake smiles and thorazine. Sonora felt queasy. Don't let them see that you're crazy.

'Sorry about your partner.'

'Thanks.' She was tired. She'd had a long drive and a shit day. 'Shooter got Aruba through the window?'

'Tore the damn thing right off. He was up here in the nut house because the security is better. No civilians.'

'Really?' Sonora looked up and down the hallway.

'Staff. They all wear street clothes on this floor, to keep the patients from getting upset. Good set-up for Aruba, 'cause they got the drugs and experience to handle a head case. Which he is, from what I can see.'

Sonora did not comment. She'd wanted Aruba in jail, not an institution, which was a moot point now.

Whitmore turned a corner, and Sonora had to do a shuffle step to follow. 'We kept two guys on it, instead of the usual one.'

'Inside or out?'

'Out. Aruba was in bed, under restraint. He never had a chance.'

'It was this or the chair,' Sonora said. But she felt cheated. She wanted the trial, and so did the DA, so did all of Cincinnati. Aruba, the bastard, had taken a short cut.

The doorway to the room was crowded. Two folding chairs in the hallway, an overturned Styrofoam cup. Crime scene guys and uniforms. People made way for Whitmore, looked Sonora up and down.

'Had a guy sitting outside the door, another guy in the room—'

'I thought you said they were both outside.'

'He'd gone in to take a leak. Better in here than leaving his post.' Sonora walked inside. Aruba was still there, arms in the leather restraints, strapped to the bed, even the one in the cast. That must have hurt. But not as much as the bullets that had perforated his chest in a close torso cluster. He could have been a police target at the firing range.

His eyes were open, glazed, a snarl on his face. No way he'd seen it coming. He'd died quickly.

Sonora was a tiny bit glad he was dead already, just for the sake of the world. Things went wrong sometimes in a courtroom; there were never any guarantees. But she still felt cheated.

'He was going to confess,' Sonora said. Stepped sideways around an IV pole connected to nothing that had crashed sideways over the bed. Aruba, in his death throes.

Whitmore motioned to a door, next to an empty closet. 'Our guy was in there.'

'He fire his weapon?'

'No. Killer used a Remington bolt-action shotgun. Same as your guy, that right?'

'Yeah, probably the same weapon. Soon as your ME digs those bullets out . . .'

'I hear you.'

Sonora took a camera out of her purse. 'Okay by you if I take a couple of pictures? For the case book?'

'Sure, go ahead. We can send you what we get.'

'I know.'

'I hear you already have somebody in custody. How's he look?'

'He'd of had to hustle to get them both, but it's possible. Eddie Stinnet, brother of one of Aruba's victims. My honest opinion is he doesn't have the brains or the discipline, but I've been wrong before.'

Whitmore looked at his watch. 'Mind if I come up, sit in on some questioning?'

'Door's open.'

'Listen, you staying the night?'

'No.' She was broke. Didn't want to spend the money, didn't want to leave the kids alone.

'Sure? I can get you a place to crash.'

'No, but I appreciate the offer.'

He put a hand on her shoulder. 'Watch yourself, driving home through Boone County.'

Sonora actually smiled. 'Don't worry, Whitmore. One cowboy a night, that's my limit.'

Chapter Sixty-Four

The house creaked in the four a.m. hush, all quiet except in the living room where Sonora, sleepless, restless, laid on the couch with a book open on her stomach. The television volume was a low murmur, an old western with a young John Wayne, *Old California*.

It should have worked for her; it should have been the video equivalent of comfort food, but the movie was too old, the cinematography too jerky, the black and white images flat and dull. The musical score was perfunctory to the point of annoying, the script and characterization a joke, and the viewer too jaded and too distracted.

Sonora took a drink from an open can of Coke. She'd tried cutting back on Coke and coffee, wondering if it was just the caffeine that was keeping her awake, but four a.m. was a good time to abandon that particular theory.

Gunfire erupted onscreen, and Clampett lifted his head and barked.

'It's okay,' Sonora said. 'They're just circling the wagons. Don't worry, they'll get those supplies to Bearclaw – unless the Duke catches the fever.'

Clampett went back to sleep.

He slept very well, Sonora thought, looking down at him. Was there such a thing as a dog who couldn't sleep? Could it be the dog food?

She stood up, took the newspaper clipping she'd dug out of

her dresser drawer off the top of the television set where she'd left it an hour ago. An old shot of Keaton, walking out of a courtroom, three years ago. He looked sad.

He still looked sad, Sonora thought. Even after four years.

She went into the kitchen, found a box of matches from Bogarts, and lit the newspaper.

It was dry and old and the flame caught quickly, catching her by surprise. She dropped it in the sink, and the rubber mat over the garbage disposer flared. The oily dark smell of burning rubber filled the kitchen, just as the smoke alarm went off.

Sonora opened the back door, waving smoke. The phone rang. She shut the door, alarm blessedly off, and turned off the water over the sink. The rubber mat was ruined, but the disposer would still work. She hoped.

'Blair.' She glanced at the hallway. No sign of the kids. What was the matter with them? Hadn't they heard the alarm?

'Hey, it's me.'

It was a universal thing with men. In their hearts, they were all named 'me'. But she knew the voice.

'Gillane. Hey. What are you doing up?'

'I didn't wake you, did I? The nurse up here on five told me you called about half an hour ago, checking on your partner.'

'Yeah, I did. How is he? Everything okay?'

'Oh, yeah, he's doing okay, all things considered. You don't need to worry.'

'Thanks. What are you doing up?'

'Working the graveyard shift. Did you get my messages?'

'What messages?'

'The ones I left with your kids.'

'You've been talking to my kids?'

'Frequently. Didn't they tell you?'

'Nobody tells me anything.'

'So what are you doing right now?'

'Ummm.' She looked over her shoulder at the sink. 'Not much, really. Watching a John Wayne movie.'

'Is it *The Sons of Katie Elder*?'

'No.'

'I love *The Sons of Katie Elder*. Look, I get off in an hour. How about breakfast? The Waffle House'll be open, you can always count on the Waffle House. And who else but me can you talk to at this time of night?'

'Nobody else is up.'

Sonora leaned over Heather's bed, and shook her daughter's shoulder. 'Hon, it's Mom.'

Heather's eyes rolled backward and she snuggled deeper in her bed.

'Heather. Come on, I need to talk to you, just for a minute.'

The little girl sat up suddenly. Blinked. 'Is the house on fire?'

'No, sweetie, of course not.'

'What's wrong?'

'Nothing, hon. I'm just going to meet someone for breakfast, then I'm going on in to work. There's lunch money in the box, and Tim will take you to school if you miss the bus, but don't miss it. Will you be okay if I go?'

'Who're you going with?'

'You don't know him.'

'Is it Mark Gillane?'

'Yes, it is. Lucky guess, Heather?'

'I forgot to tell you, he's called a lot.'

'Heather, will you please write my messages down?'

'Sorry. Mom?'

'What?'

'You know if you want to ever get married again, it's okay with me. I wouldn't mind, so long as he doesn't try to boss me around.'

Sonora gave her daughter a hug. This was the third time they'd had this conversation. Sonora was curious about Heather's criteria.

'Thanks, hon, but I don't have any wedding plans right now. And you might not like some strange guy in the house.'

'If I knew him, he wouldn't be strange. And he might cook

me an egg in the morning, or give me a ride to my friend's house.'

'I'll cook you an egg!'

'No, Mom, go on and go.' Heather kissed Sonora's cheek and pulled the covers back over her head.

Chapter Sixty-Five

The Waffle House was well lit and almost crowded. Gillane was waiting for her, in a booth near the back, sitting so he could watch the door, which you could do from almost any booth or table. Something out the window had caught his attention. She'd expected him to be in scrubs, straight from the hospital, but he'd taken time to change into jeans, hiking boots and big socks, and an oversized gray sweatshirt that looked spotless but comfortable.

He turned then, and saw her, stood up and held out his arms. She did not have to tell him that yesterday had been horrible.

He took her jacket and folded it next to him on the seat. 'I've got coffee for you, and a menu whenever you're ready. How are you, sweetie?'

Sonora settled into the booth, thinking she felt surprisingly well. It was warm inside, and familiar, plenty of construction workers, farm laborers, students and hospital employees going off shift. She decided she liked the five a.m. ambiance, now that she was sampling so much of it. Still dark out, and quiet, nobody around, but morning on the way. She could not quite put her finger on what she liked about it, but she liked it.

And she was glad to see him. Scary, that.

'I checked on your partner before I left. He's in some pain, but that's about par. I made sure they gave him something before I left, and he's probably sleeping it off right now.'

'Thanks, Gillane.'

'My first name is Mark.'

'Thanks, Mark.'

She looked down at the menu, saw him peeping at her over the top of his. 'What?'

'Nothing. You know what the best thing is to get here?' He pointed to a section on the plastic menu. 'You get everything with that. Waffle, bacon or sausage, eggs. Hash browns, which are by the way a specialty of the house.'

'I couldn't eat all that.'

'You don't have to. Just a bite of whatever you want. It's just the most *fun* thing to order.'

'Gillane, sorry, Mark. Where have you been the last ten years? Eating isn't supposed to be fun.'

'You don't strike me as one of those women who order dressing on the side for dipping lettuce edges.'

'Why not?'

'Too sensuous.'

She let that pass. 'Okay, let's order fun.'

It was getting to be that the less she ate the more she ordered. A smack in the face to the anti-eating crowd, which was almost everyone, these days. She would eat two bites of anything that had any hope of pleasing her, but these days it all tasted of anxiety and ashes, and her hunger was an elusive thing. Her stomach had this new attitude that food was a chore.

But she was getting good at shoving her food and rearranging it so it would look eaten. Sort of.

The waitress seemed to know Gillane. She looked grand-motherly, and she had the comfortable air of being in her own kitchen. She brought them orange juice that tasted suspiciously of Tang.

'This is one of the few places where they know how to cook bacon,' Gillane told her.

'As in?'

'Chewy. I don't like it to crunch.'

'*Me either!*' she said, in her best Valley Girl voice. '*We're so much a-liiike!*'

'You do that very well. You're not *from* California?'

'No, but we all watch TV.' Sonora added another bucket of half and half to her coffee.

'How'd it end with the Duke?'

'Oh, the movie? He got the wagons to Bearclaw. And I do remember *The Sons of Katie Elder*.'

'What's your favorite movie ever?'

The food arrived. White plates, thin ceramic coffee mugs. She opened two buckets of half and half, poured them into her coffee.

'*Witness*. You?'

'That looks good.' He put cream into his coffee. She noticed strawberry syrup on his spoon.

'Was that intentional?'

'What?'

'The strawberry.'

He looked into the coffee cup. 'Now I'm in a bind. I think I'm going to say, yes, it was intentional. And my favorite movie is *The Princess Bride*. It used to be *Animal House*, but that's sort of dated. Are you a Jackie Chan fan?'

'Yes.'

'Really? You like guy movies?'

'Yeah. You like chick flicks?'

'No. Why are you smiling?'

'No reason.' When she was younger, and not so wise, she used to wonder why a guy could not be more like a girl. Keep a clean house, never mind that she didn't, she was busy, okay? Like Fred Astaire movies. And when she did, at last, meet men like this, she found they did have a lot in common, including an appreciation for the romantic company of other men. 'Do you like Fred Astaire movies?'

He paused, a forkful of hash browns halfway to his mouth. He clearly felt he was on dangerous ground. 'I don't mind seeing the clips,' he said carefully.

Sonora smiled again. Perfect. She ate a bite of fried egg, cooked over easy, and shoved some food around her plate while she chewed. She glanced at the other women in the restaurant, few and far between at this time of the morning. Something in the face of the girl in the nurse's uniform, long brunette hair with blonde streaks, green eyes, attacking her food like it was her enemy, the irresistible lover who calls you and hurts you and won't go away.

Eat, Sonora told her, in silent communication. Eat all you want and fill up, it's okay. Don't be like me. If you lose your hunger, you can lose your life.

Gillane smeared butter over his waffle.

'I know somebody who makes the best biscuits,' Sonora said.

'Who?'

'A lady I met a few days ago. Mrs Cavanaugh. She knew . . . she knew the family that was murdered.'

'Still not sleeping?' he asked.

'Now and then. Thanks for bringing me that Benedryl, by the way.'

'Helping at all?'

'Some.'

'Who was that guy who was at your house?' He dumped Tabasco on scrambled eggs.

'Old friend. Ancient history.'

'When was the last time you were in love?'

'Elementary school. A boy named Rocky Newman. I keep looking for another one just like him, but so far, no luck.'

'Your luck could change.' He smiled at her over a mouthful of sausage. 'How are your children, how are your mice, how is your horse?'

'The mice are *thriving*. I came home last night and Tim was sitting on the floor, watching TV, feeding one of them a Dorito.'

Gillane grinned. 'I don't think you're supposed to feed them if you want them to leave. You better be careful, Sonora, or word will get out and every mouse in America will be at your kitchen door.'

'Now he tells me.' Had she checked to see if the kitchen window was locked? She was sure she had.

'Clampett must be having a heyday.'

Sonora ate a bite of bacon. Chewy. Perfect. She was actually feeling a tiny bit hungry. 'You'd think so, but he's stopped chasing them. It's like he's gotten used to them, or signed a no-interference treaty.'

'A laissez-faire kind of dog?'

Sonora nodded.

'Must be a lot of golden in him.'

She set her fork on the plate. The hunger had vanished, like it did these days, no rhyme or reason. Gillane put a hand out to touch her sleeve, but whatever he was going to say went out of his mind. He looked at her, and she felt the chemistry, so strong and sudden she wondered the sprinklers didn't go off.

'How long before you have to be at work?'

'Two hours.'

'You up for another cup of coffee? I grind my own beans.'

She thought about it.

He took her hand. 'We'll keep the lights low.'

'To be romantic?'

'That, and because I haven't vacuumed.'

The house had been built in the forties, a dream rental near the hospital, with an arch over the porch, red brick, red tile roof. Small. A narrow, newly blacktopped driveway that led to an old-fashioned free-standing garage.

Gillane pulled the caddy three-fourths of the way into the drive, and led her up the concrete steps to the front porch, which had been coated in blue enamel. It reminded Sonora of her grandmother's house.

The living room had hardwood floors, and a blue and tan oriental carpet, just like one Sonora had almost bought at Wal-Mart. A huge brown leather couch took up one side of the room, there were bookshelves, a gigantic big-screen TV. Black and white photos on the wall, and some Wyeth prints. An old marble fireplace with a brass grate took up one corner. A beautiful room, decorated in busy male. Gillane was clearly passing the *I am a heterosexual* decorating test.

His stereo system was fabulous. The best speakers. He hit the CD, and 'Last Train To Clarksville' filled the room.

'Oh, hell, I thought that was the Sheryl Crowe CD. Great makeout music.'

'No, leave it on, it's been years since I heard the Monkees.'

'Did you used to watch their show?'

'Sure, didn't you?'

'If I did, I'm not telling.' He headed for the stereo, stopped when he was walking past. 'Take your jacket?'

It came in a wave, the heat between them. In the back of her mind she'd been thinking makeout only, a nice cup of coffee, talk before work. But, God, he walked her backward to the wall, and she wrapped her legs around him, and he snuggled his body into hers like he couldn't get close enough.

He kissed the side of her neck and she laughed because it tickled, but felt so damn good. And there she was, sliding down the wall. He grabbed her by the waist, pulled her close and kissed her again. He was leading her down the hallway, taking the time to kiss her slowly like he was learning her from the lips.

'Come on, twenty more feet, we can make it to the bed.'

It struck her funny, somehow, like they were cartoon characters trying to make the oasis.

'We could crawl,' she said, which set him off and he led her to the bed, started unlacing his boots, laughing and trying not to. She pulled the Reeboks off, tossed them, one hit the wall. 'Oh, hell, sorry, Mark.'

He threw his boot against the wall next to the shoe, and that made her laugh again.

He took a breath. 'This is not cool. Giggling. Our *first* time.'

'I'm sorry, I think it's just . . . I haven't had any sleep, and neither have you.'

He kissed her, pinning her arms gently to the bed. She pushed him away and he pulled up. 'Okay?'

'Okay.' Just testing. Making sure he kept things gentle.

He got up. 'Music?'

'The Monkees?'

'No, dammit, Louis Armstrong. It's sexy, unless you don't—'

'I do.'

He fumbled for the CD, put it in a black boom box on the dresser. And condoms. She saw the flash of a foil pack and felt relieved. No speech required. He hit a button on the boom box, there was a pause, then the pure filling notes of a master making a presence in the room.

Big bed. Brown bedspread. Unattractive that, but so guy. If it had been purple or pink she'd have run. It felt so weird taking off her clothes, and she slid under the blanket, shy, still wearing panties and a demi-bra. It was a rule with her – all lingerie from Victoria's Secret. No point wasting money on dull stuff when you could be pretty every day.

He laughed again; they were both weirdly nervous, like it mattered and like it didn't. She felt lightweight. Nobody was here for a performance, and being close to him felt so good. He pulled the covers back, slid in beside her, then tucked the covers back up because it was cold in the room. His body was so warm beside hers, and he, no shy boy, not a stitch on.

He slid a hand along her spine, and she arched her back and snuggled closer to his chest. He pulled a bra strap down over her shoulder, kissing her up and down her neck.

And suddenly no one was laughing. He unfastened the back of her bra, and pushed it away, rolling on top of her. God, how good he felt, warm and heavy and smelling so guy, the faintest scent, Obsession. She buried her face in his neck and ran her hands down his chest to his thighs. He sighed and moved closer, kissing her, shifting his weight carefully till he was on top of her, and *there* he was, hard and ready and she didn't think she could wait. He hooked a thumb in the lacy edge of her high-cut panties and pushed them down and away, and then he was inside, and Jesus, he felt so good.

Chapter Sixty-Six

Sonora was driving to the hospital, taking her time, smiling and listening to the Beach Boys sing 'Little Surfer Girl' on the radio. She found Sam in the intensive care unit, and had to wait forty minutes until he could have ten minutes of visitation. She napped while she waited, feeling peaceful. Woke up for no particular reason, and headed into the bathroom before she lined up at the door like all the other intensive-care cattle.

The bathroom was a two holer. She checked her hair, added the red lipstick. Turned away, checking her watch, glanced back in the mirror, and saw her mother.

It stopped her.

She stood in front of the mirror, one eyebrow arched, checking herself from the left side. Just for a moment there, the resemblance had been startling. Similar features, yes, but it was more the way she held her head, and something in the eyes.

It gave her an odd feeling, part of her afraid, part of her proud. She and her mother had been close, but knowing then what she knew now, she would have been closer. You never knew what a gift the unconditional love thing was, until you lost it, or had children of your own, and gave it away.

Sonora stood outside the tiny cubicle where Sam lay sleeping, leg raised by an intricate pulley and weight-driven torture device that likely came with a nightmare owner's manual, leg swathed in an armor of bloodstained bandages. Various lines of wire and tubing ran to and from his veins, connecting him to machines that kept track of heartbeat, respiration, blood pressure, temperature. Vital signs that could be noted every hour with more accuracy and a great deal more comfort through the attentions of a human being called a nurse. Medicine had been overrun by engineers, a fate worse than death.

Death before discomfort, that was Sonora's motto.

She had been wondering about Sherry, Sam's wife, but there she was, a privileged person, allowed to sit round the clock by his bed. She was sleeping upright in a small hard chair, her hand entwined with Sam's, lines of worry and fatigue in her face like a sign that read *Do Not Disturb*.

Sonora felt the strangeness, the distance.

She dropped the cherry pie she had brought him from McDonald's at the desk with a nurse and left quietly.

Chapter Sixty-Seven

Kinkle's small suite in the good old Heartbreak Hotel took away the last of her good, peaceful feelings. She felt lonely, here without Sam. Dammit, she had only given him half of that cherry pie from McDonald's. She wished she had let him have it all.

She was moving slowly, her heart not in the work. From the looks of things, Kinkle ate a lot of Morton Pot Pies, chicken, yet she knew the beef was better. Economical too, at sixty cents a pie. To his credit, he managed to cook them in a toaster oven, no small feat. The freezer, full of the pot pies, also held vanilla-chocolate, vanilla-strawberry swirled ice-cream in little plastic cups. There was pepper loaf and the remnants of take-out in the tiny fridge.

The room stank of lonely male. Clothes and a plaid blanket on a bare mattress. A television. Shelves made with bricks and raw wood planks, holding clothes, very few, and comic books, tons. Tennis shoes, Vans, three sweat-stained ball caps in a stack.

Not a glove in sight, or out, and she had gone through everything – jacket pockets, the toilet tank, the underside of the less than pleasant mattress, and the clothing wadded on the floor.

She held up the key-ring that had been confiscated during Kinkle's arrest in Kentucky. A chain, dangling a small plastic Wylie Coyote, left ear missing. For herself she would have chosen Rocky and Bullwinkle.

There were keys for the Impala, ignition and trunk. A key

for the Heartbreak Hotel. Leaving two keys unaccounted for. One fit a deadbolt, one looked made for a spring lock. Sonora fingered them, wondering. *Where do you guys go?* she thought. Anybody who could tell her was dead.

Chapter Sixty-Eight

Sonora was sitting in the Sonic parking lot, looking at a menu to see what she didn't want for lunch, when the cell phone rang. She flicked a glance at the clock on the dash. Yeah, probably the kids; they'd been home from school long enough to be tracking her down. She'd had more freedom as a teenager.

'Would this be Heather or Tim?'

'Hi, Mom, it's Tim. You had a call.'

Gillane? 'Man or woman?'

'Some woman.'

The side speaker crackled and a voice asked her what she'd like to order. She closed the window.

'She said her name was Belinda and you would know who she was.'

'Belinda? I don't know any Belindas.'

'Okay. Bye.'

'Wait, hold on, what did she say?'

'There's no need to yell at me, is there?'

'*What* did she say?'

Pause. 'She said to tell you that one time she was with Lanky and Barty up in Cincinnati—'

Lanky and Barty? Of course. Belinda Kinkle, Lanky Aruba's sister. Step-sister. Word was out, Lanky was dead. Belinda was safe now. Sonora's heartbeat picked up.

'—and that she and Lanky sat in the car one time while Barty got out and went inside some big warehouse office building thing. She said it was old brown brick with a big window in the front that had paper over it so you couldn't see inside. She thinks Barty might have been meeting that man you wanted to know about.'

The third man. Sonora dug her fingernails into her palm. 'She say where the building was?'

'She said it was big.'

'That's helpful.'

'Oh, and it was next to the Olden Brewery. It may have been part of the brewery a long time ago, but she thinks it looks empty now.'

'That it?'

'That's it. She called collect, was that okay?'

'Yeah. What made you take it?'

No answer.

'Tim?'

'I met this girl in jail, and her name was Belinda. I thought it might be her.'

'Well, Jeez.' She wondered how to field this one. Didn't have a clue.

'*Mom*, don't hang up. Heather wants to know if she can have one of your shoeboxes.'

'What for? I have shoes in them.' One of the few areas of her life where she was organized. Certain high-heeled dress shoes stayed in the box. High heels and Reeboks, no in between. Except there were barn boots now. Life grew ever complicated.

'She needs it for James Bond.'

'James *Bond*?'

'Mom, she's adopted one of the mice.'

Chapter Sixty-Nine

Sonora cruised by the warehouse parking lot, counting four cars. One looked abandoned, had a sticker on the window for pickup. She parked in the Olden Brewery lot next door, up along the curb, so she could watch. Belinda was right, the first-floor windows were opaque with yellowed curling sheets of paper, plastered up from the inside so nobody could see in. Frustrating, because she wanted to see in.

She picked up her cell phone, called Franklin Ward, brought him up to date. 'One other thing,' she said, before he could hang up. After a sudden thought. From what Mrs Cavanaugh told her, Ward could use the money, and she could use the place. 'Mr Ward, don't hesitate to turn me down if you don't like the idea, but you remember that I told you I have a horse of my own? I don't know what you're planning to do with Joy's horse, sir. If you're even thinking you'll keep her. But I need a place for Poppin, and I would pay you full board if you want to take on a buddy for Abigail. He can stay out quite a bit, so you don't have to clean a stall every day. But you may not want to take this on. I just—'

'How about we give it a try? A month or two, see if it works out?'

'You don't think it would be too much for you?' What was the matter with her, the man was ancient.

'No, I like the idea of you bringing your kids out to ride, having people around the place. And Mrs Cavanaugh's granddaughter likes to come down and ride Abigail – she'll do those stalls. Hardly be much work for me, and that old mare is awful lonesome.'

Sonora felt lightweight all of a sudden. 'That's great, really great.' Poppin, little devil, was saved. For the moment anyway. 'How soon can I bring him out?'

'Any time, Detective. Come on out here whenever you like.'

'He, um, he can be kind of a pig, I better warn you.'

Ward seemed amused. 'I'm not worried. We run into a problem, I'll call George.'

'George?'

'George Smock. Horseman from Kentucky. If there's any kind of trouble, George will sort it out.'

Sonora rang off. Watched the lot a while longer. Took down the license numbers of all the cars and called them into her favorite clerk at the DMV.

Decided, after a while, she was wasting her time. She had that old bad feeling. This case was over. This was one of the ones that was getting away.

Chapter Seventy

Inside the bull-pen, on the board, Sonora saw the Stinnet homicide listed as solved. She turned away, almost ran into Crick coming out of the men's room, drying his hands on a paper towel.

'You're up, Sonora, for the next corpse that comes in. Partner up with Molliter.' He held up a hand. 'I know you don't like it, but try to get along. We've released the Stinnets' bodies to Amber something or other—'

'Wexford.'

'Yeah, Wexford. She's making the funeral arrangements. Give her a call, and be sure you're there, be the PR piece for the department.'

'What about Eddie Stinnet?'

Crick tossed the paper towel into the trash can by the coffee pot. He snatched a junk memo off the bulletin board and crumpled it up like it was an enemy to his peace of mind. It followed the towel into the trash. 'Had to cut him loose, but I've got Gruber and Sanders working it.'

'Gruber and Sanders? You're cutting me out?'

'You're off it.'

'I'm off it? Aruba and Kinkle were mine. Why am I off it?'

'Whitmore's following Aruba up in Kentucky—'

'But aren't we coordinating—'

305

'We as in Gruber and Sanders. Sonora. It's your partner that got shot, you're too close to this. Makes for bad police work. You're off, let it go, and get back to work.' He headed for his office without a backward look.

Sonora looked for Gruber, but he wasn't there, desk abandoned. Off working her case, she guessed. Molliter walked over to the coffee maker, and filled her favorite mug, adding cream and a scoop of chocolate flavoring from his personal stash. 'Here, looks like you could use this.'

Molliter being kind? What was the world coming to?

She thanked him stiffly, moved like a zombie, heading for her desk, but never making it.

Crick's door slammed open and he took a step into the bull-pen, tight-lipped and focused. 'Detective Blair?'

'Yes, sir?' What now, dammit?

'*In my office.*'

In she went, stiff-legged and wary. Everyone in the bull-pen staring.

'Shut the door,' he told her, before she was halfway in. He turned and faced her. Studying.

Sonora watched him back, all instincts sizzling. He might be a stranger, the feelings she was getting, her internal reality shifting, the nerves up and down her spine going tight and prickly. Something was off here. Nothing felt right.

'Is this yours?' His voice was low and icy hot.

'What are you talking about?'

'You tell me.' He handed her a computer printout. A fax, from the DMV, the license plates she'd run from the warehouse lot.

Was that all? Her knees went soft with relief. 'It's just some plates I ran, some stuff from—' And then she focused, took in the names on the printout. 'Jack Van Owen's name is on here.'

'That it is.'

Sonora took a step backward, studied the sheet in her hands.

'Why are you running Jack's car, Sonora?' The voice was so soft, so angry.

'I didn't know it was his car.'

Crick settled ever so slowly in his chair, voice going all at once gentle. 'Sit down, please, Sonora. I think you better explain.'

She obeyed. 'It's my third man theory, sir.'

There was no explosion, which surprised her. So she told him. About Kinkle's reaction under interrogation. Quincy David's rumors about an angel who forgave debts, about a check-cashing service run by an enigma, and an angel was nothing if not an enigma. And finally, a break in the wall around the man behind the scenes. Aruba's step-sister, Belinda. Sonora was proud that she had established rapport with the woman, that it had paid off. She had led her to the warehouse.

'Why did you run the cars?' Crick asked, off-handed.

'Routine.'

'Routine.' It was strange, the way he said it. Sad, in a way, very distant. 'Okay, Detective, you can go.'

'What, you mean, that's it?'

He opened his arms wide. 'What else would there be?'

'But don't you think it's strange that Jack Van Owen's car was there?'

'Maybe yes, maybe no. There could be a million reasons.'

'How about I ask him?'

'How about you don't?'

'Well, I'm going to.'

'Sonora. What do you know, I mean really know, about Jack Van Owen?'

'Not a whole hell of a lot, sir, just that I like him, and as far as you're concerned, he's a fucking saint.'

No reaction. 'Eleven years ago Jack and I walked into a domestic – a man holed up with his wife and five kids, the three still alive crying their heads off, the wife still alive, but a mess, broken arm, smashed ribs, probably not a tooth left in her head.

'And in walks Jack. Two years before, his wife, Lacy, hit a coal truck head-on, killed instantly. His son, Angelo, dead too. And you could see it in his eyes, he was going in there, and he was going to bring out those kids. He talks his way in, negotiates hour after hour, trades hostages for Slim Jims and Root Beer; he brought those babies out one by one. And then he went in for the wife, me at his back, waiting. He fought for her, Sonora, talked himself hoarse, but it all came down to a gun at her head.

'She didn't even cry. Just lay there, waiting, almost like she wanted to die. But Jack wasn't going to let her go. Mom's with kids, he couldn't stand it. He jumps the guy, the gun goes off . . .'

'So what happened?'

'The mother lived.'

'And the guy?'

'He didn't live. I shot him. And Jack took a bullet in the head and the rest, as they say—'

'Is history. Anything else, sir?'

'Leave Van Owen to me.'

Sonora told Molliter she was going to lunch and if he thought it was odd at four o'clock in the afternoon to be taking a second lunch he kept the opinion to himself. She went straight for a pay phone, got the number she needed from information.

'Detective Blair?' If Quincy David was surprised he didn't much show it. 'Haven't been arresting any of my clients, have you?'

'Not a chance. I have a question for you.'

'You got me.'

'That check business down in Indian Hills, the one on Delaney, the one where you're trying to find the owner. I give you a name and a social security number, would that help you nail it down?'

There was a long silence. Then, finally, 'It couldn't hurt, none, could it?'

'Confidentially?'

'Confidentially.'

'Jack Van Owen.' She reeled off the social. Gave him her cell number. 'You want to get in touch use that number and that number only.'

Chapter Seventy-One

The building was a good ten stories high, brown brick, dirty, dark windows. A light shone from the top of the building. Sonora counted windows, decided the light came from the seventh floor. A warehouse from hell. There was one car in the parking lot around back, other than Sonora's. A battered silver Mazda, 1992, registered to Jack Van Owen.

No car ego, Sonora thought. What did Van Owen care about? She had seen no sign of a woman in his life, though the vibes he gave off were strictly heterosexual. Did he take ballroom dancing every Wednesday night, race stock cars, sit around and watch the sports channel?

There was a padlock on the back door. Sonora tried the mystery keys on the Kinkles' Wylie Coyote key-ring. Promising, but not quite. She jiggled the one in the middle that made a pretense of fitting, and the padlock clicked and sighed a rusty release. She was in.

She debated whether or not to lock the door behind her, decided not. A quick exit was a wonderful thing. She had a flashlight, and turned it on. Same flashlight she'd stolen from a uniform a year and a half ago. He was a nice guy, and she'd put a word in for him. He'd never come back for the flashlight. Maybe he figured it was a good trade. She'd heard rumors that he was up for his shield.

She shut the back door, aimed her light everywhere. It was hard to get a feel for the place, dark as it was. She missed Sam.

Her heart was beating, swift and terrible. She was afraid, more of the dark empty building than of finding Jack Van Owen. And of course, if Crick found out, her ass was grass.

She moved forward, looking for a stairwell. Her Reeboks made soft little squeaks on the linoleum.

Downstairs there was a large desk countertop, like you would see in a bank, standing like an island in the center of a large empty room. She kept moving, found a bank of elevators.

Not even an option, she told herself, and laughed just a little. Imagine, getting into one of those things. Imagine getting stuck. No one would ever find her. And considering her state of mind these days, she'd last maybe fifteen minutes tops before she went totally insane.

And she didn't even like watching movies where the hero went through the top of the elevator and climbed up the black oily cables. The staircase was a wonderful invention and she intended to make full use of it. Provided she could find it.

Not easy in the dark. She opened doors, found empty storerooms, a weird sort of utility room. Then, at long last, the stairwell.

She could go up or down.

There seemed to be no reason to go into the dark basement, and she didn't think she had the courage. She headed up the stairs, counting two landings for every floor, and made her way to the light on floor seven.

She went steadily and methodically and was a little winded, but not a lot. Her clothes were loose; not eating could have that effect. The lack of sleep lately gave her a fuzzy, tired feeling.

She opened a door to a pitch-dark hallway. Did she have the wrong floor? Had the light been turned off? Was there anybody there?

She stood for a minute, listening. It was so bloody dark.

She took a step forward, keeping the door to the stairwell open with her left foot, maybe not logical but it sure made her feel better. Shone her light on a door that had a brass number that said nine. Nine? She hadn't come up that far. Had she?

She studied the number, realized it was a six, swinging upside down. She wasn't up far enough. One more floor.

She went back into the stairwell, pulled the door quietly closed behind her. Headed up another flight of stairs.

Her gun was tucked securely in the back of her jeans. Other cops might creep through the building gun in hand, but she knew her limitations. Knew she was likely to trip or shoot at shadows. Never would have admitted it to anyone.

But she had lost enough weight that there was a real danger of the gun sliding down the back of her pants. Talk about embarrassing. Cop injured in the line of duty. Gun in her pants.

Make that killed in the line of duty. That way she wouldn't have to endure the teasing.

She kept hold of the railing, feeling the dust accumulate on her fingertips. Thinking that the best and worst part about death was that you died. It jarred her to know that she no longer viewed death as the worst possible thing that could happen. It was the comfort and it was the curse. The beauty of death was that the struggle was over. Hopefully.

She ought to have expected it eventually, this thing within her, this darkness. She'd been depressed before, plenty depressed, plenty of times. Despair was not unfamiliar to anyone at some time in their life. Her brother had died four years ago, she'd been devastated.

But this was different. This was new and unhappy. This was please. She had never, ever, thought *please* before, not on this subject, not for days on end.

Definitely not good. But saying so did not make the feeling go away.

Maybe it was a best, Sam not being with her.

The door to the seventh-floor stairwell was locked. Twisting the knob, meeting the resistance, made her heart jump. It made it definite. It made it real. Someone was up here. Someone who did not want to be disturbed. Sonora tried the keys on the ring. Dammit, she did not want to walk back down those damn dark stairs.

Key number three fit just fine and popped a lock she could

have picked with a bobby pin, if she had a bobby pin, which she did not. She shut the flashlight off.

The door creaked when she opened it, and she kept hold of it, easing it shut softly, holding her breath and fighting the hinge.

And she heard music. Light shone from an open door like a beacon in the dark, dirty hallway. The music came from the open door.

She knew the voice. Jimmy Durante, singing 'As Time Goes By'. Had she landed in some episode of *The Twilight Zone*?

The music covered her footsteps. Her gun started to slide and she rescued it from the back of her pants, and held it with palms growing wet and slick. She wished her breath was not coming so quickly, her heart not beating so hard.

It was a long walk down that corridor – God knew she wasn't moving very fast. She did not like alone. Not here, not tonight.

Sonora took a breath, and moved to the edge of the doorway.

From her narrow field of vision, she couldn't see a soul. She peered around the corner – it was an office, thrown together with an old, overlarge oak desk, a wood swivel chair with a leather seat, wooden slats like a birdcage, old-fashioned. She wanted to sit in that chair and spin around and around.

A free-standing old mahogany wood coat hanger supported a tan windbreaker and a black wool coat, towering over two oak file cabinets, legal size, and a brass umbrella holder held, naturally, a large black umbrella. Which looked dry, from where she stood.

She took a step inside. A phone, a computer, wood trash basket discreetly by the file cabinet. A fresh white orchid floating in a bowl of water on the desk.

A boom box sat in the corner, the CD light glowing red. The music. And photos on the wall – maybe ten or twelve. Tina Stinnet, bloody on the pink canopy bed. Carl Stinnet turned sideways in the chair. Crime-scene photos of the Stinnet home invasion.

Sonora heard the flush of a toilet and the creak of a door and she looked behind her to see Jack Van Owen stepping out of a small room, closed off by a door with a frosted-glass window, still wiping his hands on a hand towel, hunter green and fluffy.

She gasped and so did he.

Van Owen put a hand to his heart. 'For God's sake, Detective. And why are you jumping three feet, you're the one sneaking up on me.'

As usual, she could not resist that smile. Dammit, she was glad to see him. Any human contact at this time of night in this part of town. He passed ahead of her and went into the office.

'Come on in and sit down. Cup of coffee?'

She did not smell coffee but she said yes, and he went to the top of a file cabinet, opened a foil packet, and went about the business of brewing a fresh pot.

He inclined his head to a khaki, overstuffed loveseat that sat in a corner in front of the battered oak desk. 'Go on and sit. You take cream but no sugar, and if there's chocolate I should add that too.'

'Yes,' she said.

'Won't be a minute.' He tossed the towel on top of the file cabinet. 'Let me go wash this mug.'

Sonora, in the act of sitting, got back up again.

He tilted his head sideways. 'Or not. I guess it's clean enough. I take it you don't want me out of your sight?'

Sonora put the gun away. 'Sorry.'

Van Owen bent to the boom box and turned it off, then sat in the wood and leather chair, rocking it back and forth.

'I thought you might come.'

She didn't say anything.

He turned sideways, looking out into the corridor. 'You alone, or should I expect some of your buddies? I just need to know if I should wash another mug or two.'

'Just me,' Sonora said.

He put his fingertips together. 'If I had to guess, I'd say you're not supposed to be here.'

'Good guess.' The coffee maker sizzled and spurted and the smell of coffee wound its way into the room. Sonora sat back on the loveseat. Resisted the urge to tuck her feet up beside her. She liked his office. She liked it very much.

He turned the chair and faced her. 'Well, my dear, and what am I going to do with you? Which is not to say that I'm not glad to see you. I'm just not sure *why* I see you.'

'I like it better when you're blunt with me. When we talk in shorthand. You know what's on my mind, and I know what's on yours.'

'Go on.'

'You could confess. Tell me everything. Spend the rest of your life in jail.'

He nodded good-naturedly, eyes alive and full of humor. 'We'll call that option one.'

Although she knew better, Sonora began to relax. He had a gentleness with her, a sort of grave sense of good manners that smoothed all of the awkward angles. Her mother had been right, manners did make the man.

'Do you know who you are?' he asked her. The coffee bubbled.

'Weird question.'

'Rhetorical question. You weren't supposed to respond.'

Sam would have laughed if he'd been here, Sonora thought. She could not sit still, she could not keep quiet.

'Yes, I know who I am.'

He stood up and poured coffee in two mugs. Doctored hers with cream and a packet of instant hot chocolate. Took his black. Went on talking as if she had not said a word.

'You are me, eleven years ago.' He glanced at her over his left shoulder. 'Okay, a female version. Prettier and softer, and I mean that in the nicest possible way. But you are me, Detective, me before . . .' He stirred her coffee, and handed her a mug, his fingers lightly brushing hers. 'You don't have the smallest idea how much I envy you.' He took his coffee mug and sat on the edge of his desk, swinging one leg. 'I was a good cop, Sonora. A good homicide cop. I didn't even grow up wanting to go into police work. I thought I'd be an actor. Don't look surprised. But when I became a cop – it was right. You know what I mean, don't you? It's the same way for you.' He put his coffee cup on the edge of his desk. 'Don't let go, Sonora. Don't blow your career, you don't know how much it means till it's gone.'

She looked at her mug. Tiny white marshmallows floated on the top, melting slowly in the heat. Sonora thought of the witch in *The Wizard Of Oz*, when Dorothy threw water and melted her. The hourglass had been running.

'I forget things.' Van Owen plucked the orchid from the clear glass bowl and pointed to his temple. 'If you ever take a bullet, try not to catch it in the head.'

He leaned close and Sonora saw the dimple in his left cheek. He looked at her so very directly, taking in her face, her hair, her neck and shoulders, and if she did not know better she would have thought he was moving in for a kiss.

He was humming under his breath, just, and he tucked the flower behind her ear, and moved her hair off that shoulder, and she felt her face go hot.

Van Owen took a step backward, cocked his head to study the effect, smiled again, just a little one, and said not a word.

And then he was gone. One moment he was there, and the next, vanished, not in body of course, the shell of the man was still there, going through the motions, but the essence was gone. He could have been a ghost.

Where did he go? she wondered.

But she knew. She knew because, just lately, she was going there herself. And she understood, now, the distance she felt with everyone, Sam, the kids, Gillane. Because where she was headed – that was a place most people knew better than to go.

Chapter Seventy-Two

It was a rare thing for Sonora, not to be hurried. She leaned back into the loveseat and sipped her coffee, and Van Owen settled back behind his desk and sipped his. They were both quiet. They were both thinking.

'Your son?' she said, almost absently, pointing to a picture in a frame on his desk. The two of them were posed in front of The Riblet, a small downtown bar.

'Yes.' He looked pained. He picked the picture frame up, put it in a desk drawer.

'He looks like you.'

'I always thought he favored his mother.' They were quiet a long moment. 'One question,' he said finally.

She looked up.

'You *have* been called off this case?'

'Yes. You talk to Crick. You know.'

'Yes, I know.' He ran a finger along the edge of the desk. 'Everyone downtown is satisfied. Crick. The lieutenant. The chief of police.'

'Everyone except me. My partner's in the hospital.'

'Any chance you might just go away?'

'You say we're just alike? What do you think?'

He was thinking, making a decision. 'I think you need to know, at least in your head. Even if you have to fade away afterward. And you will, Detective, you will. Are you wearing a wire?'

'No.'

'Show me?'

She stood up. Unbuttoned the white cotton shirt, took it off, and stood in loose jeans and demi bra. She was not sure what she would do if he asked her to go any further.

But he did not ask. Jack Van Owen, the gentleman, Jack Van Owen, the man with style and panache.

She put the shirt back on, fingers a little shaky, pleased to be spared any lewd commentary.

'You shivered. Are you cold?' He stood up and handed her the tan windbreaker.

She put it on, thinking she was less mobile now, with the cuffs hanging a good six inches below her wrists. She folded them back, inhaling the stimulating essence of Jack Van Owen that was embedded in the cloth, smelling cologne which she had not noticed before now. She could only just catch the scent of the orchid, tucked wetly behind her ear.

'Once upon a time, Sonora Blair.' Van Owen leaned back in his chair. 'Let's say that I am an actor, playing the part of a very dedicated homicide cop named Jack Van Owen.'

Sonora sat back to listen. Clara Bonnet would have a field day with this dissociation. An actor, playing a part.

'If Jack Van Owen is such a nice guy, why, when he gets pensioned off from the force – a tragedy, that, but things happen – why does he become a loan shark? Because that's what it is, Detective Blair, this check-cashing service. We're both cops and we ain't stupid, and we know bad when we smell it. Most of the guys run places like this. Sooner or later the law's going to catch up with them, but until then? It's wide open.'

'I've looked into this, Jack, and there are plenty of laws that apply.'

'Yeah, but the wiseguys don't think so, and half the commonwealth attorneys haven't figured it out either. I'm not arguing with you, Detective. No point in you and me going over the fine points; if nothing else you've got the moral high ground.'

'Then what are you doing in this line of work?' She was

slipping, letting the disapproval show. My God, she had her arms folded – she knew better. She was letting her guard down.

He swiveled his chair, crossed his legs in a manner that was oddly effete. 'I used to have a wife and a son, and I loved them very much. That much I remember. But I got hurt. And I lost my . . . grief for them. Grief is an odd thing to miss, don't you think? But it was all I had left of them.'

He looked at her, expectantly.

She heard Joy Stinnet's voice in the back of her mind. *Hail, Mary, full of grace.* 'Why the sidetrack, Van Owen? Looking for the sympathy vote?'

'You see, I had this prejudice, when I got into this business. I thought the majority of the clients were . . .' He waved a hand. 'Deadbeats. People who run up bills, people who have no intention of paying, cons and criminals, people on the fringe. Guys who, if they weren't actively working the underbelly, have connections to that world, leanings if nothing else. I figured I'd get the debts paid, maybe give these jokers a break for information, pass it along to my old buddies on the job. Keep my hand in, even make a sort of living in the only world I know.'

'And what about the people who are just hitting a rough patch. People like Joy and Carl Stinnet?'

He raised a finger. Gave her a crooked half smile. 'Ah, yes. But I had that covered, or so I thought. *Those* people would be treated with kindness, Detective. Hell, I've been there myself; there were times when my son was young, Lacy and me scrambling for groceries, packing lunches. I planned to let it go, forgive debts, when I could swing the finances. Plenty of times I let people off the hook. Check it out if you don't believe me.'

'I did.'

He lifted his chin. 'Of course you did. Of course you did, Detective. But there were so many of them. So many good people, all in some kind of a bind, medical bills, work layoffs. People dying of cancer. Single mothers struggling in shit jobs with low pay and child support coming about as often as a blizzard in July. How could I collect from people like that? I kept . . . losing track.' He tapped the side of his head. 'I have good days and bad days. Some days, would you believe, I have no sense of smell? Other days, it's so acute it's unbelievable, I'm like a basset hound, it's wonderful.'

He pointed at the flower in her hair. 'Can you smell the orchid? It's a beautiful scent, a delicate thing. I always keep one on my desk. One, because my wife loved them. I know this because I have it written down. And two, because if I can smell it then I know I am together, and I can face the day. When I can't smell the orchid, I stay in the shadows.'

Sonora leaned forward, elbows on her knees, empty cup dangling from her fingers. 'You have it written down? That your wife loved orchids? What do you mean by that?'

'Haven't you been listening? Detective, have you ever lost anyone close to you?'

She knew he had checked her out, researched her. She knew that he knew about Stuart. 'Don't play with me, Van Owen.' A dangerous button for him to be pushing. His first serious misstep.

'Four years ago you lost your brother to a serial killer.'

'Everybody knows that.'

'Everybody does. Were you close?'

'Not playing.'

'Close.' He tapped a finger on the desk. 'As much as your grief . . . pains you, wouldn't it be worse if his name was only that? A name? And you lost all your memories of him? There are worse things than losing someone to death, Detective.' He pointed to the left side of his head. 'Lose their memory, and then they're really gone. When my wife and son died, I was . . . I went under. It was like a wave over my head. But bad as that was, I see it now as something precious. For years that grief was my companion, it was my twin, it looked out at me in the mirror every morning when I shaved, every night when I brushed my teeth.' He massaged his temples. 'That bullet didn't just take my job, it took my grief. You, who lost your brother, you can understand about missing grief. Sometimes I remember my wife, and it's like I lose her all over again. But the pain is worth it,

Sonora, because I get her back here.' He put a fist over his heart. 'And that, Detective, is a pain that I cherish.'

She did not want to understand, but she did. *He is weirder than shit*, she told herself, in a hard inner voice, looking for distance as fast as she could. She set the coffee cup on the floor, at the edge of the brick-red rug.

'How could you let it happen, Jack? Aruba and Kinkle? Turned loose on people like the Stinnets? You knew better, you had to know. A cop like you, with your street smarts, your instincts. Crick says you were damn near psychic. And it's not just Crick. You are, you were, a legend, Jack. I never hear your name without reverence. You've been gone for eleven years and they *still* talk about you, dammit.'

'Kinkle worked the phones and the desk in the storefront on Delaney Avenue. He wasn't ever supposed to leave the office. I never figured on Aruba.'

'You didn't hire him?'

'*Aruba?* I didn't even know he was out of jail.'

'He was Kinkle's uncle.'

'Step-uncle.'

'You sent them out to do collections, Jack. How could you?'

He was shaking his head. 'No, Sonora, no possible way. They were screwing me, the two of them.'

'What do you mean?'

'I mean that when I would let a debt go, Kinkle and Aruba would collect and pocket the money. It worked like this. I tell Kinkle to erase a debt. He says okay, boss. And then he and Aruba go door-to-door to collect what they can. They pocket the money, and nobody's in the loop but them. I'm not looking for the money. The client pays up and tries to forget.'

'Not the Stinnets.'

'No. Not the Stinnets.'

'Why didn't you see it, Jack? You're not dumb, you're a cop for God's sake.'

'A cop on disability.' He touched the side of his head. 'I told you, didn't I, that I have bad days? Kinkle knew that. Knew I didn't always . . . have a handle on things. Do I think he would have done it without Aruba? I don't think he had the nerve, but the idea had to be his. Maybe they hatched it together. It's too easy to underestimate Kinkle.'

'There was a third man, that day at the Stinnets,' Sonora said.

Van Owen's face stayed impassive. 'No.'

'Somebody punched Aruba. Somebody stopped him from raping that girl.'

'Kinkle.'

'Kinkle, my ass. Joy Stinnet saw him. She called him the angel. That was you, wasn't it, Jack? You're the angel.'

Van Owen smiled with a self-confidence that was unsettling, that told her she was wrong, wrong, wrong, she didn't have it yet.

'Detective, we are talking about a woman who was near death. A woman who was saying her catechism. Maybe she was having a religious experience. Maybe she *saw* an angel.'

'How did you know that?'

'Know what?'

'That she was saying her catechism.'

A pause. 'I read it. It was in the report.'

'No, it wasn't.'

'It was in the report.'

'If it wasn't you, Jack, who then? Who are you protecting?'

'Give it up, Detective. You've got your men, Aruba and Kinkle.'

'Both dead.'

'They deserved to die.' He waved a hand at the wall. 'Look at that. I've looked at it every single morning since it happened. I face that every day and know it was my fault and my responsibility. I will never take those pictures down and I will never forget. And I take care of my responsibilities.'

'It was you, Van Owen. You're the angel. You set this up, you made it happen, you walked that crime scene and you made it stop, you were just too damn late.'

'I was shopping at Wal-Mart, Detective, like the rest of the population. I wasn't there. And I guarantee you that you have not found one piece of evidence, one strand of hair, one drop of blood, one tiny little scrap of DNA that puts me there, because if you had, you wouldn't be sitting over on that couch all by yourself. It's time to let go, Detective. I read you the last page, I showed you the end, now walk away.'

She stood up. 'I am not going to let this go.'

He looked tired, suddenly, almost uninterested. He rested his elbows on the top of his desk and looked up at her. 'You have a life, Sonora. You have kids, you have a career and a mortgage and a horse. Walk away.'

Chapter Seventy-Three

Sonora felt the chill the minute she walked into the bull-pen. She'd been suspicious when Ellen in reception pretended not to see her good-morning wave. Now, she stood by the coffee machine, stirring, stirring. No one looked up. No one said hello.

'Gruber?' she said.

He gave her a quick glance, as if it hurt him to look at her. 'Morning.' Quick, curt, embarrassed.

'You break the Purcell alibi?'

He didn't answer. Selective hearing. Molliter got up, walked casually to the coffee machine. Handed her his packet of chocolate. 'I'll keep you in my prayers.' But there was satisfaction in his eyes.

'Where's Crick?' She said it loudly, to no one in particular. No one in particular answered.

'Fuck this,' she said. 'If anybody wants to know, I've gone shopping.'

Her voice sounded so normal, edged maybe with anger. No indication that her hands were shaking and her chest felt like it was under two tons of steel.

In all her years on the job, she never would have thought she'd land here. She never would have believed that the worst of it would be her feelings. Very hurt.

She felt small and instantly worthless. Like every collar, every case, came down to those looks, that chill. What if she wasn't a cop any more? What if she couldn't go back to the way it was? What if she was a civilian?

Sonora took the Visa card she had paid down, kept it tight in a sweaty fist, looking at all the pretties. She took her time, bought two portable CD players that were on sale for sixty-nine dollars and ninety-eight cents a piece. Imagined Heather and Tim's faces when they saw them. Then she went to Abercrombie and Fitch and bought both of them a flannel shirt, gift-wrapped for no particular reason. She stopped at the pet store and got pig ears for Clampett.

She was home before the kids got out of school. Walked in through the garage, saw Clampett stretched out in front of his water bowl, watching a mouse perched on the edge, drinking tiny mouse sips.

'You are way too kind, puppy dog.' She sent him straight to dog heaven with three pig ears all at once.

For some weird reason she was crying as she arranged the gifts on the kitchen table, a big surprise for the kids. Something out of the blue, because Mom loves you.

This business with Crick was a hard one. She felt bewildered, and oddly hurt. She had always looked up to him, admired him. He was a tough boss and a good cop and kind of scary to work for, demanding and cynical, but with an ethical core she could depend on. He protected his people, ran interference, no one could have been kinder when Stuart was killed. And now. Now she didn't know what to think. Maybe best if she didn't.

On impulse she called Gillane, caught the message on his machine. 'Hi,' she said. 'Just called to say hello.'

Chapter Seventy-Four

That night she worked alone, sitting behind her desk in the bull-pen in the middle of the night, feeling weirdly nostalgic. Her life seemed divided now, to before and after the Stinnets. She missed the before, missed the time when being behind that desk in the dead of night felt like overtime, not refuge.

She missed the hell out of Sam. She was odd man out now – she knew she was watched, suspected, banished from the inner circle. It would not be possible to feel more alone.

And when he did come back, would it rub off on him? It wasn't going to be helping his career any, being partnered with her.

Sonora rubbed her face, stared at the computer screen. She had the accident report, she had gone through every death certificate in every relevant year. Lacy Van Owen had died thirteen years ago in a car accident in Union, Kentucky, but there was no mention of son Van Owen, and no death certificate that she could find. She did, however, find a birth certificate, dated 1972. Angelo David Van Owen. AKA the angel?

Chapter Seventy-Five

Sonora stood alone, barely breathing, in the hallway on the seventh floor of Van Owen's warehouse. There was no light, except what leaked in through the grime-soaked windows, neon and moonlight, the uncaring eye of the city. This was, indeed, a place that she knew, a place she did not want to be, but a place she had known was coming. Portents.

Her night vision was not good. She gave her eyes time to adjust. For once in her life she was not in a hurry. She had come before, in her mind, many many times. And she had never, in her mind, come back out again.

Some people never made peace with death. It was not a bad place to be.

Sonora was aware of the beat of her heart. The crumbling black plastic quarter round at the base of the brick walls. The mildew-stained linoleum. She smelled the accumulated filth of the institution. She smelled the years of minimal, uncaring upkeep combined with heavy, indifferent use which had left layers of scent and fatigue. No one had ever loved this building.

She walked slowly, listening. She had her barn boots on, worn brown Ariats, and they gave her an elusive frisson of good feeling, bringing to mind the smell of horses, the feel of old tack, the sweet scent of baled hay. But they also made her footsteps loud. She crouched close to the floor, unlaced the boots, and left them behind.

Before, she had been like a swimmer, not wanting to touch

her feet to the bottom of that dark place, struggling up to the surface for light and air and relief.

She would not struggle, no longer willing to make that particular effort. She would let her feet touch bottom and she would be still. There was no light in the depths where she was, but she could still breathe, slowly and quietly; she could feel her way, blindly and, wonderful this, peaceful now, and not at all afraid.

Chapter Seventy-Six

Sonora had passed him by before she paused, and headed back two steps, drawn by the black-shaded lamp and the man who sat alone behind the desk, contemplating the pool of light. He was as still as death; she thought for a moment he was dead. All she could see was the back of his head, the battered brown leather chair, his feet flat on the floor.

'Your feet must be cold, Detective.'

The chair turned ever so slowly. She could only think, as she always did, how easy it was to watch Jack Van Owen. Wondering what he would do next, wondering what he would say.

What was it about him that drew the eye, even in a room full of people? How could he generate such presence? Was it a natural attribute. Did he do it on a conscious level?

Perhaps it was a primitive and subconscious recognition that this man was way ahead, having thoughts and opinions you definitely wanted to know. Intentions it would be safer for you to be aware of.

Perhaps it was a recognition of danger. No point in watching your back if this man was in the room; better for you if you watched him.

Sonora curled her toes. Her feet were indeed cold, and it was a shocked joyousness, that cold through the socks on her feet.

Either way she could not take her eyes off Jack Van Owen.

She listened for footsteps behind her, and heard nothing with a strong relief. She did not think she would have looked away.

So familiar now, the roundish face, the stocky build, five feet ten inches tall. Thinning black hair, brown eyes that went flat with danger, but were warm now with an intimacy he could project from across the room.

He had a spark, a crackle that told you the man inside was brighter than most, quick on his feet, one step ahead.

And there he was smiling at her, and she caught herself smiling back. There was something in his eyes, an attentiveness she craved.

'You think about it a lot lately now, don't you, Sonora?'

Sonora swallowed, and she knew exactly what he meant. She should arrest him now, and end this. She couldn't. She wanted to hear more. He was talking about her now, the inside of her, like he knew. And she believed that he did know. And she could not help but wonder if he had some kind of insight here, or if he knew something that might help. That somehow, maybe, he could save her. That maybe it was not too late.

He shook his head ever so slightly. 'Don't be embarrassed about this, Sonora. Every really intelligent, thinking person comes to this, sooner or later. Or over and over, for ones like you and me.' He grinned, just a flash, to let her know, believe me, that he understood.

'Over and over, Sonora, the thoughts just won't go away, will they?' His face changed. He held up his wrists, looking as weary as she felt. 'Are you here to arrest me? Or are you here to return my jacket?'

'To arrest you.'

'You have no proof.'

'I have proof and you know it. I'm wearing it.'

'I'm not following you, Sonora.' But he was. She wondered when he'd realized the mistake, a fatal error, generated by kindness and good manners.

'You left your gloves in the pocket. The gloves you were wearing when you hit Aruba. The gloves you were wearing when you went into the Stinnets' house.'

'Try to do a good deed. How about this? They're not my gloves.'

'Don't embarrass yourself.'

'I don't particularly care any more, you know that, don't you? But don't you want to know what happened?'

She didn't answer. Didn't trust herself to play these games and win.

'Follow me, then.'

He led her down the hallway like the Pied Piper, and she followed him like a child.

Chapter Seventy-Seven

He led her the length of the wasted hallway, till they faced a freight elevator, metal sides painted black years ago, with paint that was peeling, showing the dull silver beneath. A criss-cross metal rack gating the dark opening, door yawning open like the gates of hell.

Van Owen stepped in and turned to face her, and she half expected something, like a gun, but no. Just that gentle, knowing smile that frightened her because it hinted at a knowledge of things she wanted to keep totally private. And promised an understanding that she craved.

'I'm a burning house, baby. Are you going to run away?'

'No, and neither are you. Come off the elevator, Jack.'

He waited, looking so . . . polite. Waiting.

'Step off the elevator, Jack. I'm not playing games with you.'

'Shoot me or let me go. Your choice.'

'Death by cop?'

'Death by perp?'

She had no answer to that one.

He waved a hand. 'I can see it, that death wish you have. It hums in the air around you like an aura. Like the sound of bees in a hive. If I were to kiss you, I could taste it on your mouth.' There was such intelligence, a knowing something in his eyes like a candle in a jack-o'-lantern. She had to watch him. It was like driving by a terrible car wreck.

'There is a third option,' he told her.

'Explain it quick, before I lose count.'

'You can find out what really happened.'

'I'm listening.'

He pointed upward. 'To the roof.'

'No.'

'We'll do it at gunpoint. You've got your weapon there, tucked in the back of your jeans, right? Get it out. Take the safety off. Point the gun at my heart. I want you to come to the roof, and I want you to feel safe.'

She did as he said. Took out the gun, so familiar in her hand. She felt better. More in control.

He smiled as if reading the thought.

She followed him into the elevator. She had a bad moment as he shut the gate, hating the cavernous freight elevator, like something out of *Angel Heart*. She stood with her back to the wall and watched him push the button for the roof.

The elevator moved slowly at first, then gathered speed. He spoke quickly, a man running out of time.

'When my son was born twenty-three years ago, Lacy and I felt so blessed. We named him Angelo, and we called him our angel. We'd been trying to have a child for five years.' He turned his head to face her, keeping his back to the wall and his hands at his sides. 'Detective Sonora Blair, you have two children. A boy, Tim, who is seventeen? And a little girl named Heather who is twelve.'

He knew her, knew the names and ages of her kids. She thought of the way her house looked, that first night when she was called out to the Stinnets, the memory like a keyhole view into the living room, brightly lit against the failing light, the living room that was probably dark now, while the kids slept in their rooms down the hall, trusting that she would come home, as she always did.

What did it mean to be a mother? Did it mean that you were sentenced to life?

'Listen to me, Sonora. Two weeks ago your son was arrested in Boone County for speeding, driving with a suspended license, and carrying a concealed weapon.'

'His license was fine, it was a computer glitch. It happens.'

'The weapon?'

'A machete he takes camping. And it wasn't concealed, it was sitting on the floor of the back seat. It's still legal, as far as I know, for teenage boys to go camping. And I checked this *weapon* myself. The edge is so blunt you couldn't cut a sandwich.'

He smiled as if making a point. 'Listen to you, Detective. To hear you talk the poor child was set up by a computer. And you dismiss the machete like it's a joke.'

'This isn't about me, and it isn't about my son.'

'It's about every parent who ever made an excuse for their child.'

'Then that's every parent, Jack.'

He turned sideways and faced her. 'Bingo.'

The gates of the elevator opened to darkness. Sonora smelled rain. She got that horrible closed-in feeling, a sense of dread in the pit of her stomach. The only light came from the interior of the elevator. Van Owen did not move, back plastered to the wall.

'You're not so different from me, baby. You can't distance yourself on this one. I loved my son like you love yours. I saw the good in him, saw it every day of his life.'

'You talk about him like he's dead.'

'He is dead.'

'He did not die in the car wreck with your wife.'

'No, he did not. He took the wheel of that car and jerked it out of her hands, sweet Lacy, and their car crossed the path of a coal truck. She died twelve hours later in Union, Kentucky. She was down there in the same place you were, bailing our son out of trouble, just like you did with Tim.'

'It's not the same.'

'I hope not. For your sake, Detective. You want to know *why* he grabbed that wheel? Because he wanted to stop for cigarettes, and she said no. He told me everything. He cried and said he was sorry. But I'm a cop, Sonora, I can't lose it, I live, eat, and breathe *cop*, and while the daddy in me saw the good in my son, the cop saw the bad boy, the antisocial, no conscience, manipulative . . . the angel, my son. Angelo.

'I had him committed to an institution in Arlington, Texas, until he turned twenty-one. It's easy enough, Detective. The definition of mental illness, and typical teenage behavior, are surprisingly similar. If you've got insurance, or if you've got money, you've got a soft little room. Drugs, shrinks and therapy. Until he turned twenty-one, two years ago. And then I brought him home. Cured. To help me run the business.'

'Where is he now?' Sonora said. 'You can't protect him, not after this.'

The look he gave her was puzzled. 'Still not there yet, Detective?'

The elevator light, keyed to a timer, blinked and went out. Sonora took a step forward and Van Owen touched her arm.

'Hold on just a minute. There's a light here, somewhere.'

She noted that he knew exactly where, that he flipped the switch like a man following a script. But she was grateful for the blinding yellow light, that showed a small room with metal doors thrown open to the roof. Jack Van Owen beckoned and she went behind him, gun steady in her right hand.

Sonora felt the bottom of her socks go instantly soggy, the roughness of wet concrete beneath her feet. A car passed on the street below, the tires making a shushing noise on the wet pavement, then the peculiar silence of a city at night. Somewhere, a long way away, she could hear a train.

'Are you afraid of heights, Sonora?'

'Maybe.'

'I am.' He walked toward the edge of the building and she followed, drawing a mental line she promised herself she would not cross. He stopped a good six feet from the edge. 'Hell of a view.'

She knew she was meant to look away, but she was too good a cop. She watched him and only him.

'My son cried when he told me about Joy Stinnet. Oh, I cried too, I admit it. He told me about the baby, and the teenage girl, and the dog. He was racked. I cried and he cried and we cried together. But I was happy, Detective. God help me, I was happy that my son had a conscience, that he had limits, that he stood up to Aruba. Angelo punched Aruba in the mouth, those are his gloves in that jacket pocket, it was Angelo that pulled him off of the girl. He tried to save her, got some towels, tried to stop the bleeding when Aruba slashed her throat. He was panicked, it was useless, but he tried.

'It takes courage, you know, something like that, when the blood is up and everyone is going crazy and is in a panic. Imagine it, Sonora. I was proud of him and ashamed.' Van Owen rubbed his temples. 'He came to me in such agony. He was in shock, he'd never seen something like that, something so brutal. He begged me to make it go away, he wanted to turn himself in. I didn't know . . . what to do. Jail – how could I send my son, my Angelo, to jail with the hard timers? But he had to be punished. Wherever he went, people died, bad and terrible things happened.'

'What did you do?' It came out as a whisper.

'I had a bucket, a metal bucket. It was a paint bucket he took from Stinnet's garage. I don't know why he took it – one of those dumb things that don't make any sense. I told him. I said for him to get down on his knees and pray. He was crying so hard, I couldn't make out the words he was saying, and then . . . and then I didn't believe him any more.' Van Owen looked up. 'Ever had one of those moments, Sonora, when reality shifts right under your feet? Those tears were crocodile tears. Oh, he was afraid, afraid of getting caught, afraid of getting punished. Daddy had to save him. So I . . . saved him. The only way I knew how.'

Sonora was afraid to ask, to press. She held her breath, waiting.

'I told him to put his head in that bucket, and I took my gun, my department-issue thirty-eight, and while he cried and begged for me to save him . . . I shot my son in the head.'

'Where is he now?'

'I buried him.'

'Where?'

'I buried him with Stinnet's bucket, wrapped my baby up in a blanket and buried him. I told myself that I killed my own son, because I had to. That it was the only way I could save him. But the truth is?' Van Owen looked up. 'I think I was just saving me.'

Sonora took a deep breath, let it out slowly. 'Come on, Jack. Come with me.'

He tilted his head to one side. 'People who are afraid of heights, these are people who know that they're going to jump.' He tapped his chest, over the pumping muscle of his heart. 'Somewhere, deep in here, you know. On a subconscious level. So the brain, not being dumb, hits that panic button when you find yourself near the edge.' He massaged his temples.

'A fear of heights is a compulsion to jump. It's that way for you too, isn't it? You don't see Sonora Blair standing at the edge like those others who approach the drop zone, waggle their butts, look over their shoulder, grinning like stupids, sticking their tongues out. Like they're brave, acting like an idiot, like they have one over on you because they dare to stand so close.

'But they're not brave. Stupid, maybe, if they're at all prone to be clumsy or trip, but brave? Not hardly.

'They don't feel it, do they, Sonora? They don't feel that sinking knowledge, that if you get too close you'll *have* to do it, if for no other reason than to get it the hell over with.

'That *panic* . . . that panic, you've felt it, that makes you grab hold and shut your eyes. That's your survival instinct kicking in. That's your mind's awareness that standing three feet away is for you the equivalent of someone else dangling from a forty-story balcony by a piece of string.'

He took a step backward, looked away from the edge. 'Where do you think the compulsion comes from? Did we fall to our deaths in a previous life? Do we just have . . . a death wish? Maybe it's simpler. Maybe it's nothing more than an absolute craving for freedom.'

'Freedom?'

'Sure. Think about the moment, Sonora. Where you step away from everything – the edge of the cliff, the lip of the brick, step away into nothing. Nothing to hold you, nothing to stop you . . . a total and complete letting go of everything. Your past, your future . . . your life. Seconds, just seconds, of absolute total freedom from absolutely everything.

'Have you never seen anybody fall to their death? They always scream. Don't they? It sounds like fear. But think about it. People scream on roller-coasters. Maybe it's not fear. Maybe it's more like . . . exhilaration.'

He moved to the very edge, tips of his shoes lined up at the very end of the building. He looked at her over his shoulder and smiled. 'Are you staying behind, Sonora? Facing it all alone?'

'Step away from the edge, Jack. Come on.'

The sound of her voice, the hoarseness, alarmed her. She read herself as if she were a stranger. Yes, this woman is considering her options. This woman is thinking thoughts. Watch her. You might want to worry here.

'What scares you, Sonora? Me? The heights? Yourself?'

'All of it.'

He smiled till his eyes crinkled. 'I'm not going to hurt you, Sonora. I'm done. I think maybe you're done too. Death isn't what scares you, is it? Not any more, it doesn't. Sonora?' Her name on his lips was like a caress. 'Take my hand?'

She shook her head. The gun felt so heavy, her arm so tired. She let the hand drop.

She wanted to take his hand. Everything went away from her, the night, the noise of the city. She saw the edge of the roof like the end of a tunnel, like there was only one way to go. She saw his hand.

'Good girl. Come on.'

It wasn't a step, it was more a movement, an inclination in his direction. He leaned toward her and her stomach jumped, then flooded with relief, because all he did was hold her hand, and his fingers were dry, strong and warm. She could feel his heat, their noses close enough to touch. He looked at her in such a way, like a man in love, like a man who has seen you from across the room and decided, come hell or high water, that you are the one.

And he kissed her, lips pressing hard against hers, warm, soft, teeth grazing her lower lip. He pulled away, opened his eyes, sighed.

'I'm going. You coming?'

She could not talk. Her tongue was heavy. Her throat was tight. She felt that sick sinking feeling you get when you have to say goodbye to someone you have loved all your life.

It felt bad. Like the death of a heart.

He smiled and dropped her hand. 'I'll go first.'

She never could place exactly what compelled her to look up and over Jack's shoulder. Never told anyone what she saw, her brother Stuart, how distinctly she saw him there in the darkness, how wonderful he looked, how he smiled at her and held up a hand as if to ward off something very bad.

It startled her. She backed away, felt, a split second later, Van Owen's strong grasping fingers as he reached out and grabbed for her, and she pulled away, socks slipping on the wet concrete, landing hard.

She watched him fall, white shirt billowing, disbelief like a hand at her throat, as if she had expected him to be more than human, as if she had expected him to fly. As if she had expected him to take her with him.

Chapter Seventy-Eight

For some reason Sergeant Crick was telling her to put her head between her knees, which she did, sitting there in Jack Van Owen's leather chair, wrapped in a blanket, shivering so hard her muscles ached, teeth chattering against the cup of coffee that she finally pushed away.

Light from the solitary desk lamp pooled at her feet. She heard men, and voices, and heavy feet, and still more sirens up and down the street.

A man's voice. Gruber. 'Can't make a positive ID, sir. He's too much of a mess.'

'It's him. It's Jack Van Owen. I was there when he went over.' Her voice sounded strange and chokey. Her voice worried her. It seemed to worry Crick. She had a weird, heightened sensibility, as if she were floating at the top of the room watching everyone and reading their thoughts. As if she were in her body, but out. Crick was unhappy with her. Gruber was worried. Did they know? Did they know what she had almost done? The guilt washed over like it was going to take her under.

'This is bad,' Sonora said. They were cops, they knew things. They would know what she had almost done.

'Get Mickey in here, with his camera,' Crick said. 'Sonora, where is your gun?'

'My what?'

He tilted her chin up so she could face him, as if her eyes were a book he was compelled to read. 'Where is your gun?'

'I had it.'

'Yes.'

'I don't know.'

'Did you fire your gun?'

'No.'

'Are you sure?'

'No.'

'You're not sure?'

'No, I didn't fire it.'

'You don't remember firing your gun?'

'No, sir.' She waved a hand, waving off the question, the irritation of details. 'Sergeant, he talked to me, he told me. There *was* a third man.'

Crick's head moved toward her like a bird of prey. 'Sonora—'

'No, listen to me. It was his son. Van Owen's son. That boy never died in the car accident, I checked.'

'What car accident? Are you talking about Lacy's accident?'

'Yes, the boy, Angelo. He wasn't killed, he wasn't even hurt.'

'I know that.'

'You . . . do?'

'Hell, yes, I was there, I was his partner then. There were problems with the boy, Sonora, this is ancient history, it has nothing to do with—'

'Sir, it was the boy that was there, at the Stinnets' house, he was the angel, he was the third man. Jack was protecting him.'

Crick pulled his chair close in and took both of her hands in his. 'Sonora, listen to me. Angelo Van Owen died at the age of seventeen in an institution in Arlington, Texas.'

Sonora wanted to say something, but did not know what.

'The boy hung himself. He seemed to be doing better, he got more privileges, and one morning they found him hanging from his sweater. A pretty determined suicide. Jack never forgave himself, but Angelo Van Owen is dead and has been for six years. There was not a third man, Sonora. Give it up. Kinkle and Aruba butchered Joy Stinnet and her family. The only connection with Van Owen was he supplied the victims. And he sure as hell felt bad enough about it, didn't he?' Crick swept an arm around the room, pointing to the walls covered with pictures. 'But that business of his was a cover, Sonora. He came up with a lot of good information over the last few years. He was a good guy. He was a good friend. He was never at the Stinnets' house, and he never would have let it happen.'

'You've known from day one, haven't you? You knew he ran the business.'

'He wasn't—'

'Involved? You going to tell me he wasn't involved? Me running around talking about this third man, like some kind of an idiot, because I was totally out of the loop, right? You don't think he was involved? Think again. Because I have it, sir.'

'You have what?'

'Proof that he was there. I've got the gloves he wore when he punched Aruba in the mouth.'

Silence like a pillow over her face.

'Where?'

'Evidence room with the clerk, and they better not disappear.'

'I'm going to pretend I didn't hear that.'

'Pretend all you want, it's been said. Jack Van Owen was there.'

'He was a good cop, Sonora, and you are dead wrong.'

'Somebody here is dead wrong, but it sure the hell isn't me, not any more. Just you remember those photos, sir. If Van Owen hadn't been there, this would never have happened. He was involved. We may never know how much, but he was involved. He was not the man you knew.'

Crick's voice washed over her, in a low tone meant only for Gruber's ears. 'Go up to the roof and look for her gun. See if it's been fired, report only to me. And clear the room. We don't need these uniforms in here. Get them busy somewhere else.'

'Yes, sir.' Gruber so quiet, so serious. He squeezed Sonora's shoulder and she felt tears stream down her cheeks. She did not care that she was crying. She did not care that it made her look weak. She would not care what anyone thought ever again.

'Where in the hell is Mickey?' This from Crick, impatient but holding rein.

'He's coming, sir. You.' Gruber was pointing at someone, but even from the top of the room Sonora could not tell who. 'Get Mickey in here, now.'

'Up to the roof,' Crick urged.

Gruber left.

Chapter Seventy-Nine

Sonora did not know the name of the uniform who drove her home, and she never found out his name, though she thought of him, afterward, mentally dubbing him the sweetest boy in the world. He was tallish and thick-chested, with skinny legs, and his short dark hair was gelled back over his bullet-shaped head.

She had thought she might drive herself home, but her knees were so shaky, and she was subject to bouts of trembling, and Crick ordered her not to drive. She wasn't much for following Crick's orders, but she did see his point.

Her only thought was that it was good Crick and Gruber had not been able to read her thoughts. Because right now she hated every single one of them.

She sat in the cruiser and did not say a word to the kind questions and offers of help. Well, one question.

'Where did you get it?' She meant the half coffee, half Jack Daniels that he handed her in a StarBucks cup.

'Don't ask,' he told her kindly. So she did not for once in her life ask. The uniform could not know that *don't* and *ask* were two words that always set her off.

She hoped, later, that he did not take her aura of rage personally. But she had been made to stand up, Crick and Gruber examining her arms, taking pictures of the unbroken flesh, muttering cop things like *no scratches*, hem haw hem. Crick had offered her the chance to call an attorney, damn his sorry ass. Mickey had cleared out under her fingernails, said 'Nothing obvious' to Crick while he put his specimens away in an evidence bag. A paramedic had drawn blood, and Mickey had done a paraffin test on her hands, right and left, to see if she had fired her weapon. Admirable thoroughness.

My God, she was angry. What did they think, did they think she had shot the man? Pushed him over the edge? Was that easier to believe than the legend going bad?

But she had not stopped him, had she? She ought to have followed procedure and tried to talk him down, or at the very least, shot him before he jumped.

Tomorrow – tomorrow when she could think she would have to come up with a story. Something better than I kissed him goodbye and he jumped off the roof.

And she closed her eyes, shivering, because he hadn't screamed, he hadn't cried. He hadn't made a sound at all.

Chapter Eighty

Sonora slammed the car door of the cruiser, stirring the neighborhood dogs, and ran across the wet lawn to her front door. She giggled for no particular reason, feeling like a teenager out past curfew. The Jack Daniels was taking effect.

The children had left the porch light on, or had not turned it off, depending upon how you looked at it. Clampett was delighted to see her, and he licked her arms and sniffed her shoes, and leaned up against her leg. She dropped her purse and key beside the front door. Staggered a little when she walked, but made a survey of the house.

Clean and neat. Dishwasher running, the light on over the sink. Tim, she guessed, currying favor after his bout of jail time, appreciating home for the first time in a long time; the same could be said for herself. The children's doors were locked, as usual, and she did not have the energy to pick the locks. She sat on the couch. Patted the cushion.

'Here, boy.'

Clampett, possibly her only friend in the whole world, jumped up beside her and licked her nose. She laid her head on his neck and closed her eyes. And saw Jack Van Owen, dropping like a rock off that building.

She was exhausted, sleepy, afraid to let go.

The headlights of a car blazed against the living-room window. Someone turning into her driveway.

Clampett growled and leaped off the couch, heading for the

front door in a scrabble of toenails and aggression. Sonora went to the window with the slightly sideways motion of the partially inebriated.

A white Cadillac convertible, top up against the rain, pulling to the front of her house. Gillane got out of the car and came to the front door, heralded by the barking of the dog. Sonora had the door open before he made it to the porch. He did not say a word or stop to pet the dog, but grabbed her and held her and led her to the couch.

'How did you know?'

'I was on duty when they brought him in. Van Owen. I was scared to death it was you.'

'Why?'

He paused. 'I don't know. But I was. Tell me everything, tell me nothing, I don't care.'

'I have pissed off every single person in my department.'

'It's their fault, not yours. You are completely in the right and they're all idiots.'

She stopped and looked at him.

'I can be efficient when the time comes.'

'Mark, I can't go to sleep ever again. I'm afraid to close my eyes.'

'No, sweetie, it's safe for you to sleep. I brought you something to help you along.'

'That damn Benedryl doesn't—'

'Something nice and strong that will put you out, if that's what you want. How much have you been drinking?'

'I don't know.'

'We'll have to figure it out. I don't want to put you out for good.'

How good he felt. How wonderful he smelled. 'I want to sit here on this couch and I want you to hold me all night long.'

'Good by me.'

'What will the kids think?'

'How nice it is that someone will make them breakfast tomorrow morning.'

'I make them breakfast *every* morning.'

'Do not.'

'Do too.' She pushed away from him. 'I saw my brother tonight. When Jack Van Owen jumped off the roof. I didn't push him, he jumped. My brother wouldn't let me jump.'

'That's what brothers are for.'

She looked at him, but he was serious. 'You do know that my brother is dead?'

'I do know that, yes.'

'But I saw him on the roof. You accept that?'

'I'm from the South, Sonora. We see our family all the time, even after they've passed.'

'But I'm not from the South.'

'It must have been quite a shock.'

She laughed, then leaned against him. 'I dreamed about him, and then I saw him. I don't think there's any question but I am going nuts.'

Gillane wrapped his arms around her. 'I'm an emergency-room doctor, Sonora. I've watched a lot of people die. We're all out there looking for signs, looking for . . . grace. Something sacred in the middle of everyday horror.'

'Every time I close my eyes I see Jack falling. Every time I fall asleep I hear Joy Stinnet saying her catechism.'

'Tonight's going to be different.' Gillane fished something out of his shirt pocket. A white shirt, Egyptian cotton, just like the one Van Owen had been wearing. 'Swallow this,' he said.

She did. A large caplet. 'How long before it takes effect?'

'Normally about twenty minutes, but you've been drinking, you don't have long.'

She sighed, and leaned against him. Smelled mint on his breath, rubbed her cheek on his freshly shaven one.

She closed her eyes. She didn't want to look at his whole face, just the jaw. The line of it, the feel of the skin, the firm chin. He did not scare her. He pulled her closer, held her with a lovely gentleness, so that she could hold him back without fear, without tense muscles warding off real and imagined pain.

'Do you mind if we go up to the bedroom? I'm a little long for your couch.'

'I don't know. I don't want to . . .' Her tongue was getting thick and she had to concentrate. 'I don't want to weird out the children.'

'It's okay. I'll be up before they are, and I'll introduce myself over bacon.'

She nodded, too tired to point out what the odds were of finding bacon in her refrigerator. 'And you're definitely not gay?'

'I am definitely not gay.'

Chapter Eighty-One

Sonora sat on top of three hay bales in Franklin Ward's barn, legs dangling, listening to Poppin and Abigail munch their hay. She could hear another horse calling from a farm nearby. It was something, for her, to sit on a stack of hay bales in the cool of the barn, a red and white plastic Super America cup full of coffee by her leg.

She liked barn noises, country noises, so different from what she was used to. Birds. The crunch of the horses' teeth as they worked their feed. Someone hammering in the distance. Cars passing now and then, sometimes pulling a horse trailer.

She had gotten up early with Gillane and polished her barn boots while he made breakfast. A man making coffee in the morning was a wonderful thing. Comfortable barn boots were a wonderful thing.

She had hugged the children goodbye and Gillane had left her with a kiss, and she had managed to get out of the house with the air of a woman who has pulled herself together. But she had been raw to the world, and had come to the barn like an open wound, a sponge to sensation. She felt every breath of air, every bend and bump in the road went through her like an electric jolt; she could not meet the eyes of her neighbors, could not bear to be looked at.

Her defenses were flayed. Her stomach felt like a sunburn that was peeling, sore and itchy and streaked with blood. There were too many images in her mind, words and snatches of remembered conversation like discordant music, jazz on the brain, experimental, demanding, giving no melody and not a crumb of comfort.

But now all she could hear was the shift and rustle of the horses. She grabbed a handful of the alfalfa and inhaled. Felt the weight go off her shoulders, a little anyway, the brain static fade to background irritation, white noise of the soul. She leaned back and rested her head against the raw and rotting wood of the barn wall, feeling like a rabbit home safe in the burrow.

She was there quite a while before she heard the barn door creaking on the rusty hinge, and she looked up and saw Franklin Ward walking in, the sun at his back, erect as always, neatly dressed in his corduroy pants, green the color of the daily flannel shirt.

'I saw your car in the driveway a while ago. Thought you might need a little time.'

'You heard?'

'Just what they had on the radio. They didn't say much. Just that a highly decorated ex-policeman named Jack Van Owen died from a fall from his seven-story office building. There was speculation about Joy's case. I almost called you up, then I thought you'd be out to tell me when you could, looked in the driveway, and there you were.'

He got out the old tack box and handed her a brush. 'Let's get some work done while we're talking.'

He went into Abigail's stall, and she headed for Poppin, whom she knew would hold relatively still as long as he had hay to eat.

'I'm trying to put some weight on that horse of yours,' Franklin said.

'Best of luck.'

Sonora took a metal shedding blade and scraped dried mud off Poppin's backside. The horse had clearly been enjoying the rain. He turned his head and gave her a look which she took for affection. Dried mud landed on her sleeve, her boots, and the shavings on the floor of the stall.

They groomed the horses while she talked, handing each

other brushes over the short partition. Ward didn't say much, other than to pass her the hoofpick to get to Poppin's feet, or repeat a phrase now and then when his hearing let him down.

She did not dress it up or leave anything out, kept her voice matter-of-fact and low-key. She found herself apologizing.

'I can't tell you for sure how bad a guy Jack was. I don't even know if he was bad. I can't tell you for sure I should have pursued him. I think he put an end to things, when they could have been worse. But I hold him accountable. He was in a nasty line of business, and if he didn't set things up, he put the elements together.'

'If it hadn't been for him, it never would have happened,' Ward said. 'But I look at it differently. She was my niece and I loved her.'

'At least it's over. The investigation, anyway. These things are never over, are they?'

Something in her voice caught his attention. He leaned on Abigail's back, and looked at her over the partition. 'Don't try and run away, Detective.'

'What do you mean, run away?'

'It's in our culture, isn't it? We're a young country, the United States of America, and that's a good thing, or it can be. We got that good old American can-do philosophy, that don't-take-no-for-an-answer attitude. It just doesn't prepare us for when the answer *is* no.

'I spent some time in Europe after the war. My war. For a while there I just didn't feel I could face going home. Felt different, and didn't want to pretend. I was homesick as hell but I couldn't go back.

'We used to make fun of the Europeans, the way they'd shrug and say, that's life. We used to think it was an excuse to be lazy and not try. I stayed in Europe till I got the point. And the point is, that sometimes the answer *is* no. Somebody dies, that's a no. Your child goes away from you, you lose your job, someone kills somebody you love. That's no, Detective.

'People run from no. They drink too much, do drugs, get so busy at work they can't see straight. They get depressed and sleep, or eat everything in sight. They cry and they scream and kick and say yes yes yes. But no matter how hard you run, no is right there, right behind you.

'Take it on the chin, Detective. Running from no puts you in a bad place. Go on and feel bad. It's part of life.'

'And *that* is supposed to make it all better?'

'In time, Detective. In time.'

Like any other intelligent person, Ward knew a good line to end on. He didn't say anything else, except to ask her to hand him a saddle, and he put the tack on Abigail and handed her the reins.

'I should go to work,' Sonora said.

'If you wanted to go to work you should have said before I got the horse tacked up. Too late now. Okay by you if I let Poppin out in the paddock?'

Sonora took the reins. 'He should be okay. How come your horse acts so nice, and my horse acts so bad?'

'I told you already. George Smock. You'll have to send Poppin to Kentucky if you want him to behave.'

'I'll just settle for lead and feed right now.'

She led Abigail to the side of the fence, and the horse stood patiently while Sonora climbed to the second wood slat and threw a leg over the mare's back. Abigail, a truly miraculous animal, stood quietly till Sonora urged her forward, then moved ahead steadily.

Sonora felt her shoulders go loose, and did not notice that Ward waited till he saw the smile spread across her face before he left the paddock and closed the gate.

'Mr Ward? Did you get a letter from Sergeant Robert J. Purcell fourteen years ago when Tina was two?'

He stopped. Thought about it. 'I did. Sent it back unopened.'

'I see.'

'There a problem with that?'

'Nope.'

'Sonora?'

'Yeah?'

358

'Mrs Cavanaugh said if you wanted to bring your children over Sunday afternoon, she'll make us a mighty fine roast.'

'Actually . . . that sounds good. Want me to bring anything?'

'Just yourselves. And Mrs Cavanaugh said if you have a young man to bring, please do.'

'I guess I will.'

'We'll set an extra place,' he said, and headed back to the house.

Sonora, feeling brave, clucked Abigail into a trot, with Poppin following like an excited puppy.

Chapter Eighty-Two

Sonora stood behind her desk, four hours late, smelling like horse, and planning to leave early. She knew better than to sit down. She tapped her finger on the corner of the desk, feeling the high-pitched tension of the bull-pen behind her. She had said hello to no one, after sitting alone in the car for thirty-five minutes, psyching herself up to be tough. It was there in the back of her mind, the doubt, making her wonder if she should have let things be.

Behind her the phones were ringing. Sam's desk was still piled with papers just as he had left it, beneath a rising level of dust. She missed him like a physical pain. A few more weeks and he'd be back. She could hang on till then, if she had to. If they let her.

There was something new on his desk, a small brown package. She picked it up curiously. Addressed to her and tossed on the wrong desk.

Probably a bomb.

Except the return address was from Pill Hill. Who would be mailing her something from a hospital?

She ripped the brown wrapping off, found a plastic-wrapped bundle of thick white cotton socks, a packet of six, and a note from Sam.

Something to lift your spirits, girl. I been hearing things. Just you remember, I'm behind you, so hang on. Will be up and around and at your back in no time. Love, Sam.

Only Sam would know the socks had to be pure white, with some elastic in the top so they could stay up, thick heavy slouch socks. Only Sam would know that to a woman perpetually behind in laundry, a woman whose children daily declared open season on her sock drawer, new socks were one of the small, but significant pleasures of her life.

She could have laughed, she could have cried, she settled for neither. She settled for going to Crick's door, and getting it over with.

He was sitting sideways behind his desk, staring out the window that was half covered by steel filing cabinets, a tiny bit of sunlight and a whole lot of dirt. The fax machine beeped, and paper rolled over the top of the basket into a pile of other papers that no one had bothered to pick up off the floor. Crick held an empty coffee cup and he did not look up, but he knew damn well she was there.

'Do I still have a job?' Sonora asked, finally. Somebody had to take the plunge.

Crick turned his chair slowly. If she had expected him to age overnight, or go gray-headed, she was disappointed. He looked like he always did. Confident to a fault and slightly dangerous.

'Close the door.'

She obeyed. 'Do I still have a job?'

'Sit down.'

'Not till you answer my question.'

She saw the tiniest half smile, and she knew that he was irritated and that he admired her nerve. She missed the friendship that they had had. Chalk another casualty up to Jack Van Owen.

'Whether or not you still have a job depends on two things. One, that forensics does not find anything to show that you helped Jack Van Owen off the roof of that building. Prelims from the MD show no evidence of a gunshot wound and your weapon had not been fired. So long as the pending investigation doesn't hit a snag, you're okay there. You'll have to talk to the IAD guys tomorrow. And you have to talk to me today. And that's part two. That's what I decide after we've had our conversation. Want to sit down now, Detective?'

'Yes, sir, I think that I do.'

He leaned way back in his chair and took full advantage of the dramatic pause and if he wanted to intimidate her it was working. She might be in the wrong here. She could not get that out of her head.

'You should have left it alone, Sonora. You let me down.'

The rage sparked, closer to the surface than might have been safe. 'You let me down, sir.'

'I took you off the case.'

'For no good reason that I understand. Or maybe I understand it all too well.'

'I do not now and never will believe that Jack Van Owen had anything to do with that butcher job.'

'That man wasn't the Jack Van Owen you knew. That man was what was left after a severe head injury.'

'Received in the line of duty.'

'It was a tragedy, sir. Just like that bloodbath at the Stinnets. What does Mickey say about the glove?'

'Too early for results.'

'What does he *think*, sir?'

'He allows the possibility that you could be right.'

'So there was a third man.'

'Who tried to stop it.'

'Who caused it.'

'What was it you wanted, Sonora? Just to bring the legend down? Do you feel good about this? Everybody's dead now. We'll never know what really happened. You didn't manage to bring him in alive, did you, so we'll never know to what degree he is or isn't guilty.'

'Who the hell do you think killed Aruba and Kinkle? More to the point, who do you think shot Sam?'

'We're looking into that. If Eddie Stinnet didn't actually do it, maybe he knew the guy who did.'

'I'll just bet.'

'Out of line, Detective.'

'It's my case.'

'Not even in your wildest dreams. Why were you two up there on that rooftop? What were you doing in the building, and alone?'

'Who am I going to call for backup?'

'I don't like that answer and I don't believe it.'

'I wanted to give him a chance to turn himself in. To cooperate with the investigation.'

He rubbed his chin. 'If I had any doubt about Jack being in the clear, morally, that Jack was involved in murdering that family, I would have brought him in myself.'

'No, sir, because when the time came, you didn't. He talked to you. You knew him. And you knew he was involved from day one.'

'On that we must agree to disagree. You have a hard shell, Sonora.'

'It was you who trained me that way.'

Chapter Eighty-Three

Sonora sat in the middle-school gymnasium, back aching on the polished pine bleachers. Tim sat beside her, waving at girls who were two years younger than he was, impressing them with his upper-class air and Brad Pitt haircut. She had expected him to be bored, but there were enough older brothers and pretty sisters to keep him happy.

He nudged her with an elbow. 'Mom, do you mind if I go sit with—'

'No, go on ahead.'

After her talk with Crick she had spent the rest of the day on the phone, researching, not caring who overheard, though it was very damn clear they were listening. No death certificate had been issued for Angelo Van Owen in Arlington, Texas, no death certificate for anybody of that name six years before or after. No record of an interment of Angelo Van Owen in any cemetery in Arlington, Texas.

Sonora realized she was chewing her bottom lip. She stopped. A bent man in khakis rolled a white piano to the left side of the gym, and children filed on to the three-tiered level of risers. A program that consisted of a piece of red construction paper folded in the middle listed the musical numbers that would be performed by the sixth-, seventh- and eighth-grade chorus, with individual names listed on the back. Sonora looked for Heather's name, like all the other mothers, saw that it was spelled correctly, and put her hands in her lap to wait.

The kids were at the most awkward time of their lives, and it showed in strange haircuts, tense faces and a certain wariness. Some of them still had that untouched baby air, some were overly made up and knowing. More than a few had the look of embarrassment kids that age get just to be alive, much less stand up in front of their peers and their parents and sing.

The chorus teacher and the pianist were both female, both dressed in severe and formal black, which pleased Sonora. She looked at the faces of her co-parents. Everyone looked tired. She recognized the interesting seating arrangements that occur at school events attended by divorced spouses and their significant others, strung together in the middle by shared children.

The chorus teacher introduced the performers, the pianist, and the man who fiddled with the microphone and speakers. She then faced the children, held up her hands, and the concert began.

The voices were young and sweet, timid at first but more enthusiastic with her kind and practiced encouragement. Heather looked way too grown up in a black skirt, white shirt and red vest. She stood carefully on the middle riser in the two-inch heels and Sonora prayed her daughter would not slip and fall, like she herself had at a concert years and years ago. She clutched the single rose she would give her daughter after the performance, a family tradition. She had been to the florist that afternoon, with two missions.

It came to Sonora that she had been much too close to the dark things. That she had come very near to something she did not even want to name.

People were smiling, the room grew warm beneath fluorescent lights. The first song stopped, everyone applauded, and Heather, looking through the audience for Mom, gave Sonora a knowing smile before her attention was gathered by the director, and the next song began.

Chapter Eighty-Four

Sonora stood alone in the cemetery. It was here, in a grave site next to Jack Van Owen's wife, that she found her last trace of Angelo Van Owen. Though there was no record, no death certificate, her request for exhumation had been denied.

In her mind, the grave would be empty. Angelo Van Owen would be buried somewhere secret, head blown apart in a metal bucket by a father who loved him too much to let him live.

Sonora's palms left sweat marks on a square cardboard box that enclosed a small white orchid, nestled in lavender tissue. She stood for a while, thinking the older she got, the harder it was to figure shit out.

She could not hate him. He had been right all along – they were very much alike, in ways that were hard to admit. What would have happened if he hadn't been shot in the line of duty, if his wife's car hadn't run into the path of that coal truck, if his son hadn't grabbed the wheel of that car?

If she had taken his hand that night at the edge of the world.

The department had finally and reluctantly abandoned Jack Van Owen. The murders of Aruba and Kinkle and the assault on Detective Sam Delarosa were still officially open.

Not enough evidence to pin it on Jack; no doubt in her mind that he'd done it, acting on information that she herself had given him over the phone when he'd called to tell her he'd found Tim.

There were those who said that she pushed Jack Van Owen

over the edge of that building. People who whispered about her as she went by, men who looked at her with a weird sort of respect and a hard-edged admiration mixed with resentment. She had taken out a home invader, people had seen the crime scene photos. She had taken out a fellow cop, and people felt ashamed.

Rumors.

Crick had been careful. Documenting the lack of scratches on her arms, making sure there were no Sonora Blair skin fragments and DNA under Jack Van Owen's fingernails, no sign of a struggle.

It didn't matter. There were those who said that Sonora had done it for expediency, that she had been pressured from higher-ups, pressured by Crick. An ex-cop going bad was an embarrassment the department did not need, not in the wake of a case that had given them warmth, approval, spotlight.

Sonora read the gravestones. 'Lacy Van Owen, beloved wife and mother, 1953 to 1987.' In the middle, the mystery, 'Angelo "Angel" Van Owen, beloved son, 1972 to 1989'.

And Jack. Buried just days ago, the ground raw, no headstone yet. She left the orchid for him.

People would believe what they wanted to believe. It was how legends were born.

LYNN HIGHTOWER

NO GOOD DEED

'Genuinely fresh and exciting' – *Observer*

'A cracking tale told at a stunning pace . . . the characterisation is great, the suspects are 10 a dollar and the dialogue worth a million' – Frances Fyfield, *Mail on Sunday*

'Sharp, shocking and shamelessly satisfying' – Val McDermid, *Manchester Evening News*

When fifteen-year-old Joelle Chauncey and the horse she is riding go missing, leaving blood and a discarded riding boot at the scene of the crime, homicide cop Sonora Blair is called in from downtown Cincinnati. Searching for a motive, she must first establish who was the target – the girl or the horse.

As events escalate at the riding stable, Sonora detects an eerie and unsettling presence. A killer who will lead her down a bizarre path of good and evil and dark compulsions, proving fear can be the most dangerous enemy of all.

HODDER AND STOUGHTON PAPERBACKS

LYNN HIGHTOWER

EYESHOT

'Suspenseful and psychologically sound, with a fierce, frazzled quality to the writing which gives it edge and credibility. Astonishingly good' – Philip Oakes, *Literary Review*

'Hightower has invented a heroine who is both flawed and likeable, and she knows how to keep the psychological pressure turned up high' – *Sunday Telegraph*

Young mother of two, Julia Winchell witnessed a murder before she died. Eight years before she died.

A murder unsolved but not forgotten. A murder where the body disappeared and no one believed her story.

When Julia returns to Cincinnati, she recognises the killer on the front page of the local paper.

Then Julia diappears. Shortly afterwards her severed leg is found alongside the interstate highway in Kentucky.

A mother of two herself, Detective Sonora Blair is determined to find out what happened to Julia Winchell – and to bring her killer to justice.

HODDER AND STOUGHTON PAPERBACKS

LYNN HIGHTOWER

FLASHPOINT

'Cleverly crafted crime story from an exciting new writer . . . frightening . . . gutsy' – *Daily Mail*

'Good frissons of psychological terror . . . Sonora is a lively and sympathetic addition to the ranks of fictional female coppery' – Marcel Berlins, *The Times*

'A powerfully original book . . . Like all the best thrillers, *Flashpoint* leaves you uneasily aware of shadows, especially those that start at your own feet' – Reginald Hill

The killer is a woman, and she knows no mercy. She handcuffs men to the steering wheel of their car, douses them with petrol, and sets them on fire. She then takes pictures and mails them to her victims' families. The media call her 'Flash'.

Homicide Detective Sonora Blair doesn't need any more complications in her life. She's a single mother with an ulcer, two kids and a three-legged dog. Getting involved with Keaton Daniels, the latest victim's brother, is a bad idea – one that could cost her her job. And when the killer becomes fixated with Keaton, it's an idea that could cost him his life.

So Sonora embarks on a bizarre and dangerous cat-and-mouse game with Flash – who wants to be her friend, but wants to kill her man.

HODDER AND STOUGHTON PAPERBACKS